MARY ALICE MONROE

"An author of power and depth."
—*RT Book Reviews*

"Her writing is always sensitive and true, and as inspiring as the natural wonders about which she writes."
—*New York Times* bestselling author
Dorothea Benton Frank

THE SUMMER GIRLS

"Monroe knows her characters like no one else could, and her portrayals of the summer girls are subtle, realistic, carefully crafted, and pitch-perfect."
—*Publishers Weekly*

"More than just a beautifully written, moving portrayal of three sisters finding themselves and each other after years of separation . . . [*The Summer Girls*] deals head-on with significant issues so skillfully woven into the narrative that I often stopped to consider the import of what I'd just read. If you're a dedicated environmentalist, this book is a must-read. If you're just someone who enjoys a good story, you'll get that, too, and much more."
—*New York Times* bestselling author Cassandra King

"This book contains drama, humor, and romance which any good summer read does. Plus it has the message about the care and treatment of dolphins. Monroe is an expert at making this blend and *The Summer Girls* is one of her most successful efforts."
—*Huffington Post*

"A song of praise to the bottle-nosed dolphins that bring so much joy to the men and women who gaze at the creeks and rivers of the low country each evening."

—*New York Times* bestselling author Pat Conroy

"Mary Alice Monroe at her best. . . . *The Summer Girls* reminded me of what I love about Southern Fiction."

—*Heroes and Heartbreakers*

"A captivating story of how the ocean and a charismatic dolphin reunite sisters in the alluring ecological setting of the low country of South Carolina. The story resonates on a personal level and, moreover, delivers a powerful reminder of the importance of protecting dolphins and the environment in which they live."

—Patricia Fair, director, Marine Mammal Program, NOAA

BEACH HOUSE MEMORIES

"In the bestselling tradition of Kathryn Stockett's *The Help*, Mary Alice Monroe skillfully weaves together issues of class, women's rights, and domestic abuse set in the tumultuous South during the 1970s. . . . Beautifully wrought, and rich with keen insight . . . an unforgettable tale of marriage, resilience, and one woman's private strength."

—*Bookreporter*

"Monroe's resplendent storytelling shines even brighter . . . [with] startling insights into the intimate connection between nature and the human heart."

—*New York Times* bestselling author Patti Callahan Henry

"*Beach House Memories* is another in a remarkable trilogy that has increased sea turtle volunteerism and conservation efforts. I highly recommend it."

—Sally R. Murphy, DNR Sea Turtle coordinator (retired)

"Fantastic. . . . The combination of an emotional story, environmental details, and Mary Alice Monroe's beautiful writing makes *Beach House Memories* a book you won't want to miss."

—*The Bermuda Onion*

"Captivating. . . . Fascinating, vivid characters. . . . Thought-provoking."

—*Booktrib*

"Mary Alice Monroe writes what she knows with the sea turtles, the tides, the beach, and the people of the area. . . . This is the kind of story that can take me away from the day-to-day of life, a story you will remember always."

—*Wordpress*

More praise for Mary Alice Monroe

"Monroe invigorates her characters with a spiritual energy that effectively drives the inspiring novel."

—*Booklist* on *The Butterfly's Daughter*

"Haunting . . . a story of past mistakes and second chances."

—*The Charleston Post and Courier* on
Last Light over Carolina

"An exquisite, many-layered novel of an unsolved mystery, an obsession, a reconciliation, and a little romance."

—*Booklist* on *Time Is a River*

The Summer Girls

MARY ALICE MONROE

POCKET BOOKS

New York   London   Toronto   Sydney   New Delhi

Pocket Books
A Division of Simon & Schuster, Inc.
1230 Avenue of the Americas
New York, NY 10020

This book is a work of fiction. Any references to historical events, real people, or real places are used fictitiously. Other names, characters, places, and events are products of the author's imagination, and any resemblance to actual events or places or persons, living or dead, is entirely coincidental.

First Pocket Books paperback edition June 2014

POCKET and colophon are registered trademarks of Simon & Schuster, Inc.

For information about special discounts for bulk purchases, please contact Simon & Schuster Special Sales at 1-866-506-1949 or business@simonandschuster.com.

The Simon & Schuster Speakers Bureau can bring authors to your live event. For more information or to book an event contact the Simon & Schuster Speakers Bureau at 1-866-248-3049 or visit our website at www.simonspeakers.com.

Manufactured in the United States of America

10 9 8 7 6 5 4 3 2 1

ISBN 978-1-4767-5883-1
ISBN 978-1-4767-0903-1 (ebook)

To Nana
Elizabeth Potter Kruesi
With Much Love and Gratitude

The
Summer
Girls

Sea Breeze, Sullivan's Island, SC

April 5, 2012

My darling granddaughters—Dora, Carson, and Harper,

Greetings, my precious girls! On May 26 I celebrate my eightieth birthday—can you believe I'm so ancient? Will you come home to Sea Breeze and your old mamaw and help me celebrate? We will do it proper with a lowcountry boil, Lucille's biscuits, and most of all, each other.

My dears, like an overripe peach, I'm past my prime. My mind remains sharp and my health is good, considering. Yet, with an eye to the future, I've decided to move to a retirement community, and it's time to sort through all that I've managed to clutter my house with all these years.

And I've realized that it has been far too long since we've been together. I know your lives are busy and your summers filled with engagements and travels. Yet—please say you'll come to my party! For the summer, if you possibly can! That is the only gift I want. I yearn so very much to share this final season at Sea Breeze with my Summer Girls.

Yours,
Mamaw

P.S. This invitation does not include husbands, beaus, or mothers!

CHAPTER ONE

LOS ANGELES

*C*arson was sorting through the usual boring bills and circulars in the mail when her fingers paused at the thick ecru envelope with *Miss Carson Muir* written in a familiar blue script. She clutched the envelope tight and her heart pumped fast as she scurried up the hot cement steps back to her apartment. The air-conditioning was broken, so only scarce puffs of breeze that carried noise and dirt from the traffic wafted through the open windows. It was a tiny apartment in a two-story stucco building near L.A., but it was close to the ocean and the rent was affordable, so Carson had stayed for three years, longer than she'd ever lived in any other apartment.

Carson carelessly tossed the other mail onto the glass cocktail table, stretched her long limbs out on the nubby brown sofa, then slid her finger along the envelope's seal. Waves of anticipation crested in her bloodstream as she slowly pulled out the navy-trimmed, creamy stationery card. Immediately she caught a whiff of perfume—soft sweet spices and orange flowers—and, closing her eyes, she saw the Atlantic Ocean, not the Pacific, and the white wooden house on pilings surrounded by palms and ancient oaks. A smile played on her lips. It was so like her grandmother to spray her letters with scent. So old world—so Southern.

Carson nestled deeper in the cushions and relished each word of the letter. When finished, she looked up and stared in a daze at the motes of dust floating in a shaft of sunlight. The letter was an invitation . . . was it possible?

In that moment, Carson could have leaped to her feet and twirled on her toes, sending her long braid flying like that of the little girl in her memories. Mamaw was inviting her to Sullivan's Island. A summer at Sea Breeze. Three whole rent-free months by the sea!

Mamaw always had the best timing, she thought, picturing the tall, elegant woman with hair the color of sand and a smile as sultry as a lowcountry sunset. It had been a horrid winter of endings. The television series Carson had been working on had been canceled without warning after a three-year run. Her cash flow was almost gone and she was just trying to figure out how she could make next month's rent. For months she'd been bobbing around town looking for work like a piece of driftwood in rough waters.

Carson looked again at the letter in her hand. "Thank you, Mamaw," she said aloud, feeling it deeply. For the first time in months Carson felt a surge of hope. She paced a circle, her fingers flexing, then strode to the fridge and pulled out a bottle of wine and poured herself a mugful. Next she crossed the room to her small wood desk, pushed the pile of clothing off the chair, then sat down and opened her laptop.

To her mind, when you were drowning and a rope was thrown your way, you didn't waste time thinking about what to do. You just grabbed it, then kicked and swam like the devil to safety. She had a lot to do and not much time if she was going to be out of the apartment by the month's end.

Carson picked up the invitation again, kissed it, then put her hands on the keys and began typing. She would accept Mamaw's invitation. She was going back to the lowcountry—to Mamaw. Back to the only place in the world she'd ever thought of as home.

SUMMERVILLE, SOUTH CAROLINA

Dora stood at the kitchen stove stirring a red sauce. It was 5:35 P.M. and the rambling Victorian house felt empty and desolate. She used to be able to set a clock by her husband's schedule. Even now, six months after Calhoun had left, Dora expected him to walk through the door carrying the mail. She'd lift her cheek toward the man who had been her husband for fourteen years to receive his perfunctory kiss.

Dora's attention was caught by the sound of pounding footfalls on the stairs. A moment later, her son burst into the room.

"I made it to the next level," he announced. He wasn't smiling, but his eyes sparkled with triumph.

Dora smiled into his face. Her nine-year-old son made

up her world. A big task for such a small boy. Nate was slight and pale, with furtive eyes that always made her wonder why her little boy was afraid. Of what? she'd asked his child psychiatrist, who had smiled kindly. "Nate isn't so much afraid as he is guarded," he'd answered reassuringly. "You shouldn't take it personally, Mrs. Tupper."

Nate had never been a cuddly baby, but she worried when his smiling stopped after a year. By two, he didn't establish eye contact or turn his head when called. By three, he no longer came to her for comfort when he was hurt, nor did he notice or care if she cried or got angry. Except if she yelled. Then Nate covered his ears and commenced rocking in a panic.

Her every instinct had screamed that something was wrong with her baby and she began furtively reading books on child development. How many times had she turned to Cal with her worries that Nate's speech development was behind the norm and that his movements were clumsy? And how many times had Cal turned on her, adamant that the boy was fine and she was making it all up in her head? She'd been like a turtle tucking her head in, afraid to go against him. Already the subject of Nate's development was driving a wedge between them. When Nate turned four, however, and began flapping his hands and making odd noises, she made her first, long-overdue appointment with a child psychiatrist. It was then that the doctor revealed what Dora had long feared: her son had high-functioning autism.

Cal received the diagnosis as a psychological death sentence. But Dora was surprised to feel relieved. Having an official diagnosis was better than making up excuses and coping with her suspicions. At least now she could actively help her son.

And she did. Dora threw herself into the world of autism spectrum disorders. There was no point in gnashing her teeth wishing that she'd followed up on her own instincts sooner, knowing now that early diagnosis and treatment could have meant important strides in Nate's development. Instead, she focused her energy on a support group and worked tirelessly to develop an intensive in-home therapy program. It wasn't long before her entire life revolved around Nate and his needs. All her plans for restoring her house fell by the wayside, as did hair appointments, lunches with friends, her size 8 clothes.

And her marriage.

Dora had been devastated when Cal announced seemingly out of the blue one Saturday afternoon in October that he couldn't handle living with her and Nate any longer. He assured her she would be taken care of, packed a bag, and walked out of the house. And that was that.

Dora quickly turned off the stove and wiped her hands on her apron. She put on a bright smile to greet her son, fighting her instinct to lean over and kiss him as he entered the room. Nate didn't like being touched. She reached over to the counter to retrieve the navy-trimmed invitation that had arrived in the morning's mail.

"I've got a surprise for you," she told him with a lilt in her voice, feeling that the time was right to share Mamaw's summer plans.

Nate tilted his head, mildly curious but uncertain. "What?"

She opened the envelope and pulled out the card,

catching the scent of her grandmother's perfume. Smiling with anticipation, Dora quickly read the letter aloud. When Nate didn't respond, she said, "It's an invitation. Mamaw is having a party for her eightieth birthday."

He immediately shrank inward. "Do I have to go?" he asked, his brow furrowed with worry.

Dora understood that Nate didn't like to attend social gatherings, not even for people he loved, like his great-grandmother. Dora bent closer and smiled. "It's just to Mamaw's house. You love going to Sea Breeze."

Nate turned his head to look out the window, avoiding her eyes as he spoke. "I don't like parties."

Nor was he ever invited to any, she thought sadly. "It's not really a party," Dora hastened to explain, careful to keep her voice upbeat but calm. She didn't want Nate to set his mind against it. "It's only family coming—you and me and your two aunts. We're invited to go to Sea Breeze for the weekend." A short laugh of incredulousness burst from her throat. "For the summer, actually."

Nate screwed up his face. "For the *summer*?"

"Nate, we always go to Sea Breeze to see Mamaw in July, remember? We're just going a little earlier this year because it is Mamaw's birthday. She will be eighty years old. It's a very special birthday for her." She hoped she'd explained it clearly enough for him to work it out. Nate was extremely uncomfortable with change. He liked everything in his life to be in order. Especially now that his daddy had left.

The past six months had been rocky for both of them. Though there had never been much interaction between Nate and his father, Nate had been extremely agitated for weeks after Cal moved out. He'd wanted to know if his father was ill and had gone to the hospital. Or was he traveling on business like some of his classmates' fathers? When Dora made it clear that his father was not ever returning to the house to live with them, Nate had narrowed his eyes and asked her if Cal was, in fact, dead. Dora had looked at Nate's taciturn face, and it was unsettling to realize that he wasn't upset at the possibility his father might be dead. He merely needed to know for certain whether Calhoun Tupper was alive or dead so that all was in order in his life. She had to admit that it made the prospect of a divorce less painful.

"If I go to Mamaw's house I will need to take my tetra," Nate told her at length. "The fish will die if I leave it alone in the house."

Dora slowly released her breath at the concession. "Yes, that's a very good idea," she told him cheerfully. Then, because she didn't want him to dwell and because it had been a good day for Nate so far, she moved on to a topic that he wouldn't find threatening. "Now, suppose you tell me about the new level of your game. What is your next challenge?"

Nate considered this question, then tilted his head and began to explain in tedious detail the challenges he faced in the game and how he planned to meet them.

Dora returned to the stove, careful to mutter, "Uh-huh," from time to time as Nate prattled on. Her sauce had gone cold and all the giddiness that she'd experienced when reading the invitation fizzled in her chest, leaving her feeling flat. Mamaw had been clear that this was to be a girls-only weekend. Oh, Dora would have loved a weekend away from the countless monotonous chores for a few days of wine and laughter, of catching up with her sisters, of being a Summer Girl again. Only a few days . . . Was that too much to ask?

Apparently, it was. She'd called Cal soon after the invitation had arrived.

"What?" Cal's voice rang in the receiver. "You want me to babysit? All weekend?"

Dora could feel her muscles tighten. "It will be fun. You never see Nate anymore."

"No, it won't be fun. You know how Nate gets when you leave. He won't accept me as your substitute. He never does."

She could hear in his voice that he was closing doors. "For pity's sake, Cal. You're his father. You have to figure it out!"

"Be reasonable, Dora. We both know Nate will never tolerate me or a babysitter. He gets very upset when you leave."

Tears began to well in her eyes. "But I can't bring him. It's a girls-only weekend." Dora lifted the invitation. "It says, 'This invitation does *not* include husbands, beaus, or mothers.'"

Cal snorted. "Typical of your grandmother."

"Cal, please . . ."

"I don't see what the problem is," he argued, exasperation creeping into his voice. "You always bring Nate along with you when you go to Sea Breeze. He knows the house, Mamaw . . ."

"But she said—"

"Frankly, I don't care what she said," Cal said, cutting

her off. There was a pause, then he said with a coolness of tone she recognized as finality, "If you want to go to Mamaw's, you'll have to bring Nate. That's all there is to it. Now good-bye."

It had always been this way with Cal. He never sought to see all of Nate's positive qualities—his humor, intelligence, diligence. Rather, Cal had resented the time she spent with their son and complained that their lives revolved around Nate and Nate alone. So, like an intractable child himself, Cal had left them both.

Dora's shoulders slumped as she affixed Mamaw's invitation to the refrigerator door with a magnet beside the grocery list and a school photo of her son. In it, Nate was scowling and his large eyes stared at the camera warily. Dora sighed, kissed the photo, and returned to cooking their dinner.

While she chopped onions, tears filled her eyes.

NEW YORK CITY

Harper Muir-James picked at the piece of toast like a bird. If she nibbled small pieces and chewed each one thoroughly, then sipped water between bites, she found she ate less. As she chewed, Harper's mind was working through the onslaught of emotions that had been roiling since she opened the invitation in the morning's mail. Harper held the invitation between her fingers and looked at the familiar blue-inked script.

"Mamaw," she whispered, the name feeling foreign on her lips. It had been so long since she'd uttered the name aloud.

She propped the thick card up against the crystal vase of flowers on the marble breakfast table. Her mother insisted that all the rooms of their prewar condo overlooking Central Park always have fresh flowers. Georgiana had grown up at her family estate in England, where this had been de rigueur. Harper's gaze lazily shifted from the invitation to the park outside her window. Spring had come to Central Park, changing the stark browns and grays of winter to an explosion of spring green. In her mind's eye, however, the scene shifted to the greening cordgrass in the wetlands of the lowcountry, the snaking creeks dotted with docks, and the large, waxy white magnolia blooms against glossy green leaves.

Her feelings for her Southern grandmother were like the waterway that raced behind Sea Breeze—deep, and swelling with happy memories. In the invitation Mamaw had referred to her "Summer Girls." That was a term Harper hadn't heard—had not even thought about—in over a decade. She hadn't been but a girl when she spent her last summer at Sea Breeze. How many times had she seen Mamaw in all those years? It surprised Harper to realize it had been only three times.

There had been so many invitations sent to her in those intervening years. So many regrets returned. Harper felt a twinge of shame as she pondered how she could have let so many years pass without paying Mamaw a visit.

"Harper? Where are you?" a voice called from the hall.

Harper coughed on a crumb of dry toast.

"Ah, there you are," her mother said, walking into the kitchen.

Georgiana James never merely entered a room; she *arrived*. There was a rustle of fabric and an aura of sparks of energy radiating around her. Not to mention her perfume, which was like the blare of trumpets entering the room before her. As the executive editor of a major publishing house, Georgiana was always rushing—to meet a deadline, to meet someone for lunch or dinner, or to another in a string of endless meetings. When Georgiana wasn't rushing off somewhere she was ensconced behind closed doors reading. In any case, Harper had seen little of her mother growing up. Now, at twenty-eight years of age, she worked as her mother's private assistant. Though they lived together, Harper knew that she needed to make an appointment with her mother for a chat.

"I didn't expect you to still be here," Georgiana said, pecking her cheek.

"I was just leaving," Harper replied, catching the hint of censure in the tone. Georgiana's pale blue tweed jacket and navy pencil skirt fitted her petite frame impeccably. Harper glanced down at her own sleek black pencil skirt and gray silk blouse, checking for any loose thread or missing button that her mother's hawk eye would pick up. Then, in what she hoped was a nonchalant move, she casually reached for the invitation that she'd foolishly propped up against the glass vase of flowers.

Too late.

"What's that?" Georgiana asked, swooping down to grasp it. "An invitation?"

Harper's stomach clenched and, not replying, she glanced up at her mother's face. It was a beautiful face, in the way that a marble statue was beautiful. Her skin was as pale as alabaster, her cheekbones prominent, and her pale red hair was worn in a blunt cut that accentuated her pointed chin. There was never a strand out of place. Harper knew that at work they called her mother "the ice queen." Rather than be offended, Harper thought the name fit. She watched her mother's face as she read the invitation, saw her lips slowly tighten and her blue eyes turn frosty.

Georgiana's gaze snapped up from the card to lock with Harper's. "When did you get this?"

Harper was as petite as her mother and she had her pale complexion. But unlike her mother's, Harper's reserve was not cold but more akin to the stillness of prey.

Harper cleared her throat. Her voice came out soft and shaky. "Today. It came in the morning mail."

Georgiana's eyes flashed and she tapped the card against her palm with a snort of derision. "So the Southern belle is turning eighty."

"Don't call her that."

"Why not?" Georgiana asked with a light laugh. "It's the truth, isn't it?"

"It isn't nice."

"Defensive, are we?" Georgiana said with a teasing lilt.

"Mamaw writes that she's moving," Harper said, changing the subject.

"She's not fooling anyone. She's tossing out that comment like bait to draw you girls in for some furniture or silver or whatever she has in that claptrap beach house." Georgiana sniffed. "As if you'd be interested in anything she might call an antique."

Harper frowned, annoyed by her mother's snobbishness. Her family in England had antiques going back several hundred years. That didn't diminish the lovely American antiques in Mamaw's house, she thought. Not that Harper wanted anything. In truth, she was already inheriting more furniture and silver than she knew what to do with.

"That's not why she's invited us," Harper argued. "Mamaw wants us all to come together again at Sea Breeze, one last time. Me, Carson, Dora . . ." She lifted her slight shoulders. "We had some good times there. I think it might be nice."

Georgiana handed the invitation back to Harper. She held it between two red-tipped fingers as though it were foul. "Well, you can't go, of course. Mum and a few guests are arriving from England the first of June. She's expecting to see you in the Hamptons."

"Mamaw's party is on the twenty-sixth of May and Granny James won't arrive until the following week. It shouldn't be a problem. I can go to the party and be in the Hamptons in plenty of time." Harper hurried to add, "I mean, it is Mamaw's eightieth birthday after all. And I haven't seen her in years."

Harper saw her mother straighten her shoulders, her nostrils flaring as she tilted her chin, all signs Harper recognized as pique.

"Well," Georgiana said, "if you want to waste your time, go ahead. I'm sure I can't stop you."

Harper pushed away her plate, her stomach clenching at the warning implicit in the statement: *If you go I will not be pleased.* Harper looked down at the navy-trimmed invitation and rubbed her thumb against the thick vellum, feeling its softness. She thought again of the summers at Sea Breeze, of Mamaw's amused, tolerant smile at the antics of the Summer Girls.

Harper looked back at her mother and smiled cheerily. "All right then. I rather think I will go."

Four weeks later Carson's battered Volvo wagon limped over the Ben Sawyer Bridge toward Sullivan's Island like an old horse heading to the barn. Carson turned off the music and the earth fell into a hush. The sky over the wetlands was a panorama of burnt sienna, tarnished gold, and moody shades of blue. The few wispy clouds would not mar the great fireball's descent into the watery horizon.

She crossed the bridge and her wheels were on Sullivan's Island. She was almost there. The reality of her decision made her fingers tap along the wheel in agitation. She was about to show up on Mamaw's doorstep to stay for the entire summer. She sure hoped Mamaw had been sincere in that offer.

In short order Carson had given up her apartment, packed everything she could in her Volvo, and put the rest into storage. Staying with Mamaw provided Carson with a sanctuary while she hunted for a job and saved a few dollars. It had been an exhausting three-day journey from the West Coast to the East Coast, but she'd arrived at last, bleary-eyed and stiff-shouldered. Yet once she left the mainland, the scented island breezes gave her a second wind.

The road came to an intersection at Middle Street.

Carson smiled at the sight of people sitting outdoors at restaurants, laughing and drinking as their dogs slept under the tables. It was early May. In a few weeks the summer season would begin and the restaurants would be overflowing with tourists.

Carson rolled down the window and let the ocean breeze waft in, balmy and sweet smelling. She was getting close now. She turned off Middle Street onto a narrow road heading away from the ocean to the back of the island. She passed Stella Maris Catholic Church, its proud steeple piercing a periwinkle sky.

The wheels crunched to a stop on the gravel and Carson's hand clenched around the can of Red Bull she'd been nursing.

"Sea Breeze," she murmured.

The historic house sat amid live oaks, palmettos, and scrub trees overlooking the beginning of where Cove Inlet separated Charleston Harbor from the Intracoastal Waterway. At first peek, Sea Breeze seemed a modest wood-framed house with a sweeping porch and a long flight of graceful stairs. Mamaw had had the original house raised onto pilings to protect it from tidal surges during storms. It was at that same time that Mamaw had added to the house, restored the guest cottage, and repaired the garage. This hodgepodge collection of wood-frame buildings might not have had the showy grandeur of the newer houses on Sullivan's, Carson thought, but none of those houses could compare with Sea Breeze's subtle, authentic charm.

Carson turned off the lights, closed her bleary eyes, and breathed out in relief. She'd made it. She'd journeyed twenty-five hundred miles and could still feel the rolling of them in her body. Sitting in the quiet car, she opened her eyes and stared out the windshield at Sea Breeze.

"Home," she breathed, tasting the word on her lips. Such a strong word, laden with meaning and emotion, she thought, feeling suddenly unsure. Did birth alone give her the right to make that claim on this place? She was only a granddaughter, and not a very attentive one at that. Though, unlike the other girls, for her, Mamaw was more than a grandmother. She was the only mother Carson had ever known. Carson had been only four years old when her mother died and her father left her to stay with Mamaw while he went off to lick his wounds and find himself again. He came back for her four years later to move to California, but Carson had returned every summer after that until she was seventeen. Her love for Mamaw had always been like that porch light, the one true shining light in her heart when the world proved dark and scary.

Now, seeing Sea Breeze's golden glow in the darkening sky, she felt ashamed. She didn't deserve a warm welcome. She'd visited a handful of times since the "Summer Girls" years—two funerals, a wedding, and a couple of holidays. She'd made too many excuses. Her cheeks flamed as she realized how selfish it was of her to assume that Mamaw would always be here, waiting for her. She swallowed hard, facing the truth that she likely wouldn't even have come now except that she was broke and had nowhere else to go.

Her breath hitched as the front door opened and a woman stepped out onto the porch. She stood in the golden light, straight-backed and regal. In the glow, her wispy white hair created a halo around her head.

Carson's eyes filled as she stepped from the car.

Mamaw lifted her arm in a wave.

Carson felt the tug of connection as she dragged her suitcase in the gravel toward the porch. As she drew near, Mamaw's blue eyes shone bright and welcoming. Carson let go of her baggage and ran up the stairs into Mamaw's open arms. She pressed her cheek against Mamaw's, was enveloped in her scent, and all at once she was four years old again, motherless and afraid, her arms tight around Mamaw's waist.

"Well now," Mamaw said against her cheek. "You're home at last. What took you so long?"

CHAPTER TWO

$\mathcal{M}$arietta Muir hated birthdays. In a few days she was turning eighty years old. She shuddered.

She stood on the rooftop porch of her beach house overlooking the Atlantic Ocean, which was serene this morning and caressing the shoreline like an old friend. How many summers had she spent in the embrace of that body of water? she wondered. Never enough.

Marietta's fingers tapped the porch railing. There was no point in fussing about her birthday now. After all, she herself had made the party arrangements and invited her granddaughters to Sullivan's Island. But what choice did she have but to make her eightieth birthday an event? How many times over the years had she invited her grand-daughters to her island house, and how many times had they replied with excuses? Marietta thought of the letters she'd received, each written in a script as different in personality and style from the others as the girls themselves, yet each filled with the same excuses. *Oh, Mamaw! I'm so sorry! I'd love to come, but . . .* The exclamation marks at the ends of the excuses made the apologies feel all the more insincere. How else could she wrangle three recalcitrant young women from all over the country to travel to South Carolina to visit?

When they were young they loved coming to Sea Breeze. Once adolescence was over, however, they all became too engrossed in their grown-up lives. Dora got married and became, quite frankly, overwhelmed with all the demands of her son and husband. Carson's ambition had her flying all over the world with her camera. And Harper . . . Who knew? She had slipped away into her mother's camp, ignoring letters, sending perfunctory thank-you notes for gifts received, never calling. The simple truth was that since the girls had become women, they rarely visited their grandmother.

Marietta's fingertips tapped along the porch railing. Well, at least they were all coming this time, even if it was perhaps her subtle promise of loot that had lured them in. The little pirates . . . It was well known that the founding father of the celebrated line of sea captains in the family's long and illustrious history was, in fact, a pirate. It was never talked about in polite society, but it was quietly understood that the family's subsequent wealth sprang from the seed of that buccaneer's bounty.

Her thinning lips pursed in worry. What she had *not* mentioned in her letter was that she would also be unearthing family secrets, especially about their father. In her long life she'd learned that those dark and musty facts always had a way of leaching out and fouling lives. Best to air them out, while she still had time.

Time—that was at the crux of her invitation. She'd invited her granddaughters to her birthday party. She hoped they would agree to spend the entire summer. They simply *had* to, she thought with a twinge of anxiety. She clasped her hands together. *Please God, let them agree to stay for one final season.*

Marietta looked at her hands, which were graced with a large, mine-cut diamond. *Ah, the ravages of time,* she thought. Back in the day, her hands had been smooth and graceful, not withered as they were now. It pained her to see the wrinkled skin, the dark spots, the way her once-long fingers curled around the railing like an old crone's claw. Old age could be so humbling.

But she didn't *feel* old—certainly not as old as eighty. That was much older than she'd ever dreamed of being. Older than her mother or father had ever been, and many of her friends. Or her beloved husband, Edward, who had passed a decade earlier. And even her darling son, Parker. She'd thought she'd die herself when he did. A parent should never have to survive the death of a child. But she *had* survived, for quite a long time. And in her mind, she was not *old* Marietta or *young* Marietta. She was simply Marietta.

The aches and pains were real enough, though, as were her fading eyesight and her inability to remember names. Marietta took in one last sweeping view. From high on the roof deck of her house, Sea Breeze, Marietta could see beyond the front row of island houses and the thick expanse of maritime shrubs far out to the golden beach. When she'd first come to Sea Breeze as a young bride, there were no houses between hers and the ocean. Now another two rows of houses crammed the narrow space before the beach. But from the roof deck she still could look over the obstructing rooftops to see the same view of shimmering ocean. The azure water mirrored a cloudless sky and white-tipped waves rolled ashore at an unhurried pace, tossing sand as ancient and teeming with mystery as time itself.

She laughed ruefully. As ancient as herself.

"Miz Marietta!"

Oh bother, Marietta thought. Lucille was no doubt upset to discover she'd snuck up to the rooftop again. Marietta turned from the rooftop railing to look anxiously down the steep stairs. When she was young she would race like a gazelle up these same stairs each morning, breathless with anticipation to peer out at the condition of the sea. *Backbone,* she told herself as she gripped the stair railing tight. Marietta tentatively, slowly, began her way down the narrow stairwell. She was met halfway by Lucille. Her maid's dark, round eyes flashed as she looked up at Marietta.

"Lucille, you gave me a start!" Marietta exclaimed, tightening her grip on the railing.

"I gave *you* a start? What do you mean, running up and down those stairs like a girl? You could fall! And with your bones, that'd be the end of it. I'm out of breath racing to get here once I figured out where you snuck off to." She climbed a few steps closer and placed a firm grip on Marietta's arm. "I can't let you be on your own for one minute without you getting yourself into trouble."

"Nonsense," Marietta scoffed, accepting Lucille's support. "I've gone up and down those same stairs for longer than I can remember."

Lucille snorted. "And you remember a long, long time, too. You ain't that young girl no more, Miz Marietta, no matter what you think. You promised me you'd let me know when you was heading up to that roof. I got to come with you, so's you don't fall."

"And what would you do if I did fall?" Marietta asked archly. "You're as old as I am. We'd both fall into a heap of broken bones."

"Not *as* old . . ." Lucille mumbled as she reached the landing of the porch, then guided Marietta down the final steps.

Marietta didn't like being watched and tended like some child. She'd always prided herself on her independence. As she prided herself on having her own opinions and not being shy to offer them. When she reached floor level, she pulled back her shoulders and shook off Lucille's hold, sniffing. "I know exactly how old you are. You're sixty-nine and every bit the old coot I am."

Lucille chuckled and ruefully shook her head. "I am that," she conceded, "but I'll take every year I can, thank you very much."

Marietta gazed at Lucille standing across from her, arms resolutely locked across her breast. They stood almost eye to eye and took each other's measure. Marietta was as long and sleek as an egret. Her cropped white hair feathered her head and when she stood silent and watching, as she did now, she appeared as regal as that elegant marsh bird.

In contrast, Lucille was as compact and stout as a well-fed marsh hen. Her once-shimmering black hair was more white now, but her large dark eyes still gleamed with the stubbornness and guile of that gregarious bird. And Lord knew her cackle was as harsh. Though she was nearly seventy, Lucille's skin was as smooth as polished ebony, and it had been Marietta's secret mission for years to get Lucille to divulge what ointments kept her aging skin so supple. Lucille had been hired as Marietta's maid some fifty years earlier and had faithfully tended the Muir home and family on East Bay in Charleston. When Marietta sold the great house and moved permanently to Sea Breeze, Lucille had come with her.

Today Lucille was more a companion than a maid. Lucille knew every secret in Marietta's life and stood as a fierce gatekeeper at her door. Marietta sometimes thought Lucille knew too much about her and her family. She felt vaguely uncomfortable that there was one person intimately involved in her life whom she couldn't hoodwink. Only Lucille was allowed to make the wry comments that could shatter Marietta's illusions or state the bald truth, no matter how harsh it was for Marietta to hear. Marietta trusted Lucille implicitly and her loyalty to Lucille was unquestioned. They were, in fact, devoted to one another.

Marietta strode from the porch with purpose. The west wing was original to the old beach house. It was a warren of three rooms: one she and Edward had slept in, one had been Parker's room, and the wide room with heart-pine paneling, bookshelves, and paintings of hunting dogs had been the den. Years later, when Marietta had expanded the house and Parker's three daughters came for summers, the girls laid claim to the west wing by virtue of squatter's rights. In her mind she could still hear the giggling and squeals. The poor men were chased out of their lair, grumbling about hormones and the vanities of youth.

"Did you get the necklaces out as I asked?" Marietta said as they walked through the den.

"They're in your room, on your bed."

Marietta walked through the living room to the master bedroom. The master suite made up the house's east wing, and it was her sanctuary. She'd restored and remodeled Sea Breeze when she'd made the permanent move from Charleston to the island. Poor Edward hadn't lived long enough to enjoy his retirement. Marietta had found him slumped over his computer only a year after Parker's death, leaving her utterly alone in her redone house.

She walked across the plush carpeting directly to her ornately carved, mahogany four-poster bed, where she saw three black velvet bags lying on the bedspread. Three necklaces for three granddaughters.

"It's high time I selected which necklace to give which girl."

Lucille crossed her arms over her ample breast. "I thought you said you was gonna let *them* pick out the one they like the best."

"No, no, Lucille," Marietta replied impatiently. "That wouldn't do at all." She paused, turning her head to meet Lucille's gaze. "It's said," she said in the manner of a sage, "that pearls take on the essence of the person who wears them." She nodded, as though adding emphasis to the declaration. She began walking again. "I've worn those pearl necklaces for decades. Why, each pearl is positively *infused* with my essence. Don't you see," she said as though it were obvious, "that by giving my granddaughters my pearls, I'm passing on a bit of myself to each of them?" The very idea of it still had the power of giving her pleasure. "I've been looking forward to this moment for years."

Lucille was accustomed to the air of the dramatic in Marietta and remained unconvinced. "They can still pick their own necklace and get that essence juju. What if they don't like the one you picked out for them?"

"Don't like? What's not to like? Each necklace is priceless!"

"I'm not talking about how much it's worth. I'm talking about liking it. You don't want them sneaking looks at each other, checking out what the other one got. Chances are, you'll get it wrong. I've never known three people more different than those girls. If you asked me to choose, why, I couldn't. Wouldn't have a clue what they like." She narrowed her eyes and nodded her head in a jerky motion. "And you don't neither."

Marietta lifted her chin. "Of course I do. I'm their mamaw. I *know*."

"Uh-huh," Lucille replied with a doubtful shake of her head as they crossed through the living room. "So much for you trying not to manipulate folks so much."

"What's that? You think I'm manipulating them?"

"I'm just saying . . . Seems to me I remember you saying how you wanted to sit back and watch the girls choose, so's you could see for yourself what their tastes were and what kind of women they'd grown up to be. You *said* you wanted to help them get close again. How're you gonna do that if you're already setting things up the way you like? Didn't you learn nothin' from Parker?"

Marietta looked away, troubled by the truth in the accusation. "My life was devoted to Parker," she said, her voice trembling with emotion.

"I know it," Lucille replied gently. "And we both know it was that boy's undoing."

Marietta closed her eyes to calm herself. Now that years had passed since her son's early death, she could look at his life with a more honest eye, one no longer blurred by her devotion.

Marietta and Edward had wanted children, expected them. Not a horde, but an heir and a spare at the very least. In retrospect, it was a miracle that Marietta had delivered a son. After Parker's birth she'd suffered count-less miscarriages and the despair of a stillborn child. She had doted on Parker . . . spoiled him. She didn't learn until years later that she was what the doctors called an *enabler*.

Edward had complained it'd cost him a fortune in donations just to get the boy through the drunken debauchery of fraternity parties and countless girls to miraculously collect a degree. After college graduation, Edward had wanted to "boot his son off the payroll" and force him to "become a man and find out what it meant to earn a dollar." To which Marietta had responded with tongue in cheek, "Oh? You mean like you had to do?"

Parker could do no wrong in his mother's eyes, and Marietta became adept at making excuses for his failings.

If he was moody, she declared him sensitive. His womanizing, even after marriage, was always the fault of his unsatisfactory mates. And his drinking . . . well, all men liked to drink, didn't they?

Parker had been a beautiful child and had grown to become, no one could argue, an unfairly handsome man. He was tall and lean, with pale blond hair and azure eyes—the Muir color—rimmed with impossibly long lashes. Combined with his upper-class Southern heritage, to her mind he was Ashley Wilkes incarnate. When Parker looked appealingly into his mama's eyes, it was impossible for her to stay angry with him for his indiscretions. Though his father had grown immune to it over the years.

Never the women, however.

Women flocked to him. Marietta had secretly loved to watch them flutter their feathers around him like plumed birds. In her vanity, she took credit for it. Yet, Marietta had never been naive. It was precisely because she knew Parker could be indifferent to consequences that she'd taken it upon herself to introduce him to his future wife.

That woman was Winifred Smythe, an acceptably attractive young woman from a fine Charleston family. More to the point, she was a woman who was malleable, of moral upbringing, and willing. Everyone who saw them together couldn't help but agree they were a "golden couple." Their wedding at St. Philip's made headlines on the society pages. When Winnie gave birth to a daughter one year later, Marietta felt it was a personal triumph. Parker named his daughter Dora, after his favorite Southern author, Eudora Welty.

It was at this time that Parker declared he was writing a novel. Marietta had been infatuated with the idea of her son as an artist. Edward saw it as an excuse not to get a real job. Parker had tried to work in the bank with his father but that had lasted less than a year. Parker hated being cooped inside a building without windows and hated numbers, suits, and ties. He claimed he needed to write.

So he was given an allowance by his parents and began writing a novel that, according to Parker, would allow him to join the hallowed ranks of celebrated Southern authors. It was the seventies, and Parker became a stereotype of an author: he holed up in his dingy office at the Confederate Home with bottles of Jim Beam and marijuana for his inspiration. He wore turtleneck sweaters, let his hair grow, and generally was self-indulgent regarding his "craft."

Two years later, Parker's novel was not completed and it was discovered he was having an affair with the nanny. Marietta had stormed to the house she'd bought the couple on Colonial Lake in Charleston and demanded that Parker leave the nanny and beg his wife's forgiveness with a significant piece of jewelry. To her shock, Parker had stood up to her for the first time and refused to do her bidding. The other woman, a beguiling French girl of barely eighteen, was pregnant, and he intended to divorce Winnie to marry Sophie Duvall.

And so he did. Immediately after his divorce from Winnie was final, Parker married Sophie. True to form, Parker's apologies and cajoling eventually brought his parents to the shack of a house he and Sophie rented on Sullivan's Island. Marietta had wailed to Edward that the only reason the house was still standing was because the termites were holding hands. Marietta and Edward did not attend the sham wedding with the justice of the peace, but they took heart when their son found his first job, managing an independent bookstore in the city. Edward had been so hopeful about his son's commitment to *something* that he'd agreed to an allowance to help support the couple after the baby was born—another girl. Parker named his second daughter Carson, after Carson McCullers, thus continuing his predilection for naming his children after Southern writers.

Poor Sophie, Mamaw thought to herself, recalling the waif of a woman. She suffered postpartum depression and eventually became Parker's drinking partner. Their lifestyle slipped from bohemian to dysfunctional. Their drinking had kept Marietta awake nights with worry. The tragedy she feared occurred four years later. No one ever mentioned that horrible fire that took Sophie's life. The circumstances were hushed and became yet another of the Muir family secrets.

After Sophie's tragic death Parker dug deep enough to finish his novel. Energized with renewed enthusiasm, he moved to New York to work as an assistant in a publishing house. He was determined to find an editor, and, Mamaw thought with a sigh, in fact, he did. Unfortunately this editor didn't publish his novel. Instead she married him. Georgiana James was an up-and-coming junior editor for Viking. She had drive, ambition, and the generous support of her wealthy British family. They'd married quickly—and divorced months later, before the baby was born. It was another girl, and in a rare concession to Parker because Georgiana approved of the literary reference, the child was named Harper after the Southern author Harper Lee.

Georgiana had proved a stalwart opponent to all things Muir. She steadfastly refused Marietta's invitations to visit Charleston, nor was Marietta invited to New York to visit Harper. But Mamaw persevered, determined not to be snuffed out of any of her granddaughters' lives.

During these tumultuous years, Carson had come to live with Mamaw in her South of Broad home in Charleston. During the summers, little Dora came to stay with them at Sea Breeze on Sullivan's Island to play with Carson. Mamaw smiled wistfully remembering those years, so long ago. The two girls were like peas and carrots, always together. Even after Carson moved to Los Angeles with her father, she still came back to Sea Breeze to spend each summer with Dora. It wasn't until years later that Harper was old enough to join them on the island.

Those few precious summers of the early 1990s were the only years all three granddaughters were together at Sea Breeze. Only three years, and what magical summers they'd been. Then the teenage years intervened. When Dora turned seventeen she no longer wanted to spend her valuable vacation time with her baby sisters. Carson and Harper became a duo. So it was that Carson was the link between all the girls. The middle child who had spent summers alone with each sister.

Mamaw brought her hand to her forehead. To her mind, all the summers seemed to blend together, like the ages of the girls when they played together. She had a kaleidoscope of memories. There once had been a very special bond between her granddaughters. It worried her to see them as near strangers today. Mamaw couldn't abide the term *half sisters*. They were sisters, bound by blood. These girls were her only living kin.

Bolstered with resolve, Marietta turned to the velvet bags. One by one she spilled the pearl necklaces atop the pale pink linen coverlet. The three necklaces shone in the natural light that poured in through the large windows. As she studied the glistening pearls, her hand unconsciously rose to her neck. Once, each of these necklaces had graced the slender length of it, back when her neck had been her glory. Now, sadly, it was an embarrassment. High-quality natural pearls, all of them. Not these modern, freshwater bits that were more accessories than treasured pieces of fine jewelry. Back in her day, pearls were a rarity, among the most valued pieces of a woman's jewelry collection.

It was traditional to give a modest, classic pearl necklace that rested just below the base of the neck to a young girl at her sixteenth birthday or at her debut. Reaching out, Marietta lifted the first necklace. It was a triple-strand necklace of pearls with a showy ruby-and-diamond clasp. Her parents had given her this choker for her coming-out at the St. Cecilia Debutante Ball. Her father loved extravagance and this had certainly been an extravagant choice, one that had made her feel like a queen among the other princesses bedecked in their white gowns and single-strand pearl necklaces.

Marietta studied the pearls dangling from her palm, considering to whom she should give this necklace.

"I shall give these to Harper," Marietta announced.

"The quiet one," Lucille commented.

"Not so much quiet as reserved," Marietta said, contradicting her. "It's the English in her, I suppose."

"Same thing to me," Lucille said. "She was like a little mouse, wasn't she? Always holed up with a book. Startled easy, too. But Lawd, that girl was as sweet as tupelo honey." Lucille pursed her lips in thought, then shook her head. "Don't know but that it's a showy necklace for a tiny thing like her."

"Exactly the point. They'll show her off. And she'll wear them well," Marietta replied, thinking of Harper's proud bearing. "You see, Harper is the closest in age to mine when I received these pearls. And I do think the cream-colored pearls will complement her creamy skin tone."

"Creamy?" Lucille's chuckle rumbled low in her chest. "She might be the whitest white girl I've ever known."

Marietta smiled at the truth in it. Harper's skin never tanned in the sun; it only burned—no matter how much lotion she applied.

"She has that fair English skin like her mother. Georgiana James," she said with a sniff of distaste, remembering the cool, expensively tailored woman who had snubbed her the last time they'd spoken. "I swear she must apply her makeup with a trowel. She looks positively cadaverous! And she claims she has royal blood," Marietta scoffed. "Not a drop of blue blood flows in those veins. I daresay not much red, either. But dear Harper really does have the most soulful eyes, don't you think? She gets that color from the Muirs . . ."

Lucille rolled her eyes.

Marietta folded the pearls into her palm and wondered about the young woman who lived in New York City and kept her distance.

"It's Georgiana who's poisoned Harper against us," she declared, warming to the topic. "That woman never loved my son. She used him for his good looks and his family name." Marietta leaned closer to Lucille's ear and whispered dramatically, "He was little more to her than a sperm donor."

Lucille clucked her tongue and frowned, stepping back. "There you go again. You don't know no such thing."

"She divorced him as soon as she was pregnant!"

"You can't hold that against the child."

"I do not hold it against Harper," Marietta said, affronted. "It's her mother, that English snob who thinks Southerners are a pack of ignorant rednecks, whom I hold a grudge against." She waved her hand dismissively. "We all know that Parker wasn't the easiest of men to live with, God rest his soul. But not to let him see the baby after she was born was heartless. And he was already so out of sorts at the time."

"'Out of sorts'?" Lucille repeated. "That's what you call him being drunk all the time?"

Marietta fought the urge to snap a stinging retort at Lucille in defense of her son, but Lucille had gone with her to New York to put Parker into the first of several rehabilitation clinics. The sad truth was that Parker, for all his charm and wit, had been a notorious lush. It was what had killed him in the end.

Marietta didn't want to think of that now and resolutely placed the choker in a velvet bag and moved on to the second necklace.

Thirty-six inches of perfectly matched, lustrous pink pearls dripped from her fingers as she lifted them from the velvet. A small sigh escaped her. She had worn this exquisite, opera-length strand of pearls at her wedding, and later for more formal occasions, when the pearls fell below her chest to accentuate countless glorious long gowns.

"This necklace will go to Dora," she said.

"She's the bossy one," remarked Lucille.

Marietta's lips twitched at Lucille's ability to nail the girls' personalities. "Not bossy, but perhaps the most opinionated of the girls," Marietta allowed. Dora had followed the course of most traditional Southern young women. She'd married Calhoun Tupper, a man from her social circle, soon after graduating from college. Dora dove headfirst into her role as wife in support of her husband's banking career, her community, her church, and, later, her son. Like Marietta, she had difficulty getting pregnant, but, again like Marietta, she at last had a son.

"The length will elongate her figure," Marietta said.

"She's a big girl. She could use that length."

"She's not big," Marietta argued for her granddaughter. "She simply has let her figure go."

"Oh, I didn't mean anything bad by that. I like women with some flesh on them. Can't stand those skinny ones with their bones poking out."

It wasn't Dora's full figure that concerned Marietta as much as her unhappiness. She wasn't just overweight, she was overwhelmed. Marietta slipped the long necklace into a separate velvet bag. Then she lifted the final necklace.

This was a single strand of large South Sea black pearls. The magnificent baroque pearls had an undertone ranging from pale silver to deep black with a layering of iridescent hues. She thought of Carson with her dark hair and skin that turned golden in the summer from hours in the ocean. With her penchant for travel, she would appreciate a necklace so exotic.

"And this one is for Carson," she said with finality.

"She's the independent one," Lucille added.

"Yes," Marietta agreed softly. Secretly, Carson was her favorite granddaughter. It might have been because she'd spent the most time with the motherless girl when she'd come for extended stays after being unceremoniously dumped by her father when he was off on a jaunt. But Carson was also the most like Marietta, passionate about life and not afraid to accept challenges, quick to make up her mind, and a tall beauty with a long history of beaus.

"Is Carson out surfing?" Marietta asked. Carson had been the first of the girls to arrive at Sea Breeze.

"Oh, sure," Lucille replied with a chuckle. "That girl is up with the birds while the rest of us are still in bed. She's not lazy, that's for true."

"She's happiest when she's on the water." Marietta looked again at the mercurial colors of the pearls and thought of that same quality in Carson. Fire and ice. She was warmhearted to the core but quick to cool. It worried her that her beautiful granddaughter couldn't find a place—or a man—to hold her. Something dark burned in her soul, like these pearls. That was dangerous for a woman's heart. Marietta let the pearls slowly slide from her finger into the velvet bag.

She looked at the three velvet bags lying on the coverlet. It was an old woman's prerogative to own up to the mistakes of her life. She recognized now that her sins of omission with her son sowed the seeds of the problems in his marriages. Yet it was too late now to worry about the daughters-in-law, disappointments all of them. But her Summer Girls . . .

This summer was her final attempt to circle back, to recognize each granddaughter with clear vision, to close the gaping distance that had been growing between them over the last decade, and hopefully to restore some measure of their affection for each other.

Three granddaughters, three necklaces, three months . . . she thought to herself. This was the plan.

CHAPTER THREE

*C*arson had always believed salt water ran in her veins. She couldn't bear to be inland too long. A day spent without her toes dipping at least once into an ocean was a day half lived. Simply put, the ocean was her life.

The day had begun as a typical May morning on Sullivan's Island. After just a couple days back at Sea Breeze, Carson was already settling into a comfortable rhythm. She awoke as the pale rays of dawn painted her bedroom walls a pearlescent pink. Soundlessly, the young woman rose from the single bed of the room she'd always claimed in her grandmother's house. This morning, her head was woozy and her mouth felt like dry cotton from the wine she'd drunk the night before. She still didn't know how Mamaw could stop after just two glasses. When would she ever learn that heavy drinking and early rising didn't mix?

Carson slipped into a bikini, still cold, damp, and sticky with salt from yesterday's late swim. Peeking out the shutters as she applied a thick coating of SPF 50 to her face, she spied the ghostly remnants of a moon in the dusky dawning sky.

She smiled at the possibility of catching a wave while the red sun broke free of the horizon. It was her favorite moment of the day.

Carson hurried, stepping into flip-flops and loosely tying back her long, dark brown hair into a sloppy bun with an elastic. The pine floors creaked in the old beach house as she crept along the narrow hall to the kitchen. The last thing she wanted to do was awaken Mamaw. Her grandmother didn't appreciate the importance of getting out on the incoming tide.

Except for the newer appliances, the ancient kitchen with its pine cabinets and flooring and multipaned windows had never changed. Lucille wouldn't allow it. Long ago the kitchen had been painted yellow, but over the years it had dulled to a hue that, in the heat of a Southern summer, always made Carson think of rancid butter. Still, Carson loved everything about this house and it pained her deeply to think that Mamaw might be selling it.

Opening the screen door, she stepped out into the morning's fresh promise. There was a hush in the air. The day was as yet cool and unspoiled. As she crossed the porch and made her way across the dewy grass, her gaze swept the leaning garage, the house, and the quaint cottage that Lucille lived in. The buildings clustered together around an ancient oak drooling long trails of moss. In the morning light, the sight looked like an Elizabeth Verner pastel depicting historic Charleston. Mamaw adored Sea Breeze and had always seen that it was meticulously maintained.

It struck Carson that now the place was as tired and aged as its matron. Carson thought again how precious each day was.

Beside her surfboard she kept a large canvas bag filled with sandals, suntan lotion, a towel, and a cap. To it she added a fresh towel and an icy bottle of water and headed across the yard to her car, nicknamed the Beast. The car smelled of salt and coconut oil and the floors were covered in sand and empty water bottles.

It was a short drive to her favorite spot on the neighboring Isle of Palms. Carson recognized the few cars already parked along Palm Boulevard near Thirty-Second Avenue. Grand houses sat side by side between the road and dunes like a pastel-colored fence blocking the view of the ocean from the street. She walked along the beach path, her heels carving deep prints in the cool sand. The dunes were alive with spring wildflowers—yellow primroses, purple petunias, and the brilliant red and orange gaillardia. She spotted the ravaged frame of a dead bird, barely visible among the blossoms. Ants were marching to and from the hollow bones while bits of broken feathers stirred in the breeze. *Poor thing*, Carson thought. Nature, she knew, wasn't always pretty.

The weight of the surfboard was heavy on her arm but she pushed on without pause up the final dune. Reaching its peak, she felt the first gust of salt-tinged air. Carson rested her board in the sand and her face broke into a wide grin as she took in the unparalleled vista of dark sea and sky melting into an endless horizon. Closing her eyes, she breathed deep the taste of home.

Carson couldn't deny the unswerving pull of the tides.

There was something about the smell here—the tangy mud mixed with salt—that sparked memory. The Southern coastline with its glassy, peeling waves was softer, more welcoming, than the rocky cliffs and powerful surf of California. Everything about the lowcountry soothed. And no matter how many times she'd left, or how often she'd sworn never to return, those deep tidal roots kept tugging her back.

The beach was dotted with a few tanned men and women waxing their boards and chatting with one another. The camaraderie between local surfers ran deep. They grew up together, and over years of seeing each other daily on the water, those loose friendships forged bonds that lasted a lifetime. Echoes of their high-pitched laughter mingled with birdcalls. Farther out in the ocean, a few surfers were already on their boards, bobbing in the lineup while waiting for a decent wave. She quickly joined them and freshened up the board wax where her back foot had worn through the last coat.

She wasted no time. The swell was two to three feet, solid by South Carolina standards. She felt her enthusiasm begin to bubble in her veins. Lastly, she wiggled into a spring suit—a short-sleeved, short-legged wet suit— that hugged her body like a second skin. It was a tight squeeze and she ignored the annoying stares from some of the men on the beach. Done with her preparations, Carson hoisted her board and took her first few steps into the brisk water.

Here we go, she thought as she plowed through the surf, paddling hard in the chilly water out to where the breakers hit. When she caught sight of the first blue wall of a good wave she gripped the sides of her board, pushed down, ducked her head, and dove under it. The board cut through the water as the cold wave broke over her. She burst from the water, hair streaming, gasping for air, droplets of water shimmering on her face in the sunlight.

Carson loved this first exhilarating immersion in the ocean. For her, it was akin to a baptism, leaving her refreshed and clean, forgiven of all sins. That epiphany was what kept her coming, morning after morning. It was addictive. Grinning, she kept paddling as she braced herself for the next wave.

Once out beyond the breakers, Carson pulled herself up to sit on her board and wait for a wave. Her long bare legs dangled in the murky coastal water as she looked out at the sandy shore beyond. From this distance, she felt more a part of the sea than of the land. There was a profound sense of solitude this far out in the ocean, an awareness of how small one truly was in the scheme of such vastness. Rather than feel small, however, in this arena she felt part of something much bigger than herself. This gave her a sense of both power and peace.

Fellow surfers joined her in the ocean, bobbing on their boards like pelicans on the water as they waited for the right wave. Surfing was a solo sport but surfers chose their favorite spots. This was hers. She'd surfed here when she was a teen, and had readily gotten to know the current community of surfers. There were even some familiar faces. Despite the fact that she was a loner at heart, it was nice having someone to watch her back out on the mercurial ocean.

She bobbed in the water for a long while, waiting for a

good wave. Looking up at the rising sun, she realized that the tide was beginning to suck back out and she was floating farther out than usual. Behind her, a shrimp boat was trawling. The distance between them was uncommonly short. In fact the trawler was so close she could hear the raucous cry of the seagulls hovering over the green nets, vying to steal a meal. Pelicans circled and a few dolphins arched nearby as well, searching for a handout.

Carson frowned with annoyance. This was a recipe for trouble. Anytime fish gathered, wildlife hovered. Instinct told her to paddle farther from the boat, but in the distance she saw a strong wave building. "At last," she murmured, and gripped her board tight. This would be her ride in. Suddenly her attention was caught by a pelican tucking in its long wings and dive-bombing into the ocean, a mere ten feet from her board.

"Whoa," she exclaimed as she felt the ripples in the water. The bird had barely disappeared under the water when from the same spot the sea exploded in spray as a massive shark burst from the water, the pelican dangling in its jaws. Carson's breath froze in her chest as she watched the shark spin in the air, a glistening gray missile, then fall with a bombastic splash mere feet from her board. Carson pulled her legs onto her board and stared in shock as she rocked in the powerful wake.

For a second it seemed as though the whole earth had sucked in its breath. On the shore, people clustered near the water and pointed toward her. Yards away, a fellow surfer's eyes were wide with fear.

"Get out of there!" Danny shouted as he paddled hard toward shore.

What do I do? her mind screamed. She was fearful of putting her legs and arms back into the water. She'd missed the wave and the shark could be anywhere in the murky water, even right below her. Carson scanned the sea. The sun glistened like diamonds on the water. Overhead, the seagulls had resumed their grating cries as they circled the receding shrimp boat. All appeared peaceful. Carson released her breath and slowly leaned forward to her belly to paddle.

Then, from the corner of her eye, she caught a swift movement. She turned to see the unmistakable dorsal fin of a shark circling the shrimp boat. *Dear God, don't let the beast be inflamed into a feeding frenzy,* she prayed, paddling hard, focusing all of her mounting adrenaline on just making it to shore. Amid the cries of the birds, Carson heard the shouts of fellow surfers calling to her to get out of there. Moments later she felt a rough bump against her right leg from a large body. It felt like wet sandpaper. Carson's stomach dropped and she yanked her legs back up onto the board, holding tight.

"Oh God, oh God," she cried against her knees. The salt water burned her eyes and her whole body shook as she searched the dark sea. She knew from beneath the surface her surfboard resembled a sea turtle or a seal—ideal prey for a shark. For the first time in the sea, Carson felt hunted and helpless.

She shivered, waiting, watching as time crept by. All seemed quiet again. The sun was changing the sky from dusky to a brilliant, cloudless blue. She raised her hand like a visor over her eyes and squinted as she scanned the blue water that went on forever. She was alone. The other surfers had made it in to shore and the shrimp boat was heading north in its leisurely trawl. For a moment Carson felt a sense of hope. Surely the shark would follow the trail of the boat's fish-chummed water.

Then her surfboard rocked as a dark shadow passed close, fully as long as her six-foot board. Carson choked back a scream as the large gray body emerged from the depths beside her, but she released her breath in a sigh of relief at the sight of the rounded head, the long snout, and the sweet smile of a dolphin.

The dolphin circled her board, arching in its typical fashion, then circled twice more before it disappeared again. Carson swiped her hair back and took a deep breath. She'd read somewhere that dolphins didn't swim near sharks. Encouraged, once again she slowly loosened her legs and began to tentatively paddle toward shore, trying not to splash. She was making progress when she spotted the shark circling to her left. Cursing it to hell, Carson jerked her legs back on her board.

The shark was maybe ten feet in length and at least four hundred pounds of hard muscle. It was a bull shark, one of the most aggressive and unpredictable sharks that prowled shallow waters. Humans were not part of their diet, but the bulls were testy and had been known to deliver fatal bites. And this predator was clearly curious about her. It advanced toward her in its unmistakable zig-zag pattern.

Suddenly, the dolphin emerged again. It swam close to her board and began slapping the water with its tail fluke aggressively, as if beating a drum in warning. It seemed to work; the shark suddenly veered away and the dolphin submerged again. Carson felt the seconds tick by, clutching her legs, teeth chattering. What was happening? She'd heard that dolphins protected humans from sharks, and she prayed that was happening in this moment.

But the shark would not be chased off. It reemerged farther out, refusing to yield. The dolphin turned and began swimming with agitation in the stretch of blue sea between her and the shark before it disappeared again. Carson kept her gaze pinned to the shark, which suddenly turned her way. At that moment time seemed to crystallize. Carson felt numb as all sound diminished into the vacuum of those soulless eyes. Her mouth slipped open in a silent cry.

Out of nowhere, the dolphin suddenly streaked past her in a straight trajectory for the shark. The dolphin was so fast it hydroplaned across the water like a missile to T-bone the shark's flank. The bulky shark seemed to fold in half under the force of the hit in its vulnerable gills. For a fraction of a second the stunned shark appeared to hang limp, suspended in the water. Then, in a swift, reflexive move, the monster swung its head, its blood-colored gums and fierce teeth exposed, in an attack. The dolphin bolted, but not before the shark's teeth closed on its tail.

"No!" Carson couldn't stifle a cry as they both disappeared again under the water. It had all happened so fast—a matter of seconds.

Her heart broke for the dolphin, but she knew she had to get away while she could. Mercifully, a decent wave was building. This would be her best, perhaps only, chance to escape. She paddled for her life, stroking deep, immeasurably grateful for the familiar feel of the water lifting her forward. Clinging tight to her board, with her eyes fixed on the beach, she rode the crest on shaky legs close to shore.

Normally Carson was careful not to scrape her board by driving it into the beach, but today she rode the wave all the way in. Her legs felt like rubber and were scraped by the sand. Her friends ran to help her up and to carry her board from the sea.

While people clustered around her, Carson stood on the shore and stared at the ocean, her arms crossed tightly around her chest, shivering violently despite the morning sun. She looked out in an uncomprehending daze. Somehow, for reasons she didn't understand, a dolphin had saved her life, perhaps losing its own in the effort. She'd heard similar tales from fellow surfers, but this hadn't happened to somebody else. It was real. It had happened to *her*.

CHAPTER FOUR

The following day, Carson returned to the Isle of Palms and stared out from the beach at the familiar vista of ocean and sky. The surfboard felt heavy under her arm, and the late-afternoon sun was hot on her shoulders, but she lingered, staring out at the expanse of ocean and the mild waves cascading ashore. Only one other surfer was out there, bobbing in the calm sea, staring out at the horizon. The surf was unremarkable, barely enough to bother with. Yet that wasn't what was keeping Carson's feet rooted to the sand.

She was afraid. Her mouth was dry. Her heart was racing, not in anticipation but in dread. As she looked out at the vast expanse of the ocean, images of the shark flashed in her mind. She saw again the death in the soulless eyes, the rolling back of the mouth, exposing powerful pink gums and razor-sharp teeth. Carson felt again the terror of floating helplessly on her board while, underneath the murky water, a frenzied beast was biding its time.

Never, not even as a little girl, had she hesitated to leap into the salt water, as eager as any other creature of the sea that had been on land too long. The ocean, the Atlantic especially, was her motherland. She knew she shared the water with countless other creatures. Sharks included. The ocean was their home, too, one she'd shared with them for all of her life. She told herself that what had happened yesterday morning was a freak occurrence.

She shook her legs, swallowed hard, and expelled a long, shaky breath. "Get back in there. You belong there. Come on . . ."

Carson rolled her shoulders, then took off into the water. The water was chilly as she splashed into the shallows. Her heels dug into the soft sand; then, when she was far enough out, she slapped her board onto the water. She felt the tingling cold on her bare skin as she lay flat on the board, then stretched her arms out and began paddling hard out to sea. *Push, push, push*, she told herself, puffing hard. The sunlight on the water was glaringly bright. Carson felt cold, and the salt water burned her eyes. The first wave was approaching. She gripped her board tight. Ducked her head. Took a breath to dive under it.

Then she bailed. She couldn't help herself. Her muscles were tightening and her heart was pounding in a panic. All she could think of was that she had to get out of the water, get back to shore. Gulping air, she paddled for her life. Once in the shallows she leaped from her board and dragged it ashore, collapsing on the sand.

Carson crouched on the beach with her forehead resting on her knees as her breath slowly returned to normal.

When she could, she wiped her face with her palms and stared out at the ocean again, stunned.

What had happened to her out there? She'd panicked for no reason she could name. Who was this girl? She had always thought of herself as fearless. But today, when the fight-or-flight instinct kicked in, she hadn't fought. She had fled.

Carson retreated from the beach, packed up her car, and headed back to Sea Breeze. Her hands clutched the wheel so tightly her knuckles were white. She told herself over and over that her panic was just a normal reaction to what had happened yesterday morning. That in time the fear would dissipate like the confusion one felt after a nightmare. She just had to keep trying.

Still, Carson felt shaken to her core. Her whole life seemed to be spiraling. She was free-falling without a parachute, and now even surfing didn't bring her the sense of belonging that it always had.

Perhaps her fear wasn't a failure as much as it was an omen.

There were no secrets from Mamaw.

Later that night, after Carson had showered and feasted on crab cakes and red rice, she and Mamaw went to sit for a spell on the back porch. Carson curled up on a large black wicker chair with a glass of wine. A candle flickered in the low light and Carson could hear the pounding of the surf in the black distance. Across from her, Mamaw sat in a rocker, wrapped like a queen in a scarlet shawl.

"Well now, missy," Mamaw said when they'd settled in their chairs. Her blue eyes shone like full moons in the candlelight. "You've arrived early looking like one of the Joad family with your car packed to the gills, you've been sulking around, and tonight you're as nervous as a long-tailed cat in a room full of rocking chairs." Her left brow arched. "Let's have it."

Carson sighed, took a sip of the cool wine, then set the glass on the table. "I'm okay. I'm just a little freaked, is all. I was almost shark food out on the ocean yesterday."

Mamaw sucked in her breath and her hand reached up to the pearls around her neck. "What? What happened?"

"It was one of those weird perfect storms of coincidences. I was farther out than usual and this shrimp boat was closer in than usual. All these gulls and pelicans and dolphins were chasing the chum."

"Not a good combination."

"Right. It was a smorgasbord."

"A shark . . ." Mamaw shivered dramatically. "Honey, I hate knowing you're out there with those beasts."

"Oh, Mamaw, they're out there all the time. It's their home, don't forget. I mean, I've seen a lot of sharks out there. A *lot*." She saw the expected look of shock on Mamaw's face and wanted to spare her worry. "We're not their usual diet and they leave us alone. But this guy . . ."

Carson paused, feeling again that drop she'd felt in the pit of her stomach after the determined bump the shark had delivered to her leg. Carson knew that most of the accidents with sharks in the surf were just that—accidents. A case of mistaken identity.

"I just got spooked." She went on to tell Mamaw the

details of the encounter, ending with how the dolphin T-boned the shark. "If that dolphin hadn't defended me, I don't know what might've happened." She paused, her hand resting on her wineglass.

"And . . ."

Carson took a small breath. "And, Mamaw . . . I can't get back into the water. I tried today, but I just couldn't do it. . . . I've never felt that. Never. You know the ocean is my lifeline. I feel lost, desperate, like I've been cut off from my fix." Her voice shook. "I don't know what to do."

Mamaw placed her palms together at her lips and considered. "But that incident in the ocean . . . That's not all that's bothering you, is it? You came here feeling a little lost already, didn't you?"

Mamaw looked at Carson in a way that made Carson squirm in the chair. It was the look of someone who was about to tell her something she didn't want to hear.

"I guess . . ." Carson admitted.

"I thought so." Mamaw sat back in her rocker and pushed back and forth, biding her time, like the waves beating the shores in the distance.

"I'm in trouble, Mamaw," Carson confessed. "I'm out of work, out of my apartment, out of money." Carson brought her hands to her face. "I'm so ashamed."

Mamaw stopped rocking. "My dear girl. I don't under-stand." Mamaw had a way of sounding both shocked and calm. "What about that television show? It seemed to be such a success."

"It was," Carson acknowledged after a shaky breath. "It ran three seasons, which is a long time by industry standards. Word that it was canceled came out of the blue.

They didn't bother to explain why." She reached out for her glass and took a long swallow of wine.

"But surely you can get another job," Mamaw said persistently. "You've been working in your field for more than ten years. You've traveled the world, worked on films. I've bragged on you to anyone who would listen." She shook her head disbelievingly. "Carson, I don't understand. You've been so successful."

She shrugged, hating to have to explain. "I don't know . . . It's a tough job market. The streets of L.A. are littered with folks like me trying to get a job. I've tried, really I have." She sighed heavily. She couldn't tell her grandmother that some of the connections she'd called on were men she'd slept with, or that she'd been fired from a gig for showing up intoxicated. Her reputation wasn't as sterling as Mamaw thought.

"It's been humiliating," she confessed. "I hung in there as long as I could, but I'm broke."

"Surely you've saved something for a rainy day?"

"I freelanced. There wasn't much to save." She looked at her grandmother earnestly. "And you know I've had a lot of experience living on a shoestring."

Mamaw nodded, confirming her understanding that her son, Carson's father, had been unreliable at best, negligent at worst, and that Carson had borne the brunt of that broken lifestyle. They'd moved from one place to another, living from check to check, always waiting for that screenplay that would make them rich to sell.

"There's nothing left, Mamaw," she said, her voice tinged with bitterness. "It's as though all my years of work amount to nothing."

"Oh, honey, I know it seems like that now. But at times like this you have to take the long view. Trust me. You don't know where this turn will take you. God never closes a door without opening a window."

Carson pinched her lips. She didn't dare tell her grandmother, a staunch churchgoer, that she no longer believed in God.

"What about that young man you'd been seeing? What was his name? Todd? Where does he fit into this scenario?"

Carson suppressed a shudder and downed the last of her wine. "I broke it off last winter," she said summarily. "He took it hard, I'm afraid. Claimed I'd broken his heart and that he'd been saving for a ring."

Mamaw sucked in her breath. "A ring?"

Carson was quick to dispel her hopes. "It's all for the best. All I could think was that I'd gotten out of that one in the nick of time." She quickly rose to her feet, in need of more wine. "Be right back. I'm getting a refill. Do you want a glass?"

Mamaw shook her head.

Carson walked swiftly across the porch to the kitchen, her thirst building. Lucille had tidied up the kitchen and retired, but she'd left a plate of homemade lemon bars on the table. Carson refreshed her glass, then, remembering where their conversation was heading, took the bottle with her. She tucked it under one arm, and with the other, she carried the cookies back to the porch. She found Mamaw looking out into the darkness with a pensive expression.

"Oh, Carson," Mamaw said with a sorry shake of her

head when Carson settled back in her chair. "I worry about you. You're over thirty, my dear, and though you're just as beautiful as ever," she hastened to say, "you *are* getting older. Perhaps you shouldn't be so quick to throw away every proposal."

Carson's eyes flashed as the arrow struck true. "I'm only thirty-four," she shot back. "I'm not the least bit worried about getting married. I'm not even sure I *want* to get married."

"Now, don't get your feathers ruffled."

"I'm not ruffled," Carson complained, shifting on her seat. It was hard to sit still and listen to someone two generations removed extolling values that no longer had any impact. She had been raised to be respectful of her elders, but this rankled. "It's just . . . I don't know, it's insulting that you think my only hope in life is to get married. Frankly, Mamaw, from where I sit that never worked out too well for Dad. You're from another era. Thirty-four isn't old. Women aren't getting married right out of college anymore. We're starting our own careers. I'm not waiting for some man to take care of me. I depend on myself."

"Yes, dear," Mamaw said serenely. "I see how well that's working out for you."

Carson squeezed her toes and simmered. "Well, I'm not going to settle just to get married. Like Dora did."

"Carson," Mamaw said with a hint of scolding. "It's not nice to say something like that about your sister. Especially not now."

"Why not now?"

Mamaw looked at her with wonder mixed with

regret. "Mercy, child. Didn't you know Dora is getting a divorce?"

Carson leaned forward in her chair and gasped. "No!"

"Oh yes . . ." Mamaw nodded sagely. "It's all very sad. Cal up and left them both seven months ago. Said how he couldn't live there anymore. Dora was devastated. Still is, I'm afraid."

This was shocking news to Carson. In her mind, Dora was the ideal Southern housewife with traditional values, involved with her husband's career, her church, her community. Every Christmas she received a beautifully engraved card with a photo of the family smiling, dressed in their red sweaters on the front porch or seated in front of the pine-strung mantel. Looks could indeed be deceiving.

"Poor Dora. They'd been married for what? Twelve years? That had to be a terrible blow. She never let on that she was having any troubles."

"She wouldn't, dear. That's not her style."

Carson thought of how her sister never revealed anything unpleasant, even as a girl. If Dora had won a prize, it would be sung from the rafters. If she failed a test, she took it to the grave.

"Did she see it coming?"

"I'm afraid if it wasn't concerning her son, Dora didn't see anything. That may have been the cause for their split. She's dedicated her life to Nate. But a wife shouldn't forget her man. Cal felt ignored, and I daresay he was."

"A woman shouldn't forget herself, either," Carson added.

Mamaw raised her eyes. "So true."

Carson sighed with sincere regret for her sister. "I can't believe she didn't tell me."

"It's not something one puts on a Christmas card, dear," Mamaw said. "Nor was it a secret. It pains me that neither of you have kept in touch. A pity."

"It is," Carson said softly, acknowledging the truth. It was a sorry statement that they'd become so estranged that her sister, even a half sister, wouldn't write to let her know she was getting a divorce. Carson had to accept half the blame for that. She'd not reached out to her sister, either, when she lost her job and was floundering. Maybe, she thought, they could help each other now.

"What's wrong with us, Mamaw?" Carson asked softly. "If someone like Dora can't hold a marriage together, what hope is there for me? I have had a long string of men and relationships." She snorted. "If you can call them that. When I'm alone at night, sitting in the dark and nursing a drink, sometimes I wonder if I'm like Daddy, missing a gene for love and doomed to a lifetime of failed relationships."

"I don't think so, dear. Granted, your father never set a good example. But you're my granddaughter, after all. And you're the most like me. I had a long string of beaus, true. But don't forget that I was married for fifty years. Edward was the love of my life." She reached out to gently pat Carson's hand. "You just haven't found the right one yet."

Carson looked up skeptically. "And Dora?"

Mamaw sighed. "Who knows? Perhaps Cal wasn't the right one after all."

Carson guffawed. "She settled."

"She made a mistake," Mamaw said, correcting her. "It happens."

"And Harper?"

"Goodness, Harper's a child yet!"

"She's twenty-eight."

"I suppose she is," Mamaw said with some surprise. "I always think of her as a little girl. Yes, well . . . Aren't you the one who just told me that you're waiting to get married? That thirty wasn't old?"

Carson chuckled. "Hoist by my own petard." She kicked off her sandals and curled her feet up onto the chair, settling in for a good gossip. "What's the story with Harper, anyway? I hate to admit I haven't kept up. Is she still living in New York?"

"Harper doesn't communicate with me much, either. I'm sure her mother doesn't encourage the connection. All I'm privy to is that she still lives in New York. With her mother," she added, clearly not approving. "And she works for her mother's publishing company. Her mother has her talons in deep with that fledgling, I can tell you. Harper's a very bright girl, you know. Went to all the best schools."

"Of course," Carson muttered, feeling an old envy rear its head. She felt burned each time Mamaw let drop what good schools Harper had attended. Carson would have given anything to have gone to a boarding school like Andover, then to a college like Vassar. Only she would have gone to California Institute of the Arts or the Savannah College of Art and Design. She'd filled out the applications but there was never any money for her. After graduating from high school, Carson worked during the day and took night classes in photography at a local community college. Any success she'd achieved came from her own talent and hard work. All she ever got from her parents were her good looks.

"Must be nice to have everything handed to you on a silver platter," she said, hearing the bitterness in her own voice.

"There are curses with that, too. And, Carson, you went to college."

Carson felt the burn and said with heat, "No, I didn't. Not really. I took classes at a local college. I never graduated." Carson shrugged and shook her head with pique. "I don't want to talk about this anymore," she said, burrowing into the cushions and taking a fortifying swallow of wine.

An awkward silence fell between them as Mamaw rocked and Carson finished her glass.

"I'm sorry," Carson said, a soft voice in the darkness. "I'm just feeling sorry for myself. I shouldn't be so nasty."

"You're not," Mamaw replied indulgently. "And I want you to feel you can say anything here, to me."

"This place has always been my home. My refuge. I need your support now, Mamaw. I'm feeling lost," Carson confessed, her voice wavering. "And afraid."

Mamaw immediately leaned over to put her long, slender arms around her. She smoothed the hair from Carson's forehead and kissed it.

Carson relaxed, feeling safe again after so many months of uncertainty. She didn't know what she'd expected Mamaw to do when she'd returned to Sea Breeze. Perhaps toss a few dollars her way, offer a consoling pat as more wine was poured. A little indulgence, certainly. Wasn't that what had always been offered to her father whenever he was down on his luck? Carson needed a little indulgence now.

Mamaw drew back and grasped Carson's shoulders and gave her a gentle shake. Carson smiled shyly, expecting one of Mamaw's platitudes to buck up her spirits.

"Now, you listen to me, young lady," Mamaw said, looking directly into Carson's eyes. "Enough of this moping and feeling sorry for yourself, hear? No more talk of being afraid. That's not who you are. You're a Muir and don't you forget it. I admit, you've had a difficult time of it with your father. I indulged Parker at such times as this and I daresay I may have made mistakes there. But I won't make the same mistakes with you, my precious."

Mamaw released Carson and sat back in her chair.

"You may not want to find a husband, and that's all right. You're a big girl now and capable of making your own decisions. But, darling, you can't lie around here feeling sorry for yourself and licking your wounds. There's no fight in that. No honor. Listen to your grandmother. Tomorrow you need to get up early and face the new day. Get back out in the water."

Mamaw pinned Carson with her gaze. "And find a job!"

The following morning, the alarm on Carson's phone sounded like bell chimes. She shot her arm out to turn it off before anyone else woke up. When she rose, she looked at herself in the mirror, saw her blue eyes bright in her reflection, and realized she felt sharp, rested . . . and good. She wasn't bogged down with the grogginess that came from her usual night of drinking. She'd gone to bed early to catch up on her sleep and this morning her head was clear and she felt a tingling of energy running in her veins. Spurred on by Mamaw's advice to stop sulking around, Carson was determined to take the first baby step and get back into the water.

She stepped outside and was greeted by the moist, fragrant morning air. It felt warmer than the day before. She could trace the advent of summer as they moved closer to June. Soon, the water would be warmer, too, she thought with a smile. Inside the house, everyone still slept soundly. She went directly to the back porch, where her paddleboard was resting. Hoisting it under her arm, she carried it to the end of the dock, attuned to the creaking of the wood beneath her feet and the lapping of water against wood. The dawn still hovered at the waterline. Carson smiled. She hadn't missed it.

Walking down the long wooden dock, Carson held her tall paddleboard with fidgety fingers, feeling the panic slowly rising in her chest at the prospect of entering the sea. It might have been just the cove, not the waves along the front of the ocean, but there was still wildlife coming and going from either place.

She cleared her throat as she faced the sea, opening her heart. "I don't know how to fight this. I depend on you to help me." She took a deep breath. "So here I am."

There was nothing left but to get wet. Carson lowered her paddleboard onto the water as she had countless times before. Her hands shook and her feet felt clumsy on the familiar board but she pushed forward. Once she found her balance on the sweet spot, she took a deep breath and lowered her paddle. *Just one stroke after another,* she told herself as she made her way away from the dock out into the current.

There was a peace and solitude in these early-morning paddling trips that was akin to meditation. She was just another creature making her solitary path along the waterway. The water level was low. White egrets stood along the grassy edges with enviable poise on their sleek black legs. A little farther up the creek, she spotted a great blue heron, majestic and haughty.

It was after six A.M. and still most of the windows of the houses along the creek were dark. Their occupants were sleeping away the best show of the day, she thought to herself. But she was glad for the isolation. It was a good idea to have a buddy watching your back when you were out on the surf. Here on the quiet waterway, however, she felt safe cruising along with only her thoughts for company. She focused on the steady rhythm of her strokes, left to right, left to right, and the rippling sound the paddle made.

She was making steady progress along the creek when to her left she heard a loud splash. Carson's rhythm broke as she swung her head toward the sound in time to spot the tip of a dorsal fin before it disappeared underwater. She felt her heart race as her body froze, paddle in midair. Then she saw the gray dorsal fin reemerge a few yards ahead of her board.

Carson sighed in relief when she saw that it was a dolphin, and chuckled at herself for being so jumpy. Atlantic bottlenose dolphins roamed these waters. These estuaries were their home. She loved these whimsical creatures, never more than since one had saved her life. Carson dunked her paddle back into the water and pushed hard, hoping to see the dolphin again. Turning her head, she scanned the flat water until she spotted the dolphin emerging with a percussive *pfoosh* to breathe. She followed the graceful swimmer as it traveled farther down the creek; then it surprised her by turning again and coming back.

Carson stopped paddling and let the current drag her along like it would any piece of driftwood. The sleek gray dolphin eased alongside the board, this time tilting its body slightly so it could peer up at her, curious. Carson looked into the large, dark almond eye and had the distinct impression that this dolphin was checking her out. Not in idle curiosity, either. She'd experienced dolphins coming close to her paddleboard many times before. But this moment was surreal. Carson sensed—she knew— that there was *a thinking presence* behind that gaze.

"Well, good morning," she said to the dolphin.

At the sound of her voice, the dolphin jerked its head away and dunked under the water.

Carson laughed at its capriciousness. How different looking into these eyes was compared to looking into the shark's. In the dolphin's gaze she sensed a curious mind, not her doom. She couldn't deny that she was as curious about this unusually friendly dolphin as the dolphin seemed to be about her.

The water level was slowly rising as the tide came in. The sun rose higher, too, and she was getting close to the end of the boundaries of the cove behind Sullivan's Island. If she didn't turn around, the tide would carry her out into the choppy waters of Charleston Harbor. She put her back into her strokes and pushed her paddle against the current toward home. It was hard work but good for that flat belly that seemed to spark Dora's jealousy.

She was focused on the task when in her peripheral vision she spotted the curious dolphin again. It was discreetly keeping abreast of her, then shot ahead several yards before turning back. Carson smiled. The dolphin clearly was following her. Carson wondered if it was actually playing with her or just curious about the gangly creature who made such pathetic progress in the water while the dolphin was so streamlined and graceful.

By the time Carson reached the dock the thrumming of boat engines could be heard in the distance, signaling the end of her peaceful time in the cove. She climbed onto the dock and pulled off her paddleboard, shivering as splashes of chilly water struck her bare skin. Hearing another percussive whoosh, Carson dropped to her knees on the floating dock, raised a hand over her eyes, and squinted. A large gray head emerged from the water a few feet away. Carson didn't move, not wanting to spook the dolphin. Bright eyes, smart and watchful, gazed at her from the water for a few minutes. Then the creature opened its mouth and emitted a series of short, squeaky sounds.

The dolphin closed its mouth, then tilted its head to peer up at her speculatively, as though to ask, *So now what?*

Carson laughed. "You're so beautiful," she said to the dolphin, reaching out her hand.

Immediately the dolphin dove, lifting its tail into the air.

Carson sucked in her breath and stared at the empty rings of water where the dolphin had been. A chunk was missing from the dolphin's left fluke, like it had been bitten off. Carson rose shakily to her feet and stood scanning the water while the memory of the shark incident flashed through her mind. She recalled how the dolphin had sped toward the shark like a bullet and rammed into its side. The shark had seemed to fold into itself for a second, and just as quickly, it had swung around in attack. She'd seen the mighty jaws lurch for the dolphin's tail as it tried to escape.

"Oh my God," Carson gasped. This had to be *the* dolphin. The one that had saved her from the shark. Could it be possible? It made sense that the dolphin would come to the relative quiet of the estuaries to heal. Her mind went over the way the dolphin had looked at her, studied her, and how it had come back a second time to check her out.

The dolphin had recognized her.

She laughed shortly, stunned by the possibility. Her rational mind told her it couldn't be true. But then again, why not? Like humans, dolphins were self-aware and highly intelligent.

Carson scanned the water of the cove. In the distance, against the blue-green water, she spotted the gray dolphin as it gracefully arched in and out of the waves. It was heading out into the harbor. Carson cupped her hands at her mouth and called out, "Thank you!"

CHAPTER FIVE

*M*amaw called an old friend and within the week Carson had a job as a waitress at Dunleavy's, a small Irish pub on Sullivan's Island. That's how things were done on the island, where family connections were tighter than a tick on a dog. Carson had to swallow her pride, but in truth, she was happy to have the job.

Carson didn't have savings, stocks—nothing. Her life on film crews had always been on the go, traveling from one exotic location to another. Some people couldn't keep up the fast pace, but living out of a suitcase came naturally to her. Her father had never let the moss grow over them, moving them from one apartment to the next. So being here at Sea Breeze the last few weeks had been a nice slowing down. She was gradually getting back into the Southern rhythm.

And she had to admit she enjoyed working at the pub.

Dunleavy's was a family-owned pub on Middle Street, a popular few blocks of quaint restaurants and small shops. The pub had great beers on tap, fresh popcorn, and a homey decor. There were picnic tables and umbrellas outside where folks could sit with their dogs. Inside, beer cans and license plates decorated the walls and the screen door slammed when you walked in.

Carson worked the lunch shift and made decent tips, but even after two weeks she had a lot to learn. She was trying to carry one too many plates from a table when her hand slipped, knocking over a beer glass and sending it shattering across the floor. Thankfully the lunch rush was over and only a few patrons remained at the small wood tables, but each of the six heads turned toward the clatter, as well as the faces of her boss and fellow waitress, Ashley.

"Careful there," Brian called out from his post at the bar. "Again . . ." he added with a rueful shake of his head.

Carson gritted her teeth and smiled at the manager, then bent to pick up the broken glass.

"What's the matter with you today?" asked Ashley, rushing over with a broom and waste bin. "Step back and don't cut your fingers. Let me sweep up."

Carson leaned against the table. Around her the few tourists went back to their plates and a soft buzz of talking resumed.

"I'm the world's worst waitress," Carson whined.

Ashley chuckled as she swept. "Well, you're not the best, but you've just started. Don't worry. You'll get the hang of it. I'll finish up here. Why don't you bring a menu to that guy who just sat down in your section," she said with a nod of her head.

Carson reached over to grab a menu.

"Put on your pretty smile," Ashley teased. "It's Mr. Predictable."

"Stop it," Carson said with a smirk.

"He always sits in your section."

"That means he likes the window, not me."

"Yeah, well, you don't see his moon eyes following you when you walk away."

"Really?" Carson asked, mildly surprised. Not that she should have been. She was accustomed to the glances of men, but her radar was off and she'd not registered this one. She turned her head to slyly check out the man in question. He was tall and lean, a little too angular, and had the slightly disheveled T-shirt–shorts–and–sandals look of a local. His hair was dark brown with curls that went askew under his cap. She couldn't remember the color of his eyes, couldn't, for that matter, remember much about him.

"He's not my type," Carson said.

"You mean he's not the cool Hollywood dream boy you usually hang out with in L.A.?"

Carson had told Ashley about some of the men she'd dated in L.A.—mostly actors and filmmakers. She got a kick out of seeing Ashley's eyes widen, impressed with the roster of men who were either movie star good-looking or very cool. Mr. Predictable was neither.

Carson smirked and tightened the strings of her apron around her uniform, a green Dunleavy's T-shirt. "Why don't you take his order? He's more your type anyway . . . the scruffy good ol' boy."

Ashley sighed lustily. "He's cute. But I've got a boy-friend. I'm off the market. Besides"—Ashley put her hand to her heart with an exaggerated expression of horror—"I couldn't do that to the poor man. He'd be so disap-pointed if he saw me come to the table instead of you."

"Well, he can look all he likes. I'm not looking for romance."

"Honey," Ashley said with a smirk before sauntering away with her broom and trash, "we're always lookin' for romance."

When Carson approached the table the dark-haired man turned from the window to her. This time Carson looked into his eyes. They were a deep chocolate color that had the power to melt when he locked gazes with someone, as he did now. He was taking her measure, she could tell, as though he were surprised that she'd finally taken notice of him.

"Well, hey," she said with an engaging smile. She'd had a lot of luck with this smile over the years and expected results. "Nice to see you're back."

He arched a brow, amused. "Yeah, well, I like it here," he said, withholding a smile. "Good food. Nice atmo-sphere."

"Uh-huh," she replied. "What'll it be? Wait, let me guess. The black-'n'-blue burger."

He glanced up to look at her from over the top of the menu. "You noticed?"

"Well, you do order the same thing every day."

"Why change a good thing?" he replied, closing the menu and handing it to her.

"Do you want a beer with that?"

"Sweet tea," they both said at the same time, and laughed.

"Coming right up."

Looking over her shoulder, she smiled, then chuckled quietly, noting that Ashley had been right. His dreamy gaze was following her. He was indeed Mr. Predictable.

A short while later she carried the pub's signature burger to the table. He looked up from his sheaf of papers and smiled too brightly when she approached. Not wanting to encourage him, she didn't smile in return and placed the food down without ceremony.

"Sure you don't want a beer?" she asked, all business. "We have Guinness on tap."

"No, thanks. I don't drink."

"Oh," she said. She felt awkward for pushing the beer if the guy was an alcoholic. "A refill then?" The ice clanked loudly in the pitcher as she poured his tea.

"Did I say something to offend you?" he asked.

"No," she replied, shifting her weight. "Not at all. I'm just preoccupied."

"Anything I can do to help?"

"Not unless you know someone looking for a stills photographer."

"So, you're a photographer?"

"Yes. But not like for portraits or weddings. Though I'd freelance those now, if you know anyone who's looking. I work out of L.A. In the entertainment business."

Understanding flickered in his eyes. He leaned back against his chair. "So you take all those publicity shots we see in magazines and online?"

"No," she replied slowly, realizing she'd have to explain

for the thousandth time what a stills photographer did. "I do anything to do with photos for marketing a film. I shoot episodes, backdrops, behind the scenes—whatever, to promote the show. It's complicated," she said, cutting the conversation off. She was reminded to check her messages to see if any of her contacts might've come through with a job possibility. "I've got to get back to work."

"Oh. Right," he said in a rush, realizing he was taking up her time.

She swirled away, stopping at tables to refill glasses, take orders, bring food in the dance of waitresses. Half an hour later he was still sitting at his table reading. Carson stopped back to check on him.

"Refill on that sweet tea?" Southerners always rolled the two words together so it sounded like *sweetie.*

He looked up from his papers and smiled. "I'm good," he replied in his easy drawl. "Just a check."

She was about to turn and fetch it, but, thinking of her tip, paused to say, "Sorry I had to run off like that before."

"I'm sorry I kept you from your job."

He really did have a nice smile, she thought. When his lips slid halfway up in that sweet teasing grin, his dark brown eyes sparked with what she knew was flirtation.

"What's your name, anyway?" she asked him. It seemed wrong to think of him as *Mr. Predictable.*

His grin widened to reveal white teeth. "It's Blake. Blake Legare."

Recognition clicked. "Are you one of the Legares from Johns Island?"

"Guilty as charged."

"No kidding? Do you know Ethan Legare?"

"Which one? We're a big family and there are a few Ethans."

"The one who works at the aquarium. Married to Toy, who's in charge of the sea turtle hospital."

"Sure do. That Ethan's my first cousin."

"Really?" She'd forgotten how living in Charleston was like living in a small town. Mamaw had always impressed upon her the importance of dressing well and speaking politely, because there were no strangers in Charleston. "Ethan and I used to surf together back in the day. I haven't seen him for . . . well, years."

"I don't figure he's got much time for surfing nowadays, what with two kids."

"Ethan has two children?" She chuckled, remembering the skinny kid who was as fearless on the water as she had been. "That's hard to believe."

"It happens," he drawled.

"What about you?" she asked him. "Are you married with kids in tow?"

"Me?" he asked, amused at the idea. "God, no. I mean . . ." He faltered, seeing her shocked reaction at the emphasis. "Not that I'm against marriage or anything, it's just, well . . . No. I'm not."

He was blushing slightly and Carson thought it was mildly beguiling.

"Do you surf?" she asked Blake, steering them into a different topic.

"Used to in high school. Don't anymore."

That was typical of a lot of men who grew up along the coast. Most boys she knew tried surfing at least once, but few really took up the sport. *Too bad*, she thought.

Blake added, "I've taken to kiting."

Carson's mind did a U-turn. "As in kiteboarding?"

He nodded. "Yeah. I like it better. I go out whenever I get a free moment and some good wind."

Carson looked at his long, lanky body, seeing him in a new light. He wasn't muscle-bound, which was never a look she found sexy. But in his dark brown T-shirt she could see that his muscles were hard and sinewy, typical for swimmers. *Who knew?* she thought with renewed interest. Mr. Predictable wasn't so predictable after all.

Condensation dripped from the iced tea pitcher down her arm. It was getting heavier by the minute. She boldly put the pitcher down, then dried her hands on her apron.

"I've always wanted to learn to kiteboard," she said, warming to the topic. "But I don't see a lot of girls out there doing it. I know they do, of course, but it looks like it takes a lot of upper-body strength to handle the kite."

"Not especially. The arms are used for control of the kite, but you're connected to the kite by a line that's attached to a harness you wear like a belt. There's a lot of core strength involved. A lot of girls are giving it a try. If you surf, you shouldn't have any trouble." He paused, then said, "I could give you a lesson . . ."

There it was. The invitation, as she'd expected. And yet, not at all what she'd expected. Going to the beach to learn how to kiteboard wouldn't really be a date—no drinks, no candles, no awkward small talk. It was a lesson, outdoors, in the daylight. If she didn't like him, they'd say good-bye and that would be it.

She smiled. "That'd be great. Where do you kite?"

"Around Station Twenty-Eight."

"Yeah, I've seen the kites out there. Okay, maybe I can—"

Her response was interrupted by someone shouting out her name.

"Caaaaaaarson Muir! Is that really you?"

She turned her head and followed the voice to the door to see a broad-shouldered, deeply tanned man with shaggy blond hair and wearing a raggedy blue polo shirt and khaki shorts. He held out his arms and stampeded her way to lift her clear off the ground.

"Damn, it really is you!" he exclaimed as he set her down, grinning from ear to ear.

Carson pushed her hair from her face, laughing, flustered by both the welcome and his staggeringly beautiful blue eyes.

"Hey, Dev!" she replied breathlessly. "Well, aren't you a blast from the past!"

Devlin Cassell had been a summer crush when she was in her teens. He had dated Dora for a summer, but there had been one hot and heavy kissing session between them on the beach one lazy summer evening after Dora had left for college and that's where it had ended.

"When did you get back?" he asked her, his eyes devouring her.

"A few weeks ago."

"You staying with Mamaw?"

"No, I'm renting a villa at Wild Dunes."

His eyes widened. "Really?"

"Would I be working here if I was? Of course I'm at Mamaw's."

"Good ol' Mamaw. There's no one like her. How is she? What's she up to? She still hosting those big parties?"

"No big soirées these days. But the family's celebrating her birthday this weekend. She's eighty years old."

"No kidding." Devlin shook his head as though in disbelief. "I'll bet she doesn't look a day over sixty."

Carson laughed. "Mamaw always said you could charm the skin off a snake."

He laughed at that, murmuring, "Yep, that sounds about right."

She enjoyed the cadence of a Southern man's chatter and realized how much she'd missed it.

"You remember Brady and Zack?" Devlin asked, stepping back and extending his arm toward his two friends, both of similar age and attire. They'd removed their baseball caps, revealing sunburned faces and salt-dried hair. She didn't know the men but smiled, lifting her hand in a casual wave. "Come on, pretty girl, walk with me," Devlin said, putting his hand on the small of her back and guiding her to the bar. "I'm so dry my throat feels like a desert."

He smelled like he'd been drinking for hours.

"I'm working," she told him.

"And I'm a paying customer." Devlin reached the bar and slid onto a bar stool. "How're you doing, Brian?" he called out. "Got a Guinness for me?"

"With your name on it," Brian replied. Devlin was a regular and welcome in the pub.

"And one for the lady."

The other two men called out their beer orders and slid onto nearby stools. Carson caught Brian's eye and lifted her brows in a nonverbal request for permission to speak to her friend. Brian discreetly nodded, then turned to work the tap.

"So, Carson," Devlin said, turning his head and searching Carson's face. "You are still the prettiest girl I've ever seen. How long are you here for?"

Carson shrugged and sidestepped the compliment. "I don't know. Till it's time to leave, I suppose."

"No man waitin' on you? No ring on the finger?"

Carson shook her head. "God forbid," she replied, then realized she'd offered the same answer as Blake Legare.

Devlin's eyes gleamed. "I always thought you were one fish no one was going to catch."

"What about you?"

Devlin screwed up his face. "Caught and set free. Divorced last year."

Brian delivered the beers to the men and moved on, though she knew he wouldn't miss a word.

"Yeah, it was tough," Devlin admitted, then took a long sip. "But I got my Leigh Ann out of the deal, so I guess it was worth it."

"You have a child, too? I'm having a hard enough time picturing you married, much less a father."

He shook his head ruefully. "So did my wife, apparently. In all fairness, it was my fault. I screwed up." His face fell and he picked up his glass for a long drink.

So he cheated, she figured. Too bad, but not entirely a surprise. Devlin wasn't a playboy, but he was a perpetual boy who liked to play. When they'd been young, he'd been popular with everyone. He was the guy with the available boat, the surfboard to share, the cold beer—the guy who always knew which beach house on Capers Island would be empty for the weekend. Most of her friends from that time still lived in the area but had settled down into jobs, marriage, children. Even Devlin had given it a shot.

She'd heard that Devlin was an extremely successful real estate maven on the islands. But seeing him here at midday, obviously just back from a fishing trip with his buddies, confirmed her suspicion that as a husband and father, he clearly hadn't been able to set aside his toys and freedom in order to step up and be responsible.

It was, she supposed, predictable.

At the word, she glanced back at Blake's table. Her heart sank to see it was empty. She stepped away from Devlin to walk to the table. There was no message scribbled on a piece of paper, no card with a phone number. Only a twenty-dollar bill that lay tucked under his plate.

Carson reached down to collect the money. It was a generous tip, but she still couldn't help but feel shortchanged.

CHAPTER SIX

*H*arper's first good news of the day came when the pilot announced that they'd caught a tailwind and that they'd made the trip from New York to Charleston ahead of schedule. But as she put away her iPad, she suddenly wished for that extra twenty minutes to wrap up her work.

She turned and looked out the window of the Delta jet as it broke through the clouds and began its approach to the Charleston airport. The descent sparked mixed emotions. From her vantage point, she could see the signature landscape of the lowcountry stretched out along the Atlantic Ocean. Long, winding creeks snaked their way through thousands of acres of green wetlands, looking like they'd come straight from a Mary Edna Fraser batik. It was a seductive landscape, undulating and lush. Even sensuous. It was no wonder the lowcountry was home to so many acclaimed authors, she thought to herself. The landscape was an inspiration.

Unfortunately, her father had never joined their ranks. *Poor Daddy*, she thought. Despite his dreams, he'd lacked both the discipline and the talent. Harper felt neither love nor scorn for her biological father. She'd hardly known him. Her mother had never discussed him or acknowledged their marriage, other than to give his daughter his name, and hyphenated at that. There wasn't one photograph of him in their apartment. When Harper was old enough to ask questions, Georgiana told her only child that she'd married Parker Muir for his charm, wit, and potential. She'd divorced him because she'd discovered she'd been wrong. With an editor's cruel succinctness, she summed it up: "Parker Muir could talk about writing better than he could write."

The only meeting Harper had had with her father had been at Dora's wedding. He might still have been handsome if he hadn't been so thin, his face marred by an alcoholic sheen. She shuddered and clutched the armrests, a last vestige of her childhood fear of flying. One gentle bump, and the plane landed smoothly on the runway. Immediately she grabbed her phone and tapped her foot as it powered up. The two-hour plane ride was an eternity to be unplugged.

Before leaving the airport she slipped into the ladies' room to take stock of her appearance in the mirror. She wanted to make a strong impression on Mamaw and her half sisters, showing them that though she was the youngest of the group, she was no longer the baby. She was an adult: successful and worldly.

Her hair hung like a sheath of tangerine silk, grazing her shoulders. Her large blue eyes stared back at her like a cat's, with slick black eyeliner and thick, dark lashes. She'd had her pale ones dyed. Before she left, she powdered her skin, covering the faint freckles that peppered her cheeks and nose.

Harper brushed away lint from the tailored black cotton jacket and gave the hem a firm tug to smooth it where it just met her slender hips. She had to look perfect when she arrived, mature and confident. She wore tight black jeans and sexy, black, strappy high heels. They killed her feet, but they looked great. At five feet two inches, she didn't want to be dwarfed by her sisters and Mamaw.

Harper would be like her mother, she decided. She needed to make an entrance.

She slipped her black designer bag over her shoulder and, with a final satisfied smile at her appearance, she muttered, "Nobody puts baby in the corner." Then she gripped her roller bag and began walking toward the taxicabs in mincing steps.

When Carson pulled into the driveway, she was surprised to see her usual spot in front of the garage taken by a Lexus SUV. Squeezing out of the car, she pulled her gear from the passenger seat, then let her gaze linger on the SUV. Unlike her dented and rusting blue Volvo, the silver Lexus with the South Carolina plates didn't have a scratch; even the black leather interior was pristine. A children's puzzle book was in the backseat, along with a red sweatshirt. It could only mean that her half sister Dora had arrived from Summerville.

Carson sighed, annoyed. Why was she here today?

Dora wasn't expected until the weekend. It wasn't that she wasn't glad to see Dora, but she wasn't feeling very social. And maybe it was selfish, but she wanted a few more days with Mamaw all to herself.

She lugged her paddleboard from the rooftop and stored it in the garage. The scent of moss and mildew made her nose tingle. Carson followed the stone path around the thick hydrangeas to the back porch, where an outdoor shower was hidden behind an enormous, blooming gardenia. Opening the door, she sidestepped the spiderwebs in the corner and the weeds poking up through the stones and turned on the faucet. The shower only offered cold water, but on the island in the summer, the water was always lukewarm. She slipped from her beach cover-up and showered in her suit, inhaling the sweet scents of lavender soap and gardenias as she felt the tension slide from her body. After she dried off, Carson loosely braided her dripping long hair, grabbed her towel and her patchwork bag, then made her way up across the porch to the back door.

There was a time when she would have dashed across the yard and burst through the door to greet her sisters. There would've been squeals and giggles and a rapid sharing of all news of the preceding year. They would speak so fast it was more a rattling off of headlines, details to be filled in later.

So it was rather a sad state of affairs that today, instead of rushing, she slowed her steps, delaying the inevitable. When Dora had turned seventeen she'd stopped coming to Mamaw's house for long stays and instead only visited on the occasional summer weekend with a friend in tow.

Even after all these years Carson still remembered the hurt and pain of being the odd man out as the older girls whispered and giggled together.

She remembered Dora's wedding to Calhoun Tupper. For her half sister she'd worn an embarrassingly froufrou petal-pink bridesmaid gown with matching dyed shoes. It was an elaborate, high-society affair, the wedding Dora had always dreamed of. It would have been Carson's nightmare. But Dora *was* a beautiful bride in a froth of white. Even if Carson cringed to think of poor Dora going home with that bore of a husband.

She kicked a pebble, wondering how the distance between them had grown so great. At best, they had little left to say to one another. At worst, each looked askance at the other's life.

Carson pushed open the back door and stepped into the kitchen. Even with the air-conditioning, the room was steamy. Mamaw used to think air-conditioning an island house was not only ridiculous but an appalling waste of money. Carson and the girls would open the windows wide and sleep on the porch under mosquito nets. When Mamaw reached menopause, however, the hot, humid weather became so unbearable she caved under pressure and installed central air-conditioning during the renovations. Still, Mamaw couldn't abide a cold house and kept it only cool enough not to perspire. When Lucille cooked in the summer, the system couldn't keep up.

Lucille stood at the stove, one hand on her hip and the other stirring a large bubbling pot. Her back had grown as crooked as a politician. Another woman with a substantial girth stood beside the wooden kitchen table, and it took a moment for Carson to realize that it was Dora. She was so much heavier than when Carson had last seen her, and so washed out. Her thin blond hair, once always so neatly coiffed, was slipping sloppily from a black elastic. Drops of perspiration formed on her neck and forehead. *And who picked out that navy polka-dot dress?* Carson wondered. It made her look older than Mamaw, who'd never have been caught in a garment like that.

Dora was fanning herself with a napkin and speaking with intensity to Lucille. She glanced up when Carson entered; her fanning stopped and her eyes widened slightly with recognition.

"Carson!"

"Hey, Dora," she called back with forced cheer, closing the door behind her to salvage whatever air-conditioning competed with the steam. "You're here!" She moved toward her sister and leaned far forward to deliver a kiss. Dora's cheek was moist from sweat. "It's great to see you again."

"It's been too long." Then Dora's smile froze as her gaze swept Carson in her bikini. "Well, don't you look cool."

Carson felt the abrupt chill stiffen her spine. She suddenly felt like she was buck naked. "I went to the ocean. You should take a dip tomorrow. It's going to be a hot one."

Dora heaved a dramatically heavy sigh. "Maybe . . . I'm a mother. I don't have the free time you do. I guess you're accustomed to swimming and going to the beach whenever you want to." She smirked. "The lifestyle of the rich and famous, right?"

Carson looked at her askance. "I'm neither rich nor famous, but I do like to swim."

Dora smoothed a hair off her face. "Why, aren't you the early bird, already here in time for a swim. When did you arrive?"

"A while ago," Carson answered evasively, leaning over to set her bag and towel on the floor. She stepped close to Lucille, who was stirring gumbo on the enormous Viking stove, to kiss her cheek. "Smells good."

Lucille smiled broadly with pleasure.

"Oh?" Dora asked. "When?"

Carson turned to face her. "At the beginning of the month."

"You've been here for three weeks already?" Dora said, surprise mingling with a hint of disapproval. "Why didn't you call?"

"I had a lot to do when I landed and you know how fast time flies once you get here. Besides, I knew you were coming for the party and that I'd see you then. And here you are!" She looked squarely into her sister's eyes and smiled even brighter, determined to be upbeat and ignore Dora's increasingly rapid fanning.

Carson prowled the kitchen table, checking out the hot sauce, the spices, the bits of sausage and shrimp. She spied a plate of cut okra and reached for it.

"You leave my okra alone," Lucille called out from the stove.

Carson withdrew her hand guiltily. "I swear, you've got eyes in the back of your head."

"I need that okra for my gumbo. If you're hungry, take some of the crackers and cheese I laid out for you." She jerked a shoulder toward the sideboard. "Lawd, child, I can't make a meal without you raiding my supplies. It's always been like that." She stopped and turned abruptly, frowning and shaking her spoon at Carson. "I opened the pantry today expecting to find a nice fig cookie to eat with my coffee and all that was left was a bunch of crumbs!"

"I was so hungry last night . . ." Carson replied, embarrassed.

"You ate the whole bag!"

Carson laughed sheepishly. "I know. I'm sorry. I'll replace it."

"Don't bother," Lucille replied, mollified, as she returned to the stove. "Just next time, mind there are other people in this house who might want some." Lucille shook her head, mumbling. "I can't understand how you can eat like a man and still look like that." She pointed her spoon toward Carson's body.

Carson just laughed, but glancing over, she saw Dora's eyes narrow as she looked at Carson's taut, flat stomach, so flagrantly displayed in the kitchen. Carson sighed inwardly. She often received jealous looks like this, from thin and heavy women alike, especially when they watched her eating hamburgers or indulging in sweets. Envy burned in their eyes, as though they were cursing God that she could eat like that when they dieted every day and still couldn't lose weight. Carson couldn't stop and tell each one of them that it might have been the only food she'd eaten that day, or that she'd just run six miles or surfed in chilly ocean water for the past two hours.

She moved to the sideboard, where Lucille had left a

plate of Brie and crackers, and helped herself to a thick chunk of cheese. "Want one?" she asked Dora.

Dora looked pained as she stared at the cheese, but with seeming restraint, she shook her head no. "I'll wait for dinner. Maybe a drink. It's almost five, isn't it? Is there wine in the fridge?" she asked, but didn't wait for a reply. She opened the fridge and found it stocked to the brim with groceries Lucille had been laying in for the party weekend. An open bottle of white wine was waiting in the door. She stood a moment in front of the fridge, enjoying the coolness, then reluctantly closed the door. She took out three wineglasses from the shelf and filled one for herself, then, looking up with a questioning glance, got a shake of the head from Lucille and an enthusiastic nod from Carson.

"What made you decide to come so early?" Dora asked, handing Carson a glass.

Carson took a long drink of her wine. She needed it to soothe Dora's cool greeting.

"Lots of reasons. It's been forever since I've visited Mamaw and time just opened up." She bit into the Brie, not willing to divulge the details. The days of blurting secrets between them were over. "Plus, I don't know," she added, her tone changing as she spoke from the heart. "Dora, I was surprised to see how *old* Mamaw is."

"She's turning eighty, after all."

"I know. That's my point. She's always been old to me. I mean, when I was ten, she was . . ." Carson paused to do the math. "Fifty-six, which isn't old, really."

Lucille huffed from the stove. "I should say not!"

Carson smiled as she continued. "But it seemed old to

me. So did sixty, seventy. But she was always so alive, so vibrant, in my mind. Ageless."

"She's not Santa Claus," Dora said.

Carson was taken aback by the derision. "No, of course not," she replied, crossing her arms across her chest. "It's just that Mamaw was always the same in my mind. Immortal. But when I came home and saw her, she not only looks older, more frail—but I swear she's shrinking." She swirled the wine in her glass. "I suppose for the first time it hit me that Mamaw isn't always going to be here, waiting. I shouldn't take for granted that she'll always be here for us. Each year, each day, is a gift."

"I don't take her for granted," Dora said. "I come out to see Mamaw every chance I get."

"You're lucky you live so close."

"Not close, exactly," Dora clarified. "With good traffic it's still some forty-five minutes away. I still have to plan. I mean, she's not across the street. But I make the effort."

Carson was silenced by the implied criticism that she had not made the effort in several years. But she couldn't defend herself.

Lucille turned and said, "You know, I can't recall the last time you came out to see Miz Marietta."

"Why, Lucille, you know we come every summer," replied Dora.

"Uh-huh," Lucille said, turning again to the pot. "When it's nice enough to visit the beach."

"You know Mamaw joins us every Christmas, Easter, and Thanksgiving. For every special occasion."

There followed an awkward pause during which Dora's cheeks flamed and Carson turned to help herself to another piece of cheese. She knew that Lucille wanted to level the playing field for her by eliminating false claims, and for this she was grateful.

"How's Nate?" Carson asked, changing the subject.

"Oh, Nate! He's fine," Dora replied robustly. "You'll see him shortly. I expect he's getting settled in his room now."

Carson paused before biting her cheese. "He's here?"

"Of course he's here. Where else would he be? I always bring Nate with me so he can visit his great-grandmother. And it's about time he met his aunts, don't you think?"

"Of course. I'm delighted. B-but . . . " Carson stammered. "I thought—"

"Thought what?" Dora asked, sensing a small challenge.

"I thought this was a girls-only weekend."

"Mamaw would be brokenhearted if her only great-grandchild didn't come."

"Where will he sleep?"

"In the library, where he always sleeps."

"Harper is going in the library. It's always been Harper's room."

"Now it's Nate's room. She can sleep somewhere else."

"There is nowhere else," Carson replied, refraining from adding *as you well know*. Dora had always been bossy, even as a child, but she was never unreasonable. "Well, Nate can share your room. You have twin beds."

Dora rubbed her hands together. "I'll just check with Mamaw. She'll know what to do."

Carson put up her hands. "Don't bother her with this. She's napping. Look, Dora, I know for certain that Mamaw planned for Harper to sleep in the library because I have the task of freshening the rooms and adding flowers. If you don't want Nate to sleep in your room, perhaps it would be best to bring him back home. At least for the party."

Dora's face flushed. "I can't," she replied in a voice laced with both resentment and distress. "There's no one else to take care of him."

Carson sighed and brought her fingers to the bridge of her nose. She had to remember that Dora was in the throes of a divorce. Lucille turned off the stove and set down the spoon with a clatter that interrupted any more talk. She faced them, lifting the hem of her white cotton apron, and began wiping her hands with agitation.

"I'll go on over and help the boy move his things to your room," she told Dora in a tone implying the matter was settled. "Carson, you best go get changed for dinner and wake up Mamaw. Dora," she said kindly, "take a minute for yourself and freshen up after your travels. Gumbo's ready!"

Dora bent over the bathroom sink and splashed water over her face. It felt so inviting that she wanted to strip the clothing from her body and jump into the shower. How lovely it would feel to dive into the ocean like Carson and wash away the dust and perspiration and memories of this horrible day.

But of course she didn't have time for a shower, much less a swim. Nate would have a hissy fit about the move to

this room and Lucille, bless her heart, would not be able
to handle him once he got in a mood.

Dora grabbed a towel and began blotting her face.
She paused, catching her reflection in the mirror, something she was loath to do. She barely recognized the puffy,
pale face she saw in the reflection. Her blue eyes, once
described by Cal as the brilliant blue of a gem, appeared
lifeless. She should stop drinking so much . . . and cut
out sweets, she told herself even as she knew she would
not. She no longer had the energy to deny herself the
small pleasure of a glass or two of wine or a bar of chocolate. She reached up to tug out the elastic already slipping
from her head and then, turning her gaze away from the
mirror, brushed her hair with quick, efficient strokes. Her
mind was already shifting from herself to Nate and what
she might prepare for his dinner. As if he would even consider touching the gumbo . . .

"Oh damn," she muttered, leaning against the sink in
dismay. She'd forgotten to stop at the grocery store on the
way to pick up gluten-free bread. Now she'd have to go
out and find a loaf somewhere or he'd not have anything
for breakfast. Nate was so fussy about his food. She often
thought that no matter how much foresight she'd applied
to her day, for her—Eudora Muir Tupper—it was always
in vain. She loved her son, wanted to be the best mother
she could be for him, but she was so exhausted at the end
of each day, many nights she just cried herself to sleep.
Sometimes she felt a prisoner in that crumbling castle of
a house that she'd once been so eager to own.

Dora went to lie down on one of the Jenny Lind twin

beds, careful to leave her shoes off the patchwork quilt. She rested her forearm across her forehead, blocking the light. Her brain told her to jump up and help Lucille with Nate, but her body wouldn't budge from the soft mattress. She felt as though she were slipping back in time, back to when she was young and on vacation at Mamaw's house and didn't have a worry and could sleep in bed for as long as she wanted.

Silence returned and slowly her muscles relaxed. Lucille was a patient woman, she rationalized, who had dealt with Nate's outbursts since his birth. Just a few minutes more and she'd get up and help. It had been a very tough day for the little guy. He didn't like change and he'd sensed something was up from the moment he awoke and spotted the suitcases in the hallway.

"No, no, no, no, no!"

Dora groaned, recognizing the fury in Nate's voice. No way Lucille could handle what Dora knew was the beginning of a full-blown tantrum. This was the real reason why she had not wanted to move Nate from the library. She should have explained right away to Carson that Nate had autism and that the library was the room Nate was accustomed to sleeping in, with his favorite books and the Nintendo he adored. How he had already been frazzled by the move to Mamaw's house.

Then the sudden sound of a crash and glass breaking forced her to her feet.

Mamaw's eyes sprang open when she heard the crash. She'd fallen asleep with her book half-open across her lap. She simply couldn't keep her eyes from drifting shut—no fault of the story line. She was simply tired so much of the time now that the lure of sleep and dreams proved overpowering.

She tilted her head, listening intently. The child's scream could only have come from Nate. She heard the rustle of feet on the stairs, then the voices over Nate's screams. Lord, that boy could holler. Mamaw sat in a tense silence listening to the uproar across the hall. In time the screaming subsided and she heard again the retreating footfalls in the hall. There was a knock on the door and the crack of light as it opened.

"Mamaw? Are you awake?"

"Carson? Lord, yes, I'm awake. No one could sleep through that racket."

She heard Carson's throaty chuckle as she walked across the bedroom in her long-legged gait, pausing to flick on a small lamp. Warm light flooded the room, revealing Carson in a long summer shift of fiery oranges and yellows. Carson had inherited Mamaw's long, lean body. Mamaw smiled and reached her arms out to her.

Carson drew near and bent to kiss her cheek.

"Mmm . . . I love your perfume," Carson said, closing her eyes. "I feel like I've always known this scent. Kind of musky. I always think of you and this scent as inseparable."

Mamaw felt a twinge in her heart and stroked Carson's long hair. "It's Bal à Versailles. Actually, my dear, it was your mother's scent. She gave me my first bottle and I've worn it ever since."

Carson's tanned face paled a shade and she slunk down to her knees beside Mamaw's chair.

"It was my mother's scent?" she asked with wonder. "How did I never know that?"

Mamaw shrugged lightly. "I can't say. We speak so seldom of Sophie. She always wore this perfume. She was French, of course," she added, as though that explained it.

"There's so much I don't know about her," Carson said in a soft voice.

Mamaw patted Carson's hand. *Oh, child*, she wanted to tell her. *There* is *so very much you don't know about your mother.*

"The bottle is on my bathroom counter. Why don't you try it? The scent is very particular about who can wear it. It must be the patchouli or the musk. It might smell very different on you. But if you like it, I'll give you the bottle. I'd like to think we share a scent, *chérie*."

Another shout of "*No!*" pierced the air.

"What *is* all that ruckus about?" Mamaw cried.

Carson rose to her feet. "Nate's freaking out because we told Dora he had to sleep in one of the twin beds in her room. He was in the library."

"Harper is meant to sleep there."

"That's what I told her."

"Dora does have her hands full, doesn't she? She ought to get more help with Nate, especially now that Cal has left. Poor dear, she's exhausted."

"I hardly recognized her. I thought she looked older."

"Yes, well, it's her weight, too. Nothing adds years to your looks like letting your figure go. Perhaps you could encourage her to go on a diet. Exercise more. You're her sister, after all."

"Oh no, I'm not going there."

"Well, you could try," Mamaw said persistently. "It's that big house that's weighing her down."

Carson rolled her eyes. "And Cal . . ."

"Hush now. You mustn't mention the divorce while she's here. She's very sensitive. She needs our support now, more than ever."

From the hall, the screaming took on the rising crescendo of a supersonic jet taking off. Mamaw felt her heart skip a beat. She threw up her hands and said in a shaky voice, "Hurry and tell Dora to let that poor child sleep in the library if it means that much to him. I'll figure something else out for Harper. I simply cannot listen to that boy scream any longer! My birthday party will end up being my funeral!"

Dora ran across the hall into the library to find Lucille holding a squirming Nate tight and speaking to him in a low voice. Nate was inconsolable, flailing his arms wildly. Before Dora could reach them, Nate's hand belted Lucille in the nose. She fell back, hands against her shocked face. Nate's face registered not even a flash of acknowledgment that he'd hurt Lucille. Instead he spied his mother, pointed at her, and shouted, "You said to sleep here. I always sleep here at the beach!"

Dora looked at Nate's wide blue eyes, more terror-struck than angry. She walked slowly up to Nate and spoke in a low, soothing voice. She reassured him with instructions. "Yes, Nate, you're sleeping at the beach house. But tonight you're sleeping in Mama's room, okay? We will bring your Nintendo to Mama's room. All right?"

"No!" Nate shouted at the top of his lungs.

From over her shoulder Dora saw Carson standing beside Lucille, her eyes wide with shock and incomprehension. Dora turned back to Nate, relieved that he allowed her to put her arms around him as she continued the soothing litany, knowing he would respond more to her tone than the words. Dora didn't have time or even the desire to explain autism to Carson. It was like when Nate had a meltdown in the grocery store. People would rudely stop and stare at his head banging or at him whining, looking at her with critical eyes as though she were a bad parent, as though it were within her power to rein him in.

Amid the chaos, no one noticed a small, redheaded woman standing hesitatingly at the door. Her large eyes were wide with shock.

"Hello?" Harper called out.

It was not the entrance she'd hoped for.

CHAPTER SEVEN

*D*inner that evening was as long as a month of Sundays. Not that the meal wasn't delicious—Lucille had put her back into preparing a spicy gumbo, crisp hush puppies, and Carson's favorite banana pudding for dessert. It was the tension at the table that Carson couldn't stomach.

It should have been a happy homecoming. A time of laughter and catching up. Instead, Carson could feel a headache blossoming from holding in the dozens of pithy comments pressing against her tight lips.

To be fair, the evening started off badly. Dinner was late and everyone was still on tenterhooks after Nate's hissy fit. Dora had prepared a special plate for him and brought it on a tray to his room for him to eat while he watched his favorite programs on television. Then Harper caused brows to rise when she refused the white rice. And they couldn't help but stare when she began daintily picking out the pork sausage from her gumbo with her fork. Lucille harrumphed loudly but everyone held their tongue politely.

Except Dora.

"Are you a vegetarian now?" she asked in a censorial tone.

"No," Harper replied blithely. "I just don't prefer red meat."

"Pork is a white meat," Dora said, correcting her.

Harper looked squarely at her sister and smiled. "Then, meat," she clarified.

When the hush puppies were passed, Harper refused those as well.

"You don't like hush puppies anymore, either?" Dora asked, clearly annoyed. "There's no meat in those."

Carson gave Dora *the look*, the one that told her to stop badgering Harper about her food, but Dora ignored her. Carson remembered Harper being quiet and subdued as a child. That, and her petite size, earned her the nickname "the little mouse." Dora could never boss Carson around the way she did Harper. In fact, sticking up for Harper was one old habit that Carson could settle back into quite seamlessly.

"It's not that I don't like them," Harper replied pointedly. "I don't eat fried foods. Or anything white, for that matter."

"What's that supposed to mean?" Dora asked, pressing her. "You don't eat anything white?"

"White flour, white rice, white noodles, etc." Harper shrugged. "It's not as healthy as brown."

"Oh for pity's sake. Lucille slaved over this dinner,

you know," Dora said, fuming. "The least you could do is try it."

"Dora, she's not your child. She can decide for herself what to eat," Carson said.

Harper's pale cheeks turned pink. She turned to Lucille and smiled sweetly. "In that case, I'll definitely try one of these magnificent hush puppies, Lucille." She pinched a single hush puppy and laid it on her plate. Then she reached for the collard greens and began serving herself a big helping. "These smell heavenly. You make the best collards anywhere, Lucille."

Lucille puffed up, her pride assuaged. "I'll make some whole-wheat waffles in the morning," she offered. Then under her breath she added, "I'll fatten you up some, don't you worry. You're so skinny I can't find your shadow."

"I, for one, am going to eat every bite," Dora said, picking up her fork.

"I'll bet," Carson muttered, then caught a warning glance from Mamaw.

"The amount of food one eats doesn't imply the appreciation of the food," Mamaw said, picking up her fork. "Harper never was a big eater, if I recall. Dora, you've always had a healthy appetite."

Dora flushed and stared at her plate, heaped with food.

The dinner conversation took a turn for the worse when Dora began to complain about how the island had changed, how much she missed its sleepier days, and how the Northerners—especially Manhattanites—

were destroying the South all over again, this time using dollars and loose morals as bullets.

Divorce or no divorce, Carson thought Dora needed to be taken down a peg. To Harper's credit, however, she seemed to have her own method. Harper ignored Dora's comments, focusing instead on cutting her shrimp and okra into ever-smaller pieces, which was driving Dora to bristle more than any comeback could.

As soon as the dessert of banana pudding was finished, Mamaw rose and announced that she was tired and going to retire. Then she suggested that the girls do the dishes, seeing as how Lucille had worked all day preparing the meal.

Dora immediately left to check on Nate, with a promise to return. Harper and Carson went into the kitchen and faced, flummoxed, a mountain of dirty dishes, pots, and pans.

"Welcome home!" Carson called out, grabbing a towel from the counter.

Harper grinned wide and walked across the room to take an apron from the wall hook. "I don't think I remember how to wear one of these things," she said with a laugh as she slipped the loop over her head. The apron was pale green with ruffles along the shoulder straps and hem. Her hands fumbled with the strings behind her back. "I haven't worn one since I was maybe ten. In fact, I think this is the same apron."

Carson laughed and stepped behind her. She tied the apron strings tight. Her sister had always been little, and it didn't look like she'd grown much since she was ten. "I think you've actually got an eighteen-inch waist."

"Me and Scarlett O'Hara," she quipped, walking to the sink.

Carson rolled up her sleeves and turned on the radio. Country music blared out.

"I see Lucille still loves her country tunes," Carson said. "Do you remember how the radio was always blasting out her music?"

"That or baseball games. I don't think I've listened to country music much at all since I was last here."

"Me neither," Carson said. She gave Harper a quick glance. "I'd forgotten how much I loved it."

"Me too!"

As they washed and dried the mountain of dishes, they shuffled their feet and sang out refrains about love lost and found, regrets and hopes, red dogs, and sexy black dresses. The time flew by as they began sharing bits of their own stories with the lyrics. Gradually, the ice that had formed over dinner began to thaw.

No sooner was the last pot washed and put away than Harper tossed the apron on the counter, turned to Carson, and said with heart to her sister, "I need a drink. Let's go out."

Carson could have kissed her. They hurried to Carson's bathroom to refresh their makeup and brush their hair. Carson was enjoying the novelty of a sisterly bond as they chatted about shoes and designers they both loved, blissfully avoiding any heavier topics. It was as though Dora's rant had bonded them, unfortunately against her.

"What's her problem, anyway?" Harper's eyes flashed in warning. "God, it burns me to admit it—and don't you dare tell her I said this—but it hurt when Dora said those things about 'Northerners' and New Yorkers at dinner. She's about as subtle as a dump truck."

"And filled with as much garbage," Carson added. "I hope you don't take her opinions to heart. I never do. Sometimes she's so stuck-up she'd drown in a rainstorm."

Harper chuckled at that. "She was always so much older than me. I think I was afraid of her at some level when I was a little girl." She paused. "But I'm not anymore," she said more boldly.

"She's in a bad place right now. Cal's left her. They're getting a divorce."

Harper paused for a moment. "I didn't know."

"I just heard myself."

"That explains a lot. Still," Harper said, "she shouldn't take it out on me."

Carson waved her hand dismissively. "Let's not think about her right now. I'm getting seriously bummed. And this is your first night here." She reached for the perfume bottle and sprayed some on her neck.

"That's Mamaw's scent!" Harper exclaimed, sniffing the air. Her big blue eyes were even wider with wonder. "How . . . what is it? Where did you find it?"

"Mamaw gave me a bottle. I'm supposed to test it, see how it smells on me." Carson sprayed a bit on her wrist. "What do you think?" She held out her arm so Harper could lean in for a sniff.

Harper sniffed, then, looking up, smiled a knowing smile. "It smells really good on you. Like it belongs on you," she said ruefully. "Very sexy." She snorted as she drew back up. "Figures."

"Why do you say that?"

"You're the one who is most like Mamaw."

"No, I'm not. I don't look like anyone. Y'all are blond and pale. I'm dark and tall and I have big feet."

Harper laughed and reached for the bottle of perfume. "Maybe not in looks." She shrugged. "I don't know. It's hard to name. You're her favorite, that's for sure."

"Not that again," Carson said with a moan.

"Let me try some," Harper said, spraying perfume on her wrist. "What do you think?"

Carson obliged and bent to sniff her wrist, then immediately recoiled. "Oh, no," she said, waving the air. The musk smelled more like body odor on her. "Really, Harper, that's just bad on you." She chuckled. "You're going to have to scrub it off if you want a guy to come within twenty paces of you."

Harper sniffed, then wrinkled her nose. "Oh God, you're right," she said, going straight for the sink and soaping up. "I'll stick to my Old Dependable—Chanel Number Five, thank you very much. Funny how that works, isn't it? A perfume can smell so dreadful on me but so fabulous on you. Like it has its own personality. Its own particular preference for people."

"Or genetics," Carson said softly, looking at the label of the bottle in her hand. She brought it to her nose, sniffed again, and grew pensive. "It was my mother's scent."

"Really?" Harper said, turning her head to look at Carson. "I didn't know that. I always thought of it as Mamaw's scent."

"I just found out myself. It's not like I remember her," she said in an offhand manner. Even as she said the words she knew that was a lie. There was indeed memory associated with the scent, unexplainable, that spoke of being cradled, sung to, loved. The scent she'd always associated with Mamaw triggered feelings of safety and comfort. These were emotions she connected with Mamaw, true. Only now she knew the memories went deeper—to her mother. And knowing this, she felt strangely uneasy, even sad, as she inhaled the scent.

"I . . . I don't think it's right for me." Carson moved to the sink and, like Harper, began washing the perfume from her wrists and neck.

"Really? I thought it smelled really great. I have to admit, I'm a little disappointed. I'd have liked to share something with Mamaw."

Carson blotted the moisture from her neck with a towel and wondered at that comment. "I'd always figured that you didn't enjoy any connections to your Southern heritage."

Harper finished drying her hands and leaned against the bathroom counter. "That sentiment is my mother's. She never wanted any contact with my father—*our* father. Or his family. I grew up thinking that to be like him, or to be attached in any way to him or his family, was some-how . . . bad."

Carson felt stung. "What a bitch," she blurted. Then quickly added, "Sorry."

Harper shook her head. "She can be a bitch. But she's my mother, so . . ." She shrugged and turned again to the mirror to smooth her hair. "You know, when I'm in New York, I don't think about the Muir side of the family. It's out of sight, out of mind." She looked down at her hands, the ring finger bearing a gold signet ring with the James family crest. "I'm proud of my family. Love them, of course. But there's a lot of baggage being a James. When I come here, I feel . . . I don't know, freer. More at ease. Always have."

"It's the humidity. Once it starts heating up you have to move slow," Carson teased. "Your brain softens."

Harper laughed. "Well, it is good for my skin. But no, it's this place. Talk about smells . . . The air here is rife with scents, and each one of them is connected to some memory. They started gushing back the minute I smelled the pluff mud. Memories of Mamaw braiding our hair, diving with us into the surf, lazily reading on hot summer days, those big container ships cruising by." Her voice shifted and she added softly, "Most of all, of you and me, Carson."

Carson was moved to see tears swimming in her sister's eyes. "I know what you mean."

"What do *you* remember?" Harper asked Carson.

Carson puffed out air, considering. "The beach, of course."

"You were always in the water. Such a tomboy."

"You know what else?" Carson asked with the sparkle of memory in her eyes. "I remember running all over Sullivan's Island like wild pirates searching for buried treasure."

"Yes," Harper agreed, her eyes widening in recognition. She raised a fist and shouted, "Death to the ladies!"

That had been their rallying call when they were kids and played pirates. They'd shouted it outdoors at the top of their lungs, and whispered it, too, in the house after Mamaw reprimanded them for being unladylike.

Carson burst out a laugh and raised her fist into the air as well. "Death to the ladies!"

The call still had the power to bond them as they laughed and shared a commiserating glance. In that flash of connection years melted away and once again they were two girls sneaking off to play pirates across Sullivan's Island, ignoring the dreaded rules of feminine etiquette, determined to discover all the treasures of the world.

"What's going on?" said a voice at the door.

Looking up, Carson saw Dora standing there, one hand clutching the frame. Her face was scrubbed clean and glowing with moisturizer and her blond hair hung to her shoulders. She had changed into a matronly nightgown that made her pendulous breasts and belly appear as islands in a sea of mauve.

"I thought you went to bed," said Carson as Harper slipped a sparkly turquoise top over her braless torso.

"No. Nate had a hard time falling asleep. I'm sorry I didn't make it back to the kitchen. I'll do dishes tomorrow night."

"No problem," Carson said, wriggling into her jeans.

"Are you going out?"

"Just for a drink," Carson replied, sucking in and zipping. Harper finished clasping on her necklace and Carson turned to admire the unusual arrangement of big chunks of turquoise stones encased in gold that blazed against Harper's blue eyes. Carson couldn't take her eyes off them.

"Isn't it kind of late?" Dora asked.

Harper snorted. "No."

"Where are you going?"

"Does it matter?" asked Harper, clearly testy. She refused to meet Dora's gaze and instead leaned over the sink to apply gloss to her lips.

"Just down the road," Carson replied, hoping to keep the peace between the eldest and the youngest. "Station Twenty-Two probably." Carson saw a longing in Dora's eyes and felt a sudden sympathy for her. She remembered what it was like to be the odd man out.

Dora reached up to tuck her hair behind her ear. "There's something I want to tell you about Nate," she said.

"What?" Harper asked as she applied gloss to her lips. Her tone implied she wasn't interested.

Dora cleared her throat nervously. Carson was combing her hair. She checked out Dora in the mirror, curious. It wasn't customary for Dora to be nervous.

"My son has autism."

Carson's hand stilled. Her glance darted in the mirror to Harper, who was applying blush to her cheeks. In that look they shared an immediate understanding and compassion.

Carson lowered her hand and turned to face Dora. She didn't know what was an appropriate response. *I'm sorry* wasn't right. What she felt was more sympathy for her sister, for what she could only assume meant more challenges.

Harper said, "Are you sure?"

Dora bristled. "Of course I'm sure. You don't think I'm making this up!"

"No," Harper quickly said, clearly embarrassed. "I mean, is he diagnosed?"

Dora still chafed at the question. "Yes, he's been to a child psychiatrist and we've been through all the tests. There's a wide range of diagnoses wrapped up in the autism spectrum. Nate has Asperger's syndrome, a high-functioning form. Don't misunderstand. He's highly intelligent. It's like he's dyslexic in reading social cues. Things like facial expressions, gestures . . . those little ways we communicate with each other." She paused while her gaze swept both Carson and Harper. "Like the look you both gave each other in the mirror—Nate doesn't get those. And he doesn't always show emotions like you'd expect." She twisted the diamond on her ring finger. "He's really a good boy. I didn't want you to think he was some spoiled brat who throws tantrums."

"Oh, no," Carson immediately replied, more out of politeness. In truth, that was exactly what she'd thought.

"There are a few other things you should know," Dora continued, intent on making them understand her son. "Nate doesn't like to be touched. So please don't hug him or kiss him. And he's very particular about things, like what he eats, and his routine. He gets very upset with any change. Which is why I didn't want to move him from his room." She laughed sadly. "You saw what happened there. When he's overwhelmed he has his little meltdowns."

Carson watched her twisting her ring. The skin beneath it was irritated and red.

"I should've told you right away," Dora added. "But I still feel very defensive about him."

"Don't be," Carson interjected. "I'm glad you told us. It helps us understand what's going on. I'm sorry, too, about your divorce."

"Me too. And I'm sorry we haven't been in touch," Harper added.

"Does Mamaw know about Nate?" Carson asked.

Dora shook her head. "I've only told my family in Charlotte and a few friends. I've been homeschooling, so . . ."

Carson looked at Dora, her face pale and tired, and thought of the beautiful, confident girl who'd dreamed of a future as the happy wife of an adoring husband with two or three perfect children and a beautiful, well-maintained home. Dora's marriage was on the rocks, her child had special needs, and she was preparing to sell her house. Talk about having the rug pulled out from under you.

"Aw, Dora," Carson said, and impulsively wrapped her arms around her sister. "This has to suck."

She felt Dora stiffen; then Dora burst out laughing. When she pulled back, Carson saw relief shining in her eyes. "It does," Dora said, choking back a laugh that sounded more like a cry. "It sucks."

Hearing the expression from Dora's lips made Carson and Harper laugh with her. It was as though a valve had opened up and let all the pent-up steam in the room release.

"Hey, Dora, come on out with us tonight. We're just going for a drink. It'll be fun," Carson said.

"Maybe another time," Dora replied. "Nate's still upset and I can't leave him."

"You sure?" Harper asked.

Carson saw longing in Dora's eyes but she shook her head. "Next time."

Harper zipped her makeup bag so fast it hummed.

"Then we're off. Oh, Dora," she added. "I totally get why Nate's in the library. That's cool. But I'm going to bunk in the twin bed in your room tonight so don't freak out if you see me tiptoeing into your room."

Carson winked at Dora as she followed Harper out. "Don't wait up."

Mamaw hid in the dim shadows behind the door of the library, a book clutched to her breast and her head tilted to catch the words of her granddaughters. She couldn't sleep and had come into the library to find a book to read. Nate was fast asleep on the pullout sofa bed, exhausted, the dear boy.

Oh, Dora, why didn't you grab the chance for a little fun and just go? She could hear the longing in Dora's voice from across the hall.

She spied Dora as she went to her room and closed the door. Then she heard the clickety-clack of high heels on her hardwood floors. She waited until she heard the front door close, then hurried to peek out the window. She watched Harper climb into the passenger seat of Carson's car, heard the pitiful creak of the rusty door as she slammed it shut. Carson gunned the engine and she heard the girls shout out, "Death to the ladies!"

Mamaw walked into the dimly lit living room and peeked around for Lucille. Seeing the coast was clear, she hurried to the small liquor cabinet. She'd had it fully stocked for the weekend. She poured herself two fingers of her favorite Jamaican rum, added ice, and took a sip. To hell with her doctor's warnings. She was about to be eighty years old and needed a little fortification tonight. The sweet burn trailed down her throat to warm her belly. She smacked her lips with satisfaction.

Back in her room, Mamaw lit the bedside lamp and climbed under the billowy blanket of her big bed. Without Edward to share it, she felt adrift in an ocean of sheets and pillows. Still not sleepy, she opened a novel and began reading. After a few minutes, whether it was the slow start or her agitated mind, she set the book aside. She just couldn't settle tonight. Her mind was running a mile a minute, going over and over every gesture, comment, and look her granddaughters had made. Giving up sleep, she climbed from her bed and went outside on the back porch to sit on a cushioned wicker chair.

The moist air did its work of softening her bones. She and Edward used to grab their pillows on hot nights and sleep out on the porch, same as their parents and grandparents did back in the days before air-conditioning. She'd rest her head on his shoulder and they'd lie quiet on the small iron bed with crisp white sheets and listen to the sounds of the night—the swell of cicadas, the chirping of crickets, the occasional lonesome call of an owl, and the muffled laughing of young girls. Sometimes Edward would say, "It's high time those girls got to sleep." But she'd hold him back, knowing how special summer friendships were.

Mamaw had hoped that she would hear that talking and laughter again this evening, as they used to. But Carson and Harper couldn't wait to escape and Dora had retreated to her room. She sighed heavily. Not that she could blame them. Dinner had been a debacle. They'd behaved like strangers. Worse than strangers. Mamaw rested her forehead in her palm. What was she to do? The weekend wasn't starting off at all as she'd planned. Harper and Dora had made clear that they were only staying for the weekend. Mamaw knew she needed the entire summer to heal the wounds that separated them. She sighed and watched the fireflies glow off and on in the dark as they drifted randomly in the night.

"Please, God," Mamaw said, closing her eyes. "I'm just asking for enough time to see these girls discover the bonds between them again. To realize that they are more than acquaintances. More than friends. That they are *sisters*."

Opening her eyes, Mamaw brought her fingers to her lips, considering her options. Her party was tomorrow night. It would be her last chance with all the girls together. She sighed. There was nothing left to do but resort to Plan B.

Station 22 was a popular Sullivan's Island restaurant. Carson felt at home in the shabby-chic decor with colorful local island art on the walls. It was the oldest restaurant on the island and known for its great seafood. And it was packed. Carson and Harper followed the noise toward the large bar in the back of the room where men with sunburns, baseball caps, and island shirts and women in slinky summer tops and heels gathered with drinks in their hands, laughing and talking. Carson searched for a familiar face and grinned when she spotted Devlin seated at a table across the room. She waved and called his name. He looked up and, spotting her, stood and called her over.

Devlin, gregarious as ever, grabbed two more chairs so they could join the already overflowing table and signaled the waitress. Introductions were made and Carson was amused to see the four other men staring at Harper's perky breasts while the women checked out her clothing. Especially her Louboutin shoes. What Carson liked best, however, was that Harper knew it and played along. The crowd was so dense and loud Carson had to shout to be heard. After a while, she gave up, leaned against Devlin's shoulder, and nursed her beer, enjoying watching Harper at the center of attention. *Who knew the little mouse could be such a party girl?* she wondered.

Devlin leaned over close to her ear. "Your little sister's a fox."

Carson looked up and saw the gleam of appreciation in his eyes as he gazed at Harper. "I see she's made another conquest."

His glance shifted to her and his pale eyes hazed with woozy seduction. "She's not the sister I'm interested in."

Carson gave a little snort of disbelief.

"Speaking of sisters, where's Dora?" Devlin asked, pulling back. "Why didn't she come out with you?"

Carson quickly got over the momentary sting of realizing she wasn't the sister he was interested in, either. "She's stuck at the house with Nate. Her son," she explained when he shook his head uncomprehendingly.

He took a swig from his beer. "Well, sure, she'd be married with children by now."

"She's getting a divorce."

Devlin's brows rose with curiosity.

"Don't hold your breath, Romeo. She's not the bar-hoppin' type."

"What type is she?" he asked, amused.

"The churchgoing, stay-at-home type."

"Really?" He considered this as he downed his beer. "That's not the Dora I remember. You know what they say about the quiet ones."

"Dora, quiet?" Carson chuckled. "I think you've got the wrong sister. Harper over there was the quiet one."

He looked at her askance. "You mean that she-cat over there holding court? I think you've got your sisters mixed up."

Carson finished her beer and wondered how well he'd known Dora and whether there was any truth in the rumors she'd heard that Dora had broken Devlin's heart. She raised her hand to attract the waitress and ordered another beer.

"You should've heard Dora at dinner," Carson told him. "*Quiet* and *shy* are not words I would use to describe the way she took Harper down. As well as"—Carson lifted her hand and began counting off—"Northerners, New Yorkers, gays, tree huggers, and Democrats."

Devlin laughed and took a swig of his beer. "I knew I liked her."

"*Please*," Carson said with a sorry chuckle. She could feel the liquor working its magic, loosening the tension. "Spare me. Mamaw's not here to stop me from wiping the floor with you."

"That I'd like to see." Devlin let his arm slide around

Carson's shoulders and he leaned in close to her again. "How about we forget about your sisters and take off?"

Her brows furrowed and she turned her head. His blue eyes were staring straight into hers with a seductive glint. She wouldn't mind going home with Devlin, she thought. It had been a while since she'd been with a man, and Lord knew she'd dreamed of being with Devlin many times back when she wasn't legal.

"Stop sniffin' around me, you ol' horndog. You just told me you had the hots for my sister."

"What is it about you Muir girls?" he said with a slow smile. "I'm just a fool for you."

"You're a fool, I'll give you that," Carson said teasingly. She drew back and stood, then felt the floor sway. She wobbled in her heels and grabbed his shoulder. "Time for me to go."

"I'll drive you home."

Carson looked into his eyes and realized he was more drunk than she was. "I'm with Harper."

"Oh, she'll be fine," Devlin argued, and his tone was persuasive. "I'll get Will to take her home. He's more than willing."

Carson checked out the big-shouldered man in a fashionably ripped black T-shirt with a beer glaze in his eyes. Harper was dwarfed beside him as she leaned against his massive chest.

"Too willing. No, I think the little lady's had one tequila too many. I'll take her home."

Devlin inched forward and let his hand slide along her thigh. "You sure?" he asked in a husky voice.

"No." She sighed and pushed his hand away. *Damn Harper,* she thought to herself as she stepped closer to her sister. Weaving slightly, she called out over the noise. "Harper! We're going."

Harper turned her head. Her hair was mussed and she moaned against Will's chest, "So soon?"

"Yep. Come on, sister mine."

She took her sister's arm and pulled her to her feet, shaking her head against the chorus of offers to take Harper home, knowing full well none of them would go directly to Mamaw's. This fun-loving, carefree woman was not the shy, retiring little girl she remembered. Carson watched with amusement as Harper laughed out loud at something the big fellow in the black T-shirt whispered in her ear, then waved a coy good-bye. Carson kept a firm grip on Harper as she tottered across the room. Once outside, the gravel and sand proved too much for Harper's spiky heels. She bent over to slip them off, and in the process began hurling out the evening's tequila.

Carson held back Harper's hair and kept a steadying hand on her shoulder until she finished. Then she settled Harper in the passenger seat and walked around the car to the driver's seat. She was fumbling for her keys in the dark when she was startled by the sound of a man's voice at her window.

"You sure you can drive home?"

At first she thought it was Devlin and she blinked in the restaurant's bright lights. It was Mr. Predictable. She racked her groggy brain for his name. Blake, that was it.

"Please," she said, trying to enunciate clearly with a thick tongue. "The day I can't drive a straight shot down

Middle Street going twenty-five miles an hour, you can take away my keys."

"I think that day has come," Blake said. He smiled but his gaze was firm. "How about you give me your keys and I'll drive you home." He opened the car door.

Carson realized he wasn't asking permission. Beside her, Harper was already snoring softly. Carson closed her eyes for a minute and felt the world spin. She didn't think she was drunk, but maybe she'd had more than she'd thought. She opened her eyes to see Blake was still standing in front of her in his blue jeans and T-shirt, his hand stretched out, palm up.

"How're you going to get back to your car?" she managed to get out.

"No problem. I don't have a car. I'll just toss my bike in the trunk."

"You can't. It's filled with junk."

"Then I walk a few blocks." He pushed his palm closer. "Keys."

"Shit," Carson murmured, defeated. She dug in her purse and found the keys attached to a big silver chain. "You know, I don't really know you," she said warily, holding the keys back.

"Sure you do. But if you feel more comfortable, I'll try to find one of your friends inside who's not too drunk to drive you home. Either way, Carson, you're not driving tonight."

"They're not my friends." Carson pouted and thrust the keys into his hand, her fingers brushing his. She climbed into the backseat and crossed her arms in a show of defiance. She knew she was being pitiful, but she had to salvage some self-respect. As he slid behind the wheel she noticed the breadth of his shoulders, his strong hands on the wheel as he fired up the engine.

The drive was less than a mile but it felt like hours as they drove in a dark silence, save for Harper's gentle snoring. Clouds covered the moon and stars and the sky was inky. Carson leaned against the cushion and looked out the window at the house lights flickering as they passed. She wondered how Blake had just happened to be in the parking lot when she'd left. It seemed every time she turned around, there he was.

"I thought you didn't drink," she said, turning her head toward him. He was a dark silhouette, so she couldn't gauge his expression. "What were you doing at the bar?"

"It's a restaurant, too," he answered. Blake drove a bit more, then added, "But I came looking for you."

Carson felt suddenly uneasy. She hadn't thought it could be just a coincidence. "Looking for me? Why?"

"I wanted to talk to you," he said easily. "But then I saw you go off with that other guy, the one who was with you at Dunleavy's, and I figured you were together. I didn't want to get in the way."

He was talking about Devlin, she realized. "I'm not *with* that guy," Carson said. "He's just an old friend. I have a lot of guy friends."

Blake brought his hand to his jaw and scratched. "Oh."

"So what did you want to talk about?" she asked, still not comfortable with his following her.

"We got cut off earlier. At Dunleavy's. We were going to set a time for me to teach you about kiteboarding. You still interested?"

"Oh. Yeah, sure," Carson said, regrouping. That made sense. It was a relief he wasn't stalking her . . . not much, anyway. It was actually flattering that he was so determined. "When's a good time for you?"

He shrugged. "I work during the day, so weekends are good. Or any day after five."

Carson considered the party this weekend. She was excited to learn and didn't want to put the lesson off too long. He pulled into the driveway of Sea Breeze and parked the car.

"Monday?" she suggested, leaning forward in the seat.

He faced her then, and in the dim light she could just see the side of his mouth curl in a smile. "Monday it is. I'll meet you at Station Twenty-Eight at five."

Blake climbed from the car to open the passenger-side door while Carson climbed out from the back. Blake was very gentle with Harper as he shook her. She awakened with an unladylike snort. Blake helped Harper out of the car, holding on tight when she hit cool air.

"I feel sick," Harper moaned.

Carson stepped a foot away, just in case. "We'll put you to bed so you can sleep it off."

She and Blake walked on either side of Harper and guided her as she wobbled to the front door.

"Do you want me to help you bring her in?" he asked.

"No, thanks, I can manage the rest of the way." Carson got a better grip on Harper's waist. "She's a little thing. I don't want to wake up Mamaw or Lucille. Harper won't want anyone to know about this."

"She'll have a hard time keeping it a secret tomorrow when she's hungover."

"Yeah. She can't hold her liquor."

"And you can?"

"So you see."

"Well, you're not as drunk as I'd feared."

"I tried to tell you."

"Still," he said seriously, "you aren't fit to drive."

"Debatable."

Harper moaned. "I wanna lie down."

"I better get her in. Thanks."

He handed her the keys, tucked his fingers in his back pocket, and backed away. "See you Monday at five."

"Come on, honey," Carson said to a softly groaning Harper. "Time to put the baby to bed."

CHAPTER EIGHT

Carson couldn't wait to slip into her swimsuit and sneak off into the cove before the others woke up. She scurried down the dock while the sky was misty gray and climbed on her paddleboard. Her paddles splashed softly in the early-morning quiet as she coasted toward the inlet, scanning the cove. Sure enough, a dolphin emerged alongside her paddleboard with a noisy exhale from its blowhole. Carson felt her heart skip and immediately broke into a smile. She knew it was the same dolphin even without seeing the damaged fluke beneath the water.

"You came back!" Carson exclaimed, calling out in a high voice.

The dolphin made a high-pitched whistle that sounded happy to Carson's ears.

The dolphin swam ahead rapidly, then leaped in the air and returned to the paddleboard with eager eyes. It was watching her, inviting interaction. There was no question that this time this social dolphin had sought her out.

And more, it was trying to communicate. Carson wanted to engage but felt deaf and dumb.

Always, in the back of her mind, a voice teased her, *This is all your imagination. The dolphin isn't trying to communicate. It's just a wild animal.* Yet another voice argued that she should ignore her rational doubts and simply accept what was happening. When she looked into the dolphin's eyes, there was no questioning the animal's intense level of awareness. And it seemed to be challenging her.

Carson decided then and there to cast away all doubts and make up her mind to believe. And this she'd have to do with her heart rather than her mind.

Carson slowly moved to lie on her belly on the board. She wanted to get face-to-face with the dolphin. The dolphin didn't swim away, as she feared it might. It lingered, tilted its head, and looked at her with keen, curious eyes.

She rested her cheek on her hands and for a while they simply watched each other in a joyful quiet. It reminded her of nights with her sisters when they were young, lying on their beds, sharing stories as they fell asleep. As she bobbed on her board, water, salty and cool, splashed in her face and formed thick pearl drops on her lashes.

To her surprise, the dolphin tilted on its side and looked at her. Delighted, Carson imitated it and rolled to her side. The dolphin slipped to its belly, then lay on its side again. And Carson did the same. An idea blossomed in Carson's mind, and this time, she turned over completely onto her back. She held her breath. After a pause, the dolphin rolled over, presenting its gleaming white underbelly. Carson saw one long line and what looked like parentheses on either side of it. They both flipped around at the same time.

Aha, Carson thought, grinning. *You're a girl. I just knew it.* Carson lifted her head and, looking into the radiant eyes, spoke the name that had been floating on her tongue.

"Hello, Delphine."

Mamaw lounged in her robe on the back porch, feet up on the ottoman, sipping coffee and reading the *Post and Courier*. Today was her birthday! Eighty years of living . . . Who'd have guessed it? She felt she'd earned the right to be decadently lazy today. Her past was behind her and she'd lived a full life. She didn't like to think her best was behind her as well, but she was realistic that this might be true. Still, it was a blessing to live long enough to see your children grow and prosper and procreate and to witness another generation carrying the torch. As it was a curse to outlive your children, your husband, your friends.

This was the hand she'd been dealt, however, and she was glad to still be in the game. Eighty years of good resolutions and failures. Eight decades of dreams and dashed hopes. When she was young she'd marked the years' successes and failures with a measure of equanimity. After all, she still had plenty of years left to set things right. When she reached sixty, she paid closer attention to the passing of the years, and now, at eighty, she didn't dare hope for another decade, but prayed for at least a few more years so she could witness these young women finding their path. Truth was, she'd be grateful to see this summer through.

From the west wing of the house a screen door creaked. Mamaw turned her head to see Nate dressed in his usual outfit of soft fabric shorts, T-shirt, and tennis shoes. He was half bent in a crouch and scuttled across the porch like a ghost crab. She watched him hurry down the long wooden dock, breaking one of his mother's strictest rules. Mamaw set her coffee cup down with a clatter and hurried as fast as her body could to the porch's railing.

What is that boy up to? she wondered. Dear heaven! He was going straight to the edge of the dock. He wasn't going to jump in, was he? Could he even swim? She felt her heart rate accelerate, was ready to call out.

Then a movement in the water caught her attention and she saw what the boy had been watching and waiting for. Carson was paddling her board toward the dock. She was dripping wet in her bright coral-colored bikini and her long dark hair was clinging to her muscled, tan body.

Just look at her, Mamaw thought with pride and wonder. With her dark looks and athletic body, she was like some exotic Amazon princess. For all that Mamaw had once been thought of as a local beauty, she wondered if she'd ever possessed Carson's vibrant vitality.

A movement beside the paddleboard caught her attention. There was a dorsal fin. Mamaw clutched her heart as the memory of Carson's shark story leaped into her mind. Mamaw squinted and leaned forward on the railing and saw that it was a dolphin! A short laugh escaped her lips as she brought her fingers to her mouth, almost slumping in relief. A dolphin . . . Nate must have spotted it from his window. It was no wonder the boy was so excited.

Mamaw continued to watch as Carson deftly stepped onto the floating dock and easily lifted her board from the water. Nate scrambled down to the lower dock and stared into the water, mesmerized by the dolphin that lingered there. She heard the dolphin's piercing whistle, followed by the high-pitched sound of Nate's laughter. Mamaw's hand slipped again to her heart, this time in a gesture of tender surprise. She couldn't remember the last time she'd heard the boy laugh.

The porch door slammed again, drawing Mamaw's attention. Dora appeared in a panic, her eyes searching. She stopped at the edge of the porch and raised her hand over her eyes, spotting the pair at the dock.

"Nate!" she called.

"Oh, leave him be," Mamaw called out to her. "He's with Carson. He'll be fine."

Dora swung her head around, startled to hear Mamaw's voice. Dora was neatly dressed in a blue seer-sucker skirt and white embroidered linen blouse. She'd taken more care with her appearance, something that spoke volumes to Mamaw.

"You look quite pretty this morning," Mamaw told her.

"He shouldn't be out there on that dock," Dora said anxiously, moving her hands to her hips. "He knows the rules."

"Oh, Dora, leave the boy be. He's having a good time. And he's in good hands. Carson swims like a fish. She won't let anything happen to him. For heaven's sake, child, take a moment for yourself and enjoy a cup of coffee. I don't imagine you get many breaks early in the morning."

Dora shifted her gaze to her grandmother. Her face appeared conflicted, as though she wasn't sure what she should do.

"Go on and fetch some coffee and join me for a spell," Mamaw told her, patting the chair beside her. "It's my birthday. And I'd love a little company."

Dora looked back out at the dock, then turned to Mamaw. Her face slowly shifted from resignation to a hesitant smile. "All right," she said, and walked back into the house.

Mamaw took a final glance at the pair at the dock, locked in deep conversation. *Good*, she thought. That boy needed some time with his aunts. And Dora needed some time to herself.

A few moments later Dora came out with a steaming mug and a smile on her face. Mamaw smiled brightly in return. Perhaps it was going to be a nice weekend after all.

When Carson climbed onto the dock, she was surprised to see Nate sitting there with his legs folded staring out at the dolphin. He was such a skinny little kid, and he had the worst haircut. It was the old-fashioned bowl style; Dora had to have cut it herself, she thought, looking at the jagged, uneven edges. When the boy's eyes shifted to her, Carson sensed nervousness, as though he feared her getting too close.

"Why, hello, Nate. What are you doing here?"

"Nothing," he said, looking at the dock.

In the distance they could hear Dora calling Nate's name. The boy tensed and picked at a scab on his arm but did not answer her.

"Didn't you hear your mother calling?"

Nate scowled but said nothing.

"You should answer her. She might be worried."

"I don't want to."

"Why not?"

"I don't want her to come here because she will make the fish go away."

"The fish?" Carson paused. "Oh." Nate meant the dolphin, which explained why he was here. "That's not a fish, Nate. It's a mammal. It's called a dolphin. Come meet her."

Nate's eyes appeared eager but tentative. Carson held out her hand, which he ignored. Instead he carefully stepped down to the floating dock and approached the edge. Delphine swam several yards away but circled back, curious as ever, making clicking noises.

"The dolphin likes you," Nate said.

Carson smiled, feeling it was true. "I hope so. I like the dolphin."

"Does your dolphin have a name?"

"She's not *my* dolphin. She's wild. . . . But I do call her Delphine."

"Delphine," Nate repeated. "That's a good name."

Carson laughed and leaned forward to hug the boy, but Nate saw her coming and immediately stiffened. Remembering Dora's warning, Carson caught herself and pulled back.

Nate didn't appear to notice her dilemma. He was engrossed with searching for Delphine, who had submerged and disappeared into the depths.

"Where did she go?"

Carson raised her hand over her eyes like a visor and searched the still water. A few minutes later she spotted Delphine far across the cove. "There she is," she said to Nate, pointing. "Straight across. Wait, she dove again." She saw Nate on his tiptoes, squinting. They watched as Delphine arched over the water, catching breaths, swimming farther away. After a few minutes, Carson couldn't spot her any longer. "She's gone. But don't worry. She'll be back."

"But I want to see her now."

Carson didn't have much experience with children and demanding ones hit a nerve. "Well, kiddo, you can't. She's a wild animal. She comes and goes when she pleases. Speaking of which, it's time for us to go. Come on." She gave him a gentle nudge, then began to walk off. A small hand gently tapped her arm. She turned to see Nate chewing his lip and looking out at the water.

"Can I see the dolphin again?"

She saw his eyes—as eager as the dolphin's—and empathized with his need to make contact with whatever it was the dolphin possessed that drew them both in like magic.

"Sure," she replied with a smile. "If she comes back. And I think she will. Maybe later today we can come back here together. Bring your life vest, and we'll go for a swim. You do know how to swim, don't you?"

Nate nodded. Then he smiled, and it was like the sun coming out from behind a dark cloud.

Later that morning the smell of bacon was wafting from the kitchen. Carson followed the scent, her stomach growling. The kitchen was empty but she saw a plate of crisp bacon and some of Lucille's biscuits laid out under a glass bowl. She was reaching for them when she heard footsteps behind her. Turning her head, she saw Harper. Her face was pale and her eyes glassy, but she'd made the effort. Her hair was pulled back in a stubby ponytail and she was neatly dressed in slim madras Bermuda shorts, a white polo shirt, and clean white tennis shoes. Carson looked down at her own green T-shirt over torn denim shorts and thought Harper looked better outfitted for Nantucket than for Sullivan's Island.

"Good morning," Carson said. "Going sailing?"

Harper shook her head dully, missing the joke entirely.

"Want some bacon?" Carson asked, taking a big, greasy, exaggerated bite.

Harper visibly paled. "Ugh. Don't mention food. Is there coffee left?"

"I'll get you a cup," Carson said, piling bacon onto her plate now that she knew she didn't have to share with Harper. She reached to open the cabinet and pulled out a large mug that bore the faded insignia of the Gamecocks. "A little too much tequila last night?"

Harper shushed her, looking from left to right. "Keep it down. I don't want Mamaw or Lucille to find out." She took a slow sip of coffee. "I have no idea how much I drank. Someone was always putting a drink in front of me. It was bottomless. . . ." She took a sip of coffee, then walked to the cabinet and prowled for a glass. Finding one, she filled it with water; then from her pocket, she retrieved two aspirin. "The breakfast of champions," she muttered, and swallowed them down with a shudder.

Carson laughed lightly, with more sympathy. "Sorry, sis. Didn't mean for you to get hungover. I should've watched over you better. You're a tiny thing." She couldn't help but snicker. "A lightweight."

"I don't need you to watch over me, thank you very much. I can usually hold my own," Harper said. "It's just that it was a crazy day and I didn't eat much." She swallowed more water. "Let me guess. You can hold your liquor like a champ."

Carson grinned and slid a long piece of bacon into her mouth. "I feel right as rain."

"Great."

"While you were snoring away, I went to town and got us some fishing poles and lures. Sister mine, put on your sunscreen, 'cause we're going fishing today."

Harper slanted a glance at her from under half-closed lids. "You've got to be kidding. Worms? Fish? Me? Not a chance."

Nate came into the room, followed by Dora. Carson felt a twinge of affection when she saw his blue eyes spark at seeing her.

"Hey, squirt," Carson said to him. "Want to go fishing?" she asked.

"Fishing?" asked Dora with surprise. "I don't remember anyone saying that was part of today's agenda."

"I wasn't aware that there was an agenda," Carson replied. As the eldest, Dora always assumed she was the one who should organize family events. And she had a naturally bossy nature.

"But of course there is," Dora said. "We have cocktails on the porch at five, for which we are all supposed to be in our dinner best so we can have our photograph taken," she added.

"Photograph? Oh, what a nice idea. I'll get my cameras ready."

"*You're* not taking the photo," Dora said. "Mamaw hired a photographer."

Carson took offense. "Why would she hire someone? I'm a professional photographer. Tell her to cancel."

"She wants you *in* the photograph, not behind the camera," Dora explained.

"Hasn't she ever heard of a timer? Where is she? I'll talk to her."

Harper spoke up. "Let it go," she told Carson. "Mamaw's made her arrangements. I'm sure she was thinking of you."

"Harper's right. Mamaw is having dinner catered so Lucille can relax and join us, too. She's gone to a great deal of trouble planning everything." She delivered a meaningful glance to Carson. "But no one said anything about fishing."

Mamaw came into the room with Lucille, her eyes gleaming. "It was meant to be a surprise, Dora. So please smile and try not to spoil it." Mamaw brandished a red fishing rod and reel. "Look what I've found!" She stroked it gently before she turned to face Nate. "This was your great-grandfather Edward's fishing rod. He loved fishing and had several, of course. But he used this one almost exclusively at the end. It was his favorite. I know it would have given him great pleasure to teach you to fish. Since he isn't here, I'm giving it to you, his only great-grandson. I hope you catch as many fish out there on that dock as he did."

Mamaw handed the rod to him with a dramatic flourish. Carson could see that this moment meant a great deal to her.

In contrast, Nate reflected no emotion at all. He accepted the rod into his arms and looked at it dispassionately.

Dora came to stand beside him, a grin stiff on her face. "Isn't that wonderful! Say thank you to Mamaw," she told him.

Still looking at the rod, Nate complied and said flatly, "Thank you."

"It's a lovely gift," Dora said, her voice high with enthusiasm. "Thank you so much, Mamaw. He loves it."

Mamaw's face fell slightly at Nate's lackluster reaction, but she rallied and offered Dora a faint smile. "I hope he enjoys it."

"Oh, he will!" Dora exclaimed. "Won't you, Nate?"

Nate did not reply. He lowered the rod and shifted uncomfortably under the attention.

Carson saw Harper leaning against the counter, studying the boy silently. Dora's determination to be enthusiastic over Mamaw's thoughtfulness was hard to witness and Carson felt a sudden empathy for her.

"You know, Nate," Carson said in an even voice, "that is a very good rod. Once you start fishing, you'll love it. Guaranteed."

"I don't know how to fish," he said with little emotion. "My father knows how to fish but he never taught me. He said I wasn't old enough and too clumsy."

Carson shot a glance at Dora to see her face twist in sorrow. Carson cursed Cal for being too damn lazy or uncaring to take his nine-year-old son fishing.

"Nah, you're the perfect age to learn," Carson said. "Did you know that Granddaddy taught me when I was even younger than you? We used to sit right out there on the dock and fish for red drum, flounder, all kinds of fish. Then we'd clean them and Lucille would cook them up and serve them swimming in butter with a little lemon and parsley. Remember, Mamaw?"

Mamaw's eyes warmed at the memory. "Your great-granddaddy is in heaven now, Nate, so it seems only fair that *we* teach you."

"What do you say?" Carson asked.

"Say?" Nate asked, not understanding the idiom.

"Do you want us to teach you how to fish?" Carson explained.

"No."

"Oh," Carson said, deflated.

"I want you to teach me how to play with the dolphin."

"Dolphin?" asked Dora. "What dolphin?"

Carson groaned inwardly. She wasn't prepared to share Delphine with anyone.

"The dolphin that comes to the dock," Nate answered in his matter-of-fact manner. "It's Aunt Carson's dolphin."

Dora looked at her with confusion. "*Your* dolphin?"

"No, of course not. It's just a wild dolphin that sometimes comes by the dock."

"Her dolphin has a name," Nate said. "She calls it Delphine. That is a very good name. Delphine plays with Aunt Carson," Nate informed them with conviction.

Carson looked around the room to see all eyes glued to her. She sighed. "It's a long story. If you want to hear it, come down to the dock. Fishing is a slow sport and we'll have lots of time to yak."

The afternoon proved to be an enormous success. Mamaw passed out large floppy hats and suntan lotion and Lucille packed a picnic lunch of curried chicken sandwiches on whole wheat bread, pickles, tangerines, homemade oatmeal cookies, and plenty of iced sweet tea. Dora prepared Nate his own picnic of accepted food, which he ate without complaint. The women feasted under the shade of the dock's roof, then began the great fishing venture.

At first there was a lackluster response from Harper. She relayed a litany of excuses—how she didn't sit in the sun, how she needed to catch up on work, had e-mails to answer. But Mamaw cajoled her to bring her laptop out on the dock, where she could sit in the shade. Harper obliged and settled under the roof of the dock with her iPad. Meanwhile, Mamaw set bait and helped Nate and Dora cast from the dock.

Carson brought out her camera and it felt good to take her first photographs since leaving Los Angeles. Behind the lens of a camera, Carson was able to catch glimpses of her family in close-up, details of their personalities often missed by the naked eye.

She noticed that Harper was skilled at being invisible. While "the little mouse" stayed quiet and tucked away in the corner, people forgot she was there, which allowed her to observe private moments. Her fingers were always tapping at her computer or phone. Carson wondered if she was writing wry vignettes to her mother, something along the lines of "Amusing Tales from the South." Or "Redneck Riviera."

Little Nate was very intense about everything he did. Every photo showed him with his brow furrowed and his gaze sharp as Mamaw taught him how to set the bait, cast, reel in. To his credit, Nate observed silently, no matter how long Mamaw took to explain things—and she could get long-winded. When it was his turn to try, his little fingers were nimble.

Dora, in contrast, did not engage. She hovered near Nate, whether out of worry or habit Carson couldn't be sure. She held her fishing rod in a listless fashion, leaning against the railing and gazing off at the sea. In a close-up shot, Carson caught Dora's beautiful blue eyes swimming in tears.

By midafternoon, the sun was high and the fish weren't biting. Not that anyone really cared. Carson had slipped a bit of Firefly sweet-tea vodka into the iced tea to give it a little kick and help loosen the tongues. It worked. As Carson set aside her camera, Harper set aside her iPad and the ladies talked amiably about safe subjects such as movies, recipes, happy memories. Only Nate remained relentlessly alert at the pole. Occasionally Carson would hop up to help him cast again, or Dora would reapply suntan lotion on his arms and face.

Suddenly, Mamaw yelped and jerked back her rod. "I got one!"

In a chorus of cheers, everyone leaped to join her. Giddy with her good luck, and perhaps a bit less sure-footed from her "tea," Mamaw hooted while the girls laughed and whistled. Carson leaped for her camera to capture Mamaw's comical struggle. Mamaw finally reeled in the smallest red drum Carson had ever seen.

Dora laughed at the sight of it dangling from the line. "Sure was a lot of fight for such a puny fish."

"Hey," said Carson defensively. "It's the only fish we caught!"

"Well, take a picture of my prize," Mamaw said, holding the little fish proudly in the air. "Before I toss it back in."

Nate was a hound on the scent, close at Mamaw's side as she grabbed a pair of pliers.

Carson wasn't sure Mamaw wasn't too woozy to wield the pliers and stepped in, but Mamaw indignantly waved her aside.

"I've been fishing since before you were even a glimmer in your father's eye. Now, stand back." She grabbed hold of the fish and deftly removed the hook. "Nate, honey, do you want to do the honors and toss this *puny* fish back into the water?"

"Yes," Nate replied in a voice husky with fear and excitement. To his credit, he reached out with both hands and clasped the fish tightly. It wiggled but Nate held on as he walked to the front of the dock with his arms held stiffly before him.

Carson followed him, hoping he didn't squeeze the fish to death before he released it. Looking over the railing, she was surprised to see Delphine, her mouth open and her gaze on Nate holding the fish over the water.

"Don't feed the dolphin!" she cried out, but it was too late. Nate released the fish.

In a flash, Delphine leaped to catch the fish adeptly in her mouth. She tossed it in the air, caught it again, and dove, disappearing with her treasure.

Nate burst out in a high-pitched laugh of delight. He leaned far over the railing on tiptoe, beaming, as he searched for signs of Delphine. Dora put her hands to her lips, eyes wide in amazement at the sight of her son's joy. This was the first time she'd seen Nate smile all weekend.

Delphine positioned herself beneath the dock and made a series of staccato, nasal calls to an appreciative audience.

Harper sat at the dock's edge dangling her feet in the water. Despite generous lotion and her floppy hat, her skin was turning pink. "I think she wants more fish!"

"She's begging," Carson said with disapproval, looking down at the dolphin and shaking her head. "She must've been fed fish before. That explains why she's so friendly. Oh, stop it," she called out to Delphine. "Ladies don't beg!"

"Is that the same dolphin that was here this morning?" Mamaw asked.

"That's Delphine," Nate announced. "She is Carson's dolphin."

"She's not *my* dolphin," Carson said again, getting the sense she was fighting a losing battle. She looked into the water to see Delphine waiting below, her dark eyes gleaming. "You're not helping," Carson told the dolphin, but as always, Carson couldn't help but smile back.

"How did she get here?" Harper asked. "At our dock?"

Carson tried to downplay the drama. "What can I say? She likes me."

Mamaw laughed with pleasure. It was a lovely trilling sound, feminine but not silly. "You always were our little mermaid." She reached out to gently cup Carson's face in her palm. Then she turned and leaned over the railing to stare imperiously down at the dolphin. Delphine tilted her head, staring back in her beguiling manner.

"You are a pretty thing, aren't you?" Mamaw declared.

As she straightened, a breeze caught her coral-colored silk scarf and sent it floating in the air. Mamaw gasped and Carson lunged to grab it but the scarf floated just out of her reach, sailed in the air a moment, then landed in the creek.

"Off it goes," Mamaw said with a sigh. "It was only a Ferragamo."

Delphine took off after the brightly colored scarf floating in the water. Curious, the dolphin poked at the floating fabric like it was a piece of flotsam, then lifted it in the air and tossed it. She grew excited by the game and swam around the scarf in a tight circle, tossing it a few more times. Then she grabbed the scarf and disappeared with it under the surface.

"You little thief!" Mamaw called out at the widening ripples.

"She's back!" Harper said, pointing to the dolphin emerging farther out in the cove. Then she burst out laughing. "Oh. My. God."

Delphine returned to the dock dragging the coral scarf around her pectoral flipper, looking like a lady walking along the boardwalk.

Everyone started laughing then, even Mamaw. She leaned over the dock railing. Beneath her, Delphine was dragging the Ferragamo scarf in her mouth. Carson lowered the camera and gazed at the faces of her family—Harper, Dora, Mamaw, Nate—recognizing that this was a singular moment for them all. Everyone was smiling and laughing, and it was this enigmatic dolphin that had appeared from nowhere to bring them to this tipping point.

"At least you display good taste," Mamaw called out in her inimitable imperial tone. "Welcome, Delphine, you little minx! I hereby declare you one of my Summer Girls."

Carson, Harper, and Dora clapped and hooted, united in Mamaw's welcome of the dolphin. The mood shot upward as Delphine paraded her scarf in the water beneath them.

"I want to catch another fish for Delphine," Nate declared, walking off to fetch his rod.

"Wait. No. We shouldn't," Carson called after him. "There are laws forbidding feeding dolphins. Fines."

"Oh, why not?" Dora asked, getting caught up in Nate's enthusiasm. "Who's going to see us? And what harm can feeding one little fish do? It's their natural diet, isn't it? Nate is so excited. I haven't seen him get so interested in anything else but his video games. And look, she obviously wants it!" She hurried over to Nate's side.

Mamaw picked up some bait and waved Nate closer. "Bring your rod. You'd better get crackin', boy. You've got a customer waiting."

"Don't worry," Harper said, tapping Carson's arm in a consoling fashion. "It took all afternoon to catch that one fish. I doubt they'll catch another."

Carson crossed her arms in worry, glancing from Delphine to her family. Mamaw and Nate were bent over a hook, head to head, attaching bait. Dora picked up her rod and began casting out. Even Harper had joined the fray, taking Carson's rod to Mamaw for bait. They were talking to each other, communicating.

Below them, Delphine was still there, head out of the water, watching them with curiosity. The scarf was gone, no doubt tucked away in some safe spot. Carson didn't have the heart to argue. After all, who was she to interfere? Wasn't Delphine free to come and go at will? Maybe Dora was right. What harm could come from offering Delphine one little fish?

CHAPTER NINE

*T*he time for her party had come at last. Mamaw rested in the coolness of her sitting room, the shades drawn against the relentless sun, shuffling a deck of cards. Her hands moved with deft skill, cutting the deck in half, making air whir against her palms as the cards fell into place. One by one, she snapped seven cards onto the small desk to begin yet another game of solitaire. Her hands stilled when she heard a soft knocking on the door.

"Come in!"

"You ready to start dressing?"

Mamaw turned to see Lucille in a blue taffeta dress with a beaded bodice. "Oh my word, Lucille. You look beautiful!"

"Don't I know it? I love the glitter," Lucille replied, preening with the compliment. "I thank you for my new dress."

"It suits you. You look radiant. Royal blue is your color."

"Now it's time to put down those cards and get you lookin' pretty."

"Are you sure we don't have time for a quick game of rummy?"

Lucille laughed and drew closer. "I never known anyone who loves to play cards as much as you do."

"Except perhaps you?"

"Even me."

Mamaw sighed dramatically and set the cards on the table. "Did you know these cards were given to my grandfather by Admiral Wood? And *he* was gifted them by Admiral Perry. This is my prize deck." She kissed them for luck. "It's a special day, isn't it?"

"It surely is. Come on, Miz Marietta. Let me help you up."

"Very well," she replied, releasing the playing cards with reluctance. "There is no more delaying the inevitable playing out of cards tonight with my granddaughters."

"No, ma'am. You're ready."

"As ready as I'll ever be. All that's left is to see if we can squeeze my largesse into my gown."

"You should've bought something new for yourself, Miz Marietta. It's your birthday, after all. Instead of buying things for everyone else."

Mamaw swept open the door to her large walk-in closet. Seeing so many clothes, hats, and shoes almost sickened her. "Oh, Lucille, I don't need another dress. I don't want one. Look at all those clothes!" She stared at them dispassionately. "Most of them I haven't worn in years. I can't even fit into most of them. I don't know why I hold on to them."

"Maybe it's time to go through and weed out some and give them to charity. Before you move on. You won't have room for all of them in your new place."

"Yes, that's a good idea. I can't take it all with me." She smirked. "Going to the retirement community is like a dry run for the final departure, eh? A downsizing? Lord knows I'm ready for it. I'm weary of taking care of this place, worrying about every storm that approaches, closing drapes against the sun, the silver, the china, the furniture. It's all such a burden now. I long to be free of all that *stuff*. To have a little fun again." She put her hand to her cheek as she gazed at the line of gowns in the closet. "But it will be hard to part with my evening gowns. Each one holds a special memory."

Mamaw sighed, running her hand along the gorgeous silks, taffetas, brocades. In her mind's eye she wasn't Mamaw but Marietta Muir, the Charleston socialite known for her glittering parties, her easy repartee, her refined tastes. "Such lovely fabrics and colors. Do you think the girls might want to scrounge through them first and see if there's something they might like? Carson is about the same size as I once was. And Harper, if they were taken in." Mamaw thought of Dora and didn't think she'd fit into any of the dresses. "Dora might like my shoes and bags."

"Could be . . ."

"There was a time when I bought a new dress for every big occasion," she said wistfully. "Edward's eyes lit up when he saw me all fancied up in my best." She paused, recalling Edward's face when she'd step out into the living room and do a pirouette for him. "This may come as a surprise to you, but I don't really care how I look anymore."

"That's a switch," Lucille murmured.

"Do you think that it's a sign I'm slipping? You know, dementia or something?"

Lucille laughed and shook her head. It sounded to Mamaw like a hen's cackle. "Mercy no!" Lucille said, waving her hand. "I 'spect you've just got more important things on your mind now than frills."

"Yes," Mamaw said with conviction, taking heart. "Yes, that's it."

"So, which dress do you want me to pull out?"

"That off-white linen gown with the black scrollwork. It should fit, don't you think?"

"Only one way to find out. Now, hold on to my arm while I fluff it open so's you can step inside."

Mamaw held tight to Lucille's arm, wobbling as she gingerly stepped inside the gown. Lucille struggled with the zipper around the waist.

"Can you suck in any?" Lucille asked.

Mamaw sucked in as tight as she could but her muscles were so atrophied that nothing she did seemed to make a difference. Once she'd had such a flat belly; now it seemed to be the spot where all her calories went. After much effort, Lucille pushed the zipper up its path.

Mamaw released a gasp, feeling the tight waist like a boa constrictor against her belly. "Lord help me, I can hardly breathe! Now I know what my ancestors must've felt like in a corset." With a rustle of fabric she took careful steps to the full-length mirror on her door. She threw back her shoulders and stood tall while she perused her reflection. The ornate black scrolls at the waist distracted the eye from the rounding of her belly, and the A-line cut flowed to the floor, giving her a sleeker silhouette.

"Not bad," she murmured, smoothing her hand over the fabric. "Not bad at all. I don't look a day over seventy," she quipped.

"Them seams look ready to burst," Lucille said, perusing the dress with her chin in her palm.

"Oh, let them," Mamaw replied, fanning her face. "I just have to take shallow breaths. I do want to look nice for our photographs. Is the photographer here?"

"Yes'm. He's been here for a while. Of course Carson's fussing that she could've done the pictures better and we just should've asked her."

"But I want her to be *in* the photographs."

"That's what I told her. But I understand how she's feeling. It's silly, you hirin' a caterer when I could've cooked up a meal better."

"What am I going to do with the two of you?" Mamaw asked, lifting her palms. "I'm just trying to let someone serve *you* for a change."

Lucille muttered something under her breath that Mamaw couldn't catch.

"Just say thank you," Mamaw teased. "Speaking of the caterer, is he here?"

"Sure he's here. Been settin' up for hours. And the girls are in the living room. Everyone's here. They're all waiting on you!"

"Oh . . ." Mamaw felt flustered. She didn't like to be rushed. "Well, it *is* my birthday party. They can't very well start without me."

She went to her dresser and pulled a small jewelry box out from a drawer. She had selected her jewelry very carefully for tonight. For all her discomfort, she did look like a queen in this gown. She wished that Edward were here to see her.

She leaned forward, closer to the mirror, to place the diamond scroll earrings, a fiftieth-wedding-anniversary gift from Edward, into her lobes. On her ring finger, she wore the antique cushion-cut diamond. The large stone caught the light and glittered like a million stars on her finger. Finally, she gathered the three black velvet bags containing the pearls and placed them in her black beaded pocketbook. Only a single blue velvet bag was left on the bureau.

She looked over her shoulder and summoned Lucille.

"I'd meant to give this to you later, when we had dessert. But I think . . ." Marietta turned to face Lucille. "Well, dear friend, you should have this now." She handed Lucille the velvet bag.

Lucille's eyes were wide with curiosity as she accepted the bag. "What's this? You already bought me this dress."

"It goes with the dress."

Lucille gave her a mock-suspicious glance, then opened the bag and let the contents slip out into her palm. "Lawd have mercy!" she exclaimed when she saw the pair of large sapphire earrings, encircled with diamonds. "Lawd, Lawd . . ." She looked again at Mamaw, this time with shock. "Are they real?"

"Yes, of course they are." Mamaw laughed. "They were my mother's. And now they're yours. They'll look wonderful with your dress. I can't wait to see them on you. Go on, put them on."

Mamaw watched Lucille stand in front of the Venetian mirror to replace her gold hoops with the sapphires and diamonds, her hands shaking with excitement. Mamaw felt a rush of love for her, thinking of how those hands formed the bedrock of her world.

Lucille straightened, the earrings flashing at her ears, but not as bright as her eyes. "How do I look?"

It brought Mamaw a flush of pleasure to see how the earrings—baubles that had been sitting uselessly in a safe—brought such pleasure.

"I think the word is . . . *sexy*," Mamaw said, and got the hoped-for blush.

Humor fled as Mamaw took Lucille's hands. "Dear friend, please accept these earrings as a small token of my love and thanks, for more than I can ever express."

Lucille pinched her lips, equally unable to express her emotions.

"Shall we go? It's time for me to lay my cards out on the table."

Lucille took Mamaw's arm and, old friends, they began walking. At the bedroom door, Mamaw stopped short and her hand tightened over Lucille's as she took a sharp breath.

"Don't be nervous. You'll do fine," Lucille said in a comforting tone. "You've been thinking on this for a long while."

"Nervous? It takes a lot more than three silly girls to make me nervous." She placed her hand on her stomach as she took a deep breath. "But there is so much at stake, isn't there?"

"They'll want the truth now."

Mamaw took another breath and looked beseechingly at Lucille. "Am I being a tad overbearing with the demands I'll make tonight?"

"You? Overbearing?" Lucille chuckled. "Heaven forbid. Manipulative, maybe. Conniving. Calculating. Controlling . . ."

"Yes, yes . . . It may be my one flaw," Mamaw conceded with a twitch of her lips. "I see now how all my meddling has only resulted in miserable failures."

"And Mr. Edward's."

Mamaw fell silent as she thought again of her husband. He had been a dear man but he did, perhaps, love her too much. His love had blinded him, and knowing it, she had taken full advantage when it came to matters concerning their son.

"Do you think Edward had, well, given up on Parker?" she asked Lucille.

"No. But I always thought he should've given that boy a good whuppin'."

"Maybe." Mamaw's thoughts journeyed down a troubled path as she absently twiddled the diamond on her finger. "Maybe he should've whupped me, too. He let me get my way too often. Oh, Lucille, I fear that I weakened both the men in my life."

"That was then," Lucille said. "This is now. Just say what you've got to say and let the cards fall where they may."

"Yes," Mamaw said, and looked at her diamond. "I must restrain myself and not offer my opinions tonight. Let them work this out among themselves."

"That's the plan."

Mamaw couldn't abide fools, and Lucille was nobody's fool. Mamaw had always counted on Lucille's ability to cut through the chaff and to give her opinion, honestly and clearly, when needed. Mamaw gathered her wits. In the card game of bridge, Mamaw annoyed her partners by taking forever to formulate how she would play out her hand. But once she began she'd snap her cards on the table with alacrity, having already thought through each trick in her mind.

Mamaw sucked in a long breath. "I'm ready. Shall we go out?"

Lucille tightened her hold on Mamaw's arm. "Let the game begin."

Her party began exactly as she'd planned. After the photographer had finished, Mamaw had her favorite brut rosé champagne served in French etched-crystal glasses, which had been in the family for generations. Mamaw preferred the wide saucers to flutes. The pink bubbles tickled her nose while she sipped. Nate was happy to scurry to his room for a special dinner on a tray and a movie. Tonight was just for her girls and she wanted it to be perfect.

The five women sat together under the glistening crystal chandelier in the sage-green dining room. Mamaw had removed the leaves of the Sheraton table to create a more intimate circle. The candlelight glimmered against the family silver and crystal. From time to time, Mamaw caught the scent of the white roses in the centerpiece.

She leaned back in her chair and looked around her table at the four faces. Conversation flowed seamlessly around stories of shared memories of summers long gone. At some point between the fishing and the champagne, even Dora had lost the chip on her shoulder and engaged enthusiastically. The eldest of Mamaw's granddaughters, Dora had a picture-perfect memory for details that brought her stories alive. Mamaw thought how she'd inherited this quality from Parker.

Carson's laughter rang out. She'd always loved to laugh and wasn't shy about it. Carson was quick with an aside that added punch to a story and was fearless with her opinions, delivered with a tease rather than a jab. She, too, could spin a yarn.

Only Harper remained reserved. Not shy, she was amiable and laughed at the stories. But rarely did she add to the conversation. Yet when she made the rare comment, it was clever and displayed a sharp wit. Mamaw listened, her eyes gleaming over the rim of her wineglass, marveling at this previously unrevealed side of her granddaughter.

Mamaw watched her girls tasting the different courses of food, sampling the wines, making surprisingly well-informed comments on the seasonings and vineyards. She felt aglow seeing them enjoying the event, smacking their lips and laughing. The mood was as bright as the flickering candles.

When the coconut cake was brought out and she'd blown out the eight candles (she'd insisted they not be ridiculous and try to squeeze eighty onto the cake), it was time for gifts. Mamaw was much more excited about what she was giving than about what she might be receiving. She'd already received many other gifts from friends. The doorbell had rung all week as the UPS and mail carriers made countless stops. Sea Breeze was filled with beautiful flower arrangements, and there were more soaps and sweets in beautiful boxes than she could ever use.

Dora nervously presented her with a beautifully wrapped box. Inside, Mamaw found a hand-knitted shawl of the softest merino wool with lovely long tassels. It was magnificent, and Mamaw was deeply moved by the handmade gift, but Dora couldn't stop apologizing for all the perceived flaws. Mamaw thought how she really had to teach Dora to take pride in her accomplishments.

Harper surprised her with some modern contraption she called an iPad. The other girls were very impressed with the gift and huddled over it, checking out all the features, but Mamaw didn't have the first clue how to use it. Harper promised to teach her and said something about helping her to be "plugged in." Whatever that meant, bless her heart.

Lastly, Carson set before her a box wrapped in purple floral cloth in the Japanese *furoshiki* style. Mamaw was amused by this exotic wrapping, so like Carson. But she was unprepared for the gift. Inside was a stunning photograph of Mamaw sitting in her favorite wicker chair on the porch overlooking the cove. Carson had employed all her considerable skills to catch just the right amount of the reds and golds of the setting sun to add a glow to Mamaw's skin, making her appear ethereal. It was a singular unguarded moment, not posed. Carson had captured a rare wistfulness in her expression, a fierce tenderness that each of the girls recognized and was deeply moved by. Mamaw looked into Carson's eyes and thanked her. As she spoke the words, she wondered at the perspicacity of the woman who could capture glimpses of someone's soul.

After the waiters cleared away the last of the dishes, Mamaw signaled for them to pour another round of champagne. At last she'd come to the moment for which she'd been waiting so long.

"Now it's my turn to give you each a present," she announced.

"We get presents?" Dora asked, brows raised in surprise.

The girls all sat straighter in their chairs, eyes as wide as saucers as Mamaw bent to pick up the black beaded bag from beside her chair. From this she retrieved one velvet pouch after the other, then handed the appropriate ones to her granddaughters. Suddenly there was a flurry of movement and high-pitched squeals as the room echoed with a chorus of oohs and aahs. The girls leaped to their feet to deliver kisses to Mamaw amid declarations of love and thanks that made her head swirl. She grinned from ear to ear, thinking how much they looked like butterflies in her garden, landing on one flower, then the next, as they whirled to help each other fasten their pearl necklaces. Then, in a rush of giggles, they ran off to admire themselves in her bathroom mirror.

Mamaw and Lucille remained at the table, smiling and raising their champagne glasses in a toast to their success. Soon, the girls returned and took their seats at the table, their faces suffused with pleasure. Mamaw eyed them carefully, to see if there was any sign of someone being disappointed, or perhaps a trade in the bathroom. To her relief, each of the girls appeared delighted with the necklace chosen for her.

Lucille and Mamaw exchanged a meaningful glance and Lucille immediately rose, tactfully excused herself, and left to handle the final details of the caterer's departure. Mamaw's gaze floated around the table, resting on each of the girls glowing happily in her necklace—Dora in her opera-length pink pearls, Carson in her dark South Sea pearls, and Harper wreathed in the creamy three-strand choker. Each girl had grown up to be a beauty in her own right. She couldn't have loved them any more than she did at this moment. Now she had to pray for the strength to challenge them. She picked up her silver spoon and tapped her crystal glass, drawing the attention of the girls. Talking ceased and all eyes turned to her.

"My precious dears," she began. She was surprised again by the nervousness that swept over her. She cleared her throat and pushed on. "It's been too long since we've spent time together at Sea Breeze. I hope that you all have felt that this was your home, a place to come to whenever you wished."

Each of the girls graciously assured her this was true.

"But time marches on. As you know, I'm not getting any younger. The ruins of Rome are upon me and I've come to accept that it's time for me to move into a retirement home, where I will live among many of my friends and, importantly, be where I can take advantage of all the amenities that make life easier as I reach that certain age."

Dora, who was sitting beside her, reached over to pat her hand. "You'll always be ageless to us, Mamaw."

"Thank you, dear. However, I'm not getting any richer, sadly. Which brings me to the business at hand. The three of you have carved out lives for yourselves elsewhere in the country. You're all busy; you have other places you want to travel to when you go on vacation instead of here. I understand this and must face the fact that your visits to Sea Breeze are few and far between. I'm not saying this to be the least bit critical. However, I've always been a realist." She spread out her palms.

"I'm selling Sea Breeze," she said with a bittersweet smile.

She saw their faces reflect a mixture of shock and sorrow.

Dora spoke first. "But it's been in the family for generations."

"Yes. True enough. I feel that burden keenly. I've done all I can, my dears."

"Isn't there some way we can keep it?" asked Carson. She looked stricken.

"I really don't think so."

"B-but," Dora stammered, "I . . . I thought . . ." She shook her head. "I don't know what I thought." She laughed with some embarrassment. "That you have chest drawers filled with money, I guess."

Mamaw smiled indulgently. "We were well-off, to be sure. But our fortune has dwindled considerably. There've been bad investments, the ups and downs of the stock market, the high cost of living, and the expenses of illness and old age. After your grandfather retired, we lived on our nest egg. There was no new money coming in as expenses went up. If you knew what it costs to insure this place today, you'd weep!" She paused, choosing her words carefully. "And there were Parker's expenses. The simple truth is that my son—your father—ate through a good deal of my money in his lifetime. It was my decision to support him, and I must accept my role in the way things turned out. But here we are."

There was a silence as the girls digested this.

"He what?" Dora blurted, breaking the silence.

Harper said more softly, "I don't understand. What do you mean, he ate through your money?"

Mamaw glanced at Carson. She sat rigid, her jaw set and her blue eyes glowing like acetylene torches.

"Parker never found himself," Mamaw said, trying to couch her words with kindness. "Bless his heart, he tried so many different projects and he had so much potential. Sadly, that potential was never realized. He needed . . ." She paused, seeking the correct word that would be honest but fair. ". . . *support* over the years. And Edward and I gave it to him."

Carson couldn't hold back any longer. "Support? He depended on Mamaw's allowance."

"Wait," Harper said, still trying to understand. "Are you saying that he didn't earn any money? That Mamaw just gave him money?"

"That's what I'm saying," Carson replied.

"What about his writing?"

Mamaw covered her eyes with her hand when Carson let loose a hoot of derogatory laughter.

"His writing?" Carson asked incredulously. "Are you serious?"

"Yes. Quite," Harper replied unflinchingly. "I always understood my father was a writer."

An uncharacteristically cruel smile eased across Carson's face. "Did you? No, Harper. *Our* father wasn't a writer. He was a writer wannabe," she replied. "Or rather, he didn't want to be a writer as much as he wanted to be famous. There's a difference."

"You don't have to be so cruel," Harper admonished her, looking Carson straight in the eye.

Carson shrugged. "Me, cruel? You know his great American novel never got published, right? You ought to know that. Your mother was the first editor to reject it." There was ringing accusation in her voice.

"Yes," Harper replied tightly, keeping herself rigid. She continued. "Mother had always been quite clear about his talent, or rather, his lack of it. But I'd always thought her judgment was clouded by her general loathing of him."

Carson appeared slightly mollified. "Well, she wasn't alone in her opinion of his talent," Carson said. "He could've wallpapered a room with his rejections."

"What about screenplays?" Harper asked persistently. "Isn't that why he went to California?"

"Oh, God," Carson moaned, shaking her head in her palm. Then, peering up at Harper, she said, "You really don't know anything, do you?"

Dora spoke up. "Apparently, neither do I. I'd always

assumed that Daddy made his living writing screen-plays."

Carson dropped her hand and turned her head to stare at Mamaw with accusation.

"They don't know?" Carson asked her.

Mamaw lifted her chin. "It was no one's business but his own."

"So the great myth of Parker Muir the artist, the author, the entrepreneur, the beloved son of the great Muir clan, is alive and well," Carson said with sarcasm. "Good job, Mamaw."

Dora clasped her hands together on the table. "I think it *is* our business, Mamaw. We're not children any lon-ger. He is our father, no matter how absent he was, and apparently he made a huge dent in the family fortune. You just told us you're selling Sea Breeze because of his debts. That affects each of us. After all, we're your heirs. After, of course, our mothers."

Mamaw drew up in her seat. "Your mothers?" she said, her tone rising with her distaste. "My daughters-in-law are nothing more than a disappointment. My son may have had three wives, but it takes two to tango."

Carson abruptly rose to her feet and reached for the bottle of champagne. She filled her glass, then went around to refill those of her sisters.

Mamaw regretted her comment and gazed at the centerpiece. The roses appeared otherworldly against the flickering candles. Her thoughts drifted back to other din-ner parties, years earlier, when Parker was young and filled with promise. He filled out his dinner jacket seamlessly, and with his sharp wit, his elegant manner, his dashing good looks—he was dazzling. She wished his daughters could have known him then.

Harper turned toward her and spoke calmly. "Mamaw, I don't know my father. Other than the few stories you've fed me, and the few choice bits from my mother, he's a complete stranger to me. From you, I heard he was a writer, a starving artist. A very romantic character. From Mother, I heard he was a raging alcoholic, a no-talent writer with an exaggerated sense of entitlement. Even a womanizer."

"I think your mother got it right." Carson picked up her champagne glass and raised it in a mock toast ringing with scorn. "To dear old Dad."

"That's enough, Carson," Mamaw said, deeply hurt. She looked at her granddaughter and wondered at the source of her deep resentment.

Carson scowled and downed her glass of champagne.

"You still didn't answer Harper's question," Dora said, returning to the sore point. "How did Daddy earn his living all those years in California?"

Carson slowly turned in her chair to face Mamaw, twiddling the stem of the glass in her fingers, waiting for—challenging—her to answer the question. When Mamaw did not reply, Carson set the glass down on the table and stared at it.

"The good mother sent her little boy a monthly allowance," Carson told them. "It was always a big deal in our house, you know. Dad waiting for his check." She looked down at her empty glass and said in a changed voice, "I know you meant to help him."

"Not only him," Mamaw interjected. "To help *you*."

Carson reached out to grab the bottle and refill her glass. "At the beginning, it wasn't too bad. We had a nice apartment. Mamaw and Granddaddy gave him a good bit of money to invest in some new venture. I was pretty young, I don't remember what it was."

"It was a movie," Mamaw said.

Carson delivered a long stare. "No, I don't think that was it."

"I should know," Mamaw replied. "I recall it vividly. He wrote the screenplay and had a producer." She waved her hand in the air. "I . . . I can't recall the title."

"I wish we could have seen it," Dora said. "A movie made of Daddy's screenplay. That's something, isn't it?" She spoke the latter like a cheerleader, encouraging the girls to feel some pride in their father.

Mamaw held her tongue. Edward had always been suspicious of the whole project but she had pushed for the financial support, believing Parker's claim that if he could get one movie done, then more would follow. It was a substantial investment, and how she'd prayed it would launch his career at last. When the film was finished, she and Edward had flown to Atlanta to see it. She'd worn a new dress for the occasion and had wanted to throw a party, but her son had been strangely against any fanfare and didn't encourage them to see it. The film was shown in a smarmy theater in a dodgy part of the city, which should have been their first clue. Mamaw was shocked and Edward so outraged by the film that they got up and walked out after the first fifteen minutes. On the way home to Charleston Edward had to explain to Mamaw what soft-core pornography was.

"Where's the film? I'd like to see it," said Harper.

"I've no idea," Mamaw said in an absent manner. "It's probably destroyed. Lost."

Carson turned and said in an easy manner, "The film wasn't saved and the bottom line is it was never a success and there were never any more. End of story."

She turned to look at Mamaw, her eyes pulsing a private message to stop. Mamaw immediately understood that Carson knew the full story but didn't want to discuss it. She was embarrassed, but she was also protecting her father's—and perhaps Mamaw's—reputation.

"From there it went from bad to worse," Carson continued. "We were evicted from our apartments more often than I can remember, each one always shabbier than the last. Daddy was a master at one thing," she said with a bitter laugh. "That was staying ahead of the collectors. Wait," she added, lifting a finger in the air. "He was good at one other thing," she acknowledged. "The man could tell a good story. It's just a damn shame he couldn't get those stories down on paper. His only audience was his bar mates." She drained the contents of her glass.

"He died alone in a bar. Did you know that?" She glanced from one sister to the other, then finally her gaze rested on Mamaw. "I got a call from the police to identify the body." She paused and, twiddling the stem of her glass, said morosely, "Not one of my happiest memories."

Mamaw brought her hand to her throat, feeling it close on her. She'd never known this. By the time Carson had telephoned her, his body had already been sent to the morgue. Edward had flown to L.A. immediately to claim the body and bring it and Carson home to South

Carolina. She'd always assumed Edward had identified the body, and he had never enlightened her, no doubt trying to protect her. That would have been so like him.

"I thought . . ." Dora began, then had to stop and take a breath, confused. "Lord, I thought it was all so different," she said slowly. She glanced up at Carson. "All these years you were out in California, I'd always imagined you living in some luxury apartment overlooking the ocean. Living it up, with movie stars and glamour. I was jealous of you, Carson. I thought that you were the lucky one."

"Luxury lifestyle?" Carson laughed bitterly. "Not quite."

"At least you knew he loved you," Dora said unflinchingly. "I knew he never loved me. My mother told me he didn't often enough. She said that I was just an annoying burden, someone he had to send a birthday and Christmas gift to, if he remembered. Which wasn't often." Dora folded her arms and looked away.

"Oh, Dora," Mamaw murmured under her breath, ready to strangle Winnie for her callousness. Horrible woman. How could a mother tell a young girl such a thing? Dora turned to look beyond Mamaw at Carson. "You know what the craziest part is? I didn't hate *him*. I hated *you* because you were the one that Daddy loved best. He kept you with him and left Harper and me behind."

"Loved me? He only dragged me along so I'd take care of him."

"Carson," Mamaw said sharply, interrupting her. "That's not true. He wanted you with him. You didn't have a mother to keep you, like the others did."

"I had you," she said, her voice breaking. "I wanted to stay with *you*. I begged you to keep me, but you wouldn't."

Mamaw gasped at the heartbreak she heard in Carson's accusation. "I would have loved to keep you with me. I wanted to. What could I do?" she cried. "You were his daughter!"

"No!" Carson cried. "That wasn't the reason you let me go. You could never say no to him." Tears threatened. "Not even for me."

Mamaw's hands flew to her cheeks. "You can't believe that! Parker . . . he loved you," she said in halting words. "All of you."

"Did he?" Carson shrugged, sniffing and swiping away the tears from her cheeks. She shook her head wretchedly. "Maybe. I don't know. He tried. But you know what? I don't care if he did. He was a terrible father. A ne'er-do-well, a lazy bum—"

"Carson, stop it," Dora snapped. "Daddy wasn't all that."

"How would you know?" Carson fired back. "You never saw him except when he flew back home to walk you down the aisle." She leaned forward, skewering Dora with a direct gaze. "Don't you remember how you said you didn't want him to walk you down the aisle because you were afraid that he'd be so drunk he wouldn't make it without falling on his ass? He knew that, you know. And it hurt him."

Dora blanched, remembering.

Mamaw felt like she was shriveling inside. She couldn't catch her breath.

Harper spoke up. "The only time I ever saw him was at Dora's wedding. I was only fourteen. I was so nervous and happy at the same time at the prospect of seeing him. But when he arrived at the church, even I could tell he was drunk. Just like my mother told me he'd be. I remember Granddaddy was so angry at him. Later, at the reception, I had to meet him. I mean, he was my father. So I stalked him. I found him leaning against the wall in the back hall. He spotted me and came up to me, smiling. My stomach was in knots and I had this dream that he'd hug me and tell me how much he loved me. When he got close he just stood there and stared at me, weaving a little on his feet while I smiled so hard my cheeks hurt. He just sneered at me and said, 'You look just like your mother.'"

Harper paused, her face pained at the memory. "I'll never forget it, the venom behind the words. He made it sound like it was the worst thing he could've said. Like it was a curse and he despised the sight of me. He just walked off. I never saw him again." She wiped the tears from her face with trembling fingertips. "Not quite the sentiment a young girl dreams of hearing from her father."

As the young women argued and rehashed painful memories, Mamaw put her hand to her chest. She felt the weight of years pressing. It hurt her to hear her granddaughters spell out Parker's faults so bluntly and with such rancor. She stared at the guttering candles while steadying her breath. Wax melted down the stooping tapers onto the crystal and linen. She didn't know if she could clean up this mess. Mamaw gripped the arms of her chair and rose unsteadily to her feet.

"I need some air," she said weakly.

Immediately all discussion ceased and Carson and Dora were on their feet, holding on to her arms. Mamaw couldn't look at them; she was too upset. "I have to get out of this dress."

CHAPTER TEN

Mamaw sat nestled in the thick cushions of the black wicker chair on the porch. Looking up, she felt comforted at the sight of the classic South Carolina crescent moon with a vividly bright Venus hovering near. Around them, more stars sparkled like fireflies, creating a moody nightglow. Lucille had helped her change out of the ridiculously constricting dress. She was shocked to find pink marks on her body from the stays that would surely bruise.

Now she was free to breathe in her flowing robe. She should have known better than to try to squeeze into a dress she'd worn back when she had a waistline. Her vanity had always been a burden. She stared out at the blackness and pondered how the dinner conversation had taken such an ugly turn. Emotions had flared much more strongly than she'd anticipated. A wildfire burning out of control . . . .

The sound of creaking wood alerted her to someone's

coming. She looked over her shoulder and saw a woman's silhouette approaching carrying a bottle and two glasses.

"Do you want more wine?" Carson asked her as she drew near.

"Heavens no, child," Mamaw replied, still feeling light-headed. "I can't drink another drop. The days of late-night carousing are long over for me. I have to worry about staying hydrated."

Carson set the two glasses and bottle on the table, took the chair beside Mamaw, and reached out for her hand.

"Mamaw, I'm so sorry for my outburst earlier. It was wrong and rude and I was raised better."

"Don't apologize to me. It's I who should apologize to you. I should have been more aware, more attentive. When I think of what you went through the night your father died . . ."

Carson closed her eyes tight. "You did your best."

"I daresay we all did," Mamaw said.

Carson's face revealed gratitude for her understanding.

"But so much anger! I didn't know you carried such a burden."

"It all just burst out," Carson said. "I didn't mean for that to happen. I didn't mean to ruin your party."

Mamaw waved that comment away. "Party . . . We're family. Don't trouble yourself about that."

"But I do. I couldn't stop. I don't know whether it was just because I'm in such a sorry place now or because I wanted my sisters to know the truth about what it was like out in California with him. To hear Dora say she thought we lived the life of the rich and famous. I had to rip away that veil and show them the true sad spectacle."

"I wish you'd have told me sooner how bad your living situation had become. I would have brought you home. Here."

"It's too late to change things now," Carson said in a fatalistic tone. "My life isn't here anymore, Mamaw. California is my home."

"Is it?" Mamaw asked.

"It's where my work is."

"Is it?" Mamaw asked again.

Carson just shook her head. "I loved him," she said in a hushed whisper. "I really loved him, despite everything."

Mamaw's heart was fit to break. "I know," she said, her voice trembling. "I did, too."

The screen door slammed and two more women joined them on the porch. Mamaw leaned back in her chair to collect herself while Carson quickly wiped her cheeks, then reached to the table to pour herself a glass of wine, right to the brim.

Harper handed Mamaw a glass.

"No more wine for me," Mamaw exclaimed.

"Me neither," Harper said. "This is water."

"Bless you," Mamaw said, and took a thirsty sip. She waited while Dora and Harper grabbed two of the over-sized black wicker chairs and dragged them closer to form a circle. Mamaw smiled, amused to see the girls in their nightwear but still wearing their pearl necklaces. Even their pajamas were different, reflecting their personalities. Harper looked sleek and elegant in her gray silk sheath and three-strand choker. Dora's opera-length pearls draped over her long, mauve granny gown. Mamaw couldn't be sure in the dim light, but it looked like Carson's black pearls hung above yoga pants and a camisole.

Dora bent to light the large candle in the middle of the table. "We look like a coven," she said.

"The three witches," Harper added wryly.

Mamaw was relieved to see them all trying to lighten the mood after the earlier explosions, but a thinly veiled tension still hovered in the air.

"Mamaw," said Carson gently, reaching out from the chair beside her to touch her hand. "How are you feeling? Do you want to go to bed?"

"No," she replied, realizing that this second gathering was, for her, a second chance. "I'm a little tired but I'm old; that's to be expected. There's been too much excitement today. And perhaps too much to drink."

"Do you want more water?" asked Dora, shifting to rise.

"No, no, stay. I don't need a thing. Really, my dears, I'm fine now that I'm free from that dress. But you must all remember to drink plenty of water while you're here. Stay hydrated. Or you'll get the worst lines on your face."

The girls started laughing, and though it was at her expense, this time Mamaw didn't mind. "Don't laugh!" she admonished them. "Someday you'll look in the mirror and see all those lines and crevices and wish you'd listened to dear Granny's advice."

"We're listening!" Carson said, still chuckling.

Mamaw leaned forward and said in a forced whisper, "If any of you can get out of Lucille her secret recipe for keeping her face so smooth, I'll reward you handsomely!"

"You're on," Carson replied.

"I don't know," Dora said dubiously. "She's pretty tight with her recipes. I've been trying to get her gumbo recipe for years."

"The old crone," Mamaw said, settling back in her cushion.

The women all chuckled softly; then Harper continued in a more reflective tone, "Mamaw, I don't mean to pry into your business, but we were talking in the kitchen—and we wondered, are you financially okay? Do you need our help?"

"Oh, dear girls, aren't you as sweet as sugar? Of all the things you have to worry about, to worry about me? That's very touching but unnecessary. My greatest glory is that I won't be a burden to you. I don't have a mind for figures, but I do have good advisers who have helped me with estate planning. And of course Edward was very conscientious when it came to banking. I've settled my affairs so that I can move into a retirement community, and once I'm in"—she laughed—"I won't leave again till the Lord calls me home."

"And that won't be for a very long time, we pray," Dora said.

"Do keep praying," Mamaw said. "I didn't mean to worry you. I'm only explaining, not very well, I fear, why I'm selling Sea Breeze." She paused. Now she was moving on to the things she'd intended to discuss.

"I wish I could leave it to you, but . . ." Mamaw looked from one granddaughter to the next. "Naturally, if any of you have any desire to purchase Sea Breeze, I will do everything I can to make that possible." She paused but there were no comments forthcoming, nor had she expected any. None of the girls was in a financial position to buy any house, much less one that cost the staggering amount Sea Breeze was worth.

"After you, I'll contact the extended family members. With the increased taxes, the skyrocketing insurance premiums . . ." She sighed. "I don't know if anyone can buy it or even wants to. I would, of course, like to keep the house in the family. But if there's no interest, I'll be forced to contact a real estate agent and let the house fall into strangers' hands." She sighed and clasped her hands in her lap. "It can't be helped."

"When?" asked Carson, stricken.

"Sometime in the fall, I imagine."

When no one spoke, Mamaw continued. "Which brings me to the next topic. Since the house will be sold, I will need to deaccess some of the more important family pieces. Here's what I propose." She looked around to discover that all the girls' eyes were shining with interest.

"I would like each of you to list the item that you most want to have. The one item you are desperate for, more than any of the others. I want to be sure you each take something from the house that you love."

"There are so many pretty pieces," Dora said eagerly. "I wouldn't know where to begin."

"You've already begun!" Carson teased. "I've caught you snooping around the house, checking out the goods already."

Dora's cheeks colored. "I was not! I haven't, Mamaw!" she sputtered.

"Oh, come now, Dora," Harper teased. "Even I've seen you lift the porcelains to check the provenance."

"There's nothing wrong with education," Dora blustered. "What about you?"

"Please . . ." Harper said with an air of condescension.

"Don't go all English royal on me. You're always on that computer. Are you Googling Early American furniture, hmmm?"

Harper barked out a laugh. "Hardly. But come to think of it . . ." she said, and her eyes sparkled with mirth. She turned to Carson and wagged her finger. "I saw you checking out the prices of vintage Cadillacs!"

Carson's mouth dropped open. "That's because I'm hoping to buy the car from Mamaw. It's a business transaction. I have to know its current value."

"Uh-huh." Harper rolled her eyes. "I'm sure."

"And your eyes didn't practically fall out of their sockets when you saw Mamaw's diamond earrings?" Dora asked.

Harper had the grace to laugh. "Score. They *are* amazing. I do so love nature's vintage carbon products." She turned shrewd eyes toward Mamaw. "That ring you wore tonight caught my fancy. Is that open for the grab?"

"No!" Dora sat straight and almost shouted the word. "That's a family ring! It's always given to the Muir sons to give to their wives. By that virtue, the ring will go to Nate. He is the only male heir."

"So far," Carson countered. "What makes you think we're not going to have sons?"

"Well," Dora said primly, "you *are* thirty-four and you don't even have a boyfriend."

"My eggs are fine, thank you very much," Carson said dangerously.

Harper said smugly, "Well, cool your jets, sisters. I'm only twenty-eight and I've got plenty of boyfriends. I'm putting that ring as my number one."

"You can't!" Dora fumed. "It was given to my mother, and she had the decency to return it to Mamaw after the divorce. It's only right that the ring go to my son."

"Dora," Mamaw said in a tone that immediately silenced her. "Your mother received a hefty settlement after the divorce on the condition that she return the ring. So I'll hear no more about her noble intentions. As for the other wives . . ." She shifted in her seat like she was sitting on a burr. "I mean no disrespect to the dead"—she looked at Carson—"but neither of the other two women deserved the ring and I told Parker that. The ring is mine. And I happen to like it. Whichever decision I make, it will be mine and mine alone. Is that understood?"

There were hesitant nods all around.

Mamaw continued in a firm tone, "My dears, you needn't worry about me. I've always managed to take care of myself. Each of you will likewise have to make your own way in this world. I can, however, offer you this advice: Friends come and go. But through the thick and thin, the good and bad, you can only ever count on your family." Mamaw took a breath, feeling more in control again. "That's the heart of it. *Family*." She searched their faces, pleased to see she had their full attention. "Which leads me to my next point."

"There's more?" Harper muttered under her breath.

"Yes, Harper dear," Mamaw said pointedly, "there's one bit more. I've given this a great deal of thought, so I hope you don't think what I'm about to say is the ram-

bling of an eccentric old woman. It worries me—deeply—
that we, the last of the Muirs, are not as close as we once
were, at least not as close as we were during our summers
here at Sea Breeze. We've become strangers. I've thought
about what I could do to rekindle that spark of family in
us before Sea Breeze is sold and we all go off to the four
points of the earth."

"It was never Sea Breeze that brought me to Sullivan's Island," Harper said. "Frankly, I'm not a big fan of
Sea Breeze. It's perfectly nice, don't get me wrong, but
it's always been you, Mamaw, that I came to see. And my
sisters." She smiled shyly.

Mamaw sat back in her chair, momentarily thrown by
this comment. She glanced at Dora and Carson and saw
that their expressions reflected agreement.

"I'm so very glad to hear that," she said slowly. "But I
fear, more deeply than ever, that once I'm gone, the connection of Muir family blood will truly dissipate."

"I don't want to think of you dying," Carson said.

"I can't live forever," Mamaw said with a gentle laugh.
"No one can. But once I'm gone, what will become of my
family? That is the worry that keeps me up at night. So!"
she said, slapping her thighs with her palms. "I've a plan.
I'm asking each of you to spend the entire summer at Sea
Breeze. Our last summer. What do you say?"

Carson leaned back in her chair and shrugged. "You
know what I say."

Dora inched forward on her seat. "I always come
for two weeks in July. I suppose I can try and extend it
another week or two, if you wish."

"I'm sorry, Mamaw. I can't possibly stay here for a

whole month, much less a summer," Harper said incredulously. "I don't even get a month's vacation! I'm sorry, Mamaw. I appreciate the invitation, I truly do. But this weekend is all I can swing. Believe me, it was tough enough. But we have this weekend, don't we?" she added, trying to spin a positive note.

Mamaw slowly leaned back in her chair and clasped her hands together. "I don't think I made myself clear," she said. "I'd hoped you'd all be delighted to accept my invitation to spend the summer. But, as it appears that is not happening, I must tell you that I'm not merely inviting you. The invitation that you stay at Sea Breeze for the summer is, well"—she tapped her fingertips against each other—"more a stipulation." She stilled her hands.

"Of what?" Dora asked.

Mamaw took a breath. "Stay for the summer, or you are out of the will."

"What!" Harper exploded, leaping to her feet.

"That's blackmail!" said Dora, puffed up and sitting at the edge of her chair. "You're saying that each of us needs to spend the entire summer here or you're essentially writing us off?"

Mamaw lifted her gaze and a coy smile played at her lips, one that her pirate ancestor would have been proud of. "I prefer to think of it as adding sugar to the pot," she replied. "Truly. Just think! A vacation together. A time to reconnect. Think of it as a gift."

Mamaw waited in the tense silence as the girls digested this ultimatum.

Dora sat back in her chair, apparently resigned. "All right, Mamaw. If it means that much to you I'll manage it somehow. And I *will* have all those workmen in the house," she added with dejection. "Besides, there's no one waiting for me at home anymore. I'll have to go back and forth from Summerville a few times, but I suppose if I juggle things . . ." Her voice trailed off in thought.

"Thank you, dear. I'd hoped you could," said Mamaw.

"I'd have to keep Nate," Dora added.

"Of course."

"I'm in," Carson said, grinning, tucking her legs up.

Mamaw looked at Harper, who was pacing the patio. Harper turned and returned to the group, standing opposite Mamaw. Her face was slightly flushed. "This is ridiculous," Harper said in a matter-of-fact tone.

Dora, who was sitting next to her, swung her head to look at Harper.

"It's not blackmail, Dora. It's bribery," Harper continued. "I see the pirate blood still runs strong in the Muir family."

"Death to the ladies!" Carson shouted, raising her fist.

She was trying to lighten the mood but her effort fell cold. Harper was having none of it. She stood straighter, her jaw clenching. She wasn't aware how very much she looked like her mother at that moment.

"You know, Mamaw," she said in disbelief, "it's laughable that you'd expect that we could drop everything and come running back here for vacation, like we were little girls again. We're not! We're grown women. With jobs. Or at least I have a job. Even if we could stay a month. But, two months, three!"

"This is not merely a vacation," Mamaw implored. "This is our final opportunity to be together."

"What do you think is going to happen?" Harper asked. "That suddenly we're all going to be close again? *Sisters*? It's too late for that. You should've thought of this long ago."

"Actually, she did," Carson interjected. She offered her sisters a sober glance. "She invited us every summer."

"Well, I'm sorry," Harper replied. "I couldn't make it. And I can't make it this summer." She reached up and fumbled at the clasp of her pearls.

Carson leaned forward and stretched her arm out to touch Harper's leg. "Harpo," she said, using the old nickname. "What are you doing?"

Harper didn't reply. When the pearl necklace slid into her palms she walked over to Mamaw and stuck out her hand. "Please take it. I don't want it."

Mamaw put out her hand to catch the pearls as they slid out from Harper's palm.

"Good night." Harper turned on her heel and marched off.

"Harper!" Carson called after her.

"Let her go," said Dora darkly.

Mamaw forced herself to keep her silence, closing her fingers around the pearls. She brought her fist close to her beating heart.

"I'd better go check on her," said Carson. She sprang to her feet and trotted across the porch and into the house.

"Well!" Dora said in a huff. "I never heard anything like that in all my life. Talking that way to you. Throwing back the pearls. She might have royal lineage, but no lady would ever talk to her grandmother like that. Let her go back to New York."

Mamaw wasn't listening. She stared into the dark night, lost in her own thoughts. The night hadn't gone at all the way she'd hoped. The house was in an uproar and her girls were more alienated from one another than ever.

"Mamaw?" Dora said, nudging her.

Mamaw shook herself to the present. Dora had moved beside her and was looking at her with worry.

"Go see if Lucille is awake, would you, sugar? That's a good girl. If she's asleep, let her be. And help me up. I'm so tired. I'm going to my room." Mamaw fanned the air. "My heart's beating like a rabbit's. I'm worn out."

"Mummy? It's me." Harper sat on her bed in the room she shared with Dora. The pillow was flat, the mattress hard, and the old pink and blue patchwork quilt frayed. It was a far cry from the chic decorator rooms in her mother's house in the Hamptons. Suddenly, she felt so alone. She longed to be on the eastern shore, far from the South, far from everyone here who could pierce the shell she'd constructed around herself. Harper looked at the screen of her laptop, comforting with its steady connection to a vast, impersonal world.

"I saw that you'd called."

"Yes," Georgiana confirmed from New York. "I called twice, actually. The most terrible thing has happened."

Harper's body tensed. "What?"

"Mummy fell and broke her hip."

Harper's eyes flashed open and she rolled to her side. "Oh, no. I'm so sorry. When?"

"Yesterday. She's at hospital now and terribly put out."

"Poor Granny. How did it happen?"

"She was preparing to leave for the Hamptons and fell down the stairs. I suppose we're fortunate it wasn't worse."

"I guess that means she won't make it to the Hamptons."

"Of course she won't make it."

Harper flushed, squeezing her eyes shut. "Of course not. Silly of me. I just meant . . ." She didn't know what she'd meant. It was just one of those inane comments people sometimes made at tense moments. Her mother didn't tolerate fools or the foolish.

"She'll need someone to stay with her when she returns home from hospital," Georgiana went on. "So, darling, I'd like you to go to England as soon as you can."

"England?" Harper exclaimed, shocked at the suggestion.

"Yes," her mother said impatiently. "Mummy will need someone to stay with her. Family."

"Shouldn't you go? She'd much prefer you to me."

"I would, of course. But I have to go to the Hamptons regardless. I've accepted so many engagements that I simply can't cancel."

"But my work . . ."

Her mother's tone grew increasingly frustrated. Harper could picture her at her desk, despite the late hour, her hair pulled back and her bifocal glasses sliding down her nose. She was in a hurry and wanted this settled and off her desk promptly, without argument.

"You work for me. Your job is to do what I tell you to do. And I wish for you to go to England."

Harper let her hand drop from her ear. *Your job is to do what I tell you to do.* Despite all her imaginings, she had to face the reality that this was, indeed, her job description.

"What about all the projects I'm working on?" she asked. She was very excited about the editorial work she had outlined for the summer.

"I'll give them to Nina."

"Nina?" Harper felt immediately defensive. "She doesn't do editorial."

"She's ready for a promotion and I think she'll do well. I've had my eye on her for a while now. This would be a good opportunity for her."

Nina was a bright and attractive woman about the same age as Harper. She made no secret of the fact that she was hungry to be an editor and took any morsel tossed her way. Harper was already envious of the number of editing jobs Georgiana had given to Nina lately, despite Harper's begging for more. Harper was tired of being relegated to duties more fitting for her mother's personal assistant—doing errands, making appointments, drafting letters.

"Why don't you send Nina to be Grandmother's nurse?"

"Don't be smart," her mother scolded. "I can see that even a few days in that company has made you snippy. I hate the effect they have on you down there. You always used to come home from Sullivan's Island all full of yourself and silly. It would take me weeks to get you back to normal again."

"That's not true," Harper protested, but in her heart, she did remember feeling bold after her stays with

Mamaw. Her heart was full of running wild across the island playing pirate, making up stories, seeking out wildlife and, of course, the sea. Summers where skinned knees went unnoticed, schedules were abandoned, and they could talk at night till they fell asleep.

"I think a good stay in England with your grandmother James will do you a world of good," Georgiana added.

"I'm not a child, Mother," Harper said testily. "I don't need to be taught my manners."

"That's debatable," Georgiana replied. "But I don't have the time for that now. I want you to book your flight direct from Charleston. Use my travel agent. Don't worry about clothes. You can pick up what you need in London. Mummy is due home day after tomorrow."

Harper swallowed again, then said, "No."

There was a pause. "I beg your pardon?"

Harper felt her body go cold. She took a breath, then repeated, "No. I'm not going to England. I think you should go. She's your mother."

There was another, longer pause. "Harper, I want you on a plane for London tomorrow, is that clear?"

"No." She felt like the mutinous child again, crossing her arms and pouting. Only she wasn't a child and the stakes were so much higher.

"You're being ridiculous. I won't stand for it. I'm your boss and I'm giving you an order."

The words floated in space between them, igniting unanswered questions. Harper took a moment to swallow them, digest them, and let them settle. She reached out to lower the computer screen. When she spoke, her voice was surprisingly calm.

"Maybe you shouldn't be my boss. Maybe you should just be my mother."

There was another long silence.

"You can give my job to Nina," Harper said. "She'll be good at it."

"You're resigning?"

"As your assistant, yes." Harper laughed lightly. "Not as your daughter."

"I don't find that the least amusing."

Harper would've been more surprised if her mother had seen the sad humor in this situation.

"Don't think you can come back to my apartment and lollygag," Georgiana said in a flare of temper.

"Well, then I can just stay in the Hamptons."

"No, you can't. It's booked for most of the summer."

"I see," Harper replied.

And she did. Clearly. At long last.

Carson had no idea what time it was. It was late, that was all she knew. She could tell by the high position of the crescent moon in the sky. She was sitting at the edge of the dock with her legs dangling in the water.

"Well played, Mamaw," she muttered. Inside the house, Harper was cussing like a sailor, throwing her clothing in her fancy suitcase, declaring she was never stepping foot back into this Faulkner novel. She didn't know where Dora had gone, and Mamaw was hiding out in her room. She raised the bottle of vodka she'd swiped from Mamaw's bar up toward the moon. "Death to . . . No." She shook her head, thinking again. "To hell with the ladies!" She weaved, almost tipping over into the water.

From somewhere in the dark water she heard the loud, percussive exhale of a dolphin. The sound was close. She instantly smiled and lifted her head from her arms to gaze out into the water. Delphine's large head came up out of the water, silvery in the moonlight.

Carson slowly reached out to let her hand lie palm up in supplication mere inches in front of Delphine. Delphine gracefully nudged Carson's palm as she swam past. One small touch, but it was a profound moment of connection and Carson knew they both felt it.

From behind her, Carson heard footfalls coming up the dock. Delphine disappeared under the water, leaving only a rippled pattern on the surface.

"Talking to your dolphin again?" Harper called from the upper dock. She stepped down to the floating dock and stood beside Carson. Then, bending down to peer into her sister's face, she asked more tenderly, "Are you crying?"

"No," Carson blurted. She wished Harper would just go away and leave her to her misery.

Harper moved to sit beside Carson on the dock, slipping her legs into the water. She kicked them lazily for a while. "And you're drinking," she observed gently, sensing Carson's distress.

"What if I am?"

"Nothing. I'm just thinking we all said some pretty emotional things tonight, and I find you out here on your lonesome with a bottle of vodka, and I'm wondering what demon you're wrestling."

"What do you care? You're leaving." Carson lifted the bottle and tipped the fluid down her throat in an *in your face* gesture. "Everyone leaves."

Harper didn't respond. She reached out to let her fingers splash the water. The floating dock creaked as wood hit wood and seawater splashed up alongside the pier.

"Do you have the family illness?" Harper asked.

Carson felt her body tense. "Illness? What illness are you talking about?"

Harper smiled ruefully. "The miracle of genetics. We all carry the gene for alcoholism. It's a loaded gun in Russian roulette. One gets it and another doesn't. Do you have it?"

"Nah," Carson replied with a wave, dismissing the possibility. "Do *you*?" she asked, her question coming more from anger than real curiosity.

"I don't think so," Harper answered in an honest tone.

Her willingness to discuss it openly, without judgment, changed Carson's attitude. "Me neither," she answered with a one-shouldered shrug. "I like to have a drink now and then. Who doesn't? It's purely social."

Harper moved her hand, indicating the vodka bottle. "Since when is drinking alone in the dark social?"

Carson pinched her lips. "Tonight's different," she replied sullenly. "A lot of bad memories were dredged up tonight."

"Yeah," Harper agreed with emphasis.

Carson looked down at the bottle, as though she could see her fortune in it. "I'm sorry I brought up all that garbage about Dad," Carson said. "Being with you again, here at Sea Breeze, all that"—she made a futile gesture—"*whatever* is bubbling back up. I couldn't stop myself. I'm sorry," she said again.

"Don't be. It wasn't fair that you had to carry the burden of Daddy's crazy life all alone," Harper told her. The dock rocked and creaked beneath them. "I only wish I'd known."

Carson shook her head remembering her father's pride in his family heritage. Despite his financial woes, he'd carried his birthright like a badge of honor. "Dad wouldn't have wanted to be shamed in front of your mother."

"Why? Do you think your daddy's better than my daddy?" Harper quipped.

Carson released a short laugh, appreciating again Harper's wit.

"Why are you always protecting him?" Harper asked, prodding.

"Habit."

Harper looked at her as though for the first time. "I can understand that."

"I took care of him. It's not something I did consciously. I was a kid. It was survival. And he had a good side, too. It's like Mamaw said: he could be so charming, so funny, even thoughtful. I loved him, you know. So much. Even when I left, it was more an act of survival than anger. He was a sick puppy. You can't hate a puppy; you hate the illness."

"So what about you?" Harper asked again, smoothing back the dark hair from Carson's tear-dampened cheeks. "Do you have the illness?"

Carson heard the question this time and rather than dismissing it angrily, she dared herself to consider it. She looked at the murky water, feeling her old fears sucking her into a horrifying vortex.

"I don't know," Carson said in a voice so low Harper had to lean closer to hear her. "Maybe it's possible that . . ." But she couldn't finish the thought.

Harper went on all fours and crawled around Carson to grab the bottle of vodka. She unscrewed the top and began pouring it into the water.

"Mamaw's going to be put out," Carson warned her.

Harper shook out the last drops and screwed the top back on. "So what's it going to take for you to stop?" she asked Carson.

"Who said I'm going to stop? You stop."

"All right. I will. Starting right now." Harper delivered a challenging stare to Carson.

Carson stuck out her jaw belligerently. "Good for you."

"Just try for a week," Harper urged her. "I do that every once in a while just to be sure I can. Like I said, it's in our genetics. If you can't quit for a week, then you have to admit you have a problem."

"You forget, I work at a pub."

"Quit!"

"I need the money."

"Oh, please," Harper interjected. "How much money can you be earning as a lunchtime waitress? You don't need that job."

Carson wiped her face with her hands, feeling the waves of sobriety wash over her. "First of all, I don't have a trust fund waiting in the wings, like you do. When I say

I'm broke, I'm really broke. Second," she said with hesitation, "I haven't been entirely honest with you."

"I don't know if I can take any more secrets," Harper groaned.

"When I told you that I was taking time off of work to spend time with Mamaw . . ." Carson took a breath and realized it was time to stop looking for exits and to just tell the truth. "The truth is I don't have a job. My television show was canceled. Before that, I was laid off from a gig because of my drinking. It was the only time," she hurried to add, "but I'm worried that word got out and I'm blackballed or something, because I haven't been able to land another job." She looked away, remembering the parties she and the rest of the crew had after shooting that got out of hand. "So I'm staying here because I don't have anywhere else to go. Pretty pitiful at my age, huh?"

Harper shifted her weight to sit up and tuck her legs in. "In keeping with the spirit of transparency," she began, nodding toward Carson in acknowledgment, "I have to admit I've not been completely honest myself."

Carson was grateful to her sister for not making her the only one to expose her underbelly tonight. "Do tell, sister mine," said Carson. "Is the royal James family in fact"—she made a face—"penniless? Are you not princes at all, but paupers?"

Harper chuckled and shook her head. "No. I'm afraid not. No worries in that corner. It's my mother . . ." She lifted the empty bottle of vodka and shook it, making a dismayed face because it was empty. "Now I'm sorry I poured it all out."

"What about your mother?"

"Did you ever see the movie *The Devil Wears Prada*?" Carson nodded.

"Remember the editor? The one played by Meryl Streep? That would be my mother."

"So does that make you the secretary girl?"

"Not anymore. I quit my job."

This was met by shocked silence. "Wait, wait, wait, I don't understand," Carson said at length. "You told Mamaw you were going home."

"Yeah, well, that was before I quit. I'm staying here, if she'll let me. I have to apologize first," Harper said, ducking her head. "Big-time."

"What about her ultimatum?"

"You mean her bribery?" Harper said with a short laugh.

"That whole thing about the will," Carson interjected, feeling the need to defend Mamaw. "It wasn't bribery as much as desperation. She was only trying to get us all to stay. She's old. She's not got that much time left. And we're all she's leaving behind."

"I thought about that tonight," Harper said in a darker tone. "I may have learned the difference between an ultimatum based on love and one based on selfishness." She plucked at her shirt. "Damn my mother," she said, her heat gaining fuel. "She treats me more like a lackey than a daughter. A lackey with no talent. She doesn't have any faith in me. Sometimes, when she looks at me and she gets this look of distaste in her eyes, I know she sees my . . . our father." Harper laughed bitterly. "And we all know what she thought about him."

Carson said nothing.

"I can't work for her anymore," Harper declared, her eyes flashing. Then, as though the ramifications of that statement had just hit her, her shoulders slumped and her face fell. "The problem is, I don't know what I want to do instead. I've always been the good little girl who did what she was told." She tossed a pebble into the water.

"But not anymore," Carson said in an effort to bolster her sister.

Harper lifted the corner of her mouth. "Not anymore. I'm done being her servant." She looked up and held Carson's gaze, as though daring her to believe her. Carson had no reason not to believe her and pulsed a message of support.

"So here I am," Harper said. "I guess I'm not much different from you, Carson. I've nowhere else to go."

Carson felt a rush of sympathy for her sister. She looked out over the black water. At the tip of the pier, a soft green light pierced the blackness. It blinked on and off, on and off, with a reassuring consistency.

When Carson turned back, weaving slightly, she wore a wry grin. "In a crazy way, I'm glad," Carson told Harper. "It's nice not to be all alone in the lifeboat."

CHAPTER ELEVEN

Dora was sitting in the living room enjoying a peaceful afternoon of reading when she caught sight of Harper walking down the hall to Mamaw's room. Dora was surprised to see her dressed in white shorts and a T-shirt rather than the usual black garb New Yorkers always wore. She glanced up at the grandfather clock and saw that it was already past three o'clock. Wasn't Harper supposed to be on a plane for New York?

Dora marked her place in the book and set it on the sofa. Rising, she quietly made her way to Mamaw's room, pausing at the door. She heard voices and strained to listen. She couldn't quite make out what they were saying, but it sounded like Harper might have been crying. Curious, Dora took a measured step into the room, cringing as the floorboards creaked beneath her foot. Easing forward, she peeked around the door. She saw Mamaw sitting in her easy chair, framed by her beautiful windows. Pink roses in a crystal vase sat on the table beside her. At her feet sat Harper, her head in Mamaw's lap, while Mamaw lovingly stroked Harper's hair.

Carson was late for her meeting with Blake.

She refused to call it a date. It was a windy day in the lowcountry. Bad for surfing, but good for kiteboarding. The fluctuation in wind made Charleston a go-to location for water sports. On any day one could ride the waves.

She followed the winding beach path bordered by an impenetrable barrier of groundsel shrubs. This barrier was home to countless animals and birds and a major source of food and shelter for the migrating monarch butterflies. A small green lizard scampered across the path and a young couple passed her going in the opposite direction. They nodded their heads and smiled in neighborly acknowledgment. Station 28 was on the northern end of the island near Breach Inlet, where swimming was forbidden due to hazardous currents. Though it wasn't officially zoned for kiteboarding, the locals quietly understood that this area was designated for the wild aerobatics of the fast-moving kiteboarders.

The shaded path opened up to a wide spread of sunny beach. Beyond, the Atlantic Ocean caressed the shoreline in foam-tipped waves. Carson stepped into the sun and stopped, taking it all in and grinning from ear to ear. She'd not been to the beach since the shark incident. She'd missed the punch she felt every time she saw the infinite vista of sky and water. She'd missed the feel of sand between her toes.

But on this beach, the sky exploded with colorful kites! Eight years back there had only been three or four kiteboarders skimming over the water. Today she counted at least thirty kites. She laughed, thinking it looked as though an entire flock of enormous, brightly plumed birds were catching thermals over the ocean.

A happy sight, and it filled her with excitement that she was going to learn the sport. Carson felt like skipping across the beach, she was so thrilled. But she strolled at a leisurely pace to stand with the other rubberneckers along the shore watching the practitioners of the popular new sport. Some of the kiteboarders were far out, hydroplaning across the water, catching air and doing breathtaking turns and lifts of their boards. Some were struggling closer to shore, just learning how to maneuver the kites and getting in the way. And still more were on the beach, pumping air into their kites and laying out long tether lines, or waiting in a queue to go out.

Carson loved surfing—was good at it. But she'd long been curious about trying her hand at this new sport that would allow her to surf the air rather than the waves. She preferred solo water sports. Out on the water you needed a buddy, but the rider caught the wave or the wind on her own. Every day was a fresh attempt at soaring. She smiled to herself, wondering if she shouldn't start applying that approach to all aspects of her life.

Holding her hand over her eyes like a visor, she scanned the beach for Blake. She noticed a man covered in tattoos glancing at her repeatedly, usually the warning sign that a pickup line was coming. She picked up her bag and began walking in the opposite direction. Across the beach she heard calls—"Launch!" "Good wind!" "What size kite is that?"

A tall, slender man caught her eye. He was holding on to the bars of his kite while at the other end of the long tether lines another man was assisting, lifting the arcing blue kite into the air. The man in the harness had a swimmer's body, broad at the shoulders and slim at the hips. Sinewy muscles strained as the kite caught the wind. A beautiful body, she thought with her photographer's eye, symmetrical and tanned. Something about the way his dark curls fell over his forehead made her look closer, squinting in the sunlight.

At that moment the man turned his head her way and their gazes met and held. Her toes curled in the sand. *Blake*. She felt a rush of embarrassment course through her veins at being caught staring. His lips turned into a confident smile, full of a rogue's tease, and he lifted his hand in a brief wave before the kite surged in the wind and his attention was riveted back on it. She watched as Blake deftly maneuvered the broncolike kite in the air, steering it as he advanced toward the water, carrying his board under his arm. At the shoreline he dropped the board and mounted it. Then he released the kite to the wind and was off, slicing through the ocean with a ruffled wake.

He was good. Or he was showing off for her, she thought with a smile. Blake took air time frequently, soaring high and doing aerial stunts that had many on the beach pointing to him. Carson looked from left to right, smiling smugly because she knew him, even in such a distant way. She spread her towel out on the sand, claiming a spot. It was a beautiful afternoon with a fine breeze. She enjoyed watching the people and, farther off, closer to the inlet, a flock of peeps running along the shore, hunting for food in their straight-legged fashion.

At last she spotted Blake returning to the coast in a diagonal line, his muscles straining as he dragged the kite in from the water. She felt her stomach flutter as she rose to shake the sand from her towel. She was actually looking forward to talking with him again. Her interest was piqued, now that she'd seen his skill on the water. Athleticism had always been a major turn-on for her. Carson tossed the towel into her bag with the water bottle, her book, and her lotion, then hastily slipped a T-shirt on over her bikini. She began walking to where Blake was rolling up his kite, though not so fast as to appear anxious. Halfway there she stopped abruptly when she saw a young, curvy blonde prance to his side and begin talking in that flirtatious way young women do, twisting on her heel and playing with her hair. The three tiny rainbow triangles that made up her bikini exposed her taut, tanned body. Blake, as any other male would have, was enjoying the flirtation. Carson's lips tightened in annoyance when the girl slipped an arm over his shoulder and leaned into him, laughing.

Without a second thought, Carson turned on her heel and detoured to the beach path. She was like a horse with blinders and couldn't get out of the area fast enough. They were supposed to meet today, and though she might have been late, she'd waited patiently while he kiteboarded. As she walked away, she grimaced. To think she'd almost embarrassed herself by going to talk to him. She made it back to the Beast, her name for the car, unlocked the door, and tossed her bag on the passenger side. It was as hot as an oven inside the car and as filled with sand as the beach. Empty water bottles littered the floor, and CDs, crumpled paper, gum wrappers, and hats covered the seats. She rolled down the windows and got behind the wheel. Her thighs stuck to the burning leather.

The engine strained and churned, but it didn't fire. "Come on, Beast," she muttered, and tried twice more. Each time the engine sounded weaker and weaker, like a beast giving up the ghost. Carson hit the wheel with the palm of her hand, then rested her head against it. At that moment, she didn't know which was the bigger loser—the car or herself.

Carson felt sweaty and covered with sand when she finally returned to Sea Breeze. She quickly showered and changed into yoga pants and a clean cotton T-shirt. The bad taste of her ruined meeting with Blake and the final insult of the death of her car made her thirsty. She opened the fridge and stared at the opened bottle of Pinot Grigio. She yearned for it. Then, bolstering her resolve, she pulled out a pitcher of sweet tea and filled a large glass. Feeling slightly more confident after resisting the wine, she went in search of Mamaw. She found her sitting with Lucille in the shade of the back porch playing gin rummy. The fans were whirring above them, stirring up a pleasant breeze. Carson pulled up a black wicker chair to join them.

"Are you two at it again?" Carson asked.

"Every day, whether we need to or not," Lucille replied with her cackling laugh.

"That's the plan," Mamaw said, and slapped down a discard. "Gin!"

Lucille grumbled, and after carefully checking to make sure Mamaw was right, she counted up points.

Carson cleared her throat. "Mamaw, I'd like to talk to you about something," she began.

"Yes, dear?" Mamaw asked, looking her way with a smile of interest.

"Do you want me to go?" asked Lucille.

"No, please stay. Actually, I need you here, too."

Mamaw and Lucille shared a curious glance, then focused on her.

"Well, see . . ." She licked her lips and dove in. "Harper and I were talking about Dad and his drinking. And about, well, about how we might carry the gene for the disease."

"Oh," Mamaw exclaimed with combined surprise and interest. "Do you think you might?"

"I don't know," Carson replied honestly. "It frightens me that I might. I drank a little too much in L.A. and may have done a few things I'm not proud of. But I don't think I'm an alcoholic," she added quickly. "I don't need a drink to start the day or anything like that. I drink socially, with friends. And at dinner."

Mamaw sat still, attentive to every word.

"Anyway," Carson said in a deliberately easy manner, "Harper and I came up with this idea. We'd like to try and not drink for a while. At least not for a week. We want to see if we *can* stop. Kind of a bet," she added, trying to make light of it.

"Oh, precious, that's so wise," Mamaw said. "If you only knew how many times I'd begged your father to stop, just for a while. He never would. He said he didn't have a problem. That he could stop whenever he wanted to."

"He couldn't stop," Lucille said. "He just couldn't admit it."

Mamaw leaned forward, cocking her head like a curious bird. "Sweet child, what can we do to help you?"

"Ditch the booze," Carson said bluntly. Mamaw's eyes widened, more from the vulgarity of her words. Carson smiled plaintively. "If you could please take away all the alcohol, hide it, do anything you like with it so I—we—can't find it, I'd appreciate it. Just for a week, maybe more if all goes well. That goes for wine, too. If you serve wine at dinner, I'll cave. I know I will. But if I eat my meals here and I don't have alcohol around to tempt me, I'll be able to really see if I can quit." She rubbed her palms together between her knees, feeling clammy. "It's not going to be easy. Just thinking about not drinking tonight makes me want a drink."

"Consider it done!" Mamaw exclaimed.

"There won't be a drop when you get back from work tomorrow," Lucille said, her dark eyes gleaming like she was a woman on a mission. She glared at Mamaw. "Not anywhere. I'll see to that."

Mamaw narrowed her eyes, catching her meaning. Carson could see Mamaw working out in her mind if she could give up her nip of rum in the evenings.

"Who's winning?" Carson asked in an upbeat voice, changing the subject.

Mamaw fluffed herself up like a queen and, with a smug smile, began shuffling the deck of cards. "I am, of course."

"Today," Lucille grumbled.

Carson was impressed. Mamaw dealt as smoothly as any croupier.

"How's your job coming along?" Mamaw asked Carson as she dealt the cards.

"It's fine," Carson replied. "The tourists have arrived in force so my tips are good. It should be a good summer."

"That's nice," Mamaw said in a distracted manner as she picked up her cards. Her fingers moved quickly, sorting her hand.

Carson took a breath, then began to play out the game of finesse that was in her mind. "Mamaw, speaking of summer . . . Do you know what would make my summer *really* great?"

"I don't really know," Mamaw replied in a distracted manner. "Something to do with the water, I suppose?"

Carson took a breath. "No. It's kind of out there, so hear me through, okay?"

Lucille kept her eyes on her cards, but under her breath she muttered loud enough for all to hear, "Here comes the windup."

"Well . . ." Carson began, ignoring Lucille's tease. She leaned forward in the manner of a salesman. "My car, the Beast, died today. On my way home from the beach. It's been resurrected more times than I can count over the years, but this time it's a goner. I think the cross-country trip done her in. At least it died here and not somewhere in the middle of the country." Carson strove for levity.

"I hope you'll remove that piece of junk from my driveway," Mamaw said, looking over the rim of her glasses. "I don't want Sea Breeze to become one of those white-trash places overrun with cars and kudzu."

"I have someone coming by later this week to tow it away," Carson assured her. "I got a hundred dollars for the carcass."

"That's good," Mamaw said, her attention returning to the cards.

"So I was thinking . . ." Carson said, her toes curling beneath the table. "Would you consider . . . well . . . how about letting me have the Blue Bomber?"

Mamaw stopped arranging her cards and looked up, suddenly alert. "What was that?"

"I need a car, Mamaw, so I wondered, since the Cadillac is just sitting in the garage . . ."

Mamaw put down her cards and studied Carson's face, her eyes narrowing shrewdly. "You want me to give you my car?"

"Not give," Carson rushed to answer. "Unless you're inclined to let me put it on my wish list?"

"I am not."

"Oh." Carson released a disappointed puff of air.

Lucille said under her breath, "Strike one."

"You're not helping," Carson said to Lucille.

"I just calls 'em as I sees 'em," Lucille replied with a slight shrug of her shoulders, still chuckling.

Carson looked at Mamaw pleadingly. "Would you let me buy it?"

"You have the money for it?"

"Not yet," Carson replied, squirming in her seat.

"Strike two," Lucille muttered.

Carson glared at her. "I've got a job and I'm making good tips," she told Mamaw. "I'll get the money."

"When?"

"By the end of summer. Sooner, if a job from L.A. comes up."

"So you *do* expect me to give it to you?"

Carson exhaled heavily with frustration. Yes, she was hoping her grandmother would give her the car immediately and let her work out the payment later. The car was just sitting in the garage most of the time anyway. She wouldn't even miss it.

"What if I gave you a down payment now?" Carson cringed. It was embarrassing to not have any money, to have to borrow and beg at her age. "Say, a hundred dollars . . ."

"That will barely fill a tank of gas in that big ol' car," Mamaw replied. "Sugar, even if I let you buy it, you wouldn't be able to afford the gas."

"I won't need a lot of gas," Carson argued. "I only need the car to drive back and forth from Dunleavy's. And I really love that old car. You know I do."

Mamaw picked up her cards and began sorting them. She took her time, flicking the edges of her cards as she moved them. "I have a better idea," Mamaw said at length. "Since you'll be here all summer and only need transportation to and from Dunleavy's, you don't need a car, either." She discarded a two of clubs. "You can ride my bicycle. In fact, you can have it. Just think of all the money you'll save on gas. And all the exercise."

"A bike?" Carson exclaimed with disappointment.

"Strike three," Lucille said as she picked up the card and discarded a jack of diamonds.

"What if it rains?" asked Carson, growing desperate as she watched the two old women calmly playing cards. "I can't show up to work wet."

"That's true," Mamaw said thoughtfully. She picked up Lucille's card and re-sorted her hand. "I know!" she said, discarding a ten of diamonds. She looked back at Carson with eyes bright. "You can use the golf cart! It probably needs a new battery. And a good scrubbing. It's been sitting in the garage unused for years, but it should still be good."

Carson frowned and remained silent.

"Carson," Mamaw said, sitting back in her chair, looking at her now with her complete attention. "I love you more than anyone or thing in the world. You know that, don't you? As I loved your dad. But I made mistakes with him. I see that now. I made life too easy for him. I was always there to smooth his path. I should've made him ride a bike to work. Mercy, I should have made him get a job!"

"Amen," muttered Lucille.

Mamaw reached out and cupped her palm around Carson's cheek. Her eyes pulsed with devotion that couldn't be denied. "My darling girl, I won't make that same mistake with you."

"Aw, go ahead," Carson said, then lowered her eyes with a laugh of embarrassment. At the moment, she wasn't joking. She'd worry about her soul later. Right now she was broke and needed a ride.

Mamaw patted Carson's cheek in a gesture of summation, drew back, and picked up and sorted her cards with quick snapping sounds. "That golf cart has a nice roof on top. It's absolutely precious. Go on out now and give it a look-see."

Carson's sigh was mingled with a moan as she rose to go. She was arrested by Lucille's hand on her arm. Carson wanted to jerk her arm away, she was so annoyed with both of the women. She glanced down into Lucille's dark eyes, not sure if the woman was being kind or was about to deliver another zinger.

Lucille patted her arm with compassion. "I know this might seem like a strikeout now," Lucille told her. "But, darlin', you just scored a home run."

CHAPTER TWELVE

*T*he following few days there was a flurry of activity at Sea Breeze. Harper waited until her mother left for the Hamptons, then she flew to New York to pack up clothes and conclude her affairs with human resources at the publishing house. Harper didn't think she would be gone for more than two weeks, and Carson believed her. Meanwhile, Dora drove home alone to Summerville to see to the many details of preparing the house for sale and to face the odious task of meeting with lawyers for her divorce. Despite her reservations, she'd agreed to let the women at Sea Breeze care for Nate until she returned.

The house seemed quiet with her sisters gone. Carson loved them, of course, but they were as yet hardly close. She lay on the iron bed, her arms folded under her head, and her thoughts turned back to those summers the girls had shared at Sea Breeze. Back when Mamaw had called them her Summer Girls.

The many summers had been a hodgepodge of visits that continued from the time each of them was very young until they'd become teens. Initially, only she and Dora had spent summers together. Carson had lived with Mamaw in Charleston, and Dora, three years older than Carson, was invited to spend the summers with them from her home in Charlotte, North Carolina. Those early years were the best for the two eldest girls, long lazy summers of playing mermaids and painting on the veranda with Mamaw. Later, those years' difference signified a lifetime when Carson was ten and Dora was thirteen. Then, Dora found her half sister annoying; she invited friends to Sea Breeze and Carson was excluded from their games.

It was a turnaround when Harper began coming to Sea Breeze at six years of age. She was so small and delicate, dressed like one of the Madame Alexander dolls she coveted.

The girls had spent only three full summers together, during which time there was an eight-year spread between Dora and Harper. Carson had been the link between the eldest and the youngest, the go-between, the popular one, the peacemaker. After Dora turned seventeen she stopped spending her summers at Sea Breeze. Carson and Harper spent another two summers together alone, which forged their bond. Where Dora loved playing dress-up and feminine make-believe games, Carson and Harper let loose their inner Huck Finns. They'd explored every inch of Sullivan's Island and Isle of Palms, searching for the pirate treasure every child on the island knew was buried *somewhere*.

Like the Lost Boys, however, eventually they grew up.

When Carson turned seventeen she got a summer job in Los Angeles and Harper's mother purchased a house in the Hamptons. This marked the end of the Summer Girls at Sea Breeze.

A few years later, the girls came together again when Dora married Calhoun Tupper in a grand Charleston event. On the heels of the wedding came two funerals. Their father died young, at forty-seven, and soon after, their grandfather Edward Muir passed away. His funeral in 2000 was the last time all three girls were together. Now, all these years later, Carson wondered if Mamaw's dream of reuniting her Summer Girls was just a romantic notion.

Carson's gaze shifted to the elaborate portrait of an early Muir ancestor that hung on the opposite wall. Her great-great-great-great-grandmother Claire Muir wore an elaborate navy velvet dress trimmed with thick layers of white lace of the quality Carson saw in history books of queens and great ladies. Her thick, raven hair was swept up and adorned with rows of pearls. More pearls, long, incandescent strands of them, fell down past her generous breasts. When Carson stared at the face, the woman's brilliant blue eyes seemed to be staring right back at her.

It had always felt like this, ever since Mamaw had moved the portrait from the main house in Charleston to Carson's room. Carson looked into the eyes of the great lady in the portrait, remembering that day.

Carson had been in that awkward transition period between childhood and adolescence and fully aware of the awkwardness of her tall, gangly body, her big feet, and her dark, thick hair. Not at all like her sister, Dora, with her soft golden hair and fair skin and breasts beginning to bud from her slender body.

Mamaw had knocked softly on her bedroom door and, hearing her crying, stepped inside the room. Carson had tried to control her sobs, but couldn't.

"Whatever is the matter?"

"I'm so ugly!" Carson had cried, and began another crying jag.

Mamaw came to sit on the bed beside Carson. "Who says you're ugly, child?"

"Tommy Bremmer," she mumbled, and buried her face in her arms. "He said my hair was a rat's nest."

Her grandmother sniffed imperiously and said, "Well, if he's a Bremmer, then he ought to know a rat when he sees one. But he doesn't know one thing about girls. Neither did his grandfather. Now, stop sniveling, child. It doesn't suit you."

While Carson tried to settle her sobs, Mamaw went into the bathroom and returned with a damp washcloth. Carson closed her eyes and relished the feel of the coolness as Mamaw gently wiped the hot tears and snot from her face. When she opened them again she could breathe easier because her chest wasn't so filled with hate.

"Muirs never cower," Mamaw told her, sitting beside her on the mattress. She began tugging a comb through Carson's long, knotted hair. "You're becoming a young lady, you know."

"Ow, stop," Carson whined, wiggling away from the comb.

Mamaw persisted. "Beauty is our duty and sometimes

it hurts. We must be stoic. Now, let me have a hand at this magnificent head of hair you have."

Carson closed her eyes while her grandmother combed her hair. After the first painful detangling of knots, her grandmother was able to run the comb smoothly all the way from her scalp past her shoulders.

"You have your mother's hair," Mamaw told her. "So thick and dark."

"I don't remember her."

"It's no wonder. You were so young when she died. Dear Sophie . . ."

"I don't even have a picture of her. Everything was lost in the fire."

"Yes," Mamaw replied softly.

"What was she like?"

Mamaw paused her hand and sighed. "She was very beautiful. Dark, provocative." She shrugged. "So French. And rather shy, or perhaps she just didn't speak English all that well, I don't know. You are an interesting combination of both of your parents."

"I wish I got Daddy's blond hair, like Dora. Not this rat's nest." She tugged angrily at her hair, hating the dark color and thickness of it, hating the way the girls sometimes called her a gypsy.

"Someday, when you're as old as I am, you'll thank the Lord for this thick head of hair when all your friends' hair is thinning. When you're a young woman your hair will be one of your best features," Mamaw told her knowingly. Then she reached up to grasp Carson's chin and peruse her face in shrewd study. "And your eyes, of course."

Carson looked at Mamaw with her face pinched in doubt. "No, Mamaw," she replied, trying to be stoic. "I know I won't be beautiful when I grow up. Not like Dora."

Mamaw huffed, releasing her chin. "Yes, it's true our Dora is beautiful. A Southern belle kind of beauty. Yours is a different beauty. One you'll have to grow into."

"Like my mother?"

"Yes," Mamaw replied. "But did you know, my dear, that you also get your dark looks from our side of the family?"

Carson's eyes widened. "But everyone's hair is yellow."

"Not everyone's. There is a line of dark Irish in our blood."

Carson didn't believe that fact would help her become a beauty, but she loved Mamaw all the more for trying to cheer her up.

The next day Mamaw dressed in a summer silk dress, coiffed her hair, and got into the blue Cadillac for a trip across the bridge to her house in Charleston. When she returned a few hours later, she carried with her a large package wrapped in brown paper. Dora and Carson were hot on her heels as she and Lucille carried the mystery package into the house. Eyes twinkling, they carried it directly into Carson's room. Carson and Dora exchanged looks of wide-eyed wonder.

Mamaw ignored the girls' questions and kept an enigmatic smile on her face as she removed the sheets of brown paper to reveal a large portrait in an ornate gold frame.

Carson gasped, unable to tear her gaze from the proud,

beautiful woman depicted. Mamaw and Lucille hoisted the big portrait and hung it with great effort. When they were done, Mamaw slapped dust from her hands, placed them on her hips, and stood back to admire it.

"Carson," she said in a tone that made Carson stand straighter, "this is your great-great-great-great-grand-mother Claire. She was considered the city's greatest beauty in her time. Quite legendary. Look at her eyes. The blue—that's the Muir blue color that's been carried down for generations. Claire was the wife of the great sea captain who founded our fortune." She lifted her hand and said in a staged whisper, "The pirate! The story goes that once he'd set eyes on Claire he gave up the life of a pirate and settled down in Charleston to win her heart. She went against her family's wishes to marry him. The rest, as they say, is history. The love of a good woman can change a man, you know," Mamaw admonished.

"But Mamaw, why did you bring the painting here from the big house?" Carson wanted to know.

Mamaw reached out to lift Carson's chin with the tip of her finger. "I saw the resemblance you share with Claire. I want you to see it, too. Every day, when you wake up, look into this portrait and see how beautiful you are. And coura-geous."

"Dear, wise Mamaw," Carson murmured, remember-ing that day. Because there was no one to share with her stories of her mother, of whom there was not so much as a photograph, this ancestor had, in her child's mind, taken on the role of her mother. At night before she fell asleep, Carson had looked into Claire's beautiful eyes and shared her secrets and believed she was heard.

Of all the treasures in this house, Carson knew that this portrait would be the single item she would request.

Carson had always seen the spark of a challenge in Claire's expression, the look of a woman who never surrendered. Looking at the portrait now, she felt herself rally. Carson took a deep breath and dragged herself from her bed. She went downstairs to gather a bucket, strong cleaning fluid, and an armful of rags, then escaped Nate's current temper tantrum to go to the garage to dig out from the ruins the promised golf cart. It was either that or the rusty bike.

Inside the garage it was as dark and ancient as an old barn. Spiderwebs graced every nook and sand filled all the crannies. The single four-paned window was so dirty, rays of light barely penetrated the grime. Carson found the golf cart parked in the far corner behind a dead lawn mower, two rusted bicycles, and a worm-eaten wood table covered with dusty brown boxes filled with assorted rusted tools that Mamaw felt had life left in them. Carson thought her time would be better spent renting a trash bin and tossing everything into it.

The scent of vinegar and accumulated dust made her sneeze and her eyes water, but she gritted her teeth and pressed on, sweeping and scrubbing the dirt, cobwebs, and mouse droppings from the white golf cart. It was a two-seater cart with a bench in back. Once she washed and rinsed it with the hose and dried it with old towels Lucille had provided, she was surprised to discover that the little cart and vinyl seats were in pretty good shape. Like the Cadillac, it was probably only taken out once in a blue moon. Carson took heart. A new battery, maybe a few other incidentals, and this golf cart might really work.

A few days later, she was rumbling in her cart along the narrow roads shaded by scores of palm trees and the graceful low boughs of ancient live oaks. She felt the breeze against her cheek, heard the crunch of gravel beneath the wheels, and likened the feeling to being on a boat in the water, closer to the world around her and not trapped behind steel doors and glass.

"Darn Mamaw for always being right," she muttered to herself, having to admit she loved it. Carson liked to name her vehicles, so she christened the cart "Bouncing Matilda." While Matilda wasn't the Blue Bomber by any stretch of the imagination, it had a certain charm all its own and did the job of getting her from point A to point B on the small streets of Sullivan's Island—at least in the daylight. As she drove along the road at a slow speed, she chuckled, remembering those two old hens sitting on the porch playing gin rummy and how they'd completely bamboozled her.

That night Carson found Nate lying on his bed already in his favorite pajamas with the spaceships-and-stars pattern. He was reading a book. He looked at her as she approached, his body stiffening in wariness. She felt immensely sad to see it. She wanted him to like her and to feel at home here. He was such a skittish little guy with his dark eyes staring up. Suddenly she thought of Delphine and, in that moment, knew exactly how to behave around Nate. They really were alike in many ways, she thought.

She walked slowly to the bed, not getting too close, not making any sudden moves. "Here," Carson said, holding out two books. "I bought these for you. I thought you'd like them."

"What are they?" he asked in a small voice.

"Well, take them and see."

Nate pulled himself up into a seated position and cautiously took the books. As he saw that they were both about dolphins, his face lit up.

"They're not baby books," she told him, getting closer but mindful of keeping her distance. "This one describes some of the research on the intelligence of dolphins. I really enjoyed it. Like, did you know dolphins look at themselves in the mirror? I mean, they know it's themselves they're looking at. That's called being self-aware."

"I read about that already," Nate said, matter-of-factly. "Mamaw gave me a book about dolphins."

"Oh. Well, there's a lot of other interesting information in it. And this other one is sort of a picture guide to all marine life. There are other animals out in the sea you might like to read about. Like orcas and porpoises and whales."

Nate began flipping through the pictures hungrily. He paused to look up and ask, "Can dolphins really be glad to see people?"

"Yes," Carson replied honestly. "I think they can."

"I've been reading a lot about dolphins," Nate said seriously. "Did you know that male dolphins are bigger than females? Large dolphins in the Pacific Ocean can weigh up to one thousand pounds. I've been thinking. Delphine is a bottlenose dolphin in the Atlantic Ocean, and she is a female. I don't know her age, though. Do you?"

"No."

Nate considered this. "She might weigh about five hundred pounds."

Carson smiled in appreciation of the boy's cleverness. "That sounds right."

Nate accepted her approval. He looked at his book a moment, then lifted his head. This time, his eyes, though they did not meet hers, were filled with worry. "Is my mother alone with my father?"

Carson appreciated the gravity of his question and responded seriously, "No, I don't believe so."

"He won't take care of her."

"Nate, your mother is fine and she can take care of herself. She's only meeting your father, packing up some things for you, and then she'll be back."

He thought about that answer. "Can you put it on the calendar when she will come?"

Carson scratched her head. She knew she had to be honest and clear with Nate. He wouldn't accept the hypothetical.

"I don't know exactly when she'll be back. But I'll tell you what I'll do. I will call your mother tomorrow and ask her. If she gives me a date, I will put it on the calendar for you. Okay?"

"Okay."

He looked so small and sad and alone, Carson wished there was some way for her to reach him.

"Let's get to sleep early tonight," she told him. "We need our rest. Because tomorrow, we're going to swim."

Nate's eyes rounded in terror. "No. I won't."

"You'll love it. You'll see."

"I won't."

Carson crossed her arms and pulled out her trump card. "Delphine will be there."

"Okay," he said grumpily, but he scrambled under his blanket.

"Good night, Nate," she said, yearning to kiss him but refraining. Instead, she tucked his blanket higher along his chin. "Sleep tight. Dream about dolphins."

"That's stupid. You can't make yourself dream about anything," Nate said, closing his eyes and yawning.

Carson watched his small body curl up and her heart pinged as she thought how hard it must be to live only seeing a world filled with rules and concrete facts, without the joy of spontaneity and imagination.

Another plus in favor of the golf cart—easy to find a parking spot!

Carson was in a cheery mood and buoyed with energy as she began her lunch shift. The schools were out and the lunch tables were packed, with a line at the door. By the final hour of her shift, however, Carson was dragging. Worse, she felt like she wanted something alcoholic to drink. The notion made her jittery and she told herself it was just a blood-sugar drop.

Devlin was at the bar as usual, having a beer with shots. He didn't usually hit the shots in the early afternoon and she was a little worried about him. When her last customer left, she cleared the table, then grabbed a moment to sit at the bar with a Coke and catch her breath.

"Hey, how are you doing?" she asked him, leaning closer.

He shrugged. "Been better." He turned and smiled lazily at her. "Seein' you makes it better."

His eyes were already glazed. She didn't want to pry and knew from experience with her father that it was best not to say anything. It was better to just be around as a pal. She pulled out her tips and began counting her day's take.

"Good day, eh?" Devlin asked.

"Decent, but I'd make more on the night shift."

"Why don't you ask Brian to change your shift?"

"I did," Carson replied. "But the other girls have seniority. He'll give me a slot when one opens up."

"Ashley doesn't want it?"

"No. She wants her nights free to be with her boyfriend."

"As a woman should," Devlin said, taking a sip from his beer.

Carson swung her head to look at him, annoyed but also wondering if his bad humor had to do with his ex-wife. She felt a bit sorry for him, sitting there staring morosely into his beer. She could tell by the condensation on the glass that it was icy cold and licked her lips.

"Man, that beer looks good," she murmured.

"Want one?" Devlin asked.

Carson did, very much. She shook her head no.

"Hey, what's up?" Ashley asked, sidling up beside Carson at the bar.

Carson saw the silent question pulsing in Ashley's eyes. She had told Ashley about her plan to stop drinking for a week.

"Nothing. Just hanging, having a *Coke*," she replied, picking up her plastic cup and bringing it to her mouth.

"I'll have a Coke, too," Ashley said in camaraderie. She poured one from the fountain and they clicked plastic cups. She looked up and Carson could see something had caught her attention. "Oh my Lord," Ashley said, moving close to Carson's ear to whisper. "Look who just walked in."

Carson turned her head to see Blake closing the door behind him. He was wearing his uniform of an old T-shirt and khaki shorts over long, deeply tanned legs. She noticed that his tan was darker and his hair was so long his curls hung low over his head. He looked up and caught Carson's gaze. She swiftly turned her head away.

"So . . . what's happened to Mr. Predictable? He's taking a table in my section." Ashley nudged Carson in her ribs. "Maybe not so predictable anymore."

"Don't call him that," Carson said. "His name is Blake."

"Okay then," Ashley replied saucily. "I've got to go see *Blake*."

Carson sat looking down at her Coke with a frown. She hated to admit to herself that Blake's taking a seat in Ashley's section bothered her. Enormously.

"What's the matter?" Devlin asked, leaning hard against her. His breath smelled of beer.

"Oh, nothing. My feet hurt."

Devlin looked across the long bar. Brian's back was toward them.

"Here," he said, sliding a shot glass toward her, moving his shoulder as though to hide it. "This'll help take the pain away. Works for me."

Carson looked at the golden liquor in the shot glass and felt an almost uncontrollable desire to chug it down. She could almost feel the burn. She took a breath and shook her head. Hell, she had to last longer than this. "No, thanks."

"Aw, go ahead," Devlin said, leaning in close to speak in a soft, secretive voice. "I won't tell."

Carson slid the shot glass back. "No, thanks."

Devlin slowly pushed the shot glass back to her, smiling like it was some kind of game. "Go on, Brian's not looking."

"It's not that," Carson said pointedly. "I'm not drinking. Period."

"Huh?" Devlin said, screwing up his face in confusion. "Since when? Go on, honey, have a drink. Looks like you really want one." He pushed the drink closer to Carson with more force than necessary, some of the brown contents spilling over. Carson jerked out of the way and in response, Devlin moved to slip an arm around her shoulders.

"I said no," she snapped, pushing back the shot glass so hard it fell over and spilled across the bar.

"Hey," Devlin sputtered.

Carson tried to shove his arm off her shoulder but Devlin was wobbly and held tight so as not to fall off his stool. "What the hell?" Devlin said, his seduction morphing into something darker, sadder. "Whaddya do that for?"

Carson had seen this switch happen before and it triggered disgust more than any sympathy. "I said *no*," she said, wriggling from his grip. "Now let go of me," Carson ground out.

Suddenly Blake was there. He pushed Devlin back so hard he slid from his bar stool. "The lady said no."

Devlin sat in a daze for a second before he pulled himself up in a rush of drunken fury and propelled himself forward against Blake, pushing him hard. Blake staggered back a few steps, then held his ground and pushed Devlin away. Devlin tottered, then held steady, his chest heaving and his fists balled at his thighs.

"Dev, stop it," Carson shouted, jumping from her stool.

Brian rushed forward to step between the men. "That's enough. Take it outside."

"I've got no beef with this guy," Devlin said to Brian, appeasing him. "He butted his nose in our business."

"Yeah, I saw that business," Brian said, his face flushed. "If this guy hadn't stepped in, I would've. You've had enough for today, buddy. Go on home."

Devlin looked at Brian and the steam seemed to seep out of him. His face fell and he took a step toward Carson. Blake took a step in front of her.

"I'm sorry," Devlin said to Carson. "I didn't mean nothin' by it."

"I know, it's okay," Carson said dismissively. "Go on home."

Brian took hold of Devlin's shoulder. "I'm driving you

home, okay, buddy? Let's go." He gave a parting look over his shoulder that told the staff he'd be back.

Ashley looked to Blake, who stood with his hands on his hips, looking uncomfortable. "Thanks, uh . . ."

"Blake," he replied, and offered a quick smile. "No thanks necessary."

"Sure they are. How about I get you a drink? A beer, maybe? On the house," Ashley offered.

"No, thanks." Blake glanced briefly at Carson. "I better go."

"Wait," Carson called out.

Blake paused and looked over his shoulder.

"Thank you," she said, and smiled tentatively.

"No big deal." Blake turned and walked out the door.

Carson met Ashley's gaze. Ashley raised her eyebrows and wagged her hand to indicate she should follow him. Exhaling a plume of air, she trotted after him out the door, where he was untying the leash of a large yellow Labrador sitting under the shade of the picnic table. The dog looked up at her as she approached and gave a short huff, of welcome or warning, she wasn't sure. Blake swung his head around. For a second, two sets of dark soulful eyes stared up at her.

"Blake, I wanted to talk to you a minute, if you don't mind."

Blake rose, the leash hanging loosely in his hand. "Sure."

"What happened in there . . . It wasn't what it looked like. Devlin was just drunk. He didn't mean anything by it."

A muscle twitched in his cheek as he paused. "He

looked like he was manhandling you and, well, I couldn't just sit by and watch."

"It was nice of you to defend me. Chivalrous."

Blake looked down at the dog and didn't reply.

"This your dog?" she asked.

"Yep," he said, patting the dog. "Meet Hobbs. My good buddy."

Carson reached out and petted the massive block head of the Lab. He was a friendly dog, as most Labs were, but he was one of the biggest she'd ever seen. "Are you sure he doesn't have some mastiff in him?" she asked, laughing as the dog's long tongue licked her hand.

"Maybe somewhere back in his lineage. He's a big boy, though. He doesn't like to be cooped up, so I take him along with me whenever I can. Time was I could bring him inside the restaurant, but the rules have changed, so he sits out here and waits."

"He won't run away?"

"Him? Nah. He's a people watcher. And he doesn't stray far from the water."

Carson spotted the steel dish filled with water in the shade. It was customary for many of the restaurants on the island.

Now that the pleasantries were finished, Carson wanted to get to the business at hand. "Do you want to talk here?"

"How about we get some coffee?"

"Hold on a minute. My shift is almost over. I just have to check with Ashley."

A few minutes later she returned with her purse.

"Ashley's covering for me. The place is pretty quiet now. So, where do you want to go?"

They walked along Middle Street to a small coffee and ice cream shop. The beans were roasted on the premises. Hobbs lay down again in the shade and waited as they took a place in the long line of adults and children looking for a summer fix of sugar or caffeine. Carson could pick out the locals in shabby cutoffs, T-shirts, and sandals from the better-dressed visitors. Glancing at Blake as he stood with his hands in his pockets, rocking on his heels and studying the enormous chalkboard with all the offerings listed, it occurred to her that he fit right in. Blake was the kind of man who didn't worry about such things as new styles or trends. He wouldn't have known a famous brand if it hit him over the head. She smiled. *Thank God*, she thought.

"Hey," Blake said, bending closer. His eyes were as dark as espresso. "You see anything you like?"

Carson regrouped and took a glance at the chalkboard. "I'll have a chai with skim milk, please."

They didn't talk while in line. Carson felt uncharacteristically nervous around him. She pressed her hand against her stomach while she steadied her breath, regaining her composure. At last their turn came and Blake gave the order. Steaming cups in hand, they glanced around the small room. Two couples with their laptops looked like they were determined to roost for hours. The other tables were filled with families and chattering or whining children.

"Let's sit outside with Hobbs," Blake said.

Outside, the tables were filled as well.

"There's the park down the block," he suggested. "Hobbs loves it there."

It was a lovely June afternoon, neither too hot nor too humid. As they walked past quaint restaurants, a few real estate firms, and a massage clinic, Carson noted that he slipped around to the street side of the sidewalk. Someone had taught him manners, she realized. Mamaw would approve. Hobbs was a gentleman, too. He didn't jerk on the leash or sniff people as they walked by. He stayed by Blake's side, content to be out and about. On the corner they stopped to gaze at the beautiful paintings in the window of the Sandpiper Gallery. She thought of Mamaw's beach house and how she'd filled it with local art.

Nearing the firehouse, they crossed the street and entered the park. Flowers were blooming and the leaves in the trees were thick and lush, offering bountiful shade. Blake led her to a quiet bench situated under the protection of a magnificent live oak. He brushed away bits of leaves and dirt so she could sit. Hobbs lay at his feet with a grunt of contentment.

"It's nice here," Carson said, admiring the peaceful setting as she pried off the lid of her cup. The spicy scent of the chai was heady. "I don't think I've been here for years. I used to play tennis on the courts over there."

"I come here often," Blake told her. He lifted his coffee to his mouth and took a sip. "I live just up the block. I have an apartment in the old officers' quarters."

"I love that building," Carson replied, seeing in her mind's eye the long, white wood building with full porches. They had once been used for the officers when the military had a base on Sullivan's Island. They'd since been converted to residential apartments.

"I'll have to show it to you sometime," he offered.

Carson's lips twitched at the thinly veiled invitation. She glanced at the man at her side. He was in profile as he drank from his coffee. If she'd snapped his picture at this moment and put it in a magazine, he wouldn't have been considered model handsome. Her experienced eye could pick out his flaws: his nose was too strong, eyes too deep, there were early crow's-feet on his sun-weathered face, and he was badly in need of a good haircut.

Then he turned his head and smiled. That crooked smile that meant something amused him, probably that he'd caught her staring at him. Again. Her heart flipped in her chest. This was what was so damn intriguing about Blake's smile. It could be so charming. So disarming. And it was never caustic. That alone was refreshing.

"You know," she said, "I had a nickname for you before I knew your real name. But I'm not sure it applies anymore."

He raised his eyebrows, saying nothing.

"Aren't you even curious what it was?" Carson said, flirtatiously tapping his arm. "If somebody said they had a nickname for me, I'd be shaking them by the shoulders to get it out of them."

He shrugged. "It's a name you've applied to me, so it's yours, not mine. You can call me anything you want."

"Fine. I'm not going to tell you," she said mockingly.

"Don't. Your call."

"I don't get you sometimes," she said. "I may have been way off on your nickname. You're surprising me all the time."

"Okay, what is it?" he said, clearly more out of empathy than a need to know.

"Forget it," she said. "That ship has sailed." She was glad it had. Not only was it incorrect, she thought, but it might have hurt his feelings and she didn't want to take the chance.

"Do you think I'm some sort of hard-ass?" he asked with mock indignation. "Someone who doesn't have a sense of humor? I've got tons of humor."

"You do, huh?"

He leaned back against the bench. "Absolutely."

She watched his lips as he spoke. She'd never noticed but the man had perfect teeth. "You have a lovely smile. It was one of the first things I noticed about you. It lights your face."

His smile came, slow and seductive. "Are you trying to be nice now?"

"When haven't I been nice?"

He shrugged. "The other day, when you blew me off. You walked off the beach without even saying hello."

"Me, not nice? Excuse me? I came to the beach to meet you. Like we'd arranged."

He raised one brow skeptically. "You were late. Very late. I didn't think you were coming."

"I got held up at work."

"So why did you walk off? I know you saw me wave."

Carson picked at the rim of her cup, suddenly tongue-tied. "I . . . well, I saw you with someone else and I didn't want to intrude." She sipped her chai, not wishing to say more.

"Someone else?" His face shifted to reveal his confusion. Then understanding dawned, and that crooked smile slowly eased across his face and his eyes sparked with amusement. "Ah, yes. Her."

Carson felt the burn of a blush beginning. She took another sip of her tea.

"She's just someone who hangs out at the beach all the time. She's a friend."

A friend? They looked more than friendly. . . . Carson didn't know if she should believe him. "Whatever," Carson said. "She had her arms all over you. I just assumed."

He didn't reply, which only made her cheeks flame brighter.

"Looks like we both assumed wrong."

Carson met his gaze and tried not to smile. "Looks like."

He reached out for her hand and turned his palm over to wrap his fingers around hers. "Friends?"

"Friends."

They slowly released hands but she could still feel the tingling in her palm. She was glad that the tension between them had dissipated, to be replaced by this new warmth that was running in her veins. She liked him, more than she'd thought she would. There was something open and honest about him that made her feel comfortable, even safe.

"Tell you what," Blake said, stretching his long legs out before him and crossing his ankles. "Let's you and me try this over again. How about I call you the next time the wind is good? Say, after work?"

Carson followed his example and leaned back, crossing her legs. "Sounds like a plan."

He pulled out his phone. "What's your number?"

So, now they were exchanging numbers, she realized. A big step. She pulled out her phone as she recited her cell phone number. "Yours?" He told her his.

"We know where we live," he said with a slight chuckle.

Carson smiled as she punched his number into her phone. "By the way, Harper said to thank you."

"No thanks needed. I think we both know I did it for you."

Carson's hand froze and all humor had fled, to be replaced by a sincerity that unnerved her. This was suddenly moving all too fast.

On the street a car backfired, causing her to startle. It broke the moment, for which she was grateful. Carson tucked her phone back into her bag. "I was just thinking, you know a lot about me, but I know virtually nothing about you."

"What do you want to know?"

"Well, what do you do for a living? How's that for starters?"

"Classic," he replied. "I'm with NOAA."

"The National Ocean . . ." She trailed off, not knowing the correct name.

"Oceanic and Atmospheric Administration," he finished for her.

She cocked her head as she looked at his face, considering. "What area? Oceans, water, reefs? Wait, are you a weatherman?"

"Would it surprise you if I was?"

She chuckled. "A little."

"Dolphins," he said.

Carson's smile disappeared and she was suddenly alert. "What about dolphins?"

He looked slightly perplexed at her reaction. "I work with cetaceans. *Tursiops truncatus*, to be specific. Atlantic bottlenose. Our locals."

Carson sat forward and turned to face him, her heart beating so loudly she was sure he could hear it. "What do you do?" she asked.

He took a long breath and crossed his arms. "Well, actually I do a little bit of everything. My primary work is research on the effects of environmental contaminants, emerging diseases, and stressors on the health of marine mammals. That's a mouthful to say I study dolphins— their health and their habitat. There's a lot to do and not enough time. Or money."

"So you're a biologist?"

"That's right. I have my Ph.D. in molecular marine biology."

She didn't respond. She couldn't quite digest that her friendly kiteboarding buddy was also a doctor—of dolphins, no less. Mr. Predictable should have been *Dr.* Predictable.

"Are you interested in dolphins?" he asked her.

Carson didn't know where to begin. "Yes," she blurted. "Very much. Now, anyway."

"Why now?"

She waved her hand. "It's a long story."

"I've got time, if you do."

Carson told him about the shark. Even on this fourth telling of the story she felt the same sickening sensations she had when she stared into the shark's deathly eye and felt the girth of the sandpaper-rough body when it bumped her. She'd never forget that sense of terror. Blake went very still and his brows furrowed as he hung on every word.

"That's a pretty amazing story. I've heard of incidents where dolphins protect swimmers, of course. They're well documented. But I've never seen it happen."

"Exactly. It's kind of like a near-death experience. It's cool to hear about, but when it happens to you, not only do you never doubt they exist, but it's life-changing."

"I guess it would be. To be honest, I'm kind of jealous."

Carson appreciated that he was taking her story seriously. She'd have been crushed if he'd laughed it off as her imagination or flatly disbelieved her.

"What kind of a shark was it?"

"A bull shark."

"Those guys can be bullies."

"This one was. It came soaring out of the water like some bullet, all spinning. Then it belly-flopped onto the ocean, making this huge slapping sound and waves."

"That's a threatening gesture," he pointed out. "A warning to the other fish. Even still, shark aggression to humans doesn't happen often. I get really pissed by those TV shows showing"—he lifted his hands to make a threatening gesture and lowered his voice like a bogeyman—"*shark attacks*. It's all marketing and the sharks get a bad rap. Most of the accidents with sharks in our waters are just that—accidents. A case of mistaken identity. That water is murky. And in your case, the shape of the surfboard might have resembled a turtle or a seal, both common prey. You weren't wearing any flashy jewelry in the water?"

"God, no. I've been surfing all my life. I know better."

"We call this kind of attack a hit-and-run. Once the shark figures out the swimmer is too big or not part of his diet, he swims off. At most there'd be a single slash."

"Great," Carson said with a roll of the eyes.

"Better than a bite."

She shuddered at the thought of even a scrape from the massive teeth she'd seen. "This shark meant business. I could feel it in my gut."

He paused. "You said you got bumped?"

She nodded.

He pursed his lips. "A bump represents serious hunting. We call this a bump-and-bite. The shark circles the prey, then bumps the victim prior to an actual attack." He rubbed his jaw. "In thinking more about what happened to you—you're a lucky girl. Sounds like you were caught in a feeding frenzy. That dolphin might well have saved you from a bite."

"I know," she said slowly, her eyes wide. "I'm so grateful. I want to do something."

"Do something?"

"To help. Volunteer . . . *something*." She kicked a pebble with her foot. "You couldn't think of something I could do?"

His smile came, slow, thoughtful. "I think I can. I do an assessment of the resident dolphins every month. We take out our boat and journey all along the waterways where pods hang out. Would you like to come along?"

She couldn't contain her excitement. "Yes!"

Blake looked at his wristwatch. "Damn. It's late. I have to run."

"I should go, too," Carson said, swallowing the thousands of questions on the tip of her tongue. In fact, she could have sat there with him in that beautiful park for hours more. But he was late and in a hurry.

Blake rose to stand and immediately Hobbs was on his feet, eyes anxiously focused on his master. Blake punched at his phone, checking his calendar. "We're scheduled to take the boat this month." He looked up. "It'll take all day. Can you get off work?"

"I'll try. Shouldn't be a problem."

"Good. I'll call you with the details."

"Okay," she said, feeling more excited about this boat trip than she had about anything in a very long time. Was it fate that Blake was involved with dolphins? Another sign?

Blake offered her a final smile and a parting wave. "Okay then. I've got your number."

She returned the smile and the wave, then watched him walk off at a fast clip, Hobbs trotting at his heels. Carson reached down for her purse, then ambled slowly along the park back to her golf cart. Oh yes, she thought to herself, swinging her arm. Blake Legare most certainly did have her number.

CHAPTER THIRTEEN

C arson arrived at the beach for her kiteboarding lesson. Her body was well primed and well fed and she felt confident with Blake as her teacher. She was ready to hit the water.

She wasn't prepared for the fact that she'd spend the day with a trainer kite on the beach.

"I don't need a *trainer* kite," Carson complained to Blake as they walked along the beach to a quiet corner. She notched her chin up in defiance. "I've done a lot of surfing. How much harder can it be?"

"Listen up, Carson," Blake told her in a firm voice. "Kiting is more about controlling the air than surfing the water. Learning to control the kite is the first step. It's major. Plus, kites are very expensive when compared to trainer kites."

"If it's just about the money, I—"

Blake's face drew tight and his brows furrowed in

annoyance. "When it comes to teaching kiteboarding, Carson, I'm not going to fool around. Kiteboarding is an extreme sport and potentially dangerous. Your surfing experience will be a bonus, but not at all enough to get you airborne safely. If you didn't know what you were doing, you could seriously hurt not only yourself, but others out there on the water. And even here on the beach. Those kites have a lot of power and you first have to learn how to harness it and control it. So we're going to practice on land today with a smaller kite. Okay?"

Blake's eyes flashed and the way he said *okay* was preemptive. He wasn't about to tolerate any more complaints. He continued. "Then we'll progress to other skills. When you master those steps, then, and only then, will I let you go out on the water." He paused. "With me."

Figuring resistance was futile at this point, Carson swallowed her pride and nodded in compliance.

Blake stepped closer, put his arm around her shoulders, and kissed her. "I don't want anything bad to happen to you."

It was a brief kiss, hardly passionate, but it was disarming. Carson suddenly understood what it meant to have the wind go out of one's sails.

Blake took her out to the beach every day there was wind, and each day she lost a bit more of her anxiety about going back into the ocean. By the end of the week, she was begging Blake to go in. Finally, he declared her ready for the water.

On the big day, they walked side by side to a quiet section of the beach, away from others. Carson felt the anticipation thrumming in her veins. Blake was her assistant for the launch. After they'd pumped air into the kite, she walked several yards away in the harness while he straightened out the long lines to the kite.

"Gear's ready. You ready?" he called out.

Carson felt her heart pump wildly in her chest. She froze in the harness, unable to respond.

"Carson?" Blake called again. When she didn't reply, he set down her kite and trotted to her side.

"You okay?" he asked, genuinely concerned.

Carson swallowed hard and shook her head. "I'm scared," she croaked out.

"Okay," Blake responded, his tone annoyingly like a therapist's, but reassuring nonetheless. He bent lower at the knees so he could gaze into her eyes straight on. "About what? Getting hurt?"

She nodded.

"You've trained for this. You're ready. And I'll be right beside you."

Carson shook her head again, trying to formulate her fears into words. "I keep seeing that shark."

Blake sighed and wrapped his arms around her, holding her to his chest. "Did I ever tell you about the time I was kiting in Breach Inlet and came down smack on the head of a shark?" She heard his laugh resonate in his chest. "I scared the shark more than it scared me, I promise you. But I just shifted my kite and in the next second I was airborne. That's what rocks about kite surfing. You ride the wind out there. That's what it's all about. You jump up, catch air, maybe grab the board, then crash to the sea. You were made for this sport, Carson. Go on out there and get stoked."

She felt a surge of adrenaline, and gritting her teeth, she nodded.

Blake trotted back to adjust the long lines that led from her harness to the bright yellow and black kite. Carson held on to her control bar and focused on the half-moon-shaped kite bobbing at the end of the line. On his count, they moved in tandem toward the water; then he lifted the kite high into the air, called out the signal, and let go.

Once the wind hit the kite, Carson felt the strong pull toward the ocean. She gripped the bar, leaned back, and felt a tremendous gust of power. In the time it took to suck in a breath, she was skimming across the tips of the waves, headed out to sea, the pilot of a single wing! It was intoxicating. More thrilling than anything she'd experienced on a board before.

Far out from shore, Carson felt secure with her wingman out there with her. Dragging her butt against the waves, Carson was reminded that she was still a beginner. Whenever she lost wind and collapsed into the water, Blake was right there to help her back up. The reputation of Charleston as the city of manners extended to Sullivan's Island. The riders at Station 28 were a kindly group—and forgiving.

In celebration of her first day on the water, Blake had invited his cousin and Carson's old surfing buddy Ethan to join them. Ethan's wife, Toy, and their children formed her cheering squad, whooping and calling out her name whenever she drew close to shore. Before too long Carson called it a day and glided into shore. She collapsed on her towel, elated but exhausted.

"My arms feel like rubber," she moaned.

"You did real good out there," Blake told her. "For a rookie."

Carson peeked out from the hand covering her eyes from the sun. "I thought you were going to say *for a girl*."

"I'm not that stupid," Blake said with a laugh.

"Good call," Ethan teased.

"There aren't hardly any girls out there," Toy added. "I'm glad to see you represent our sex. *Woot, woot*," she called out, rolling her arm in the air.

Carson really liked Toy Legare. She was cute in a Christie Brinkley kind of way, all wild blond hair and curves. She wore a modest, one-piece black swimsuit and was attentive to her children, who were busy building a sand castle a few feet away.

Ethan and Blake grabbed the gear and took their turn to go out for some serious kite surfing. Carson and Toy sat against the beach chairs and watched from their island on the sand as the two men sprinted to the water.

"Those two are just kids when they're near the water," Toy said, slathering suntan lotion on her arms.

"They look more like brothers than cousins," Carson said, watching them head to the sea. Both men were tall and lanky, had brown eyes and heads of dark curls. But it was more than just looks. The way they moved, the swagger of their hips, the sinewy arms. "Maybe even twins."

"A lot of the boys in that family have that brown curly hair. But those two really are like peas and carrots," Toy replied. "Their mamas used to claim they each had gained another son, they were at each other's houses so much."

"It's interesting that they went into the same line of work."

"Marine biology?" Toy asked. "Not so surprising. They're both water bugs. Blake's working with dolphins and Ethan works for the SC Aquarium." She added with a smug smile, "With me." Toy applied lotion to her legs. "Ethan's in charge of the big tank, so he's into fish of all kinds." She laughed lightly. "Me, I'm all about sea turtles." She handed the tube of lotion to Carson, then leaned back, pressing her palms on the towel as she faced the sky, eyes closed.

Carson knew that Toy was being modest. She was the director of the sea turtle hospital at the aquarium, an impressive and high-profile position.

"How long have you been married?" Carson asked her.

"Oh, gosh, it's got to be seven years already. Goes fast."

Carson looked over to the two children playing in the sand. The little boy couldn't have been older than six. But the girl, even though she was petite, had to be double that.

Toy opened one eye and followed Carson's gaze. A crooked grin eased across her face. "I know what you're thinking. That's my little girl, Lovie. She's my daughter from before we got married. Ethan's her daddy in all ways that count, though. He's a great father. You know," she said coyly, "Blake will be a good family man like Ethan, too."

Carson squeezed some lotion onto her arms. "Why hasn't Blake married yet? I'd expected he'd be snatched up by now."

"It's not for lack of girls trying, let me tell you!" Toy

said with a laugh. "I don't know. He traveled around a lot with his work. You never saw a mama so happy to see her baby come home as Linda Legare was when Blake announced he was going to study here with NOAA. Girls started dropping by the house like flies on a sugar cube. He dated around, of course. There was one girl we thought might be the one, but they broke up last year." She leaned in closer. "I was glad. She was pretty, but she wasn't the sharpest tool in the shed, if you know what I mean."

Carson laughed and was secretly pleased to hear this. She could well imagine that Blake would eventually grow bored with someone who was not well-read.

Toy continued. "Blake says he's just waiting for the right one." Her eyes pinned Carson with a tease. "Maybe he found her."

Even knowing it was a tease made in jest, Carson was annoyed. She handed the tube of lotion back to Toy. "Let's not get ahead of ourselves. Blake and I are just friends."

"Just sayin'," Toy said with a smirk. "Besides, you've already been preapproved by Ethan. Be right back." Toy rose and went to sit beside her children at the sand castle. The little girl silently submitted to the slathering of lotion over her body, but predictably the boy groused and tried to squirm away. Toy was quick and efficient, and in a flash her two young ones were coated in the thick white lotion.

"Those two keep me busier than a moth in a mitten. Want some water?" Toy asked, wiping the lotion off her hands on a separate towel. She pulled a large thermos out from her bag.

"Love some," Carson replied, helping her with the

four cups. She marveled at Toy's mothering. Her enthusiasm for her children and Ethan, for life, hummed around her, creating a cool and confident aura.

Toy poured cold water into the red plastic cups, then screwed the top back on the thermos and put it back into her enormous beach bag. She rummaged through it and extracted a plastic container. Opening it, she set out crackers and cut celery and carrots. In another bag were sugar cookies. These she carried to the children, along with cups of water. "Don't you throw those cups away," she ordered.

"I don't use plastic bottles anymore," Toy explained to Carson. "When you've pulled out as much plastic from a turtle's belly as I have, you learn to not use plastic bags, bottles, or whatever."

"You are an amazing mother," Carson told her.

Toy's face lit up. "Thanks. If you knew my mother, you'd know how much that means to me."

"Did you always know you wanted to be a mother?"

"Oh, Lord no," Toy said, putting on her head a navy cap emblazoned with the South Carolina Aquarium logo. "I was a mother before I was old enough to even wonder about it. I had little Lovie when I was nineteen. Her father was a no-good scoundrel. But even being with him was better than being with my mother."

Carson realized she'd met someone whose childhood was probably worse than her own.

"But once I looked into Lovie's eyes"—Toy's own eyes took on a wistful expression—"I knew I was home. That's what I always wanted, you see. A home. Course, then I met Ethan and that was that." She looked out at the water and tracked her man's ride on the waves. "Will you look at him," she said, her face a vision of infatuation. "He's just showing off for us." She turned to Carson. "And it turns me on like nobody's business."

Carson spotted Ethan riding close along the beach, kicking up a large spray. She scanned the water and farther out she caught Blake catching air. He soared high into the sky and at the peak he lifted his legs, arching to bring the board high behind his back.

Toy giggled and pointed. "Ethan's not the only one showing off." She turned her attention back to Carson. "I see the way he looks at you. I'd say that's one fish that's been hooked."

Carson's gaze drifted away from Blake to Toy, grateful for the sunglasses covering the discomfort she knew was reflected in her eyes. The comment both delighted and troubled her. When people started pairing her off with someone, that was usually her cue to cut and run.

Later, Toy suddenly straightened on her knees, laughed, and pointed to the ocean. "Here come those two rowdy boys, back from the war. Take off your hat, girlfriend, 'cause they got up-to-no-good smirks on their faces. You just know they're going to drag us down to the water." She squealed as the men rushed toward them.

Carson looked up to see the two men bearing down on them at full speed. She went into a defensive crouch. "Don't you dare," she warned as Blake grabbed her by the arms and gave a tug that had her on her feet. Ethan went straight for the two children, hoisting one under each arm. Toy had no choice but to run after them, laughing and crying out to Ethan that little Danny wasn't a very good swimmer yet.

The tide was in and the sun shone high in the cloudless sky. The group caught their second wind, splashing in the waves while the children laughed and squealed in delight. Blake and Ethan put the children on their shoulders and had a chicken fight while Carson and Toy cheered them on. Danny crowed like a rooster with triumph when he and Blake toppled Lovie and Ethan into the surf. As the afternoon waned and the children began shivering, their fingers and toes wrinkled from the time in the water, they returned to their towels, where Ethan and Toy rubbed their shoulders dry. The women gathered the supplies and the men packed up the kite gear. The two children stood, towels wrapped around their slender shoulders and dragging in the sand, their damp hair sticking out at odd angles, nibbling cookies. Their eyelids were drooping like lowered awnings.

Carson watched them and felt a strange ache in her heart. She'd never seriously considered having children. All her life she'd been consumed with whatever project she was working on, the glamour of traveling to exotic places, meeting famous people. Today, however, she'd had a lovely time playing with these two little ones on the beach, enjoying their squeals and refreshingly honest comments. She'd enjoyed spending time with Nate at Sea Breeze. This past month she'd rediscovered a different, quieter kind of happiness in the lowcountry with her family, new friends, and Delphine.

They formed a ragtag army as they left the beach. Blake and Ethan carried kite gear and bags like pack mules. The two children trailed behind them, dragging their heels. Carson and Toy brought up the rear with the rest of the bags. Carson's gaze followed the men. Blake was taller than Ethan, but not by much. They shared the same easy gait and the same devotion to these lowcountry waters.

Blake turned his head to check on her. They made eye contact and smiled a message that spoke volumes. He was unlike other men she'd been with, and she'd dated a lot of men. Or, was he really that different? she wondered. Was the difference in her? Or was it simply more about the place and the timing?

They had been blessed with sunny days and balmy breezes all week. In addition to spending time on the beach with Blake, Carson had spent an hour every day bringing Nate to the dock and slowly getting him acclimated to the seawater. Once the boy got over his initial fear, Carson discovered, Nate loved being in the ocean. There was something about the rocking motion of it and the tightness of his life preserver that he found soothing. She was patient, helping him with rudimentary strokes and the art of kicking, unabashedly using the lure of Delphine for motivation.

On the first day Nate complained about everything— the temperature of the water, how dirty it looked, the greasy feel of suntan lotion, and that he simply couldn't do what she'd asked. She turned a deaf ear to his complaints and kept up her encouragement. She moved forward at his pace and gave him lots of praise, careful not to push him too hard. Nate needed to be allowed to trust himself in the water. As the week progressed, every day he complained a little less. And every day she kept her eyes peeled for the sleek gray dolphin.

Delphine didn't appear. With a stranger in the water, it was no wonder that the wild dolphin kept her distance. Carson knew she was checking them out, however. Once she'd felt the unmistakable tingling of echolocation on her legs. On the seventh day, however, Delphine made her appearance.

"There she is!" Nate called out, almost leaping from his preserver.

Carson shared his joy at seeing the large head emerge alongside them, Delphine's dark eyes following their every move with great attention. She released a big bubble of air from her blowhole and hung back a bit, both curious and shy.

"Where have you been?" Carson asked Delphine.

Delphine tilted her head to peer at the boy as she swam past them, graceful and sleek. On the second pass, they heard the soft buzzing noise.

"That feels funny," Nate told Carson.

"She's checking you out. It's okay. You're feeling her echolocation. It's kind of like an X-ray."

"You mean sonar," Nate corrected her.

"Yes," she replied, thinking she had to be on her A game with Nate. He spent every night studying his books.

As had she. Carson had read that dolphins liked children, and it was clear today that Delphine was curious about the boy. Delphine dared to come closer to brush Nate's leg with her pectoral fin. Later, she swam closer again and nudged Nate's leg, this time with her rostrum. Carson held her breath, knowing Nate didn't like to be touched. It was a miraculous moment. Nate not only tolerated the dolphin's touching his leg, he reached out and let his fingers graze her body as she swam by. *He'd touched the dolphin.* And Delphine had allowed it. Carson knew she'd never forget this moment. Some barrier had been broken. A connection made. She wished Dora was here to see it.

They spent a heavenly afternoon in the cool water with lots of splashing and laughter. Nate clearly adored Delphine. The dolphin seemed to be the center of his world, and Delphine seemed to be equally fascinated with the boy. She was very maternal. The dolphin swam close to his side, as though allowing him to swim in her slipstream. She circled him, very attentive to his whereabouts and whistling frequently. When Nate swam too far out, Delphine slapped the water with her chin, chattering, and steered him back to the dock.

Carson hurried to the dock, climbed up, and retrieved her camera from its bag. She felt again the creative urge to capture images of Delphine. She brought the camera to her eye and began clicking wildly, capturing the priceless moments of communication between the once-uncommunicative boy and the dolphin. It appeared to Carson that the dolphin recognized that Nate was a child and vulnerable, and, as she would have with any young dolphin in her pod, Delphine was acting as another auntie.

Carson lowered the camera and looked out at the boy and his dolphin. In this cove, with Delphine and Nate and herself, there was no doubt there was something going on that she could only call magic.

Later that afternoon, when Lucille called them in for dinner, Carson had to practically drag Nate out of the water. "You look like a prune," Carson told him, pulling him onto the dock. Wrapping a thirsty, warm towel around Nate's shivering shoulders, she laughed. "A stewed prune."

"I am not a prune, I am a mammal," replied Nate.

Nate was agreeable as she brought him upstairs to shower and shampoo. His soapy skin smelled sweet when he changed into his clean pajamas. He allowed her to comb his hair without the usual complaints.

Lucille had cooked Nate's favorites. She carefully laid three pieces of plain ham on his plate with three pieces of broccoli, making sure they didn't touch. Then she came up to him and set a separate plate beside him. On this she put a heap of mashed potatoes. She didn't say a word but stepped back and clasped her hands, waiting. Carson and Mamaw exchanged worried glances as Nate bent close to the potatoes in close inspection. This wasn't an item on Dora's specific list of approved foods, but Lucille had told them earlier she wanted to give the boy the chance to reject it. It was white and only had butter on it, so she was hopeful. They held their breath as Nate dipped the tip of his spoon into the soft mass, tapped it on his tongue, tasted it. Without another word, he dove in. They all exhaled. Lucille's chest expanded and she took a seat at the table.

Throughout the meal, Nate shoveled food into his

mouth and regaled them with dolphin facts. He wasn't a good conversationalist. He didn't ask questions, nor did he care about their opinions. Rather, he ignored them as he went on and on, dispensing a seemingly endless number of facts about dolphins he'd read about in his books. But Carson and Mamaw were just relieved to see him so open and animated.

"My, but you're a fountain of information!" Mamaw exclaimed with a roll of her eyes.

Later that night, Nate was so tired from all the physical exercise and sun that he offered no resistance to going to bed. "All the exercise and excitement took the contrariness right out of him," Lucille commented.

Carson tucked him in, and as she walked to the door, he called after her in a sleepy voice.

"Aunt Carson?"

"Yes?" she said, her hand on the light switch.

"Tonight I would like to dream about dolphins."

Carson smiled, surprised. He had never referred to his dreams before. She didn't even know if he had dreams.

"Me too," she answered softly before giving a prayer of thanks. Later, as she lay in her bed, she closed her eyes, picturing Nate's face in the ocean with Delphine, their eyes sparkling with happiness.

The following day Dora returned to Sea Breeze and found her grandmother sitting in the shade of the porch like a queen bee in her yellow cotton tunic.

"Darling girl!" Mamaw called out, raising both arms out. "You're back. Give me some sugar."

Dora was surprised to see her grandmother looking so vivacious and tan. In contrast, Dora felt pale and exhausted.

"How did everything go?"

Dora had spent hours with her lawyer preparing the divorce settlement. It was an emotionally draining experience. Then she had to hire painters, plumbers, and electricians to get the house in decent enough shape to put on the market. In truth, she was glad to pack up her and Nate's clothing and hightail it back to Sullivan's Island again. She found the house she'd once loved depressing now.

"As well as can be expected," Dora replied evasively.

"And the house? When will the painting start?"

"I got a slot the week after next. There's so much to do but we're only able to afford the minimum. I hate to sell it *as is*." She sighed. "Too poor to paint and too proud to whitewash."

"Do whatever you must. It'll be cheap in the end."

"Where's Nate?" Dora asked, sitting in a chair beside Mamaw.

"He's out in the water with Carson."

"Nate's in the water?" Dora asked, alarmed.

"That little boy is another fish out there, I swanny."

"He's swimming in the cove?" Dora asked again with rising horror. She stood, fixing her gaze on the dock, squinting. "He's not a good enough swimmer for that!"

"Calm yourself, Dora," Mamaw told her. "Carson's with him and she's been giving him swimming lessons. He's doing marvelously."

Dora slipped back into the chair. "Swimming lessons?" she repeated, trying to make sense of it. "He takes lessons . . . without complaining?" She had persevered for years taking Nate to swimming lessons at their local country club and he'd hated them, hated the teacher, hated everything about it. He'd had temper tantrums each time they went.

"Not a peep. He's been such a good boy," Mamaw said. "He thrives on the new regimen. I daresay we all do!"

"What new regimen?" Dora sputtered.

"You'll have to follow it, too, my dear. We're all committed. I feel wonderful! No fatty foods. No alcohol." She smirked. "Or almost none. And the schedule . . . Honey, you're going to love it. Carson is our early bird. She rises before the sun to go paddleboarding. Can't help herself, bless her heart. The rest of us get up after the sun rises, around seven."

"Nate too? He gets up on his own?" Dora asked, thinking of all the mornings she had to wheedle and cajole him out of his bed. "Is he sleeping well?" she asked.

"He sleeps just fine!" Mamaw exclaimed without guile. "All through the night. Why do you ask?"

Dora, mouth agape, just shrugged. At home, he often awoke during the night.

Mamaw went on. "He *is* particular about his food, as you warned, and we've been trying our best to stick to his diet. But once the food gets past his radar . . ." She shook her head and said as an aside, "No easy task, I tell you! He should be hired by the Department of Homeland Security. Anyway, once it's approved, he gobbles it right up. And his appetite! It's something else!"

Lucille came out carrying a glass of iced tea. She handed it to Dora. "That boy loves him some mashed potatoes. Can't get enough of them. He'll eat them at every meal if we serve them. And we do," she chuckled as she walked off.

"Mashed potatoes . . ." muttered Dora.

"That's right, dear. He doesn't object to the texture," Mamaw said knowingly. "You'll be so proud of his swimming, too. He's made such progress! And in such a short period of time. I always said that Carson was a mermaid and now your son is too. Or should I say a merman? I have no idea what to call him, but he hates to leave the water. We have to drag that boy out. Then when Carson goes to work, I mind him. Sometimes I take him fishing. Lord, that boy loves to fish. He won't eat it though, which I find peculiar. Lucille's been cooking up the fish for the rest of us, but he'll just stick to his ham without complaint.

"Sometimes Lucille and I take him to the market, which he does not like." She leaned closer and told Dora confidentially, "I don't think he likes crowds. They make him nervous, especially when they bump him. But I needed to buy him a few things, like a new swimsuit and some sandals. And books. I've never known a child who loves to read so much. Except perhaps Harper," she recalled as an expression of fond memory flitted across her face.

Dora only nodded, taking it all in.

"Then, in the late afternoons," Mamaw continued, "we're all tired and hungry and have a little quiet time in our rooms. At night, Carson does some work in her room and Nate cuddles up in front of the television to watch Animal Planet or something about nature." She smiled.

"He's a natural-born Jacques Cousteau." Mamaw sighed and shrugged, seemingly tired by the long presentation. "Then it's dinner and bedtime," she summed up.

Dora listened to this recitation, stunned to silence. All this time she'd been worried witless about how Nate was faring at Sea Breeze, fearful that she'd put too much stress and responsibility on Mamaw and Lucille's shoulders, concerned that Carson would resent an interruption in her and Mamaw's private time at the house, and here they were, happy as a bunch of campers without mosquitoes.

"I—I don't know what to say," Dora stammered.

"No need to say anything, dear. Why don't you take these towels down to the dock and see for yourself? Those two have been in there for hours. Be a dear and call them in for dinner."

Dora made her way down the long wooden dock toward the water, her mind trying to grasp all that she'd been told about schedules and swimming and good times. When she reached the end of the dock, she stopped short, unable to believe her eyes.

Out in the water Nate was swimming like a seal with strong strokes, despite his life preserver, chasing down a red ball bobbing in the water a few feet away from him. He'd almost reached it when a gray shadow shot past him and popped the ball out from the water. It was the dolphin! Dora's heart nearly stopped. That animal was right beside her son.

She almost shouted out a warning but the expression on Nate's face silenced her. Her son was laughing. Nate burst forward and swam after the ball again, grinning from ear to ear. Carson wasn't far from his side, calling out encouragement. This time Nate grabbed the ball and held on to it, beaming, while Carson whooped and the dolphin made nasal sounds that she'd have sworn sounded like laughter.

Dora leaned against the railing. From below, Carson spied her up on the dock.

"Dora!" she cried out, raising one arm from the water and waving. "Nate, look. Your mom's here!"

Nate swung his head to peer up and saw his mother on the dock. Dora waved her arm and grinned. "Hi, honey! I'm here!"

Nate frowned and held the ball closer to his body. "Go away!" he shouted.

"Nate!" Carson scolded him. "That's not nice. Say hello to your mother."

"I'm not getting out!" he shouted angrily.

Dora stared at her son glaring at her. She cringed, as though she could physically feel the delicate string that bound her to her son being ripped from her heart. It hurt, so badly.

She saw Carson out in the water with her head bent close to Nate's, coaxing him to come out of the water to greet his mother. She saw the way Nate listened to her, then begrudgingly acquiesced. He swam with strong strokes beside Carson, their pace evenly synchronized. Like she'd always wished her son would swim with her.

Dora stood alone in the shade of the dock staring at the fast current in the water rushing past her. She had spent a dreadful week in appointments with her lawyers to begin divorce proceedings. She'd made temporary settlements and arrangements with the bank, and cried, desolate and alone in that empty Victorian house, packing up her and Nate's things for the summer in anticipation of selling it. Her whole life seemed to be rushing past her. Calhoun had left her. They were selling her house. All she had left in the world was her son. And now he wanted nothing to do with her, either.

She watched Carson climb from the water onto the dock. The water streamed from her taut, beautiful body. She leaned over to help Nate climb up, he allowing her to touch his hand, his arm. He looked so much stronger, healthier. He had blossomed without her.

Dora wrapped her arms around herself, trying to contain the emotions spilling over. Carson . . . she had so much. She could have anyone. Dora tightened her fingers around her arms. Why was Carson trying to steal her son's affection?

CHAPTER FOURTEEN

Blake picked up Carson in a green four-wheel-drive jeep. Mud splattered the sides and wheels, and the rear was plastered with stickers from NOAA and the South Carolina Aquarium, and one that said DON'T FEED THE DOLPHINS.

It was only eight A.M. and she'd hoped to sneak out of the house without notice, but Mamaw had seen Carson peeking out the front window and her antennae were up. When the doorbell rang Mamaw was on her feet and at the door faster than a tick leaping on a dog.

"Why, aren't you the nice young man who is teaching Carson to kite surf?" she asked in her hostess voice, ushering Blake into the house.

"Yes, ma'am, I am," he replied, smiling politely. Blake was a well-brought-up Southern boy and Carson knew he would give Mamaw his full attention. He was wearing nylon fishing pants, the kind with pockets and zippers everywhere, and the ubiquitous T-shirt, this one a Guy Harvey. Most notably, and to Carson, regrettably, he'd cut his hair. The curls had been shorn like a sheep's wool and his hair was close-cropped around his head.

"Now, where are you two off to, so early in the morning?" Mamaw asked him.

"I thought I'd take Carson on a boat ride," he replied.

"How thrilling!" Mamaw exclaimed. "Where?"

"We're going to cruise all through the local rivers—the Ashley, the Cooper, the Wando, the Stono—checking out the resident dolphins. That's a lot of water to cover, so we'll be out the whole day. Don't forget a hat," he reminded Carson. She responded by lifting her hand, already carrying a cap. "I've packed us a lunch," Blake told her. "Are you ready?"

"I'm ready," Carson replied. She moved to kiss Mamaw on the cheek. "I'll see you later."

"Did you pack a rain jacket?" Mamaw asked. "It looks a little cloudy."

"I'll be all right. Bye, Mamaw."

Blake stepped forward. "It was nice meeting you, Mrs. Muir."

"Now, you children have a good day, hear?"

Blake leaned closer to Carson as they walked to the car. "I see where you get your charm from."

"Mamaw was quite the socialite in her day. She's active in conservation, too. She's a terrier with a bone when it comes to preserving the wild landscape of Sullivan's Island. She attends every meeting. I hope I'm so involved when I'm her age."

Blake opened the car door. "I wouldn't be at all surprised."

They didn't talk much as they drove over the bridges

crossing the Cooper and the Ashley Rivers on their way to Fort Johnson on James Island. Harbor View Road curved along the water, revealing vast expanses of verdant wetlands, and wound under huge live oak trees dripping with moss. When they passed through the South Carolina Department of Natural Resources gate onto the grounds of Fort Johnson, Blake asked, "Have you ever been to Fort Johnson?"

She shook her head. "Never."

"It's a pretty cool spot with a long and illustrious history. The first fort was built in 1708 and named for the proprietary governor, Johnson. That fort's long gone now. A later fort was built and used by the British in the Revolutionary War. That one is gone, too. Then, years later, in 1861, South Carolina state troops erected two batteries here and it was from this spot that they opened fire on Fort Sumter, the shots that began the Civil War."

Carson looked out at the vast expanse of land on which clustered a number of modern, government-style buildings nestled between ancient live oaks and countless palmetto palms.

"When did it become all this?" she asked, indicating the development.

"Well, not a lot happened here after that until around 1970, when the bulk of the property was transferred to the DNR. It's become a major marine research area for several organizations." He pointed. "Over there is the Marine Resources Research Institute. Then there's the Hollings Marine Laboratory. Another portion belongs to the Grice Marine Laboratory, and the Medical University has a marine science department."

"And that?" she asked, indicating a beautiful white plantation house.

Blake looked to where Carson pointed, then chuckled. "Lots of folks get confused seeing that here among all these office buildings, like a diamond in the rocks. That there's the original plantation home of the Ball family. It was built on their plantation, Marshlands, along the Cooper River. Some time back, the College of Charleston saved it from being torn down and had the house moved here, where it was restored. It's used for offices now, and not a day goes by that I don't drive by it and smile and thank God for preservationists."

He pulled into a large parking lot. "And this," he said, indicating a spreading, expansive office building, "is my home away from home." Without ceremony they gathered their cooler and bags and she followed him into the modern building. It was spare and sprawling, a maze of long linoleum hallways. Peeking in some of the rooms, she glimpsed crammed offices, laboratories, computer rooms, and storage rooms; in the hall, she saw rolling carts with specimens en route to one of the labs. It was a beehive of activity, everyone already hard at work or walking somewhere with papers in hand and a purpose. At last they stopped in one of the identical small offices, this one with two metal desks and crammed with computers and equipment.

"I just have to grab a few things," he told her, clearly preoccupied. "Make yourself at home."

Carson was intrigued at this peek into Blake's life. His shared office was far from glamorous, but she could tell from the photos of dolphins posted on the walls, the awards he'd won, the maps of the Charleston-area rivers with red pushpins marking coordinates, that he was committed to his research. When she spotted a hoard of photography equipment, however, she zeroed in. It was an impressive, quality array of cameras.

"Pretty top-notch equipment. Who's the photographer?" she asked him.

Blake was searching through files. "I guess I am," he replied. "We're collaborating on the research project."

"What are you studying?" she asked.

"It's a long-term study," he replied, walking over to rummage through his desk. "It's similar to several photo-ID studies being conducted along the southeast and Gulf coasts of the United States."

He picked up a piece of equipment and, satisfied, smiled. "As you'll soon see."

"I didn't know you were a photographer."

"I'm not," he answered, grabbing the bag of camera equipment. "But I'm good enough to get my job done. Here, take this," he said, handing her the red cooler. "Come on, we're wasting daylight."

She had to rush to keep up with his long strides down another maze of institutional halls. He pushed open a pair of double doors and suddenly they were in the back of the building on a boat ramp. Several large research boats were docked out here. Another man, tall and broad-shouldered, was unhooking the trailer of a boat.

"That's our ride," Blake said with obvious pride, pointing to the large black Zodiac. "Pretty cool, huh? It's fast and handles the chop like a champ."

Carson heard the awe in his voice and thought he was

just another Southern boy, in love with his boat. But she had to admit, this one was very sleek looking.

He handed her a personal flotation device. "You have to put this on," he told her. Then, "You don't get seasick, do you?"

"It's a little late to ask that question," she said with a laugh, then shook her head. "I was born to be on the water."

A half hour later, Carson was holding tight to the rope in the Zodiac as it sped through Charleston Harbor. The Zodiac was an inflatable marine craft over twenty-three feet long and outfitted for research rather than comfort. It was thrilling to hear the roar of the outboard motors and feel the spray as they cut through the chop of the harbor water like a knife through butter, low in the water. She got weary of holding on to her hat, so she stuck it between her knees, smiling with a giddy feeling of euphoria as they streamed across the water.

She looked to Blake standing wide legged at the wheel of the boat. She couldn't see his eyes behind his sunglasses but knew they sparked with excitement, like hers. From time to time he'd check papers as he steered the boat, reminding her that this wasn't a joyride for him but part of an important, multiyear research study.

They left the harbor and the water calmed as they entered the first of a myriad collection of rivers and waterways that made up the heart of the lowcountry. The tides breathed in and out of the wetlands, their rhythms as complex and interconnected as the veins in her body. Overhead, she saw a line of pelicans fly in formation, and in the grasses, herons and egrets hunted. They passed under bridges she'd crossed countless times in her car. From beneath, she heard the rumble of the cars overhead and wondered if the people in the cars even looked out at the magnificent water below. Had she? How different it was to be below in a boat, skimming across the water like a fish.

Blake abruptly slowed the engine and pointed. "Dolphin. Twelve o'clock."

Carson sprang to attention as Blake jumped for the camera and immediately began clicking. "There are two," he called out. "Adults."

Carson raised her hand over her eyes, squinting, but she couldn't see anything but water.

"Where?"

He ignored her question, lowering his camera to scan the water. After another minute, Blake shouted, "Three o'clock."

By the time she turned her head in the right direction, at best she caught the tail fluke of a dolphin diving. She turned her head to see Blake standing at the podium recording the sighting.

"That was number ninety-eight for sure. And eighty. Those two guys are pals," Blake added. "They've been hanging around together for years now."

"You know the dolphins?" Carson asked.

Blake nodded. "We've been doing this for years, so we're at the point where we can recognize them on sight. The dorsal fin markings are as unique as fingerprints."

"But you only saw them for maybe, what? A second?"

"That's enough."

Carson felt like a rank amateur. "I can't even see a dolphin in the time you spot it, identify it, and take its picture."

"The pictures are critical. When I return to the office later, the team will study the photographs, search for scarring and injuries, to solidly identify the dolphin. We know then the status of the pod, which dolphins are missing, sick, or additions."

Carson's fingers itched to use the camera. This was her area of expertise, after all. Something she could do to help. "Why don't you let me take the pictures?" she begged. "Really, I know the camera. At least then I can feel like I'm doing something to help."

"Sorry. Can't," Blake replied, returning to the rear of the boat. He was all business now, not allowing argument. "Insurance won't let anyone but us handle the equipment. It's expensive. And it's not as easy as it looks to get the shot fast enough." He waved his hand, calling her closer to the center podium. "But you can help."

Holding on to the rope, she carefully made her way across the rocking boat to his side at the wheel.

"I can always use another scout. Try to keep your gaze on the distance," he instructed. Blake kept one hand on the wheel and pointed out with the other. "Let your gaze scan in a sweeping motion. You'll be able to catch any movement, even out of your peripheral vision. Then you can zero in." He turned to look at her face. Their gazes locked; then he smiled.

Another boat zoomed by, creating a wide wake that rocked the Zodiac. She lost her footing and Blake's arm dropped to grab her around the waist, steadying her.

"Wouldn't want to lose you," he said.

She brushed the hair from her face and smiled self-consciously, hating that the man made her feel like a shy teenager. She was in new territory here and wasn't sure she liked not being in control.

Blake released her abruptly and reached for the gear-shift. "Hold on."

Carson grabbed the platform as he pushed the engines and the Zodiac took off again across the water. She'd given up wearing her hat and let her hair stream behind her. For the next few hours they traveled up and down the different rivers. It was a mystery to her how Blake knew where he was going; so much of it looked the same to her. They passed countless miles of muddy banks and acres of dark green cordgrass. From time to time they passed a cluster of houses, some of them modest campgrounds, others stunning homes with docks. Most of the time, however, it was like they were in *The African Queen*, journeying alone in the jungle, miles from civilization.

She saw small groups of female dolphins that included mothers and their young. The young calves stayed close, dorsal fins and glistening gray backs rising and falling together in the water as in a choreographed ballet. One curious youngster swam closer to the boat, its bright eyes gleaming with curiosity. Carson leaned over the side of the Zodiac, watching with delight and calling to it.

"Sweet baby," she crooned.

"Don't encourage him," Blake called out with a shake of his head. A moment later the mother swam up to steer her calf away, making loud clicking noises that sounded to Carson like she was scolding.

Whenever a dolphin was spotted, Blake killed the engines and grabbed for the camera. Carson eventually got better at sighting the dolphins as they rose and dipped in the water. To her chagrin, she only caught a fraction of the dolphins that Blake did, but when she spotted one, she felt a rush of adrenaline and shouted out the location.

Other times, however, she sat with the roar of the engines in her ears and watched Blake. His boyish enthusiasm was beguiling. More intriguing, however, was that his fervor was for something other than himself. This was in sharp contrast to so many of the men she'd dated before. Wealth, position, power—none of those things mattered to Blake, she realized. He wasn't looking at what he was going to get—more money, a new car, a vacation, or some fancy bottle of wine. She watched him, his hands on the wheel of the boat as he scanned the sea. Blake was looking at what he could give back.

And that spoke to Carson. Because of Delphine, she could understand what that passion felt like. She put her hand in the water and let it drag in the wake. She felt its coolness and felt connected to this water and everything in it. She gazed up into the infinite sky and felt connected to the birds of the air, the clouds, the grass that surrounded her, and the creatures of the sea. She felt this in her deepest nature. She was part of something so much bigger than herself. And this realization simultaneously made her feel more vulnerable and stronger than she ever had before.

As she bounced along the waterway in the boat, her face in the sunshine and the wind in her hair, Carson looked out at the natural beauty that surrounded her and it dawned on her why Blake had wanted her to see this. He was offering her a window to look through and really *see*. Not through a lens, but with all of her senses. To appreciate the significance of what was *wild*.

And in doing so, he was sharing with her a vital part of who he was.

A short while later Blake slowed the engines and brought the Zodiac close to a very small beach, larger than many of the sandy spits they'd passed that morning. The engines growled low as he brought them near, then suddenly all went silent. The Zodiac rocked while Blake hurried with the speed of experience to drop anchor. Carson listened to the sound of the gentle lapping of water against the boat and the creaking of the rope she clung to that ran along its sides.

"Ready for some lunch?" he asked her, offering his hand.

"Starving," she replied, taking it.

"Do you mind getting wet, or do you need me to carry you ashore?"

Carson smirked and for a moment thought she'd have him carry her, just because she could. The flat bottom of the Zodiac allowed Blake to get them close to shore. They only had to wade through knee-high water to get to the beach. After all the kite surfing, she'd have been too embarrassed not to wade in this short distance herself.

"I think I can manage it," she said with sarcasm.

"Careful of the mud," he cautioned her. "It can be slippery. And deep. I knew a guy who got stuck up to his knees in that slime. Had to lie on his back to pull his legs free."

Carson, swinging her leg over the edge of the boat, paused. "Are you trying to scare me? So you can carry me?"

"Just being a gentleman," Blake replied. "And did I mention the critters?"

Carson stiffened and drew her leg a bit farther back into the boat. "Critters?"

"Oh, sure," he said in a grand manner. "All kinds of insects call this mud home. And snails and fiddler crabs, of course." He shook his head. "Yep. Countless crabs. What do you think all those birds are feeding on?"

Carson looked down at the mud, squinting as she tried to see if anything was moving under the water.

"Thinking twice about my offer of a ride?"

"No, thanks anyway, Captain." Carson held firm to the rubber side of the boat and let her other leg swing over. "I'll take my chances." She scanned the water beneath her, then, taking a breath, let gravity do its job. She slid with a splash into the water. Her feet sank a few inches into the mud, but nowhere near as deep as Blake had implied.

"Oh, wow, I wonder how I'll ever make it to shore," she teased him.

"You never know," he said with a twinkle in his eye, then laughed. He put his sunglasses on, picked up his backpack and slung it over his shoulders, grabbed a large towel and draped it around his neck, then slid off the boat into the water.

They strode together through the muck to where the mud was dry and sandy. Blake chose a dry patch and spread out the towel, dropped his backpack, and indicated she should join him. She sat next to him on the towel and stretched her mud-and-sand-streaked legs out in the sun to dry.

They were enclosed in a private world rimmed with sparkling water and brilliant green grasses and trees. Above them was a vast azure sky dotted with thick white clouds. While Blake unpacked the food, Carson leaned back on her arms and listened to the sound of wind in the spartina grass and the occasional plop that could've been air bubbles in the banks, shrimp, or even a fish jumping in the distance. Above her she heard the piercing cries of the osprey, and looking up, she saw a black and white fish hawk circling.

"It's so peaceful here," she said with a sigh. "I feel a million miles away."

He smiled, pleased to see she was having a good time, and handed her a brown paper bag from the local island deli. She sat up, surprised at how hungry she was. Inside she found a thick turkey sandwich on whole wheat bread, a large chocolate chip cookie, and an apple. Blake opened a large thermos and poured her cup full of chilled sweet tea.

"I'm surprised you haven't gone out here before," Blake said.

"I've been out on boats many times, but never in this area." She looked around uncomprehendingly. They'd journeyed so far and so long. "Wherever we are," she added with a light laugh. "And it's been a long time since I've been in the lowcountry." Her voice turned wistful as she gazed out for the thousandth time that day. The view never got old. "I'd forgotten how beautiful it is . . ." She let her voice trail off.

"These waters have always been my backyard," Blake said, then bit into his sandwich.

Carson chewed and imagined him as a boy out in this great playland. No doubt skinny and as brown as a berry, his wild curls framing curious black eyes. He and Ethan were probably a lot like she and Harper used to be, only, even then, those two ruffians would've known every twist and turn of these waterways, where the sandbars were and the shallows. The best spots for fishing, swimming, and as they got older, tossing back a few cold ones. She smiled at the thought.

"What're you thinking?" he asked.

Startled, she realized she'd been daydreaming. She saw him sitting beside her with a huge sandwich in his hand, his cap over his head, and his cheeks slightly pink from the sun, and she could see the boy in the man.

"Were you a rebellious kid?" she asked, a gentle teasing tone in her voice.

Blake barked out a laugh. "Me?" he asked, his eyebrows raised, pointing to himself like the little boy she'd imagined.

"Yes, you," she replied, laughing.

"Yeah, I guess I was. A little. In a good way. Never broke the law or anything like that." He took a hearty gulp of his tea, then wiped his mouth with his hand. "I might've bent it a little."

"I'll bet," she said with a chuckle.

"What about you? Were you a wild child? Or were your parents the strict type?"

She drank some of her tea, thinking about how while Blake had been riding the water and kicking up a little dust on the roads, she had been in L.A. taking care of her father, cooking meals, cleaning their apartment, and shopping for food. The wildest it got for her was when she had to rise from her bed late at night, put on a coat, and go out alone to fetch him home from the bar.

"When I was a girl, Harper and I ran amok on the island, but the most trouble we ever got into was for exploring the tunnels of Fort Moultrie by ourselves. I only spent summers here when I was a girl. After that, I was in L.A. I didn't have much time to fool around. My mother died when I was four. So it was just me and my father. He depended on me."

Blake's brows gathered. "I'm sorry about your mother."

Carson shrugged the apology off, not wanting to spoil the mood. "I didn't really know her." Deftly, she turned the subject back to him. "What about your mother?"

Blake settled back and launched into stories about the big and boisterous Legare clan. She listened, mesmerized by the idea of having such a large family. He had the soul of a Southern storyteller. He could embellish colorful details and string her along in his easy cadence, all while she was laughing so hard tears came to her eyes. She could see these people, knew them as she'd known so many good, decent people coming up on Sullivan's Island. Even though she was here now, his stories made her feel homesick for the years she'd missed while away.

Carson was wiping a tear of laughter from her eye when she caught Blake watching her, a faint smile on his lips, his eyes as dark and full of mysteries as the creek mud. She felt a shiver, what Mamaw might have called a palpitation, and felt the zing of connection. In the quiet between them she was suddenly aware that she wanted this man, wanted to feel his lips on hers, more than she'd wanted a man for a very long time. Her gaze turned sultry in invitation as she pondered the thoughts that were surely running through his mind at that very moment.

Blake stirred and abruptly looked at his watch. "I guess we'd better be heading back. The clouds are moving in."

Carson felt a sudden deflation even as a gust of cooler wind stirred her hair and blew grains of sand in her face. She wished they could have stayed longer and talked more. They'd crossed some line and she would have liked to see where that led.

Then she looked up at the gathering clouds and roused herself to action. As she collected their trash and put it into the backpack, he shook the sand from the towel and once again tossed it around his shoulders.

Back in the boat, Blake was all business again, with one eye on the sky. His muscles strained as he pushed the boat off from the mud with a long metal pole. Once it was free, he rushed to the controls and opened the throttle. The big engine roared to life. Carson held tight to the rope and they took off in a spray of water. They rode without stopping, bouncing hard across the choppy water, making it back to the NOAA dock just as hearty, cool winds gusted through the grasses and the first drops of rain splattered hard, making pockmarks on the water.

Harper paid the cab fare as thunder rumbled overhead.

"That storm is moving in fast," the cabdriver said, handing her back the change.

"Yes." She took the receipt. "Thanks." Harper climbed from the cab and stood for a moment tasting the sweet moisture that always filled the air moments before a storm broke. She let her shoulders lower for the first time since she'd been away and just stood with her arms hanging at her sides, closed her eyes, and let the lowcountry breezes wash over her.

It had been a soul-wrenching ten days in New York. Her mother, in a fit of fury, had thrown Harper's clothing from her closet onto the floor. She'd ransacked her jewelry box and taken back any of the pieces that she'd given her.

Harper felt a drop of cold rain on her face and her eyes opened. From where she stood in the driveway, she saw the quaint white wooden cottage with its red front door under the arched cupola and the wide welcoming stairs. Though thunder rumbled overhead, Sea Breeze appeared nestled safely between ancient oaks, the boughs of which seemed to cradle the house like the gnarled fingers of some ancient guardian. Harper imagined them beckoning her to come inside, where soft golden light flowed from the windows, inviting her in from the storm.

Harper swayed on her feet as drops of rain splattered, cold and wet. She didn't move. She couldn't. She let the rain wash away the dust of the city, the grime of travel, and the stench of disillusionment. As she stood and stared at Sea Breeze, she felt the ice she'd formed around her heart begin to crack. She could almost hear the crackle as it splintered and melted to form tears that overflowed from her eyes and mingled with rain.

CHAPTER FIFTEEN

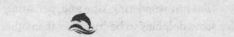

*T*he windshield wipers clicked at a steady rhythm as Blake and Carson headed back across the rivers, this time over the bridges in Blake's jeep. It had been a long, full day and Carson was exhausted, but exhilarated, too. Skimming the waterways in a boat, she'd felt like a visitor in the dolphins' world. The estuaries were their kingdom, where their families thrived. Blake had explained how a single pod could extend for miles and how they communicated by sonar across long distances and called to each other through a language of whistles and clicks. The resident dolphins were also intricately connected by elaborate social rituals.

All this made her wonder about one dolphin in particular and why she would part from her dolphin community to befriend a lonely human.

"I'm curious about something," she said, turning in the front seat to look from the road to Blake. The interior was dimly lit by the lights on the dashboard. "What about the dolphins that come close to humans? To the boats or docks. What makes them seek out human company?" She was glad he was driving so he couldn't meet her gaze, fearful that he'd read more into her question.

Blake groaned and shook his head. "Don't get me started."

"I'm just wondering," she said, persisting. "Is it normal for some dolphins to be friendlier than others?"

"If you can call it friendly. I call it begging. Dolphins aren't different from most other animals. If someone offers them food, they'll take the easy way out. When it happens over and over, they learn to beg for a living and lose their fear of humans. Think of the bears at Yosemite. It's no different here. They can become full-time moochers."

"Is it so bad to feed them? Even a little bit?"

He swung his head from the wheel and she saw fury flash in his eyes. "Yes, it's bad," he said with heat. He turned back to the road. "Feeding wild dolphins disrupts their social groups, which threatens their ability to survive in the wild. You saw those mothers with their young calves today?"

Carson nodded. It was a tender sight she'd never forget.

"They were teaching their young how to forage and hunt. If they beg, their calves grow up as beggars and never learn those skills. How well do you think they'll fare on a diet of hot dogs, pretzels, cookies, and candy? The calves won't survive. Not only that, going near the boats and docks puts the dolphins in danger of getting hurt by propellers, or entangled with fishing hooks and line. It's damned dangerous for the dolphins and heartless of the humans."

Carson didn't respond.

Blake tapped his fingers on the wheel. "I'm sorry," he said. "I didn't mean to get so hot under the collar."

"It's okay. . . . It's just, I don't think the people who feed the dolphins mean to hurt them."

"Maybe not. They think they're being kind. 'Just this one little bit.'" His face hardened. "We put signs up all over the place stating in bold letters, 'Do Not Feed the Dolphins.' We have educational pamphlets, ads on TV explaining how it hurts the dolphins. But if one person thinks it's okay if she does it, add that to a thousand others and you get the picture of how much feeding is going on."

"Right," Carson said, feeling deeply uncomfortable and not wanting to discuss this any longer.

Blake took his eyes off the road for a moment and looked at her. "I see the other side of the picture," he said in a calmer tone. "I have to necropsy the dolphins that wash ashore. The calves are dying at an alarming rate. Maybe if we put those pictures out, people would see just how those 'treats' are hurting them. No, Carson, feeding dolphins is not kind. It's self-indulgent. Selfish. People are thinking of themselves, not the dolphin."

Carson shrank back in her seat, silenced. She was one of *those people*. While she didn't feed Delphine, she looked the other way if Nate tossed her a fish that he'd caught. She saw in her mind's eye Delphine swimming gracefully in the water, the picture of health. Blake made her wonder if, in fact, Delphine was healthy. Was Carson drawing her away from her pod? Was Delphine becoming one of the dolphins increasingly dependent on human interaction and handouts from the dock?

"You look tired," Blake said, glancing at her.

"I am tired," she admitted. She felt flat, like a balloon that had deflated.

Blake turned on the radio and they listened to music the remaining distance to Sea Breeze. When Blake pulled into the drive the rain had dissipated to a soft drizzle.

"Would you like to go out again?" he asked.

"Sure," she replied. "When will you go next?"

"Next month."

So far away, she thought. "I'd love to. If I'm here next month."

"Where might you be?"

"Hopefully L.A. Or wherever I get a job."

He nodded his head but didn't reply.

"Or I may be here for months," she tossed into the mix. "I don't know."

"I see." He opened the door but she reached out to grab his arm, stalling him.

"Don't get out. It's raining. I'll just jump out." She offered a parting smile, but inside, she was cringing. She couldn't wait to flee the interior of the jeep and the guilt trip she'd just taken. "Thanks again."

"Bye," he said, and smiled, but his face appeared crestfallen.

The house felt strangely dark and empty. She heard the tinny voices from a television coming from Mamaw's

room. The kitchen was tidy but the scents of a fish dinner lingered. She looked at the fridge and thoughts of a
glass of chilled white wine caused a physical ache in her
body. She opened the door and peered inside. It was with
a mixture of relief and regret that she saw that Lucille
had been true to her word and had scoured the house to
dispose of all alcohol. Damn her efficiency. Carson stood
in front of the open fridge and just stared in, hungry but
not knowing what for. She was beyond tired and her eyes
felt gritty; she wondered if she wasn't coming down with
something. She reached for the filtered water and poured
herself a glass.

Her sandy heels slapped on the wood floors as she
made her way down the narrow hall to the west wing of
the house. As she approached the bedrooms she heard soft
music and the sound of fingers tapping a keyboard. Peering
in, she saw Harper sitting on a twin bed, head bent over a
computer. Delighted her sister was home, Carson pushed
open the door.

"Harper?" she exclaimed, bursting into the room.

Harper swung her head around and her face lit up
with genuine happiness at seeing her sister. "Carson!"

They leaped into each other's arms, Carson spilling
water from her glass. She set the glass on a dresser and
they commenced hugging and laughing, then moving to
the bed to curl their legs close and bubble over with news.

"How's the battle of the booze going?" Harper asked.

"Pretty well, actually. Still resisting."

"Really?" Harper asked, instantly intrigued. "The bet
was to give up booze for a week."

"I know, but I've managed to push on. I'm kind of

testing my will. I can't say I still don't want a glass of wine or a margarita, but I can resist. Good to know."

"Maybe then you're not an alcoholic after all?"

"Maybe. And just maybe the slower pace and my general sense of well-being doesn't demand the alcohol the way my life—and my lifestyle—in L.A. did."

"Doesn't really matter, does it? I'm proud of you. Really. And by the way, you won the bet. I drank my weight in wine dealing with my mother in New York."

The girls erupted in laughter.

Down the hall, Mamaw heard the commotion and crept on slippered feet from her room toward the west wing. Her hand rested on the wall and she leaned forward, tilting her head so her ear was closer to the noise. Mamaw heard the high-pitched voices rise and fall in conversation, punctuated with laughter. Her face softened as images from the past flitted across her mind. She didn't mean to pry but she couldn't help lingering a little while longer. She leaned against the wall and closed her eyes. She wasn't able to comprehend the words but listened to the cadence of the sweet music of reconciliation and reconnection. Mamaw's lips curved in a smile of deep satisfaction.

Carson was roused from a restless sleep by the ding of her telephone, signaling that a message had been received. She stirred and reached out to the bedside table to retrieve her phone, blinking to adjust her vision. The text was from Blake.

Dinner tonight?

Carson fell back against her pillow and looked out the plantation shutters to the first gray light of dawn. Of course he'd already be awake . . . She lifted her phone and punched in her reply.

Yes.

"Want to go to Dunleavy's?" Blake asked later that evening.

Carson winced. "No, let's not."

Blake grinned. "How does barbecue sound?"

"I never say no to a good barbecue."

They were lucky to find a parking space in front of the restaurant. People of all ages overflowed from all the restaurants, filling the night with the low murmur of conversation and the occasional piercing laugh.

The Home Team restaurant had tables outside under the awning that were open. Blake hustled to claim one. The waitress was a perky young woman with enormous blue eyes and red hair that made Carson think of Harper. They'd spent hours the night before talking, mixing giggles with tears. Her sister had turned out to be a deeply emotional girl. This surprised her. As a woman, Harper struck Carson as the kind of person who preferred to keep her distance. A watcher instead of a player. Her style of dress enhanced that impression. She was as sleek and refined as a Siamese cat. There was almost a tangible chill around her that kept others from invading her space. Other than when she drank, Carson remembered with a smile. Then it was as if she let down her barriers and became a girly girl.

Last night, however, there had been no alcohol.

She'd been animated and forthcoming, and funny as hell. Who knew the girl had such a wit? And she was observant. When they talked about their childhood summers together, Harper remembered so many more vivid, telling details than Carson did. She had the memory of a scribe.

The waitress came up and whipped out her pencil and pad. "What would you like to drink?"

"Iced tea," Carson ordered. "Unsweetened."

"Make that two," Blake said. "And we can put in our order, too. Two pulled-pork sandwiches, sides of sweet potato fries, fried tomatoes, coleslaw, and collards. And don't take all night; this lady's always starving."

The waitress laughed and collected their menus.

"Well played," Carson told him.

The waitress was quick to deliver the drinks, along with a basket of hush puppies.

"On the house," she told them, taking an extra-long look at Blake.

Carson and Blake reached for the hush puppies simultaneously.

"Oh God," Carson groaned as she bit into a soft, hot fried ball of corn bread. "I don't know if these aren't the best hush puppies I've ever eaten."

"Agreed," he said while chewing. They popped hush puppies into their mouths and looked out at the tourists laughing and talking as they paraded past.

She stirred her drink, wondering if they were friends enough for her to ask this question. "Blake, I hope I'm not too forward, but why don't you drink?"

"I'm not an alcoholic, and it's not a religious thing or

anything like that. I'll have a drink from time to time. It's no big deal."

"You don't like the taste?" she asked, genuinely curious.

His face clouded and he looked at the tea. "It's not that. I like it fine, I reckon. I don't like what it does to me," he answered.

Carson remained silent. The laughter and noise of the bar diminished to a white noise around them as she focused on the man. She leaned forward, not willing to miss a word.

"I used to drink a lot," Blake said. "You know as well as I that if you get a bunch of good ol' boys together, they're going to be up for a good time. And it usually involves alcohol. When I was a teenager, I wasn't a bad kid, but I was fearless. What kid isn't when he's eighteen, driven by his testosterone, and believes he's immortal?"

"I dated a lot of guys like that," she replied. "I think Devlin is still like that."

"Yeah, well, some guys never grow up. Me, I grew up fast when I was eighteen."

She watched as his long, tanned fingers wrapped around his glass and he stared at the dark tea. And waited.

"It was a rainy week up at Clemson, and while some of the kids grumbled about the rain, my buddy Jake and I grabbed the keys to his Bronco and headed out mudding. We met up with some other guys and had a helluva good time out on some country road. If I was fearless, Jake was überfierce. He loved that damn Bronco." He lifted the tea to his mouth and took a drink.

"I don't know if it was because we were drinking or

if it was just one of those things, but Jake veered off the road and that Bronco overturned." Blake paused. "Jake wasn't wearing his seat belt. He got ejected from the car and pinned by that damned Bronco. I was wearing my seat belt. I was injured pretty bad but I survived. I was in a kind of harness he'd put in; he'd bolted those mounting plates himself. I hung there trapped for what seemed a lifetime, pinned and helpless, listening to Jake's life ebb out of him."

"I'm so sorry," she said, unable to even imagine the horror.

He was quiet and stared at his plate. "You never forget something like that. I still wonder why Jake didn't wear his seat belt that night. I mean, he retrofitted that Bronco for safety." He shook his head. "I can only figure it was because we were drinking so much. He didn't use good judgment." He lifted his head and looked at her. "I just lost my taste for the stuff."

Carson desperately wanted to reach out and touch him but felt it would be too forward.

"Thank you for sharing that," she told him.

The night sky was darkening and the light in the bar was attracting suicidal moths. The waitress returned with their dinners, breaking the awkward silence between them.

After they dove in and slaked their hunger, Blake turned the question back to her. "How about you? Did you swear off the stuff, too?"

Carson set down her pork sandwich and picked up a paper napkin to dab at her mouth. "I'm just not drinking now. It's kind of a bet I had with Harper. We wanted to see if we could stop for a week. Then one week went to two. Now we're seeing if we can go for the summer." She shook her head. "I don't know if I'm going to make it. A beer tonight sure would've tasted good with this barbecue."

"You stop missing it after a while. You lose the taste for it," Blake said.

Carson added artificial sugar to her unsweetened tea and stirred it with her straw. The ice clinked tantalizingly and she took a sip. It was good. Delicious even. But it wasn't a beer.

"I hope that's true. To tell you the truth, right now, a day doesn't go by when I don't crave maybe just one beer or a glass of wine."

She let her fingertip collect the condensation forming on her glass of iced tea while inside, her heart was racing as she wondered how much she should tell him. Her eyes flicked to the bar, where a line of people sat on stools, chatting with glasses in their hands; to the row of potted shrubs outside the porch; to the shellacked table, searching for anywhere to look except at him.

"I know that as long as I have this craving, I haven't answered the bigger question. Whether or not I can really stop."

The words sounded so matter-of-fact, but glancing at his face, she saw that he was listening carefully without emotion or judgment.

This encouraged Carson to continue. As the small votive candle flickered between them, she told him about her father, how his drinking had interfered with his life and talent. As her food went cold on the plate, she fleshed out the skeleton, giving him a glimpse into her life caring for her father, how she'd left him at eighteen to fend for herself, only for him to die alone a few years later. She began drinking socially, but in her line of work, people drank socially around the clock. It was only recently that she'd begun wondering if she carried the family gene for alcoholism.

When she was finished, the other tables on the porch were empty. Only the bar was still crowded, and more rowdy as well.

"Want to take a walk on the beach?" Blake asked.

Carson exhaled heavily and nodded. She had the uncomfortable feeling of having just exposed her underbelly, and the thought of stretching her legs sounded perfect.

They headed toward the beach, walking close. He matched his long-legged pace to her slower one. The moon was bright, and once they broke free from the streetlights and their feet hit the sand, they could see the wide swath of velvety black sky over the ocean and the stars twinkling. Blake surprised her by taking her hand.

Carson was keenly aware of his closeness as they walked side by side. The moon was full and the sky littered with stars. Not too far away, the surf rolled in and out in a sleepy rhythm. She almost laughed, thinking how if this was a job she'd be shooting a commercial for a romantic island weekend, complete with two lovers strolling the beach. Except that they weren't lovers. This thought rankled. When was he going to make his move? She wanted to feel his arms around her, his lips on hers, to make love with him.

She became increasingly aware of the feel of his hand over hers, of each neuron aflame in that small area of skin. As they walked in the uneven sand, their hips or shoulders would bump, sending shivers of awareness down her spine.

Then he stopped and turned to face her. His thumb lightly rubbed the top of her hand. "Carson, yesterday, when you said you might be leaving . . . Did it occur to you that I might care if you leave?"

She put her hands on his chest. "I hoped you might care."

He stood just a few inches away in the darkness, so close she could see his lips curve into a slow, pleased grin. "Carson," he said with a hint of exasperation, "I've been caring for weeks now."

Carson was thirty-four years old. She'd had multiple lovers over the years and considered herself well experienced in the ways of men. Even jaded. So what was it about this man that had her blushing like she was a ridiculous teenager?

He reached out and let his fingers trail gently up her bare arms. Her breaths traced each millimeter of the slow and deliberate journey, marking the path with goose bumps. His hands slid behind her back and tugged her closer.

Carson reached up to slip her own arms around his neck, pressing herself against him in invitation. But he was not to be rushed. He lowered his lips to her neck and tasted her there, then made a deliciously slow journey along her jawline toward her mouth. It was as though he'd waited so long for the feast, he was in no hurry.

When at last he brought his mouth over hers, she opened her mouth in welcome and pressed against him. He was gentle at first, testing. Then his arms tightened around her, crushing her against him. She felt devoured by his mouth. As the kiss deepened she felt his hands roam from her back to slip under her T-shirt to her breasts. Her nipples hardened and she groaned slightly.

He pulled back, letting his hands slide to her forearms but keeping his hold on her. "We should go," he said. He took her hand again and they retraced their steps along the beach at a more determined pace, through the darkened access path, and up the streets of the neighborhood to his car. He opened her car door, then made his way around the front and climbed in behind the wheel. He turned to Carson.

"Will you come by my place?"

His hands were on the wheel and he wasn't touching her, but her body felt aflame. The attraction between them was so thick, it felt almost like she was still kissing him.

"Yes. Yes," she repeated.

Blake smiled and lifted his hand to smooth a lock of hair from her face. He leaned toward her and his lips grazed hers. She thought he'd meant to just kiss her softly, but his touch was explosive and ignited their passion like a spark on dried tinder. They lunged for one another, each hungry for more. His hands trembled as they rounded her shoulders, pushing her back, then slid along the curve of her back, then up again as he pressed tighter. Then, in sudden decision, he drew back.

Carson gasped, her lips still tingling. As Blake fired

the engine, Carson leaned back and closed her eyes, and though she'd not had a drop to drink, she felt like she was high. As they drove off, her blood was racing and her heart palpitating, making her feel carefree and giddy, like she was riding in the Zodiac again.

Carson awoke with a start. Her head shot up and she sucked in her breath. Her eyes searched the small room, the tilted blinds at the window through which gray morning light seeped, revealing clothes littered on the floor. Some of them were her clothes.

She heard a low, rumbling snore beside her, and turning her head, she saw Blake asleep on his belly, his mouth slightly agape and his hair disheveled. The sheet barely covered half of his butt. It was a nice butt, she thought with a smile as moments from the previous evening began to work back into her consciousness. Blake was as good as his kisses promised. Slow and deliberate, he liked to take his time.

She rose slowly, careful not to wake him. Carson tiptoed around the room, picking up her clothes and slipping them on, each creak of the wood floor sounding like an alarm in her head. It was a typical bachelor pad. Clothes strewn about the furniture; keys, pens, soda cans, and bits of paper scattered on the dresser; a poster of NASCAR on the wall.

The rest of the apartment was a continuation of the bedroom, an eclectic array of confusion. She thought this was very unlike the perception she had of the man, who in her mind was fastidious and precise. The furniture was functional without thought to color, design, or size. Bookshelves along the wall overflowed with books, and the small wood table was covered with books and papers and a laptop, turned off but open. The bicycle by the front door was a nice touch, she thought with a chuckle.

In contrast to the rest of the place, his kitchen, though cluttered, was clean. She gave him high marks for not having dirty dishes in the sink. With trepidation, she peeked in the fridge, expecting a withered apple and sour milk. At the sound, Hobbs trotted across the room to her side. She was relieved and impressed to find fresh organic milk, a plastic jug of filtered water, a bag of crisp carrots, celery, cheese, and some fresh fruit.

While rummaging through the man's refrigerator, Carson heard a footfall from behind. She turned, slightly embarrassed. "Pillaging your fridge." She smiled.

Standing in his boxers, Blake scratched his belly and yawned. When he drew near, he reached out to pull her close and lightly kissed her.

"Good morning, beautiful," he said.

He really did look cute in the morning, she thought, letting her hands slide up his hard chest. "Morning," she replied.

Hobbs pushed his head against Blake's thigh to be patted.

"Hungry?" he asked her. "Hobbs is."

She didn't know whether he was teasing her about finding her searching his fridge, or whether he was beginning that silly game of innuendo and she was supposed to reply with something banal about how she was hungry for his kisses. Though she was, she couldn't utter the corny words.

"I'd surf with a shark for some coffee," she replied.

He smirked. "Coffee. Right." He kissed her nose and released her to fill the coffeemaker with water.

"Can I help?"

"There's a bag of ground coffee in the fridge," he told her. "And pull out that bag of grits, too, will you?"

She liked where his thoughts were heading.

They worked in tandem, putting together the grits, butter, milk, and water. When Blake pulled out a chunk of cheddar cheese, Carson balked.

"No cheese," she said, grabbing the cheddar and holding it close. "It ruins the taste of the grits."

"Does not," he said, reaching for the cheese.

"Does too," she said, laughing now as he gripped her, manhandling her in the tussle for the cheese.

Blake won and stepped back, triumphantly holding the cheese in the air, out of reach while Hobbs barked.

"Really, Blake," she moaned, "grits are best plain with lots of butter."

"Trust me," he told her, lowering his arm. "With eggs, you want the cheese."

"So much for showing a girl a good time," she quipped.

"You'll see," he said, smirking.

While Blake stirred the eggs, they sipped hot coffee and shared some of the twists and turns of their lives, the crazy chapters, the poignant moments. All part of the usual dating interrogation. His fascination with marine life had been lifelong and marked most of his memorable moments.

"Aren't you still tempted to explore other areas?"

He stirred the grits, considering. "I still travel a lot, to conferences or to study. I spent several months volunteering in the Gulf after the oil-spill debacle. We're seeing a significant increase in untimely deaths of dolphins in that area and I fear we'll see repercussions from that disaster for many years to come."

"No, I mean to just pick up and go. To travel for the sake of traveling."

He shook his head. "I'm thirty-seven. I got that out of my system. My head's in a different place now." He looked up at her, suddenly serious. "What about you?"

Carson sipped her coffee, unsure of her answer. "If you'd asked me that question a month ago, I wouldn't have hesitated. I liked to say I went wherever the wind blew. The minute I heard about a photo job, anywhere in the world, I'd be on the first plane out. I spent the last four years based in L.A. with a TV series. It was a change for me. I thought I'd love staying in one place, going out with the same people, maybe save a few dollars."

"I take it you didn't?"

She shook her head. "Actually, I did. For a while. But by the time the series was canceled I was already feeling the wanderlust. I hated my apartment and had broken up with my boyfriend."

"Maybe L.A. was the wrong place," Blake suggested. "I loved the Bahamas, but it wasn't home."

Carson caught the faint whisper of hope in his tone. "Maybe," she said, but she was unconvinced.

"Stir this for me?" Blake said, handing her the spoon. When she took the wooden spoon he grabbed hold of her waist and lowered his head. "I needed to kiss you just now."

She laughed lightly, feeling a bubbling of interest. When his lips touched her, it was spontaneous combustion all over again. Blake reached over to turn the heat off the grits. Then he reached down to lift her off her feet in his arms.

"Wait," Carson called out, waving the spoon, dripping grits on the floor that Hobbs quickly dispensed.

Blake walked her to the sink, where she dropped the spoon. Laughing, she ducked her head on his shoulder as he carried her to his bedroom. Suddenly all the terribly corny comments about being hungry for something other than grits easily flowed from her tongue.

CHAPTER SIXTEEN

*T*he following day Carson sat on the dock, her feet dangling in the water, waiting for Nate. The seawater was warming as summer progressed. She knew that by September the ocean would feel like bathwater to her. She'd developed a routine with Delphine. If she whistled and banged on the dock, Delphine would often appear. Carson longed to see her, and knew that Nate would be eager as well. Yet today she found she could not call her.

Blake's words came to mind. *Feeding dolphins is not kind. It's self-indulgent. Selfish. People are thinking of themselves, not the dolphin.* Carson kicked the water mulishly. Sure, she'd heard the warnings about not feeding the dolphins. She'd seen the signs. She'd just thought that her bond with Delphine was special. She'd rationalized that it was okay for her, even if it wasn't okay for everyone else. The trouble was, she still wanted her relationship with Delphine. She didn't know if she could give it up. She was torn about what to do. As she sat, swinging her legs in the water, one word played over and over again in her mind. *Selfish.*

The reverberations of footfalls on the dock drew her attention. She looked up to see Nate negotiating the step down to the lower dock. He was filling out; his life preserver didn't hang so pitifully from his shoulders. He was also tan and his light brown hair was turning blond from the sun. She smiled, thinking how much her nephew looked like a typical beach boy.

"Hi, Nate," she called out. "Ready to swim?"

Nate looked out over the water. "Where is Delphine?"

Carson paused, knowing full well that his fixation on the dolphin was not going to be easy to dampen. Still, she'd made up her mind to do the right thing.

"She's out there somewhere. Either playing with her friends or hunting fish. Let's just go in the water and have a good time."

"Call her, Aunt Carson."

"I already tried," she lied, not wanting a meltdown. "Come on, let's jump in the water. She'll come if she wants to."

Nate searched the water again while Carson held her breath. Then he seemed to accept what she'd said at face value and began to climb down the ladder into the water.

Carson followed him, realizing she might have come upon the solution to her moral dilemma. She wouldn't feed the dolphin any longer, nor would she call her to the dock. Delphine would come *if she wanted to.*

That evening Mamaw was in the kitchen getting a glass of milk when she heard a strange creaking and rustling outside on the porch. She set down the glass and walked to the door. Darn raccoons were back again, she muttered to herself. She flicked on the light and opened the door. She was startled to see Nate. He froze with eyes wide like a deer in the headlights. In his arms he precariously balanced three fishing rods and a bait box.

"What on earth?" Mamaw asked.

Nate didn't say a word. He only lowered his arms and squinted in the bright light.

"Nate, what are you doing out here?" she asked him, her tone scolding. "Do you know what time it is?"

"It's eleven thirty," Nate replied.

Mamaw couldn't quite get accustomed to how literal the boy was. "Yes, and that's way past your bedtime."

"I know."

"What are you doing? Are you going fishing?"

"No. I'm setting out my rods."

"At this time of night?"

"I had to wait until everyone was asleep. It's a surprise. I want to have fish for Delphine in the morning so she'll come. I'm going to set my rods the way the old man told me that he did. He set his rods and left them, and when he came back he had a fish."

A few days earlier Mamaw's neighbor Mr. Bellows had been fishing on his dock. Mamaw had gone over to talk to him. They'd known each other for years. When she returned, she told Nate that he could go to the neighbor's dock and watch him fish. When he'd told her he was afraid, she'd said the best way to learn the ropes of fishing was to watch those more experienced. Then she told him that the old man—Mr. Bellows—had been a good friend of Papa Edward, and that if Papa were here, he would have taught him how to fish, just like he'd taught Carson how to fish.

"Nate," Mamaw said gently now, "I understand it's a surprise. But you know it's against the rules to go out on the dock alone."

"That is my mother's rule. It's not Carson's rule. I've decided I don't want to be with my mother anymore. Or my father. I don't like it when they fight. I want to stay here with you and Carson. And Delphine. So I have to obey Carson's rules. And Carson never told me that I can't go out on the docks alone. So I'm not breaking Carson's rules."

"Well, if that doesn't take the cake," Mamaw muttered to herself. To Nate she said, "Dear boy, you present your argument logically. However, your basic premise is wrong. You do not get to decide if you're going to stay with Carson or your mother. Your mother is your mother. Period. That will never change. Secondly, when it comes to you, your mother's rules are the rules of this house as well. Thus, there is no going out on the dock alone. Not tonight. Not ever."

Nate's shoulders slumped. "But I must set up my rods. I already made my bait balls. I spent four dollars and twenty-three cents on the ingredients and hooks. That leaves me with only seventy-seven cents of my five dollars. I don't have any more money for another batch."

In for a penny, in for a pound, Mamaw thought to herself, and closed the door behind her. Besides, what was the harm? He was filled with all the crazy dreams and schemes of a boy.

"All right, Nate. If I go with you, then you won't be breaking the rules. Hand me a few of the rods."

The night was cooler than expected. The stars and the moon were blocked by cloud cover, so it was especially dark. Nate carried a flashlight, which lit their way along the stone path. Mamaw had never liked traipsing in the wild at night. She couldn't see the snakes and spiders and other creepy-crawlies she knew were in that grass. When her feet stepped onto the wood of the dock, she felt much better. She followed Nate just a short way down the dock; then he stopped and put down his gear.

Mamaw held the flashlight for Nate as he pulled a plastic garbage bag out from his tackle box.

"These are called mud balls," Nate told her, lifting the mushy balls from the bag. Mamaw had to lift her nose higher, they smelled so bad. "The old man next door taught me how to make them. He told me to use cat food and bread mixed with mud. He said this'll sure bring them around and to make sure I used the damn cat food."

Mamaw chuckled to herself. That did indeed sound like Hank. "His name is Mr. Bellows."

"Mr. Bellows," Nate repeated as he worked.

"You're very good at that," Mamaw told him. "Did you ever do it before?"

"No. Just with the old man, Mr. Bellows. My father has some good poles and rigging in the shed at home, but he only took me fishing one time. That was two years ago when I was seven. He got mad when I made mistakes. He doesn't know how to make mud balls. He didn't catch any fish, either. Mr. Bellows catches many fish. He's a much better fisherman than my father."

Mamaw sighed, feeling for the boy. She didn't interfere as Nate carefully attached a leader to the bottom of the line. When he pulled out the hook that looked like a fish with bulging red eyes and several claw hooks, he looked up at Mamaw and smiled. She had purchased that one for him, not having a clue what kind of a fish it caught, just because she thought it was so comical. She stepped in to help him bait the hooks.

Nate cast the lures out and spent a good deal of time spacing the rods evenly along the deck railing, making sure that they were each approximately two feet apart.

"The old man, Mr. Bellows, said a tangled line is the kiss of death," Nate told Mamaw. "I know it isn't really a kiss. It means that it's a bad thing for the line to get tangled."

"I see." Mamaw found it fascinating how Nate took the details of his task so seriously. She watched as he carefully tied each of the poles by the handle to the railing of the dock with a piece of nylon rope. He tied double knots, saying he wanted them to hold the fish until he got back in the morning.

"Looks good and tidy," Mamaw told him. "I think it's time we went back to our beds."

As they walked up the dock, every few feet Nate looked back to make sure the poles were where he'd left them.

"I'm sure we'll catch something," Nate told her as they entered the house and closed the door behind them.

CHAPTER SEVENTEEN

*C*arson woke from a strange dream about her mother with her heart pounding, tears running down her face, and a profound sense of longing. She blinked heavily in the dim light of predawn. In the dream it was foggy and she was swimming through choppy water. Her mother was calling to her but she couldn't reach her. She hardly ever dreamed of her mother, but this time . . . even awake, it still felt so real.

A strange ear-piercing noise echoed from outside. Was it a bird? Or someone crying? Waking further, she lifted her head, alert, and sharpened her listening. That was no bird. That was a dolphin's scream!

Carson whipped back her blanket, thrust her feet into her flip-flops, and tore through the house, out the door. Outside, the dolphin's screams pierced the air, frantic and fearful. Nothing like she'd ever heard before. As she ran she cried out, "Delphine!"

The sky was overcast and the water was rough with

the current and wind. Her heart was pumping hard in her chest as she raced to the end of the dock. She searched but didn't see the dolphin. Then she froze and listened hard. The screaming was not at the end of the dock at all. It was behind her, nearer the shore. She gripped the railing and looked over the side.

"No!" Her heart rose to her throat at the sight.

Delphine was in shallow water, close to the dock, struggling like she was caught in something. The dolphin saw Carson on the dock and began flapping her tail and screaming louder in a panic. Squinting, Carson could see that the dolphin was ensnared in loops of fishing line, barely able to move. There was so much of it! Like a spider's web, and Delphine was caught in its center. Two fishing rods were floating in the water beside her. Stepping back, she saw a third was wedged in the railing of the pier.

"Delphine!" she screamed as a thousand thoughts ran through her mind. She brought her hands to her cheeks. *Calm down. Focus*, she told herself. What should she do first?

Carson raced back into the house to the kitchen phone. On the bulletin board, Mamaw had a list of emergency numbers. Then she remembered. Blake. Where was her phone?

"Mamaw!" she cried as she raced down the hall to her room to grab her purse. "Dora! Harper! Someone help!"

She found her phone and her hand shook as she punched in Blake's number. She heard the phone ring, her heart pounding, and prayed he'd answer. The line picked up.

"Blake?"

"Carson?"

"Come quick. Delphine is caught in the fishing wire. You've got to help her!"

"Delphine?"

"The dolphin!"

"Let me get this straight." His voice was more alert now, focused. "You have a dolphin entangled with fishing line at your dock?"

"Yes. Hurry."

"How bad is it?"

"Bad. It's cutting into her flesh."

"Right. I'll be there as soon as I can. Carson, listen to me. No heroics. Stay away from it." He hung up.

Carson could hear Delphine's screaming. "Forget that," she muttered, and pulled out the desk drawer as Harper ran into the kitchen.

"What's going on? God, what's that god-awful noise?"

"It's Delphine," Carson said, grabbing a pair of scissors. She raced back to the water with Harper at her heels. There were sharp pebbles on the shore but she plowed through the cold sand and chilly water without pause.

Harper stopped at the water's edge. "Carson, don't go near her."

Carson ignored her. She was fueled with adrenaline. Delphine, seeing Carson approach, began to squirm.

"I'm here. Shhhh . . . settle down," Carson called out, slowing down as she drew near Delphine. The dolphin's watery eyes looked into hers. Carson wanted to cry when she saw the devastating damage. The fine line entangled Delphine from pectoral to dorsal fin to fluke. Every time the dolphin had to come up for air, she'd strained against the line, forcing the wire to slice deeper into her flesh like a razor. Carson reached out to lift Delphine's head and hold her blowhole above the water. All around Delphine's once-pristine, gleaming body she saw lacerations crisscrossing the flesh, so deep the lines were invisible.

Worst of all, though, was her mouth. The crazy-looking hook that Mamaw had given Nate as a joke, the one that looked like a small fish with a freakish eye and two multipronged claw hooks, was deeply embedded in Delphine's mouth. Carson wanted to scream in fury at seeing the tender flesh ripped to shreds. Blood dripped into the water and Carson knew she had to worry about sharks as well. She studied the wire and began to cut as many of the lines as she could, but some of them were so knotted and close to the wounds, she thought she'd better leave them for Blake.

"I'm here," she told Delphine, close to her face. It felt to Carson that the wires were slicing her own heart as well. "Don't worry. I'm here for you. No matter what, I won't leave you."

"Carson!" Harper called with uncertainty from the shore.

"Go keep an eye out for Blake," Carson called back.

Harper turned on her heel and hurried back toward the house.

Delphine began to calm when the clouds opened up and dumped a pounding deluge of rain. Carson bent over Delphine to shield her blowhole. The pelting rain stung her back like tiny balls of ice. Carson coughed and spat out salt water as the wind swept waves into her face. She wouldn't leave Delphine. She had to keep the blowhole above the water.

Mercifully, the cloud was typically fast-moving, on its way from the mainland to the ocean. The driving rain slowed, then dwindled to a faint drizzle. Her thick hair streamed down her face, the salt water stinging her eyes, and her T-shirt clung to her like a second skin, but she didn't let go. Looking up, she sighed with relief to see the soft light of dawn rising in a pale pink and blue clear sky. She held on to Delphine and prayed it was an omen.

The government-issued jeep skidded to a stop alongside Sea Breeze. Carson looked up from the water and in the distance she saw a door slam and a man leap from the car. Harper was pointing toward the dock. Blake swung a backpack over his shoulder as he trotted down the sandy incline toward the dock.

Mamaw, dressed in a flowing robe, also came running from the house, followed by Dora, still in pajamas. They stepped out of the way as Blake ran past them to the dock. Carson heard the dock reverberating with the weight of the footfalls, echoing below where she stood. Startled, Delphine struggled anew to free herself, causing the monofilament to cut deeper into her skin.

"Down here! Hurry!" Carson called out. At her shouting Delphine squirmed again. "Shhh . . . stop, Delphine," Carson cried, desperately holding the dolphin's massive head out of the water. Her arms felt numb and screamed with pain. But it was nothing compared to the pain she knew Delphine felt. "Please, stop moving. It's okay. Someone's here to help. Hang on a little longer." Her back ached from bending over in the awkward position and her arms were clamped like vises around the rubbery dolphin.

She almost wept with relief when she saw Blake rushing around the dock. He was in his blue NOAA T-shirt. Blake tossed his backpack on the ground and plowed into the water. As he drew near, his dark eyes flashed in fury at seeing her in the water, then swiftly shifted to the dolphin. He cursed when he saw the monofilament line cutting into the dolphin's flesh.

"What happened?" His voice was rough with worry.

"I heard the dolphin screaming when I woke up," Carson told him, speaking rapidly. "I came running. I found her all tangled up in the fishing line. That's when I called you. I cut away as much as I could."

"What idiot left this line out?" he shouted. "I've never seen such a bad case. And this goddamn hook!" He almost sputtered in fury when he bent to investigate the large, multipronged hook deeply embedded in Delphine's mouth.

He didn't wait for an answer. He left Carson's side and pushed through the water to retrieve his pack and dig out his cell phone. His whole body radiated wrath as he stared at the dolphin and talked rapidly on the phone.

"Legare here. I got a dolphin seriously tangled in fishing line. It's bad. Very bad. Large hook embedded in the mouth. Dolphin's movements are severely restricted. Deep cuts. I need a vet ASAP. And wet transport. Meanwhile, check availability for rehab. Location is Sullivan's

Island. Sea Breeze . . . Yeah, that's the one. How long? . . .
He is? Good. This is a priority situation. Thanks." He put
the phone in his bag and came directly back to the dolphin's side.

"I've got this," he said as his long arms reached under
the dolphin in support. "Go on. Carson, take a break.
You're shivering."

"I'm not leaving her," Carson said.

Blake returned a firm stare. Gone was the easygoing,
smitten man she'd spent the night with. There was no
room for flirtation in this man's demeanor. He was in
charge and clearly not happy to see her in the water.

"Look. This is a dangerous situation. With her thrash-
ing, you could get seriously hurt."

"She wouldn't hurt me."

"She wouldn't, huh?"

"No," Carson said. "We're friends. Why can't you just
cut the lines off?"

"They're too deeply embedded and if I loosen them
she might try and swim away. We don't want to lose her
in this condition. She wouldn't survive with all that line
around her. And she'll need a vet to cut that hook out.
Shit, what a bloody mess. He should be here soon." He
squinted his eyes and said with impatience, "Why are we
having this conversation? Get out of the water, Carson.
It's not safe."

He turned his attention back to Delphine, gently
stroking her body, her face. He didn't coo or offer any
words of solace. But she did stop fighting and Carson
thought that somehow, Delphine understood that Blake
cared and was here to help.

Then, as if her words had suddenly sunk in, he turned and asked, "What do you mean, you're friends?"

"I *know* this dolphin. She comes to the dock."

"Delphine . . ." he said, repeating the name he'd heard on the phone.

She nodded.

"You don't *name* a wild animal. That can only lead to something bad, like this." His voice grew dark with suspicion. "Tell me you didn't *feed* her."

Carson felt hunted and looked away from his critical gaze. Her silence was his answer.

"Great," he shot out. "Damn it. See what you've done? This isn't Flipper. This is a wild animal! You don't *feed* a wild animal. You don't *swim* with a wild animal, and you sure as hell don't *make friends* with a wild animal."

Carson was stricken. "I know!" she cried. "*Now*. I never thought anything like this could happen." Looking at Delphine's ravaged back and listening to her labored exhales, she felt Blake's words cut as deeply in her mind as the fishing line. "She came on her own. She found *me*. I'd never hurt her."

"You wouldn't, huh?"

His words cut so deep she felt her knees weaken. She clamped her eyes shut to keep the tears from coming as she clung tight to Delphine.

His anger diminished somewhat. He took a breath. "I'm sure you didn't mean to hurt her. I don't believe anyone who feeds a wild dolphin means to hurt it." He looked down at Delphine in his arms. "But this is what happens."

Carson couldn't respond.

Delphine squirmed again, attempting to flap her powerful tail. With each push the slender, invisible fishing lines dug deep through the flesh like a razor.

"Hold her steady!" Blake shouted, struggling with Delphine's head.

"I'm trying!" Carson shouted back at him over the dolphin's body. It was near impossible to restrain Delphine's power, even wounded. She brought her face close to Delphine's eyes and murmured soothingly to calm her. "Delphine, it's going to be all right. We're going to help you. I won't leave you." Delphine responded to her voice and ceased struggling.

"Good. Keep it up. It's working," Blake acknowledged.

"I love her," Carson choked out, looking up into his dark eyes, still so deeply distrustful.

She saw the scorn dissipate in his gaze, but his face was still taut. "I believe you. But frankly, so what?"

"I know. God, I know and I'm so sorry." She couldn't stop apologizing. "What's going to happen to her?"

"We'll find out after the vet gets here. And I hope it's soon. Every time she moves, those lacerations get worse." He glanced up and searched her face. His own reflected worry. "You're shivering, and your lips are turning blue. Why don't you get out for a while?"

"No. She'll get upset if I leave her," Carson said, even though she didn't know how much longer she could hold on. She felt Delphine's energy waning as the minutes ticked by. "When are they going to get here?"

"They'll be here," he answered. As though in reply, they heard the loud beeping of a truck backing up. He looked over her shoulder. "That's them now."

Carson looked up to the house to see a yellow Penske truck backing in. The rear lights flashed as it parked and the doors swung open. Two young men came running toward them, each wearing a diver's top over a swimsuit. They were carrying a bright blue stretcher.

"Carson, you can let go now. Go up and get something warm on. You'll just be in the way."

"No, I—"

"Carson," he said firmly, cutting her off. "Let us handle it now. It's best for the dolph— for Delphine."

Carson nodded and carefully released Delphine. Blake held tight as Carson stepped away. The muscles in her arms felt like they were being pricked by a thousand needles. As Carson left Delphine's side and stumbled out of the water, Delphine squirmed in Blake's grasp and screamed out in distress. Hearing her, Carson doubled up in anguish at the shoreline.

Mamaw hurried to her side and Carson at last released her tears.

"Come inside and get some dry clothes on. You're soaked to the skin."

"I can't leave Delphine," she replied, shivering, her eyes glued to the veterinarian at Delphine's side.

Harper ran from the house to the end of the dock carrying a towel. Mamaw took it and wrapped the towel around Carson's shoulders, gently rubbing them, getting the circulation going.

Harper stood helplessly at their sides, a pained expression on her face.

Carson kept her gaze on the team in the water as the veterinarian, his assistant, and Blake maneuvered the blue stretcher under Delphine. It came up along the dolphin's sides to hold her steady. Then the vet pulled out his pack full of supplies and at last started cutting away the deeply entangled lines. Carson couldn't see much between the trio of broad backs huddled around the dolphin. When it looked like they were finished, the vet was talking intently to Blake. Carson didn't like the way he was shaking his head.

Lucille came from the house carrying a tray with biscuits and cheese. Dora was behind her with a thermos and Styrofoam cups. Lucille set the tray on the edge of the dock, took the thermos and poured out a cup, added plenty of sugar, then handed it to Carson. "You drink this, hear?"

Carson took the cup gratefully. It tasted sweet and hot. The liquid scorched a welcome heat into her bloodstream. Her fingers were wrinkled like prunes around the warmth of the cup. The heat seemed to seep right into her bones.

"Carson!" Blake called.

She dropped the towel, handed the cup to Lucille, and ran back into the water.

"We're going to carry her up to the truck. Can you take a side?"

"Of course. But now that she's loose, can't you just let her go?" Carson asked.

"No," the veterinarian replied abruptly. "These injuries need medical attention. Okay, on the count of three."

Each of the four grabbed a handle of the flexible stretcher. Then, on the count, they synchronized their movements and gently lifted the stretcher. Carson's muscles shook as she determinedly kept her side of the stretcher level, step by step. At the water's edge Harper and Dora each grabbed a side to assist on the agonizingly long trip up the steep slope to the truck, then up the metal ramp to lay the dolphin in a special transport carrier.

Carson slumped back, exhausted, as once again, she was ignored. The men huddled over Delphine, Blake and the other man working in tandem as the vet treated her. Carson walked down the ramp to Mamaw and huddled under her towel, waiting. After a short while, the vet got back on his cell phone. Blake jumped down from the truck.

Carson walked toward Blake, who was wringing out the bottom of his shirt. Behind her, Lucille brought the tray filled with steaming black coffee and food. She held the tray up to Blake and he took a cup, gratefully. Lucille proceeded to the truck and offered the same to the other men.

"How is she?" Carson asked Blake.

Blake's eyes narrowed over the rim of his cup as he sipped. He shook his head. "Not good. We prefer to treat and release a dolphin after we get the wire off, but there are too many injuries. And there's that damn hook. It's in deep. She needs to go to a hospital."

"Oh, no." Carson felt the news like ice water in her veins.

"And that's not even the worst part. Now, the remaining requirements have to be met."

"And those are?" Carson asked, feeling her stomach tighten.

"It's complicated," he began, shifting his weight to lean against the truck. "First we need to find a facility that has space. He's on the phone now. It looks good for an availability in Florida, either Sarasota or the Panhandle."

"Why Florida?" Carson asked. "Isn't there someplace closer? What about your facility?"

Mamaw came up beside her to listen.

"Only dead animals come to our place," he said ruefully, and took another sip of coffee.

Carson's knees went weak.

"Lord help us," Mamaw murmured, patting Carson's back reassuringly.

Blake continued. "South Carolina doesn't have a dolphin rehabilitation center." He swiped a lock of dripping hair from his face. "Which brings us to our next requirement. We have to transport her to the facility. Unless a military or USGS chopper is approved and available, which is unlikely, the animal would normally have to be transported in a truck. With the water-to-water time in between here and anywhere in Florida being ten to twelve hours plus . . . the vet doesn't think she'll make it. Sometimes we're lucky and get a donor, like FedEx, to fly a dolphin in." He blew out a stream of air.

Carson felt a new chill enter her body. "What if you can't do all this? What if she can't be relocated . . ."

Blake's eyes looked pained. "I think you know the answer to that."

"No!" Carson cried. "You can't."

Blake turned his head to look out at the sea.

"Will any plane do?" Mamaw asked.

Blake swung his head back to answer Mamaw. "As long as it can fit a wet transport."

"Hold on a bit, hear? I may know someone." Mamaw patted Carson's arm, then went marching with purpose back into the house. Lucille promptly followed her.

Carson and Blake didn't talk anymore. Blake turned and went back into the truck to confer with his colleagues.

Harper and Dora came to Carson's side and guided her to the dock. Her legs felt weak and her guilt and worry mingled to make her feel she could collapse in a corner somewhere and cry. But she wouldn't leave Delphine. She sat on the edge of the dock wrapped in a towel and kept vigil while the NOAA team worked on Delphine and made more phone calls.

It seemed a long while before Mamaw came back out. She walked briskly, carrying a sheet of white paper that flapped in the air beside her. Carson jumped to her feet to meet her.

"I have a plane," she announced with pride. "A jet, actually."

"What?" Blake said with surprise. He turned to call out to the others, "Hey! We've got a plane!" He hurried to meet Mamaw. "What've you got, Mrs. Muir?"

"I called in a favor," she replied, her eyes shining with satisfaction at having succeeded. "My old friend Gaillard has a jet he uses for business. He's a true gentleman and right neighborly. He didn't hesitate one moment when I told him our situation. Nobody loves our coastline better than he does and he won't have this poor dolphin die on his watch. Here's the information," she told Blake, handing him the paper. "Just call that number. Gill said the plane's ready when you are."

"This is major," Blake said, taking her hand and shaking it. Hope entered his voice for the first time. "Thank you. You may have just saved this dolphin's life."

He turned and raced back to the truck. Once there, he handed the paper to the vet and climbed into the truck. "Let's go!"

"Wait! I'm going with her," Carson called out, the towel falling from her shoulders as she ran to the truck.

Blake's eyes flashed. "You can't."

"She needs me."

"You've done enough," Blake said bluntly.

Carson cringed under the sting of the double entendre.

"You're wasting precious time," Blake said. "Time this dolphin doesn't have. You can't come, Carson, so drop it." He paused, then offered, "I'll call you and let you know how she is."

"Let them go, darlin'," Mamaw said at her side. "You'll just be in the way. Sometimes the best support is a retreat."

Carson nodded her head reluctantly and looked up at the truck. All she saw was the box that carried Delphine.

Blake's face softened as he stood at the edge of the truck. "We'll take good care of her. I'll call you."

He reached up to slide down the back gate. The metal slammed loudly in her face. The truck's engine fired. Mamaw took Carson's hand and they stepped back away from the vehicle.

A gut-wrenching sob erupted from her mouth when she saw the truck drive away. She felt as though part of her soul was being torn from her, leaving her raw with loss.

Carson turned to Mamaw. "How did it happen? The fishing line . . . where did it come from?"

Mamaw's eyes flickered and she looked away. "He meant well. He was trying to catch fish for her."

Carson felt the blood drain from her face as she stared at the empty space where the truck had been parked. She swung her head to look at the dock. Blood still tinged the water where several long pieces of fishing line from several rods caught the wind and blew gaily like streamers. Carson felt a sudden and overwhelming surge of guilt. It roiled in her stomach like nausea. Followed quickly by a white-hot fury that blinded her. And her rage had a target.

CHAPTER EIGHTEEN

"*N*ate!"

Carson felt like a demon licked at her heels as she stormed through the wild grass to the house. Her heart was pounding in her ears, blocking out the cries of Mamaw and her sisters as they followed her.

"Carson, wait," Mamaw said, reaching out to grab her arm. She was pale and breathless from the exertion. "Don't do anything in anger. You'll regret it."

"I already regret it. I'm sick with regret," she said, choking out the words. She pushed on out of Mamaw's grasp and bolted through the porch door. "Nate!" she called out, so loudly her voice was raspy. "Nate, where are you?"

Dora was at her heels as she marched through the living room. "What do you want with Nate?" she cried.

Carson wiped the damp hair from her face as she continued down the hallway, her feet dripping mud and sand on the Oriental carpet. She pushed open the library door without knocking. The curtains had been pulled and the room was darkened. She found Nate sitting on the edge of his bed, his hands clasped between his knees. He was rocking back and forth, keening in a low wail.

She went to stand wide legged in front of him. Nate didn't look at her or acknowledge her presence.

"Do you know what you did?" she screamed at him. "Do you have any idea what you did to Delphine?"

Nate continued rocking, his eyes focused on the floor.

Dora ran into the room, blustery with outrage. "What are you doing? Don't you dare yell at my son!"

Mamaw, Harper, and Lucille were right behind her

Carson swung around and faced off with Dora. "Stop protecting him. You're always protecting him! Do you even know what he did?"

"No! What did he do?" she shouted back, near tears of worry. It was a standoff between the two sisters, face-to-face with eyes raging.

"Your son set up all the fishing rods out on the dock. He left them out there all night."

"*So?*"

Carson's eyes flamed. "*So*, that's how Delphine got caught in the wire. She's severely hurt, maybe dying. And it's his fault! He knows better than to leave his gear out. He practically killed Delphine and he doesn't even say he's sorry."

"He won't say that. Don't you get that yet? Stop yelling at him!" Dora yelled, the irony lost on them.

"I'm so angry!" Carson cried, fisting her hands at her sides.

"Well, *you* taught him how to fish," Dora said accusingly.

Carson took a step back. "That's just great. Blame me. The truth is, he was having a good time out there, without you, and you can't stand it." Her voice was rising. "He has to accept the blame when it's his fault."

"Look who's talking about accepting the blame!" Dora shouted back at her. "Who was the one who brought the dolphin to the dock in the first place? *You*, that's who! Not Nate. You're the one who calls for it to come, and swims with it. It's *your* fault that dolphin got caught. That dolphin had no business being by the dock in the first place. Stop blaming a nine-year-old boy. Grow up for a change and put the blame where it belongs. On *you*!"

Carson stepped back as though she'd been struck, hearing the echo of Blake's accusations in Dora's words. A silence fell between them as, for a moment, the pain literally took her breath away.

"Okay. Fine," Carson said, admission in her voice. "But I'm not the one who put the hooks on the line and left the fishing rods out there like some trap," she cried. "Goddamn, Dora, you can't always protect him. He hurt Delphine. He almost killed her. She may not live. And he doesn't even acknowledge what he did." Tears sprang to Carson's eyes as she glared at Nate accusingly, but his eyes wouldn't meet hers. She knelt down and placed her hands firmly on his upper arms, forcing him to look at her.

Nate reared back and struck out. There was a collective gasp as fist met skull. Carson saw stars and fell back, cradling her cheek.

Nate leaped from the bed, running for the door, but Lucille reached out and caught him. He flailed his arms, screaming hysterically. Dora ran to his side and wrapped her arms around him, trying to calm him. Everyone started yelling then as the room erupted in chaos. Nate put his hands over his ears, slid to the floor, and wailed.

Dora turned on Carson, her eyes flashing with fury. "Get out of here," she shouted over her shoulder. "Haven't you done enough damage? The last person I need mothering advice from is the daughter of an unfit, husband-stealing, drunken suicide!"

Carson's face grew ashen. "What did you say?" she sputtered.

Dora's face looked as though she knew she'd crossed a line, but it was too late. "It's true. Everyone knows it's true. No one believed that lie about the lightning. Except you." She turned her back on Carson and tended to Nate, speaking in a low, calming voice as he wailed.

Carson didn't respond. She stood staring blindly, feeling the sting from the slap. Something in that accusation niggled at her, like a ghost howling at the window. Bewildered by Dora's accusation, she instinctively looked to Mamaw. Mamaw's face drooped with sorrow and she looked every bit her eighty years. She shook her head slowly, then motioned for Carson to follow as she left the room. Harper stood by the door, her eyes wide.

"Harper," Mamaw said, "go on and bring your sister and Nate a nice cool glass of water." She turned to Carson. "You come to my room. It's time you heard the truth from me."

The thick, creamy matelassé curtains fringed in blue tassels were still drawn, leaving the room cool and serene.

Mamaw sat in her favorite upholstered wing chair and motioned for Carson to sit beside her. Carson shut the door, silencing the sound of Nate's keening wail, and joined Mamaw in the sitting area. She slid soundlessly into the soft cushions, utterly exhausted and yet still bristling with pain from the nightmare of the morning.

"Do you want something to drink?" Mamaw asked her.

"No." Carson closed her eyes, trying to calm down. Trying to focus. She was so upset she had to concentrate to get the words out. "What I want is to know what Dora meant about my mother. She said *suicide*." Carson opened her eyes and stared at Mamaw, demanding the truth.

Mamaw's hands fluttered in her lap. It unnerved Carson to see her nervous and she tensed, sensing another hurt coming.

"Is it true?" Carson asked. "Did my mother kill herself?"

"It's not a yes-or-no answer," Mamaw began hesitatingly.

"She either did commit suicide or she didn't."

Mamaw looked at her. "No, she didn't."

Carson reconciled this in her mind. "Then why did Dora say she did?"

"She was wrong. That's just malicious gossip."

"Gossip . . ."

"Listen to what I have to tell you, Carson. It's the truth."

Carson clenched her hands tightly on the arms of the chair.

Mamaw sighed, then began in a slow cadence. "It was all such a long time ago, but I'm still haunted by it. Carson, your mother's death was a terrible, terrible accident.

Sophie had been drinking. She had a problem with alcohol, you see. Like Parker. She was in her bedroom, in bed, watching television or reading, I don't know. But she was smoking. She smoked quite a lot." She stopped and took a little breath. "A lot of us did back then. The fire department concluded that the fire started in her bedroom. The likely explanation was that Sophie passed out while smoking—that's what the coroner determined. Your mother never meant to die in that terrible fire." Mamaw paused. "I pray to God she died quickly."

"But . . . but I always thought . . . you always told me that the fire started from a lightning strike," Carson said.

Mamaw put her hands together in her lap. "Yes. That's what I told you. There was a storm that night, true enough, with a lot of lightning. Edward and I talked about it and together we decided that you didn't need to know the unsavory details. You were only four years old, after all. Your mother had just passed away. That was enough for you to deal with."

Carson listened, pressing her fingers to her eyes, trying to make sense of it. "But later, when I was older. Why didn't you tell me?"

"What good would it have done? I don't know, maybe I should have. It just never seemed the right time."

"My mother was a drunk, too?" Carson asked, stunned by the enormity of that fact. That really stacks the deck against me, doesn't it? When I came to you and told you I was worried I had a problem, *that* would've been the time to tell me about my mother. Don't you think?"

Mamaw sighed and nodded her head.

"But how did Dora know?"

Mamaw's eyes flashed. "She should never have said what she did to you. It was wrong of her. Wrong that she even knew. Her mother must have told her. That horrible gossip. Never forget that in life there is gossip and there are family secrets. We can tolerate the prattle, but to break the bonds of family is unforgivable."

"Don't defend the secrets!" Carson cried.

"I'm not," Mamaw told her. "If we've learned nothing else this summer, haven't we learned that secrets in a family are like a disease? One lie on top of another. The truth always comes out in the end."

"I'm sick to death of secrets in this family. Why don't we try honesty for a change?"

Mamaw's eyes filled with tears. "I was with Nate when he put out the hooks."

"What?" Carson stilled.

"Last night," Mamaw said, holding back tears. "I caught him sneaking out to the dock with the fishing rods. So I went with him. I helped him set the bait and put out the line. We both left the rods there. I didn't see the harm in it. He wanted to catch fish for Delphine, you see. He was trying to do something for *you*."

Carson stared at Mamaw. "Why did you let me yell at Nate if you were the one who let him put the rods out in the first place?"

"I . . . I don't know, I didn't fully understand what the commotion was about until it was too late. . . . I . . . I feel so terrible," Mamaw said. "And when I saw that poor dolphin . . . I know the boy must feel terrible, too. He cares so deeply for the dolphin, and for you, Carson. You need to know that."

Carson let out a guttural groan and rose from the chair. "I don't know what to say. My head and my heart *ache*," she cried. "They really, physically hurt." She stopped and glared at Mamaw, her mind reeling from the string of revelations. It was all too much to take. It felt like the room was closing in on her, and she stumbled running from it.

By the time Carson got to Dunleavy's the ovens were lit, the fryers jump-started, and the coffee made, and Ashley was covering both of their tables. After punching in, she almost tripped over the liquor shipment that had come earlier that morning. The top box nearly tipped but she grabbed it just in time.

"What happened to you?" Ashley asked when she burst into the kitchen to deliver an order.

Carson was tying her apron around her waist. "Don't ask," she said. She grabbed a stack of menus and headed out to face the lunchtime rush. She needed to keep busy or she'd go crazy with worry over Delphine.

Brian gave her several of his punishing looks during the shift but Carson felt too numb to care. She went through the motions like an automaton, not laughing at the cornball jokes the patrons made, answering the monotonous questions that she'd heard a thousand times with a dull voice. Ashley sensed something was wrong and gave her a wide berth during the shift.

When the last customer finally left, Brian waved them over to the bar. He was drying a glass with a towel.

"Ashley, you can go home early," he told her. "You covered the shift. Carson, you close up. Any complaints?"

"I don't mind helping close," Ashley said, but her hesitancy was polite more than altruistic.

"Go on," Carson told Ashley. "Thanks for covering for me."

Carson began stacking dirty glasses on a tray.

"What happened to you today?" Brian asked her when Ashley walked off.

Carson shrugged. "I got held up. Family problems," she replied.

Brian studied her face, then let the matter drop. "Okay, then," he said, and went back to drying his glasses. "Don't make a habit of it."

Carson ran the cocktail trays through the dishwasher and put away clean glasses so hot she had to pull them out with a towel. After that she got the restaurant ready for the evening shift. Brian had left the bar and gone to pick up something from the grocery store. Carson was alone in the pub. She stocked the waitress station with ice and wiped each table, making sure the condiments were filled.

The last task was cleaning the bar. She walked behind it, polishing the lacquered wood clean. Wiping the liquor bottles was next. Her hands ran along the bottles one by one as a sudden thirst felt like it was burning in her throat. Her hands shook on the bottles, the urge suddenly so strong. Looking around, she saw that she was alone. Quietly, she reached under the bar for a shot glass and grabbed a bottle of tequila from the shelf. She filled the shot glass, her hand shaking so hard she spilled some. She took a deep breath and paused, staring at the glass.

Her mind railed at her not to drink it, to fight the

temptation to fall off the wagon. Yet even as she heard the voice in her head, she knew she would do it. She didn't care anymore about sobriety. What did it matter? Her mother was a drunk. Her father was a drunk. So was she.

Ducking low, she drank the tequila down in a gulp. Carson winced at the jolt of what felt like needles flowing down to her stomach. Brian would fire her if he caught her. But Carson was far from caring at this point. Without thinking further, she poured a second shot and, closing her eyes, sent it down the hatch. Licking her lips, she screwed the top back on the bottle, rinsed the shot glass and wiped it with a towel, then neatly put all back in order. Reaching for a lemon slice, she popped it into her mouth to mask the scent of tequila.

The clock over the bar was neon with a beer logo surrounding the casing. Brian had told her that the distributors coaxed him to put it up there with season tickets to the Citadel games. Glancing at it, Carson saw it was time to go home. She went to the back room to get her bag and lock up.

Home. Where the hell is that? she wondered bitterly, putting her fingers to her forehead and pressing hard. The one place she'd always felt was her home—Sea Breeze— was the last place she wanted to go to now. She felt adrift without an anchor. Desperately sad and lonely. She just wanted to forget this horrible day. Forget Delphine and Nate and Mamaw. Forget Blake.

And her mother. A horrid image of her mother burning in her bed flashed in her mind.

Oh God, she needed another drink. A real drink.

She spied the shipment of alcohol waiting to be

shelved. The top box was open and partially emptied. In a rush, Carson pulled out a bottle of Southern Comfort and quickly wrapped it in one of the dirty towels. Looking over her shoulder, she stuck it in her purse, locked the back door, and walked directly to the golf cart. She opened up the small metal trunk in the back. Carefully she set the bottle next to her beach bag. When she turned back toward the restaurant, her heart leaped in her chest. Brian was a few yards away, walking back to the pub. He was carrying the mail and shuffling through the envelopes.

Carson didn't wave or shout out a hello. She slipped into the cart and fired the engine, her heart racing. She'd never stolen anything before in her life. Not even when she was a kid and her friends shoplifted for fun. Carson had never been able to do it, because she knew it was wrong.

As she drove down the street, farther from Dunleavy's, she was surprised how, after a morning of ragged emotions, she now felt absolutely nothing.

The floating dock was rickety, bobbing in the small waves. Carson stepped carefully on the creaking wood. She'd been drinking all afternoon, knew she'd had too much and it was not a good idea to be on a floating piece of wood when you'd had a few too many.

She sat in a gloomy funk and let her legs dangle in the water. She heard a fish jump and swung her head around, instinctively searching for Delphine. The black water of the cove was bleak and empty.

"Delphine!" she cried out.

Tired, woozy, she laid her head on her arms, awash in loneliness. She longed to hear Delphine's nasal whistle, to see her sweet face. Carson turned her head and stared out at the water with longing. How was she? What was she doing now? When was Blake going to call and tell her the status?

Carson dragged herself back to sitting position, cradling the bottle of Southern Comfort in her arms. She brought the bottle to her lips and drank. She had no idea what time it was. It had to be at least nine o'clock, because the sun had set and the sky was turning that deep purplish gray that heralded night. The current was running with the tide, churning the mud and water into a brackish brew. In the far distance she could make out the small, twinkling lights on the bridge that joined Mt. Pleasant to Charleston. Carson wished she were a kid again, swimming with her sisters, innocent and full of hope for the future, rather than sitting on a dock with a bottle of Southern Comfort, a bitter old woman at only thirty-four, trying to make sense of how it all went wrong. She took another sip of SoCo. Could she ever forgive Dora for flinging those hateful words at her like stones—*husband-stealing drunken suicide.*

She lay on her back and stared up at the stars, as yet faint in the periwinkle sky but still pulsing. She'd known that her mother had died in the horrible fire that destroyed the small house they'd rented on Sullivan's Island. She'd accepted the fact that her mother died in a fire the same as if she'd died of cancer or a car accident. The salient point to a child was that her mother was gone, not how she left. Tonight, however, she was haunted less by Dora's words and more by Mamaw's. They floated in her mind, creating macabre images. *I pray to God she died quickly*.

Carson closed her eyes and brought her arm up over them, shuddering. Death by fire had to be one of the worst possible ways to die. She felt physically sick as she thought about the unspeakable terror of being burned alive. Carson shivered in the night, feeling a fine sweat break out on her skin. She closed her eyes and somewhere in that blackness a memory hovered close. She could almost grasp it, like a hand in the thick smoke. She was groping for it like a frightened child. It was so close. If she could only reach it.

"Dad!" she cried aloud.

The smells were bad. And there was a hissing sound and loud noises that woke her. Carson was only four years old. She didn't know what the noises came from, but even with her head under the sheet, the bad smells made her cough. They made her afraid. She pushed the sheet from her face.

"Mama!" she cried. "Daddy!"

When no one answered her, Carson climbed from her bed to go to their room. Everything felt hot, the floors, the air, the door handle. It burned her hand when she touched it. A mean gray smoke was sneaking in from under the door and it frightened her. It was not supposed to be there. She ran back to her bed and pulled her blanket over her head. She heard glass breaking, like her mama might have been in a bad mood and breaking something.

"Carson!" It was her father's voice.

"Daddy!" she cried, and her heart leaped with joy in her chest. "Daddy!" She pulled off the blanket again and hurried to the door. This time she opened it, burning her hand as she turned the knob. But she had to get to her daddy.

Smoke poured into the room. It was thick and black and it burned when she breathed and made her eyes burn. She coughed and rubbed her eyes but that only made them worse. Crying now, she knew she had to get to her parents' room, where it was safe. She groped her way down the hall, her palms flat against the wall. Even the walls felt hot to the touch.

Then she saw him, standing in front of his bedroom. He wasn't moving. She wanted to cry that she was so glad to see him, knowing soon she'd be safe in his arms.

"Daddy!" she cried, her voice cracking in the dry heat. She stumbled toward him. He turned but she could barely see him through the smoke. She reached out to him.

Instead of grabbing her hand, he turned in the opposite direction and fled. Carson's last vision of him was his back disappearing in the smoke as he ran down the stairs.

She dropped to her knees, crying and coughing. She couldn't call his name; her throat was too raw. All she could think to do was to follow him. She crawled to the stairs. Sparks were flying everywhere. It hurt so bad when they burned her skin, like sharp teeth biting her. She crawled as fast as she could to the stairs. At last she saw that the front door was open. A man in a big hat was standing there.

"Daddy," she cried, but it came out more as a cough.

But the man in the big hat heard her and ran up the stairs and scooped her up in his arms. She buried her face against his rubbery coat as he carried her outdoors.

Suddenly the air was cooler and didn't burn her skin, though it still hurt to breathe. She coughed again and blinked open her eyes. A lady took her from the big man's arms and was carrying her to a red truck. She smiled at her, but Carson was afraid and cried for her father.

"He's all right," the nice lady told her. "He's right over there. See him?"

Carson looked to where the woman pointed. She saw him kneeling on the grass. He was all dirty and his body was bent, with his face in his hands like he was praying. Only he wasn't praying. He was crying.

She reached for him. *Here I am, Daddy,* she wanted to tell him. *Don't worry about me, I'm here.* But her throat hurt too badly to talk and the nurse was carrying her farther away from him into the little red truck. The nice lady laid her on a cot with clean white paper on it and she was saying things like how everything was going to be all right.

"I want my mommy," Carson croaked.

The nurse's face stilled and she had that *uh-oh* look in her eyes that told Carson something bad had happened. Then she put a plastic cup over Carson's mouth and told her it would help her to breathe.

"You just rest, sweetheart," the woman told her. "I'm going to take good care of you. Don't you worry. Everything's going to be all right."

But Carson didn't feel like everything was going to be all right. She felt a terror engulfing her, squeezing her heart, that was worse than the evil smoke in the house. And she was afraid.

Carson coughed and gasped for air, opening her eyes and staring wildly into the night while her heart beat hard in her chest. For a frightening moment she didn't know where she was. Then, as her heart rate settled, she heard the lapping of the water and felt the rocking of the dock and remembered she was outdoors, at Sea Breeze, on the floating dock.

She struggled to sit up, her head reeling, and wiped her face with her palms. She felt hot and afraid, like she was still trapped in the blinding smoke. She'd remembered that terrible night of the fire—remembered it like it was yesterday. It was so vivid, she could almost feel the burning of the heat and sparks on her skin. Had she tucked it far into some dark corner so she'd never have to face it again? Why had she blocked out that memory?

Then, with a sudden chill, she knew why. She closed her eyes and saw again her father's back running down the stairs. He'd left her there, in the fire. He abandoned his child to die, just so he could make it out of the house faster, saving himself. What kind of father did that? What kind of a man? Carson felt a fierce stab of betrayal. Throughout her childhood she'd stuck by his side. Every day, he'd told her that he loved her.

It was all just lies. How could he have loved her if he'd abandoned her to burn to death? Then, with a bitter twist of the knife, she realized that abandonment was what he'd practiced all his life.

Carson struggled to her feet. Her whole body felt hot, as though she were back in the fire. She picked at her sweaty clothes. They were soaked and sticky. She needed to cool down. The lights appeared a little more blurry, and the dock seemed to rock a bit more strongly. She slipped off her T-shirt and unzipped her shorts and kicked them off beside her flip-flops. Teetering at the edge of the dock, she stared into the water. The blackness called to her. With a push, she dove in.

The water was blessedly cold. She kicked her legs and pulled her sopping hair back. She felt oddly weak, so she did the breaststroke, flexing her legs like a frog. She trusted her swimming, always strong and sure, and started off toward the next closest dock. There weren't boats cruising by this late at night, and it felt safe to stretch her arms and swim farther out.

After several strokes, she noticed that the next dock was farther away, not closer. She'd gone too far out. The current was carrying her in the wrong direction. Turning her head from left to right, she focused on her own dock and stroked toward home. But the current was a steady and powerful force. She told herself not to panic. She knew this patch of water like the back of her hand. But she also knew she'd been stupid to come out here alone. At night. Especially after drinking.

Focus, she ordered herself, and pushed to stroke harder. But her arms felt so weak and, gasping, she swallowed a mouthful of water. She had to stop, dog-paddling as she choked and spat out water, trying to catch a breath. Oh God, now she was in trouble. She could feel her heart begin to race and she started stroking again, this time without precision. She wasn't trying to get back to the dock anymore. She just wanted to make it to the muddy hammock so she could climb out. She stroked as hard as she could but she couldn't make any headway. She was like a piece of driftwood in the mighty current, being dragged to the open harbor.

Dora stood on the back porch and sipped her coffee as she looked out at the cove. It was an inky night. Moving clouds were obscuring the moon and stars. *What a night*, she thought, yawning. It had taken hours to get Nate to sleep. He'd been withdrawn all day, the poor little guy. He wouldn't talk, wouldn't eat, wouldn't leave his room. Dora didn't know what could have compelled Carson to grab him like that. Hadn't she told her that Nate didn't like to be touched? With all that had happened to that darn dolphin, he was beside himself. She wished that dolphin had never come to the dock. They had enough family issues to deal with without adding a wild dolphin to the mix.

Though, she thought with a pang of guilt, she shouldn't have said what she did to Carson. That was mean and thoughtless. Mamaw was upset, Lucille had given her the evil eye, and Harper wouldn't talk to her. Dora hadn't meant to be cruel. She'd blurted it out without thinking. She'd been so mad, she'd seen red. Like Carson had been. She'd wanted to hurt Carson the way Carson had hurt her son.

A shadowy figure out on the dock caught her attention. It was a woman. Peering out, Dora recognized Carson. So that's where she was. She'd gone off to work around noon and no one had seen her since.

Dora took a few steps to the edge of the porch, watching the figure on the dock. It was odd. Carson seemed to be staggering and . . . What was she doing? Good Lord, she was taking off her clothes. She couldn't be thinking of going swimming now? Alone in the dark?

Then another thought struck. She was drunk.

"Carson!" she called out. She watched Carson standing at the edge of the dock, weaving and staring into the water. *What in all that's holy?* "Carson!"

Dora set the coffee mug on the table, and when she looked out again, Carson was gone. Dora's heart jumped and she took off running for the dock, her heeled sandals slowing her down. She kicked them off and ran. When she reached the end of the long dock, she couldn't spot Carson in the water. A cloud passed, allowing a window of moonlight to shine on the water. Dora squinted her eyes as she peered out and spied a shimmer of skin in the moonlight farther down the cove. Dora cursed. The idiot was caught in the current.

Adrenaline raced through her veins as Dora sprang into action. She punched the motor to lower the boat from the raised dock, pacing while keeping her eye on the figure in the water. The motor churned as the boat lowered at an agonizingly slow pace into the water. She moved quickly now, untying the lines and jumping into the boat. She'd always been the boater in the family, the one who'd rather tow the skis or the rubber raft. Dora powered the engine and took off toward Carson. She searched the dark water, stopping the engine abruptly when she spotted her

bobbing in the water. The boat floated in the drift as Dora
hurried to grab the life preserver.

"Carson!" she called out over the side.

"Here!" Carson called back.

"Grab hold." Dora tossed the preserver into the water.
It landed close to Carson. She kicked and stroked and
grabbed on, coughing. Pulling hard against the current,
Dora cursed and sweated as she drew Carson to the side
of the boat.

"Give me your hand," Dora called out.

Carson released the preserver and lifted her hand to
her sister. Holding tight, Dora leaned far back and pulled
Carson into the boat. Carson landed gracelessly on the
seat like a beached seal.

Carson bent over on her knees, coughing up water;
then she leaned over the side of the boat and vomited.
Dora held her long hair back from her face as Carson
heaved the alcohol and salt water from her stomach.
When finished, she slipped weakly down on the padded
bench and rested her forehead on her hands, shivering.
Dora went to fetch the boat's emergency blanket and
wrapped it around Carson's shoulders. Carson had always
been the strong one, the athletic one, and yet now she was
as weak and frightened as a drowning kitten.

And Dora knew it was her fault.

CHAPTER NINETEEN

"*A*h, you're awake."

Carson awoke, seeing the world through a cottony veil. Her eyes were dry and gritty and she blinked heavily. The shadowed stripes of the closed blinds revealed bright daylight.

"How long did I sleep?" she croaked.

"Thirteen hours," Mamaw answered. "But who's counting?"

Carson shivered under her thin cotton sheet and blanket. Every bone in her body ached. "I'm so cold."

Mamaw rested her palm against Carson's forehead, testing for fever as she had when Carson was a little girl. Carson thought her palm felt cool and comforting and her lids drooped.

"You still have a fever."

"I feel awful."

"It's no wonder," Mamaw answered, going to the closet and pulling out a patchwork quilt. She shook it out, then laid it atop Carson. "You were in that cold water for hours in the morning, then you go out swimming late last night. What were you thinking? You know that's feeding time for the sharks. And alone! Lord help us, anything could have happened. And almost did. If it wasn't for Dora just happening to be out there on the back porch . . ." Mamaw reached for the glass of water on the bedside stand. "Here, darling. I've a few aspirin to help bring the fever down. Let's see if you can't drink a little bit, hear?"

She helped Carson rise to her elbows. The movement brought a ricochet of pain in Carson's head but she managed to swallow the pills. After a few sips she collapsed back down on the bed.

"That should help you feel better. Do you think you can eat something?" Mamaw asked, setting the glass down. "Lucille made a pot of chicken soup, just for you."

"Maybe later," Carson replied, licking her moistened lips.

Mamaw's long fingers tucked the quilt around the bed. "You're still so warm. I'll get you a cool cloth for your forehead."

Carson reached up and clutched Mamaw's hand. "Don't go."

"All right, dear," Mamaw replied, a little surprised. "I'll stay, if you like." Mamaw sat on the edge of the bed. She was wearing one of her tunic tops, this one in a pale coral that matched the coral earrings in her ears. "What's the matter, child?"

"Mamaw, I . . ." Carson's face crumpled. She closed her eyes and once again saw the nightmarish image she'd conjured of her mother burning in bed that had kept her tossing and turning all night. Her brain felt scorched, as though the memory was a brand that had burned into her every waking thought. She shuddered and turned to curl up closer to Mamaw, putting her arms around her with a soft cry.

"Carson!" Mamaw exclaimed as she smoothed away the hair from Carson's forehead in a soothing rhythm. "You haven't held on to me like this since you were a little girl."

"Mamaw, last night," she said tremulously. "I remembered the fire."

Mamaw's hand stilled. "Oh, child . . ."

"After all these years, I remembered. I must have blocked it out of my mind."

"What do you remember?"

"I remembered the fire and waking up in that awful smoke. It was so hot and it burned. I heard Dad calling me. I went looking for him, but I was so afraid. But I kept going. Then when I saw him . . ." She stopped and clutched Mamaw tighter.

"Saw him? What happened?"

"He turned away. Mamaw, he left me there, in the fire. I was just a kid and he left me there. I'll never forget the sight of his back as he ran down the stairs." Her voice caught. "How could he have done that?"

"Oh, Carson, Carson," Mamaw murmured. "How can I explain what happened?"

"You can't. It's too awful. I'll never forgive him."

Mamaw rose slowly and went to the window. She adjusted the blinds enough to allow a bit more light into the room. She looked for a moment out the window, at the gentle rain that pattered against the glass. The earth needed the rain, she thought. Carson's tears were good for her, too. Cathartic. How could she help her get through this storm?

She turned and held her hands together. "Carson, your daddy came to see me after the fire. He was sick, as you are now. Sick in his body and sick in his soul. He'd just lost your mother. For all that they were not good for one another, they did love each other. He mourned her." She paused. "And he mourned what had happened to you. He lay in my arms and cried like a baby. He was riddled with guilt that he didn't go back into that burning house and search for you. When he saw that fireman carrying you out, all smudged with smoke and burns, he dropped to his knees and gave thanks."

"But he saw me," Carson cried, turning to look at Mamaw. "You can't always defend him. I was there. He saw me. And he ran away."

"No, child, he didn't see you," Mamaw told her in a resolute tone. "Parker told me how he came home and saw the fire in the upstairs windows. He went running up in a panic to fetch you and Sophie. By the time he reached their bedroom the room was in flames. The bed." She made a small, desperate gesture. "He saw her." Mamaw shook her head sadly. "He saw her body burning on the bed. Don't you see? He was in shock, honey. He didn't know what he was doing. He just turned and ran out of the house and probably would've kept on running if a fireman hadn't stopped him. He was out of his mind, honey. He never saw you."

Carson closed her eyes and brought to mind that horrid night. She remembered how she'd called out to him. How she'd seen him standing in front of his bedroom, still as a statue, before he turned and fled down the stairs.

She'd never reached him. He'd never reached out for her. What Mamaw told her was possible. Her heart wanted to believe, but her mind fought it.

"He was still a chicken shit not to come for me. I was only four years old."

"Oh, Carson," Mamaw said wearily. "It's so easy for us to judge now, in hindsight. We think we know what we'd do in an emergency. But one never knows until one is tested. I couldn't say what I'd do in that situation."

"*Nothing* would stop me from going after my own child."

Mamaw patted her shoulder in consolation. "Perhaps not. You're stronger than him. Always have been. You're the strongest woman I know. Child, you didn't give up in that fire. You were only four years old but you found your way out. You're a survivor."

Mamaw sighed wearily; the past twenty-four hours had taken a lot out of her. She sat down in the chair beside Carson and once again gently stroked her hair with her fingertips.

"Trauma is a hard, hard burden to bear. You suffered it and endured. Perhaps now that you understand the trauma of what your father went through at that moment, you might be able to forgive him for what he did. And forgive your mother's part in this tragedy."

"I don't forgive either of them. They both abandoned me," Carson said angrily.

"Sophie was a lost soul. She took a risk with her own

life and the life of her child. And paid the highest price for it. There's nothing more to say about that." Mamaw looked around the room, at the portrait of her ancestor hanging on the wall. She prayed she could find the words to bring the confidence of that ancestor back into her granddaughter's spirit.

"As for Parker," Mamaw continued, "he, too, paid a high price for his failures. He never forgave himself for not helping Sophie with her drinking, or for leaving you behind in that burning house. It haunted him till his dying day. I fear your father never really made it out of that fire. Why do you think he wouldn't leave you with me? I begged him to leave you with me, to let me take care of you, but he said he was your father and he wouldn't leave you behind ever again."

"He should've," Carson ground out against Mamaw's lap. "I wish he had."

"I do, too. But he was your father and for all his faults, he loved you. Try thinking on that, honey, and let go of the anger."

Carson felt weakened by the emotional onslaught. She closed her eyes. "I don't want to think about it. Or him. I just want to forget all of it. Forget everything."

"That's denial, dear," Mamaw said. "You are not that little girl any longer. You're a woman. At least now you know the truth, and in time it will help you gain perspective."

Carson turned her head away on the pillow.

"Listen to me now. I know you harbor a guilt, undeserved, for not being with your father when he died. You poor, motherless child. Who was taking care of *you*? You were not Parker's parent. That was not your job. That was mine. Release that guilt from your heart. Release your anger at your father. Let it all go."

Carson squeezed her eyes shut and felt the heat of tears pooling against her pillow. "I can't," she said as a whimper.

"You must. If you keep your guilt and anger festering inside of you, they will poison your life. You must find it in your heart to forgive your father . . . Nate . . . your poor dead mother." She paused. "Me. And yourself. For your own sake."

Mamaw patted Carson's hand and rose to her feet, spent. She felt ancient, like some old relic whose bones were about to splinter into dust. Before leaving the room, she turned at the door and looked once more to her granddaughter. "Remember, my darling. Your father didn't save you. But you saved him."

A spell of bad weather had moved in. Three days of non-stop rain. Dora stepped from Nate's room and quietly closed the door behind her. She slumped against the door. He was always sensitive to noises, and the thunder that rumbled all night long had kept him awake. That merely added to the meltdown Nate was suffering.

Dora straightened, wiping her face with her palms. She looked across the hall to see Carson's bedroom door was closed. From the room she shared with Harper, she heard the click-clacking of fingers against a keyboard. Dora sighed with annoyance. Harper had been holed up in there for days, either on her phone or her iPad or her computer. Hiding out.

Dora went in search of Mamaw and found her sitting in the living room. She appeared to be absorbed in her book and didn't respond to Dora calling her name. When Dora drew near, however, she saw that Mamaw was nodding off. Dora turned to leave but her foot accidentally bumped the coffee table. Mamaw awoke with a start.

"I'm sorry," Dora said, cringing. "I didn't mean to disturb you."

Mamaw was blinking heavily. "No, no, I just dozed off." She smiled wobbily. "It's the rain. The steady pitter-patter always makes me sleepy." She breathed deeply. "I love a good summer rain, love the green smell of the earth and the rumbling of thunder in the distance." She reached out to pat the sofa cushion beside her. "Come, sit down. It's nice to have some company. The house feels as quiet as a tomb."

Dora came to sit beside her grandmother. She turned her head to see Mamaw studying her clothing. Despite the rainy weather, she was wearing white pants and an aqua tunic top covered in white starfish. Being with her more stylish sisters, Dora was trying to take better care of herself. She no longer merely slid into elastic-waistband pants and a baggy top.

"You look very pretty today," Mamaw complimented her. "Cheerful. We could use some cheer around here."

"Thank you," Dora replied, pleased that her effort was noticed. "How's Carson?"

Mamaw's smile slipped. "Not very well. And Nate?"

"The same. That's what I've come to talk with you about. Mamaw, I'm worried that he's regressing. He won't come out of his room and he just sits on his bed, reading books about dolphins. He doesn't talk, except to ask about Delphine. Have we heard anything?"

"No," Mamaw said. "We haven't heard a word. Blake promised to call. I expect they don't know yet."

Dora considered this. "That can't be good. Mamaw, what if they can't save her?"

"I don't think we've reached that point yet."

"I have to prepare for the possibility. I've been thinking . . . Perhaps it's best to get Nate home, away from here, where all he thinks about is that dolphin. If the dolphin should die, I don't want him here."

"Will it make any difference?"

"There's everything here to remind him of her."

"I really think he should stay here, at least until he learns what happened to Delphine. You know he'll wonder and worry if you don't. He's not one to simply forget about it."

"No, I suppose you're right." Dora wrung her hands in indecision. She felt lost, unable to navigate through these choppy waters.

Mamaw paused, dreading going into the discussion, but she had to know. "Do you think Nate realizes what he did? That's a large burden for such small shoulders."

Dora felt herself go under the wave of worry. She sighed heavily and sank back against the sofa cushions, shaking her face in her hands. "I don't know! I just don't know if he understands guilt. He can't communicate that with me." She took a calming breath, realizing that Mamaw couldn't understand fully what she was going through with Nate.

"He understands that Delphine is hurt," Dora tried to

explain, "and that she went to the hospital in Florida. He feels very badly about that." Her eyes began to tear. "He has such a hard time regulating his emotions normally, and now . . ." She threw up her hands. "It's all such a hot mess."

Mamaw reached out to pat her hand. "It's always hard to see your child in distress."

"I know, Mamaw. But it's so much more intense with a child with autism."

"I'm sure that's true. Nonetheless, Nate has to learn to face the consequences of his actions. You will not be able to protect him from all of life's difficult moments, you know. No parent can. All we can do is to let him go through them and learn from them. To give him the tools he needs.

"Dora, I don't think you should leave. Really I don't. For Nate's sake. He's developed a good routine here. And you can't go back to your house. Didn't you say that the workmen are there, fixing it up for sale? How will you manage with the fumes of paint and varnish? Surely that can't be good for you or your son. Just think of the upsets! Granted, we've had a bump in our routine, but now we all have to pull together and start anew."

"I suppose," Dora replied, lackluster. She hadn't thought this through, and as usual, Mamaw had.

"Will he see Carson?" Mamaw asked.

Dora shook her head. "No. He doesn't want to see her."

Mamaw *tsk*ed and shook her head. "That's too bad. They'd been doing so well together. Making such progress. What a muddle this has all become." She looked at Dora. "Well, dear, you go on and take a peek in her room and see if she's sleeping. I know she'd feel bad not to see *you*."

Dora hesitated. She didn't really want to see her sister. "I wouldn't want to wake her."

Mamaw shrugged. "You should. Her fever's gone. It's what's ailing her inside that I'm more worried about. She just sleeps and sleeps. When she's awake she just stares at the wall. She won't even open the blinds."

"I feel so bad that I stirred up bad memories," Dora said. "It was thoughtless of me. I was caught in the emotion of the moment. Sometimes I speak first and think later."

"Yes . . ." Mamaw pinched her lips.

"I'm going to try and change that."

"That's good, dear," Mamaw said, then sighed. "I suppose it's just as well the truth surfaced at last. Though that particular hurt runs very deep. Carson just needs to come to terms with what happened in her own time. And she will." She patted Dora's hand, more briskly this time. "Now go on and see your sister. I think she needs you now more than ever."

Dora knocked on the bedroom door. "Carson? Are you awake?"

"Come in," Carson called back without enthusiasm.

She thought Carson's voice sounded weak and on opening the door, Dora saw her lying on her back on the bed in the dim room. Her eyes were closed, the blinds were drawn—the atmosphere was as gloomy as a hospital room.

"Hi, honey," Dora said, stepping in. "How're you doing?"

"Okay." Carson's voice was flat, lifeless.

Dora came to stand by the bed and stared down at her sister. "Honey, you look like I feel."

Carson opened her eyes and smirked. "Good one."

Dora sat on the side of the bed, took Carson's hand and squeezed it. "I hate to see you like this. Don't be sad, sweetie. It'll be all right."

"I know . . ." Carson replied weakly, without conviction.

Dora felt the weight of remorse pressing down on her heart. She hadn't come here to make a scene, but seeing her sister like this was more than she could bear.

"I'm so sorry," Dora cried, bursting into tears. "I'm so sorry I said those horrible things to you. Oh, Carson, I never thought you might . . ." She sniffed and wiped her eyes. "Nothing's worth taking your life, Carson. You have your whole life in front of you."

Carson lifted her head and looked at her like she'd gone crazy. "Wait, wait just a minute. Do you think . . . do you honestly think I was trying to kill myself out there?"

Dora wiped her eyes and stared back at her. "Weren't you?"

"No!" Carson exclaimed, pulling her hand from Dora's grip. "Good God, no. Why would you think that?"

"I—I don't know," Dora stammered. "I guess because, well, you were so sad about that dolphin and I told you about your mother. I just . . ."

"You thought if my mother committed suicide, then I would, too?"

"No, not when you say it like that." She'd done it again. Put her foot in her mouth. "I don't know what I thought."

"Jeez, Dora . . ." Carson looked away.

"I just saw you disappear into the water and my instinct kicked in."

Carson erupted in a short laugh that surprised Dora. When she turned to face Dora again, she didn't appear angry or upset. In fact, she looked vaguely amused. "Oh, Dora," Carson said. "I guess I should just thank the Lord for your instinct."

Dora heaved a sigh.

Carson's eyes grew haunted. "I *was* in trouble out there. I knew better than to go in alone but I was fool drunk and did it anyway. I got caught in the current. It's a miracle I didn't drown. But *no*, Dora. I was *not* trying to kill myself." She ran her hand through her hair. "And let me make this clear. My mother did *not* commit suicide, okay? She was drunk and smoking and passed out. Okay?"

Dora's eyes were wide with attention. She nodded her head.

"Shit," Carson said morosely. "But I guess you were right about me after all. I fell off the wagon. I am a drunk. Just like my mother."

Dora felt the shame of her callous words burn again. "Don't pay any mind to what I said. I didn't know your mother. She was my nanny but I was so young, I don't remember a thing except that she was pretty. So don't listen to what I said. I was being mean and hateful because I was so angry at you for hurting Nate. I wanted to hurt you back. That's no excuse, I know." She looked away. "And who am I to talk about mothers, right? I know you think I'm a terrible mother. Overprotective, smothering."

"I never said you were a terrible mother," Carson said. "You're an excellent mother. The best. Just a bit . . . over-protective."

Dora released a short, desperate laugh. "Cal tells me the same thing. He said that's why he left me. Or one of the reasons, anyway. He said I gave so much to Nate I left nothing for him. And that even Nate didn't like him. At first I denied it. But lately, I've had some time to think about it and I realized he was right. Not that he's been a prince." Dora's lips trembled and she reached into her pocket to pull out a tissue.

"But suddenly, I'm losing everything. My husband, my house, my life." She looked at her belly. "Hell, even my figure. Everything I cared about is just slipping through my fingers. I'm scared. You know, sometimes, when I'm all alone, I put my face in the pillow and just scream until I've got nothing left in me." She sniffed. "What do you think that means? Am I losing my mind, too?"

"No," Carson said, rising to sit. "Who cares about that damn house? It's been an albatross around your neck for years. Frankly, so was Cal. I never thought he was worthy of you."

Dora laughed lightly with disbelief. "Now you're starting to sound like Mamaw."

Carson's brows rose. "Then you know it's true. Mamaw's never wrong."

Dora shared a laugh with Carson and felt the tension ease between them.

Carson said, "I'm serious. Good riddance."

"Then why do I feel so sad?" Dora asked tearfully, plucking the tissue.

"You and me," Carson said earnestly, "we're both in a bad place right now. Harper, too. But we'll get through this. I promise you. Dora, you threw me a life preserver and pulled me in when I needed you. Let me do the same for you." She reached out to grab her sister's arm and give her a loving shake. "I'm here for you, okay? You're not alone, either."

The long-awaited phone call came at four o'clock the next day. Carson had risen from bed and showered, and was standing at the porch door, looking out, when Lucille knocked on her door.

"You got a phone call. It's from that dolphin fella," Lucille said. She watched as Carson darted past to the phone, then, with a small smile, closed the door behind her.

"This is Carson."

"Carson, it's Blake. I'm calling from Mote Marine Laboratory hospital in Sarasota."

She clutched the phone tighter. "How's Delphine?"

"Better. It was touch and go there for a while, but she's young and strong and held her own. The monofilament fishing line was embedded deeply and required surgery for removal. She's been started on antibiotics and fluids. At first she showed no interest in food but she could swim on her own, which was a good sign. They performed a second surgery to remove all of the monofilament encircling the base of the tail, which was already mangled from the shark bite. But today she turned a corner. Her blood work this morning looked significantly improved and she started eating. Even her swimming looks better. She's not out of the woods yet, but we're hopeful."

Carson began to cry. She hadn't expected such a visceral reaction. Clutching the phone, she slid down along the wall onto the floor, great heaving sobs pouring out that embarrassed her on the phone with Blake, but she couldn't stop herself.

"It's okay, Carson," Blake told her, his voice reassuring. "Delphine's one feisty dolphin."

"I'm so happy," she choked out. "You . . . you don't know what it's been like."

"I have a pretty good idea."

"Thank you, Blake. Thank you so much."

"Don't thank me. Thank this incredible team here at Mote. They deserve the credit."

"I will. I'll write to them today."

"It'd be nice if you sent a donation. The cost of caring for Delphine will be very high."

"Of course," she agreed. "I'm so grateful."

"Well, I'd better go. I've got a plane to catch. I just wanted you to know."

"You're coming home?"

"I'm done here."

"When will Delphine be coming back?"

"I can't say. We'll just have to see how she does. It's out of my hands now."

"Blake . . ." She hesitated. "Will you call me when you come back?" she asked. "I'd like to see you."

He paused.

"Please," she added.

"Yeah, sure," he said, though she heard no pleasure in it. "I'll give you a call when I get settled. I've got a lot of work piled on my desk. But I'll call."

She heard the click of the phone and hung up. She was worried about Blake's tone. He'd sounded so distant. She'd rather he'd sounded angry.

But Delphine was going to be all right. Then, for the first time in days, Carson smiled.

Carson knocked on Nate's door. There was no answer.

"Nate?" she called out.

There was no response.

Carson turned the handle and gently pushed open the door. She didn't want to startle the boy, nor was she sure how he'd react when he saw her. He might begin screaming again.

His room was dimly lit. Dora had told her that he kept closing the shutters, preferring to watch television or play his games in the dark. She found him as Dora had predicted, sitting in front of the screen, playing a video game.

"Nate?"

Nate swung around, startled. She saw the wariness in his eyes again, the same distrust that she'd seen the first time she met him. It pained her to see it.

"Can I come in?"

"No." He turned back to his game.

Carson hesitated at the door. "I have some good news."

"Go away."

"It's about Delphine."

Nate's fingers stopped manipulating his game. "What?"

Carson took a few steps toward him. "I got a phone call from Blake. He's the man who came when Delphine got sick and took her to the hospital in Florida."

No response.

"He said she's feeling much better. Delphine is going to be all right."

Nate remained expressionless, but his hand lowered as he set the game controller down on the floor. "What about her cuts?"

"Well," Carson said, "the doctors had to give her medicine and it's going to take time for her to heal, but they think she will. It's just going to take some time."

Nate said nothing.

"I wanted to tell you that. And that I'm very sorry I got angry and grabbed you. That was wrong of me. Sometimes, people get angry and do things they shouldn't. Things they regret. I'm sorry," she repeated.

Nate said nothing.

"Okay then." Carson ventured a smile, then turned to leave. As Carson walked across the room, she hoped Nate would call her back, that he'd say he was happy that Delphine's wounds were healing. But he did not. The boy only raised his controller and returned to his game. As Carson closed the door behind her, she realized that Delphine's wounds weren't the only ones that needed to heal.

CHAPTER TWENTY

A week later Carson hurried to the Medley coffee shop on Sullivan's Island. She'd waited by the phone and Blake had finally called her after he'd returned from Florida. There was a definite shift in his attitude toward her since the accident with Delphine. On the phone he'd sounded formal, even impatient, when she had asked him to meet her.

She stepped inside the coffee shop to see Blake already standing at the counter. He was dressed in the usual khaki shorts, brown T-shirt, and sandals. He looked more scruffy than usual. His dark hair was longer and he'd started one of those trimmed beard/moustache looks that she found very cool for the non-fashion-forward man. Knowing Blake, he was probably just tired of shaving. Seeing him again, it was disturbing to feel the punch of attraction and to realize she liked him more than she wished she did. He was staring up at the large chalkboard on the wall with the day's offerings written in white chalk.

"Hey," she said, drawing near.

Blake looked over his shoulder at her greeting. His immediate reaction was to smile, his dark eyes lighting up. Then it appeared as if he'd suddenly remembered he should be angry and his smile fell.

"Hello," he said in a cool voice. "Nice to see you again."

So they were back to being strangers, she thought with a twinge of regret.

"Thanks for meeting me."

"No problem," he said in an offhand manner. "It's part of my job."

She sucked in her breath. "Do you have to be so nasty?"

"I didn't think I was being nasty."

"Never mind," she said in a huff, turning to go. "I can see this wasn't a good idea."

"Wait," he said quickly.

She turned back, glaring at him with a hurt expression.

"Okay, I'm still angry."

"And I'm still devastated," Carson replied, her voice shaky.

Blake's brow furrowed in reflection. He asked in a conciliatory tone, "Want a coffee?"

Carson regrouped and glanced briefly at the menu written in chalk on the immense blackboard. "Latte, please."

Blake turned to give the order. Carson pressed her hand against her stomach while she steadied her breath, regaining composure.

Cups in hand, they glanced around the small room. There weren't many people in the coffee shop at this midmorning hour on a beautiful beach day. They claimed a small café table by the window.

"Blake," she began. She dreaded going into this discussion, but knew it couldn't be avoided. Better to dive right in than to endure painful chitchat. "I asked to talk to you today, because I wanted—needed—to tell you personally how badly I feel about what happened to Delphine."

She glanced up at him and saw him sitting with his hands around his mug, looking at it.

"I couldn't breathe until you'd called and told me that Delphine was going to be all right. If she'd died, I don't know what I'd have done. I feel like I've been given a second chance," she continued. "Yes, it was Nate's fault to leave the fishing lines out. But the bigger fault was mine for luring Delphine to the dock in the first place. I know that now. I wanted her there for my pleasure. And for whatever reason—believe it or not—she wanted to be there, too. Still, that's no excuse. I know now that she came where she wasn't supposed to be."

"And the dolphin got hurt."

"Right," she replied. "I'm so sorry."

"I understand this kind of thing happens," he said. "What I don't understand is how it happened with you. I thought you understood. I thought you were on my side."

"I *am*."

"Are you? Then how, despite all we'd talked about, all we'd seen together, did you never once mention that you had this friendly dolphin coming to your dock? You fed the dolphin. You swam with it. You acted no better than those guide boats that chum the waters for the tourists. I feel betrayed, Carson. I feel—"

"Hurt," she said for him.

He tightened his lips and nodded. "And disappointed."

Carson had no defense. She could handle his anger, but his disappointment and hurt were devastating. "Blake, I am so sorry."

He looked in her eyes, as though gauging her sincerity. She saw his eyes flicker. "Okay."

Carson knew that *okay* was something you said to someone when you really had nothing left to say. She'd not yet earned his forgiveness.

"And now?" she asked.

"Did I mention that under the federal Marine Mammal Protection Act, it's illegal to feed dolphins, and doing so can be punished by a fine of up to twenty-two thousand dollars in a civil case or up to a year in prison and a twenty-five-thousand-dollar fine in a criminal case?"

Carson paled and stared at him. "Did I mention we're making a significant donation to the hospital?"

Blake half smiled. "Glad to hear it. They need it."

"You're not going to—"

"Not if you don't continue to—"

"I won't," Carson promised.

"So, if Delphine is released to the cove," he asked her, "you won't call her back to the dock? Or feed her. Not ever?"

The image of Delphine flashed in her mind and she felt again the power of the bond of their relationship. Just the thought of what it would be like to not continue that association brought a raw pain that was unexpected.

"It will be hard," she said slowly. "I feel like I'm losing my best friend. But I never want to see her hurt again.

What if she comes by on her own? Can't I at least say hi to her?"

"Of course you can. As long as you don't start feeding her or swimming with her. Or let anyone else feed her."

"I'll just be so happy to see her again. I miss her terribly." She stopped, realizing she was treading on fragile ground. She didn't want to start crying again. "You can check on me if you like."

He withheld that crooked smile. "I just might do that." Blake looked at his watch and folded his long legs in. "I have to go," he said with finality, and picked up his cup to leave.

Carson was caught off guard by his sudden decision to leave. Impulsively she reached out to grab his hand. "Wait."

Blake paused, then settled back in his chair and waited.

Carson drew back her hand and looked at it on the table. "Look, I know I disappointed you. Where do we go from here?"

He shrugged. "I don't know."

Carson glanced at him and felt a shiver of fear. In that moment she knew she didn't want him to walk away. It was a new feeling for her. In the past if there was any discord or trouble, she was the first one to sprint. But now, for the first time, she didn't want to see this end.

"I made a mistake. I own it. Haven't you ever made a mistake?"

"Sure I have. It's not that." He paused and it felt like

eons before he spoke again. "I just don't know if we want the same things. I thought we did, but now . . ."

Carson felt her spine stiffen as she gathered her tumbling thoughts. "I am the same person today I was yesterday, and the day before that. But I've gone through a lot in these few days. Learned a lot. So much."

Carson began to speak and suddenly it was like she'd opened up the dam and the words came flowing out. She spared no detail as she told him how she'd awakened to the screams of Delphine, her horror at finding the brutal lacerations, the hook in the mouth, how desperate she felt when Delphine had to be flown to Florida. Carson told Blake about her fury at Nate for leaving the rods out, what Dora had said about her mother and Mamaw's explanation, and how she'd remembered, after all these years, the night of her mother's death. Finally, she was honest in describing how, desperate, she got drunk on the dock.

"I know I can't change the past. Not my mistakes or the mistakes of others. But I can begin by changing me. Blake, I feel like I'm at the threshold of a new beginning for myself. It's a time for second chances. For Delphine and for me both." She took a deep breath. "I'm asking for that second chance with you."

Blake rubbed his jaw, clearly giving her confession due diligence. When he spoke, his voice wasn't condescending. Carson blessed him for that.

"I know I was rough on you that day in the water. It's not that I would've been short with anyone who was down there. I was especially mad to see *you*."

"I know," she said, feeling defeated and looking out the window. "Because you felt betrayed."

"Because I was scared."

She swung her head to look at him. He was tearing at the edge of his paper cup.

"I was scared you'd get hurt. Dolphins are powerful wild animals that can be very aggressive. They can seriously bite—there are lots of incidents on record. If I sounded angry, it was because I saw you in the water and was worried."

She felt sure he saw the relief on her face. "The only one who can hurt me is you."

"I don't want to hurt you."

"Then don't."

After she'd said good-bye to Blake, Carson walked directly to Dunleavy's. There was one more atonement she had to make.

The pub was quiet, in the lull period between lunch and the cocktail hour. A few regulars sat at the tables. She spotted Devlin at the bar. There was no way to avoid him and get to Brian behind the bar. Brian looked up when he saw her and stopped polishing the glass.

"Hey, Brian," she called out as she approached.

"Carson," he replied, strangely aloof. "You're feeling better?"

"Yes, thanks," she replied, nervous at his obvious coolness.

Devlin's eyes sparked at seeing her. "Hey, stranger," he said, leaning over the bar. "Glad to see you back.

Missed your pretty face. It's tough staring at Brian's ugly mug."

She looked at Devlin, not entirely surprised that he wasn't the least bit sheepish about his bad behavior. She wondered if he even remembered it.

"Hey, Dev," she replied casually, then looked again at Brian. "Can I talk to you? In private."

"Sure." He set down the glass and towel. "In my office," he said, directing her to one of the booths.

She followed him to the booth farthest away from the bar and slid in opposite him. Devlin followed them with his gaze, perplexed. Carson sat on the booth bench with her knees tight together and her hands clasped in her lap. She looked across the wood-slab table at Brian. He'd leaned back, hands laced on the table, waiting.

"Brian, I'm ashamed of something I've done," she began haltingly. "You might've heard what happened to the dolphin at the Sea Breeze dock?"

He nodded soberly. "It's a small island. Very sad."

"I loved that dolphin and it was my fault. A few other things went down that day and I was hurting. Bad. When I came to work, I wasn't myself. Not that it excuses what I did," she hurried to add. She swallowed hard. She had to stop scurrying around the truth and just spit it out. "Brian, I stole a bottle of Southern Comfort from you."

Brian was quiet a moment. "I feel a little sick about it," he said, looking at his hands.

"That makes two of us," Carson said. "Would it make you feel better if I told you it was the only time I ever stole anything? Like ever, in my life?"

He looked up and saw the sincerity in her eyes, but his

jaw was clenched. "Would it make you feel any better if I told you it didn't matter?"

Some of the color drained from her face and for a moment she thought she might get sick. "I'll pay for it," Carson said.

Brian looked at her with an *oh, come on* stare. "Yeah, then everything will be fine. We'll just go back to the way it was."

Carson looked at her hands, feeling her heart sink. "No, I know that can't happen."

"I know how drinking can seem to put problems on the back burner." Brian pulled at his nose. "No back burners, kid. You're turning a blind eye, that's all. It's no solution."

"I figured that out. You seem to be familiar with this stuff," she said cautiously.

"Twenty years sober," he said. "And yes, I am an alcoholic."

Carson was caught off guard by his admission. "Then why work at a bar?"

He half smiled. "Look, kiddo. I've been doing this a long time. I know I can be around liquor and not drink. You don't know that. You can't be around liquor."

Carson watched Brian as he leaned back in the booth. He was a caring, honest man who didn't deserve what she'd done to him.

"So, what's next?" she asked.

"About stealing or drinking?" he said in a soft voice, not sarcastic.

"Both."

"I'm not going to sit here and tell you everything is

going to be okay, because it's not," he said. "Believe it or not, you're not the first person to steal from here. I've seen it all. Stuffing things, booze and food, into plastic bags. Then pretending to take out the garbage. Hell, I had one cook put twenty steaks in a plastic bag in the garbage, and his friend came by and picked them up. Clever, but desperate. I wasn't so nice to them. A restaurant is one of the toughest businesses to keep afloat. Each nickel and dime counts."

Truth was, she hadn't given much thought to any of the restaurant's profits or losses. *What employee really does?* she thought. She hung her head. She hadn't known it was possible to feel worse about stealing than she already did.

"I don't envy you having to face this problem," Brian said. "But I don't need to tell you, I can't have you working here anymore."

"I know," she said. "I'm grateful, Brian. For the job and for your kindness."

He offered some in return. "You're not a little girl, Carson. This is your decision. But if you think you might have a problem with alcohol, I hope—I pray—you'll look into AA. I think you're strong enough to fight it. I'd be glad to take you to a meeting. But if you'd rather go alone, there are a lot of meetings around the area. But go. At least once."

"I'll look into it, Brian, I promise. I appreciate your kindness. About the stealing and for caring enough to suggest some help."

Brian reached over and shook her hand. "I appreciate

you had the courage to come speak to me first. I knew you took the bottle."

Carson paled at the admission as she shook his hand.

Brian smiled. "You're welcome here anytime. And bring Mamaw. I haven't seen that renegade in ages."

CHAPTER TWENTY-ONE

A few days later, Carson peeked through the window and was surprised to see Blake at the front door. She'd spent the night with him and they'd said good-bye after coffee that morning. Blake had headed off to work at Fort Johnson and Carson had returned to Sea Breeze. She wondered what Blake might have forgotten that brought him back to see her.

"Hey," she said with a welcoming smile, opening the door.

Blake's smile was tight and his dark eyes troubled. "Hi," he said.

"Come on in," Carson said, her face clouding as she stepped back. "What's the matter?"

"Do you have a minute to talk?"

Now Carson's thoughts roiled. "Uh, sure. How about right here?" she asked, indicating the living room.

She followed him into the room and they each took one of the wing chairs. Blake sat stiffly, his pale blue denim shirt frayed at the cuffs, exposing tanned hands that lay flat on his thighs. Carson raked her hair from her face.

"It's so humid today," she said, initiating conversation. "Mamaw won't boost the air-conditioning. She claims she likes it."

He laughed but his heart wasn't in it. He clasped his palms together and stared at them.

She crossed her legs, holding her lips tight, feeling her stomach clench.

"Carson, I've got something I need to tell you."

"Okay," she said warily.

"It's about Delphine."

"What about her?"

"These past few days I've been going through all my photo files on the dolphins we've recorded in our area for the past five years, trying to find a match with the photos you sent me. Carson, I've searched till my eyes were blurry. Eric did, too. There's no record of Delphine in our data files."

Carson's brow furrowed. "What does that mean?"

"It means that she isn't classified as resident to the Charleston estuary system. She's not one of ours."

"How can that be? She was here, wasn't she?"

"There are several possibilities. She could have just been migrating along the coast when she got mixed up with that shark and was injured. That might've brought her into safer waters for a while. Then she found you and a free meal and decided to stay."

"Do they do that? Do coastal dolphins roam into the rivers?"

He nodded. "Yes. Most have a preference for one area or the other, but a few go both ways. There are always those that follow a shrimp boat from the coast into the harbor, too, and you said there was a shrimp boat around that morning. My guess is that she wandered into the cove for whatever reason and just stayed."

"So, she's alone out there?" Carson said, feeling a pang for Delphine. "It's no wonder she befriended me."

"Or she stayed *because* you befriended her. There's a difference."

"You are always so damned quick to remind me of my mistake."

"I don't mean to be harsh. I just don't want you to slip into that sentimental thinking again. For both your sakes."

"So, what do we do now? When she's returned, will she eventually become a member of the local dolphin community?"

He rubbed his hands together, as though upset that he wasn't handling the situation well. "That, Carson, is the problem."

Carson sensed the change in tone and felt the tension radiating from Blake's body. She quieted her emotions and listened attentively. "What problem?"

"Carson," he began on solid footing. "If Delphine is not part of the resident population in this area, the Mote Marine Laboratory's hospital will not release her back into our estuaries."

"What? They can't do that. This is where she belongs. We brought her to them to heal her. They can't keep her!"

"They won't keep her," he said, trying to calm her.

"They can't release her in Florida! That's ridiculous. She is not a local resident there, either. What's the point? At least here she has me. She knows me."

"Carson, listen to me. It's more complicated than that. First of all, the fact that she isn't a resident in our estuarine system means she won't have a support system. That's the first problem. The second is what you just said: that you'd take care of her. That can't happen. We've discussed that. Frankly, Carson, Delphine's extreme friendliness made us concerned that she has already learned to depend on humans. She's a possible candidate to be another beggar, and that's bad for her. Third, and most importantly, her wounds were intense, and add to that her already mangled tail fluke and you have a compromised dolphin."

Blake puffed out a plume of air and his eyes searched hers. "We've considered all the factors. NOAA doesn't make the decision lightly. We all want the dolphin to return home to the wild, if that's possible. The decision is still out, pending how well she heals. And," he added soberly, "brace yourself. There may be a fourth problem. Delphine is not progressing as well as they'd hoped. She is not eating well and is increasingly listless."

Carson was taken aback. "How long have you known this?"

"A few days."

"And you've waited until just now to tell me?"

"I didn't want to upset you. We were all hoping she'd come around."

Carson tried to picture Delphine—her curious eyes, her persistent friendliness—listless and injured in some strange holding tank. She felt her palms go clammy and drops of perspiration formed on her brow. She swiped the moisture away, cursing the humidity.

Blake said, "Some dolphins become listless because they're in an unfamiliar environment, and sometimes there's an underlying medical cause—but we don't know for sure what is going on with Delphine. In the end they may need to transfer her to another facility."

"They can't!" Carson cried. She rose to pace the room, horrified—threatened—by this new development. "I don't get it. Why did you take me out to see the wild dolphins? You showed me how much better it was for them to live in the wild, to socialize, to hunt. Now you're telling me that they won't release Delphine back into the wild? That they're putting her into a facility? And you're going to go along with that? She won't understand why she was put there. It's too cruel."

Blake reached out for her. "Carson."

"Don't touch me!" she exclaimed, lifting her hands into an arresting position. "I don't understand why you're letting this happen. You're with NOAA. You can stop this. You can make them bring her back here."

"No, I can't. I don't have that authority. And even if I did, I wouldn't."

"Why not?" she said through clenched teeth.

"Because it's always got to be what's best for the dolphin."

She sputtered as she bit back her words. She wanted

to shout at him that she hated him, but of course she didn't. She hated the situation. She hated her role in it. She hated to see Delphine in this state of affairs.

But she still couldn't bear to look at Blake, to be in his proximity. She had had it with his rules and regulations, his inability to understand her relationship with Delphine. His insensitivity. She was done with him, done with all of it. She stopped pacing, feeling once again the walls of the room closing in on her. The old panic built in her chest and all she knew was that she had to get out of there.

"I need to be alone for a while," she said. She jerked her arm toward the door. "Please, see yourself out." Carson turned and hurried from the room, despising herself for her emotional outburst. She rushed through the humid house, desperate to get outside and into the fresh air, to regain her composure. She had to get to the water.

The sky over the mainland was like a purple wall of rain. On the island it was still sunny. Bolts of lightning ripped the clouds, followed by the low growl of thunder. In contrast, it was still blue-skied over the islands. Carson ran down the dock, her heels hitting hard, thundering on the wood. Once on the floating dock she tore off her clothing to her bra and underwear and stood perched, her toes dangling at the edge.

Carson took deep breaths and calmed herself as shafts of sunlight pierced the water. From the depths, along the moss-covered pilings, she spotted a long, dark shadow. Her heart skipped as she instinctively thought of Delphine. Stepping closer to the edge to peer over the dock, Carson searched the waves. She saw nothing out of the ordinary, merely the rise and fall of a living, breathing body of water.

Something indescribable happened to her when she stared into the blue depths of the ocean. She could feel her anxiety slowly drain from her body. It was akin to pushing a delete button on the litany of worries she'd stored in her brain. Before long her breathing matched the rise and fall of the gentle waves. Her thoughts grew calm and rational.

The sea was, she knew, home to countless living creatures. Small fish darted between the safety of the pilings, nibbling algae. Along the shoreline the black, pointed tips of the oysters, one on top of the other, formed a dangerously delicious, barbed bed. Staring at the sandy bottom of the cove, she wondered if she'd imagined the dark shadow.

Carson wrapped her arms around her chest and chewed her lip in thought. How long would she stand trembling at the edge?

She remembered Mamaw's words to her. *You're the strongest girl I know*. She recalled the brazenly bold, self-assured look of her ancestor, Claire, in the portrait. Finally, Carson thought of her mother, and the courage it had taken for the young woman to travel alone to America to start a new life.

She had to find that courage within herself again. Sure, she was still scared of the dark shadows in the water. She'd be a fool if she wasn't. But this sea was her territory, too. Over five hundred million years ago we all called the sea home. Our bond to the ocean was personal. The connection flowed in her memory, deeper than her mother's milk.

Standing on the dock, Carson shook her legs, feeling the blood flow. She felt the sun on her face as she lifted her arms over her head, then marked a spot in the water. She took a gulp of air, that one act defining the major evolutionary difference between her and the fish in the sea. Yet it was that same need for air that bonded her with dolphins. Carson dove into the water. The cool liquid enveloped her, welcoming her.

Home, she thought as her arms stretched wide and her mouth released a stream of bubbles. Kicking hard, she burst to the surface, gasping for air. Drops of water ran down her smiling face as she thrust her arms forward and kicked again, hard. One stroke after another, she swam without pause against the current, heady with triumph. She swam straight to Mr. Bellows's dock and rested, feeling her arms tired after so many days without exercise. *I made it*, she thought exultantly. She looked at the Sea Breeze dock, marking it, gauging the distance. Now to return.

Pushing off, she began her swim back. She took it at a more leisurely pace, enjoying the sensation of stretching her arms as far forward as she could, feeling the sun on her face. She imagined Delphine swimming with her, saw her eyes eager and bright, curious about what adventure was next. She felt the dolphin's energy radiating through her. These waters held memories, Carson realized, and in that shining moment she knew that Delphine would always be with her.

As she drew closer to the dock, she saw Blake standing, waiting, his hands on his hips. He bent to offer his hand to help her up. The hurt and anger she'd felt had dissolved as another part of her—the stronger, more confident part—welcomed the sight of him. There was no room in her heart for petty peevishness. She reached for his hand and felt his strong fingers close around hers.

Blake wrapped a towel around her shoulders, then stood a polite distance back, no doubt still tentative after her flare-up.

"Can we talk about this?" he asked. "Please, Carson. This is too important."

"Yes, of course," she replied, her tone conciliatory. She began rubbing her body with the towel. "I'm sorry about my outburst earlier. I'm still tender when it comes to Delphine. But what's left to discuss? You just told me that it's all been decided already." She paused, breathing in slowly. "That they're moving Delphine to a facility."

"No, that's not what I said," he answered, enunciating clearly. "I said Delphine is not doing well. They are *considering* putting her in a facility."

"And without an ID of her being part of our resident community, that was likely to happen anyway," Carson added succinctly. She sighed and tightened the towel around herself, feeling a wave of dejection. "What's the difference?"

"There is a difference and it's what I want you to understand." Blake shifted his weight, put his hands on his hips, a move Carson recognized now as indicating he'd given the matter a lot of thought and was about to explain himself. "The place Delphine is slated for is very unique. It's located in the Florida Keys and has natural lagoons with the sea flowing in and out. She'll still be in the Atlantic Ocean, her home. It's not a cement pond. And they'll be introducing her to their pod family. They know what they're doing. Delphine will be welcomed by a devoted staff and eventually by the dolphins, too. If she goes there, she'll belong to a new family. I've seen it happen with other dolphins."

The thought of Delphine being welcomed into a family of dolphins took the steam from her sails. It was so like Blake to listen to her concerns, to offer intelligent answers. His reaction was quiet, subtle, and persuasive. She slumped down onto the dock, folded her legs close and wrapped herself tight in the towel. She stared out at the cove that still felt so empty without Delphine.

Blake moved to sit beside Carson. All was silent save for the soft rumble of thunder as the storm clouds drew closer. Choppy gray-green waves slapped against the docks.

"I thought you were against dolphins in captivity?" she asked him in a small voice, striving to be fair and realistic.

Blake seemed to appreciate her effort, understanding at last that, to her, this was not black and white; this was an issue layered with complicated emotions. "If you ask me if I'm opposed to dolphins being captured from the wild, I'd unequivocally say that yes, I'm opposed. No wild dolphin should be removed from its natural habitat for any reason. Not ever. On the other hand, the fact is there are aquariums and facilities that provide a place where injured, nonreleasable dolphins can live out their days, well cared for and loved. These dolphins would likely end up shark bait or starve if released." He paused. "The Dolphin Research Center is such a place. This is where they will send Delphine, if they deem her nonreleasable."

A gust of cooler wind sent the spray from a wave sprinkling over them. She shivered and her teeth began to chatter.

Blake's brows furrowed and he reached to put his arm around her shoulders. She resisted marginally but he murmured her name softly and pulled her closer. Carson felt the strength of his arms and relaxed against him, felt his arms slide around her, holding her tight. She breathed deeply, smelling the faint scent of his body in the well-worn shirt. He didn't speak and instead rested his chin on the soft hairs of her head.

She reached up to tuck her hair behind an ear. "I've been thinking and thinking . . ." Her voice trailed off.

"Thinking about what?"

"It's like I'm putting the pieces of a puzzle together, a puzzle that's baffled me for years. It's beginning to make sense to me now." She paused. "The fact that I'm always avoiding relationships, never counting on anyone or anything to come through, running from commitments—it might not have been something I was aware of consciously, but looking back, how else can I explain it? I didn't even want to own a condo, for God's sake. I've always had this . . ." She groped for the word. ". . . this *compulsion* to be unfettered, to be free from anything or anyone that could tie me down."

She took a breath. "Until Delphine. This summer, for the first time, I've formed a real attachment to, of all things, a dolphin." She laughed, still amazed at the miracle that she'd experienced. "She changed me. There's no other way to explain it. I don't know how to make you understand. All my life I've kept so much at bay—my emotions, the people I care about, my responsibilities. With Delphine I couldn't do that. To communicate with her, I had to move from the inside out." She shook her head.

"I couldn't fool her. I couldn't come to the water angry or sad. She forced me to raise my vibrations; she made me happy." Carson groaned and put her face in her hands. "I feel embarrassed saying these things to you. You must think I'm some *woo-woo* chick from L.A." She dropped her hands and looked into his eyes. "But it's true. And I'm not prepared to face life without Delphine in it right now."

"I know."

Carson sat up again to face him. "I feel like I'm abandoning her. All I've ever done is abandon things—jobs, relationships." She shook her head. "I won't do it. Blake, you know that is a cardinal sin in my book."

"She is not being abandoned, Carson," Blake said, pleading with her to understand. "Quite the contrary. They're eager to have her. And it wasn't like you had a hand in the decision. She was hurt, and you helped save her life."

"Can you explain that to her?" Carson asked. "In a way she can understand? You can't," she answered for him.

"Just as you can't understand what I'm feeling. You see dolphins as fascinating, intelligent creatures. But you stop there. You won't even consider the possibility that dolphins and humans can connect in a very real way that's not scientific. It's something I feel in my heart, not my head. I don't have studies to share with you. But I know our bond is there. I *know* it."

"But I *don't* doubt you shared a bond," Blake replied. He held her gaze. "I believe you."

Carson sighed, relieved that at last he validated her feelings.

"You're shivering," Blake said. "We should go."

"You're right," Carson replied, coming to a decision that had been forming in her mind since Delphine was first taken away. "I should go. To Florida. I need to see Delphine again. To see with my own eyes that she's all right."

"Carson . . ."

"If she's depressed, she'll be comforted to see me. She knows me. I might be able to help. I have to try." She took Blake's hand. "Can you help me with at least that much?"

"You want to go to the Dolphin Research Center?"

"No, I want to go to the hospital. To the Mote Marine Laboratory, where Delphine is now," she replied.

"Treatment may take weeks. Months."

"I'll stay only as long as it takes her to turn the corner."

"Where will you stay? How can you afford it?"

"I'll get a job. Get a cheap place to stay. I know how to do that."

"You won't gain access. Only the staff can see her."

"Then help me get a job there. Or an internship. Or

a volunteer position. I'll sweep the floors, scrub tanks, whatever they want. Anything that lets me in the door to see her."

He frowned. "You won't sway their decision regarding the facility."

"That's not my intention. I only want to see if I can help save Delphine. I think I owe her that much."

Thunder rumbled, closer now and louder.

Blake looked out at the sky, his profile illuminated by a crack of lightning. "You're asking me to help you leave," he said.

"Yes."

"And then what?" he asked, turning to face her. "Now, I'm asking *you*. What about us?"

The wind gusted and Carson felt filled with purpose. She reached out and took his other hand in hers and, holding tight, looked into his eyes.

"I'm not going to lose us, either," she answered. "Blake, I care about you. Deeply. I know we have something special. But I know in my heart if I let this go, if I don't see for myself that she's okay and make her understand that I'm not abandoning her, I'll never be able to move on. I'll just be running away again. Don't you see? That's what I do *every time*. I cut my losses and leave. But I'm trying to break that pattern. Only if I see this through with Delphine is there any hope for you and me."

He leaned forward so that their foreheads touched.

"Just say you'll come back."

"I'll come back."

He moved his head to kiss her, slowly, possessively.

A clap of thunder roared and echoed above them, warning them that the heart of the storm was overhead. Blake cupped his hands to frame her face, as though capturing her image, then rose and pulled Carson to her feet. Clasping hands, they ran down the dock to the shelter of Sea Breeze.

CHAPTER TWENTY-TWO

"You wanted to see me?"

Mamaw looked up from the small gaily wrapped box she held in her lap. Carson stood by the door, her expression curious, perhaps a bit anxious at being called to Mamaw's room. Carson was leaving for Florida the following morning. All day she had been a whirling dervish packing and preparing for the trip. The house was quiet now save for the murmurs of the girls out on the back porch and the clinking of ice in their glasses. Mamaw surveyed the young woman dressed in what she had come to accept were Carson's pajamas—men's boxers and an old T-shirt. Her long hair draped her shoulders like a black velvet shawl.

"Yes, come in," Mamaw replied, waving a hand to usher in Carson. Then she patted the chair beside hers.

Carson smiled and joined Mamaw in the small sitting room that adjoined her bedroom. A small lamp with a blue-fringed shade spilled yellow light on the chintz fabric covering the table and the matching chairs. This was Mamaw's favorite room, a perfect spot for a tête-à-tête. She idly let her fingers smooth the collar of her pale pink silk robe as she measured Carson's steps toward her.

Carson bent to kiss her grandmother's cheek. "This is nice."

"I wanted to have a little chat before you leave," Mamaw began.

"I'm all packed and ready to go, just like the song," Carson told her.

Mamaw searched Carson's face and saw the familiar signs of pending departure—the excitement in her eyes, the fission of energy radiating from her pores. Why were her loved ones always so eager to leave? The open road had never called to Mamaw. She'd never understood why anyone would want to leave the sultry winding creeks, the phenomenal sunsets, or the song of the surf in the lowcountry. There was more than enough culture in Charleston for even the most discriminating tastes. What the lure of foreign cities was, Mamaw was sure she didn't know.

Carson must have seen the anxiety in her face, because she leaned forward to place her hand over Mamaw's. "I'll be back soon. I promise. I'll only be gone a few weeks. I know how important this summer is to you. I won't disappoint you."

"Oh, child," Mamaw said, patting Carson's hand, "you've never disappointed me."

Carson looked at her askance. "Never? But I feel like I've just made a mess of things. Again."

"Never," Mamaw replied firmly. She hated to see any

sign of defeatism in her granddaughters. She was quick to ferret it out.

"Quite the opposite. That's what I wanted to talk to you about. Carson," she began, looking squarely into her granddaughter's eyes, wanting to be heard. "This has been a very difficult month for you. Yet you've weathered this emotional roller coaster of family secrets, confronted your drinking, shouldered the responsibility of this terrible accident with the dolphin, all with a grace and courage that not many women possess."

She paused to see Carson's eyes widen with incredulity, and in that moment saw again the little girl who had come to live with her after the fire, her burned skin bandaged, her hair singed, and her blue eyes wide with a vulnerable hope that had made Mamaw's heart go out to her.

"I am very proud of you," Mamaw said with emphasis, wanting the words to sink in.

Carson shut her eyes for a moment and then opened them again. "I'm not sure I deserve that," Carson said in a stumbling manner. "And as for my drinking, I'm just taking it day by day."

"That's all any of us can do, my dear. We wake up, bolster our resolve, and rise to face the new day. Or else lie in bed and waste our lives."

Carson nodded her head, listening. "Now you sound like Blake," she said. "He's very, shall we say, optimistic."

"Oh?" Mamaw said, her ears instantly perked to any mention of a young gentleman caller. "How is that nice young man?"

Carson's smile was all-knowing. "He's fine, Mamaw."

Mamaw waited but nothing more was forthcoming. She couldn't help herself from continuing. "You're still seeing him, then? After the incident with the dolphin?"

"I think I'm on probation," Carson replied with a light laugh.

"How does he feel about you leaving?"

"He's not happy about it," Carson replied honestly. "But he understands why I have to do this. He arranged for me to see Delphine. I could never have gained access if he hadn't."

"I see. Well, he's a very nice young man."

"You've already told me that, Mamaw," Carson said with a gentle nudge. "Seriously, I do care for him. A great deal. More than I've cared for anyone before. And I'm quite certain he feels the same way. It's like you said. We're taking it day by day. Okay?"

Mamaw tried to disguise her pleasure in this revelation by looking down at the package in her lap. "*So*," Mamaw said in an upbeat tone, straightening in her chair and taking hold of the box. "I have a little gift for you."

"A gift? It's not my birthday."

"I know very well it's not your birthday, silly girl. And it's not Christmas, Fourth of July, or Arbor Day." She reached out to hand Carson the small box wrapped in shiny blue paper and a white ribbon. "Can't a grandmother give her granddaughter a gift if she wants to? Open it!"

Carson's face eased into a smile of anticipation as she bent over the box and tidily unwrapped the ribbon, rolling it in a ball, then slowly undid the tape, careful not to tear the paper. Mamaw enjoyed watching her open the gift delicately, recalling once again Carson as a little girl. So unlike Harper, who ripped through the paper, shredding it and letting the bits scatter around her.

Before opening the lid, Carson shook the box by her ear, eyes skyward in mock appraisal. "A bracelet, maybe? Or a brooch?"

Mamaw didn't reply and only lifted her brows, her hands tightening together as her own anticipation at Carson's response mounted.

Carson opened the box, then lifted the corners of the yellowed, fragile cotton handkerchief, one that Mamaw had tucked in her sleeve on her wedding day, delicately embroidered with the initials MCM. Then she went still. Wrapped in the cotton was a key attached to a silver key ring in the shape of a dolphin. Carson looked at her grandmother with an expression of disbelief.

"Are you kidding me? Is this . . . is this the key to the Blue Bomber?" Carson cried.

"The same."

"But . . . I thought you said . . . I don't understand," Carson stammered.

"There's nothing to understand," Mamaw said with a light laugh. "It's my gift to you! That Cadillac might be old, but she's in perfect condition. She'll take you to Florida and back safely. And anywhere else you might want to go. It's yours now. I want you to have it. You've earned it."

Speechless, Carson leaned in to wrap her arms around Mamaw's shoulders and squeezed tight. Mamaw caught the scent of her own perfume on Carson's skin—their scent now—and felt the age-old bond she'd always felt with Carson.

"I don't know what to say," Carson said, sliding back in her chair. She stared at the key in disbelief.

"'Thank you' is usually appropriate." Mamaw winked.

Carson laughed, then smiled at her. "Thank you."

Mamaw felt a rush of emotion mist her eyes. "Oh, I do hate to see you go. Well, kiss me good-bye now, my precious girl," she said with false bluster. "Then off to bed. You'll need your sleep for the long drive."

"I'll kiss you good night now, and kiss you good-bye tomorrow."

Mamaw shook her head. "No, all now. I hate good-byes." She sighed. "There have been too many in my life."

Carson kissed her grandmother's cheek, lingering at her ear. "I'll be back soon. I promise."

It was a fitting morning for travel. The sky was cloudless and the air was clear, free from the heavy Southern humidity that made one feel drenched by nine A.M. Mamaw stood on the widow's porch, her hands clutching the railing, looking at the scene unfolding below.

"You sure you don't want to go down and join them?" Lucille asked by her side. "We're like a couple of old hens roosting up here."

"Quite sure," Mamaw said, feeling again the twinge in her heart that she always felt at partings. She rallied, straightening her shoulders, and said archly, "We've said our good-byes, and you know how I despise melodrama."

"Uh-huh," Lucille said with heavy sarcasm. "You sure do hate any drama."

Mamaw had the grace to chuckle. She directed her gaze to the cluster of young women gathered around the blue Cadillac. The car was packed; the top was down. For a moment she recalled herself as a young woman standing in that very driveway, laughing, hugging, kissing when she'd said numerous good-byes to Parker as he followed his wanderlust, and the forced smiles that belied her heartbreak each time her Summer Girls returned to their distant homes at summer's end. And, too, the dreadful, final farewells to her husband and son. Such was the burden of a long life. There were too many good-byes, so many sunrises and sunsets, memories joyous and painful.

Carson was the tallest, dressed in faded jeans and a pale blue linen shirt. Her dark hair was bound in a braid that fell down her back like a long rope. Over this she wore a straw fedora-like hat with a bright blue band. She was leaning against the big car with a proprietor's air, dangling the keys in front of her sisters' faces. Dora stood beside her in pink Bermuda shorts and a floral T-shirt, her blond hair flowing loose to her shoulders. She sipped from the mug in her hands as they talked. Harper was as sleek as a little black bird in ankle-length pants and a shirt, her coppery hair pulled back in a ponytail. How she could stand in those high-heeled sandals, Mamaw didn't know.

"They're as different from each other today as they've ever been," she said to Lucille. "And yet, in the past few weeks, I believe they've discovered that they're not without some rather profound commonalities. Don't you think?"

"If by 'commonalities' you mean they're not at each other's throats and are beginning to like each other again, I'll give you that," Lucille replied.

"That, too, of course," Mamaw said with a hint of impatience. But it was so much more than this, and yet too difficult to put into words. Though the girls were still negotiating the delicate bonds of sisterhood, in the past weeks she'd heard in their voices, and seen in small gestures, the beginnings of reconnection. A rediscovery of the magic they'd once shared when they were together at Sea Breeze during those long-ago summers—the three of them huddled on the beach under a single towel, whispering together in their beds, sipping from three straws in a single root-beer float, exploring the mysteries of the island and beach. Her prayer was that as the summer unfolded and the women shared time again at Sea Breeze—the very name implied a breath of fresh air— they would discover the life force that would give their lives purpose and meaning.

The sound of laughter swelled from below, drawing Mamaw's attention again. Something had stirred the girls to that belly-holding, bent-over laughter that brought tears to the eyes. Their high-pitched hoots were louder than the piercing call of the osprey circling above them. Mamaw's heart swelled and her eyes grew misty again.

"Look at them," she said to Lucille. "That's how I *always* want to see them. Happy. Bonding, supportive of each other. After we're gone, that's all they're going to have. Is that too much to ask?"

"I reckon that's every mother's prayer," Lucille said.

"I'm worried about them," Mamaw said from the

heart. "They look happy for the moment, but they're still so unsettled. All of them. I wonder what I can do to help them."

"Now don't you start up on that again. Remember the trouble that caused? You got them all here. You got them back in the game. That's all you can do. Now it's up to them to play out their own hands."

"But the cards are still being dealt," Mamaw cautioned.

Lucille shrugged. "Sure enough. Till the game is over." She turned to Marietta and they exchanged a look that spoke of a lifetime of shared worries. "You win some, you lose some."

The symphonic honk of the Cadillac's horn brought their attention back to the girls below. Carson was looking up to the rooftop, her arm straight in the air, waving. Mamaw and Lucille raised their hands and enthusiastically returned the wave. They watched as the big car pulled slowly out of the driveway with Dora and Harper trotting after it, shouting "Death to the ladies!" With a final honk, Carson hit the gas. The engine roared and she took off, disappearing around the hedge of greenery.

Dora and Harper remained at the end of the driveway waving for several moments. Then they linked arms and began walking together toward the beach.

"My, my, my," Mamaw muttered at the sight. That was a first for those two. She looked beyond to the sparkling blue ocean. The waves rolled in and out in their metronome rhythm. Maybe Lucille was right, she thought, though she'd never admit it to her. Life really was just a game of cards.

Mamaw turned to Lucille. "Time to get out of this sun. Are you up for a game of gin? I'll spot you twenty points."

Lucille harrumphed. "The day I need you to spot me is the day I take up checkers."

Mamaw laughed, feeling suddenly buoyed with hope. She grasped the stair railing, but before leaving the porch she paused, lifted her gaze, and took one final, sweeping look toward the sea. The blue Cadillac was nowhere to be seen, but in the distance she caught sight of the two women making their way together down the long, winding path.

ACKNOWLEDGMENTS

*T*he world of dolphins is fascinating and complex, and I owe a debt of thanks to many people for sharing their knowledge and expertise, and for enlightening me about these intelligent and charismatic creatures.

I owe a huge debt of thanks to Dr. Pat Fair, director, Marine Mammal Program, NOAA, for serving as my mentor, friend, and editor for all things *Tursiops truncatus*. Also, my appreciation to Eric Zolman of NOAA for memories on the Zodiac. And to Justin Greenman and Wayne McFee.

My sincere gratitude goes to all the dedicated staff at the Dolphin Research Center, Grassy Key, Florida, for an education of the mind and spirit. Special thanks to Linda Erb, Joan Mehew, Becky Rhodes, Mary Stella, Rita Erwin, and Kirsten Donald for answering my countless questions, and providing keen insights, for their support, and for dolphin experiences I'll cherish forever. And to all my fellow volunteers—Sarah, Candace, Stacy, Nate, Lindsey,

Ryan, Alice, Marissa, June, Clare, Arielle, Abby, Jeanette, Donna, Abby, Debbie, Viv, and Misty—who helped me go through the paces of animal care. A big hug and thanks to Joel Martino, who made my stay at Port Kaya note perfect.

A special thank-you to Stephen McCulloch, Harbor Branch, Florida Atlantic University—your expertise and imagination are amazing and inspiring. Sincere thanks to Lynne Byrd, Randall Wells, and Hayley Rutger of Mote Marine Laboratory and Aquarium, to Shelley Dearhart at the South Carolina Aquarium, and to Ron Hardy of Gulf World for all their help and advice during the writing of this book.

As always, heartfelt thanks to the fabulous team at Gallery Books for continued support. I'm blessed to have the talent and great heart of my editors, Lauren McKenna and Alexandra Lewis; my publisher, Louise Burke; and in publicity, Jean Anne Rose.

I send my deep appreciation to my agents, Kimberly Whalen and Robert Gottlieb, and all the team at Trident Media Group, and to Joe Veltre at Gersh, for wise advice and guidance.

On the home front, my continued love and thanks to Marguerite Martino, James Cryns, and Margaretta Kruesi for all their critiques, brainstorming, and support. And to my team: Angela May, Buzzy Porter, Kathie Bennett, Lisa Laing, and Lisa Minnick.

Finally, to Markus—let me count the ways.

Dear Reader,

Dolphins are beloved around the world. From the dawn of history stories have been told about the intelligence, beauty—that deceptive smile!—and curiosity of dolphins and their enduring connection with humans.

Yet, despite our love for dolphins, mankind is their greatest threat. Hazards include injury and mortality from fishing gear, such as gill net, seine, trawl; marine debris; longline commercial operations; and recreational boats that lure dolphins near with food. Other perils include exposure to pollutants and biotoxins, viral outbreaks, and direct harvest.

How can you help? Be SMART.

S   Stay back—fifty yards—from dolphins.
M   Move away if dolphins show signs of disturbance.
A   Always put your engines in neutral when dolphins are near.
R   Refrain from feeding, touching, or swimming with wild dolphins.
T   Teach others to be dolphin-smart.

If you'd like to learn more about dolphins, you can visit www.education.noaa.gov.

We can all do our part to protect these "angels of the deep."

Mary Alice Monroe

DOLPHIN FACTS

• The Atlantic bottlenose dolphin (*Tursiops truncatus*) ranges in size from 6.0 to 12.5 ft (2–4 m) and in weight from 300 to 1,400 lbs (135–635 kg).

• Dolphins live in fluid social groups called pods. The size of a pod varies roughly from two to fifteen individuals. The natural diet of the bottlenose dolphin consists of fish and crustaceans. They do not chew their food but swallow it whole. Dolphins usually forage for food in groups and use their intelligence to cooperate in hunting strategies.

• Coastal bottlenose dolphins are very social animals. Groupings of females with calves are called maternity pods or nursery groups. Female dolphins help rear pod dolphins as babysitters or "aunties." Mature males congregate in bachelor groups and sometimes two to three individuals form what is known as a "pair bond." Pair-bonded males will stay together for an extended period, if not all of their lives. Both young and old dolphins chase one another, carry objects around, toss seaweed to one another, and use objects to invite each other to interact.

• A bottlenose dolphin pregnancy lasts twelve months. Being mammals, dolphins bear live young and nurse them for about two years. Mothers remain with their young, teaching them foraging and social skills, for an average of five years.

• The average lifespan of a coastal bottlenose is twenty-five years. Though it is uncommon for them to do so, dolphins can live into their fifties.

• Vision: Dolphins have highly specialized eyes that accommodate changes in light in and out of the water. Bottlenose dolphins can see up to nine feet underwater with good visibility and up to twelve feet in the air.

• Hearing: Sound travels farther and faster than light in the ocean. Dolphins have highly sensitive hearing. They create and listen for sounds in order to detect prey or predators, to navigate, to communicate, and to determine the location of other dolphins.

• Vocalization: Dolphins produce clicks and sounds that resemble moans, trills, grunts, and squeaks. Above water they make sounds by releasing air through their blowholes. Dolphins develop signature whistles, or "names."

• Echolocation: Clicks emitted by a dolphin strike objects in the underwater world and bounce back as echoes that are picked up through the dolphin's lower jaw. From the returning echoes, dolphins can tell the size, shape, distance, speed, direction of travel, and density of the object, thus allowing them to "see" underwater. Dolphin echolocation is considered to be the most advanced sonar capability, unrivaled by any sonar system on earth, man-made or natural.

POCKET READERS GROUP GUIDE

The Summer Girls

MARY ALICE MONROE

SUMMARY

Marietta Muir is worried that her much-loved granddaughters, though as different as can be, are estranged. Now fully grown, Carson, the free spirit; Dora, the Southern-belle-turned-stay-at-home-mom; and city girl Harper haven't spent time together since their long childhood summers with their Mamaw at Sea Breeze, the beach house on Sullivan's Island, South Carolina. But when Marietta schemes to bring her girls back together for her eightieth birthday party, the women's differences threaten to tear them apart once and for all.

An L.A. photographer, Carson feels most at home when she's in the water. But the ocean's magic isn't enough to keep her emotional demons at bay. When she comes to Sullivan's Island, Carson is offered a fresh start . . . with some help from a marine biologist, a dolphin named Delphine, and her sisters—the Summer Girls.

QUESTIONS AND TOPICS FOR DISCUSSION

1. Dora's initial reaction to Mamaw's plan to bring the Summer Girls together for the season is to call it "blackmail" (p. 173). Do you agree with Dora, or are you sympathetic with Mamaw's scheme? Why or why not?

2. Besides Harper, Carson, and Dora, Mamaw and Lucille have perhaps the most complex and important female relationship in the book. Describe their friendship. How do the two older women serve as role models to the younger three?

3. Mamaw plans to give her granddaughters their pearl necklaces early in the book, before we know Dora, Carson, or Harper very well as characters. What could you assume about each of the Summer Girls based on Mamaw's choices for them? Were those assumptions accurate?

4. Carson is Mamaw's favorite granddaughter: "It might have been because she'd spent the most time with the motherless girl when she'd come for extended stays after being unceremoniously dumped by her father when he was off on a jaunt. But Carson was also the most like Marietta, passionate about life and not afraid to accept challenges, quick to make up her mind, and a tall beauty with a long history of beaus"

(p. 37). Which of the three sisters did you relate to most, and why?

5. Dora has not been open with her sisters concerning Nate's autism. Do you think this was a decision on Dora's part, or simply benign silence? What would prompt this? Do you think her hesitancy was ultimately more helpful or harmful for Nate?

6. Discuss how Parker's legacy affected his mother and each of his three daughters. The negative sides of his alcoholism and abandonment are obvious, but can you identify any positive effects of his actions?

7. In addition to their individual conflicts with each other, Harper, Carson, and Dora each have a complicated relationship with their grandmother. While they love her, they each feel guilty about being gone from Sea Breeze for most of their adult lives and, at times, resent Mamaw for her meddling. What are Mamaw's biggest faults in this novel? Why do you think Mamaw has decided to try "tough love" with her granddaughters?

8. Blake has to explain to Carson why befriending wild dolphins is dangerous not only to the dolphins themselves, but also to humans. Do you agree that Blake's anger with Carson over Delphine's life-threatening injuries is justified? Who do you think is most to blame?

9. Forgiveness is a major theme in this novel. Consider Carson's history with her father and her mother and all the years of secrets, silence, and enabling. Carson

has confrontations with Blake (over Delphine), Brian (over her theft), and Dora (over what Dora reveals about her mother's death). How do all of these scenes lead to her growth as a character?

10. Carson and her grandmother are the two characters who were closest to Parker. How did Parker's actions impact Mamaw and Carson's relationship with each other, even after his death?

11. Throughout the novel, Carson is fearful of attachments—to a place, to a job, and especially to a man. Why do you think she suffers from an inability to commit? What role does Delphine play in helping her to connect again with her sisters? To Blake? To herself? What is Carson's challenge at the end of the book?

12. *The Summer Girls* is the first book in Mary Alice Monroe's trilogy about Sullivan's Island. Predict what the next two books will have in store for Dora and Harper, Carson, Blake, and Delphine.

1. In *The Summer Girls*, Carson befriends Blake, a scientist with the National Oceanic and Atmospheric Association, which has ocean, weather, and fishery branches in every state. Research the NOAA, and explore their Volunteer website, http://www.volunteer .noaa.gov/, and also see Mary Alice Monroe's Conservation page, http://www.maryalicemonroe.com/site/ epage/116387_67.htm. With your book club, plan a group outing or fund-raiser to support the NOAA or another local wildlife preservation organization.

2. "I would like each of you to list the item that you most want to have. The one item you are desperate for, more than any of the others. I want to be sure you each take something from the house that you love" (p. 169). Mamaw lures her girls to stay for the summer with keepsakes from her home. Monroe reveals through flashbacks why Carson selected her treasure—the portrait—and how monetary value played no part in her decision. Every family has their unique "treasures." Discuss with your book club the family heirloom that means the most to you. Suggest that each member bring in a picture of her "treasure" to share and tell why that item has value. What would you like to leave to future generations, and what treasured mementos are most precious to you?

3. Evoke the book's setting by channeling Lucille's home-style Southern cooking. Plan to host your book club as a potluck, with each member cooking one of Lucille's signature dishes, like mashed potatoes, lemon bars, hush puppies, gumbo, and sweet tea. Make copies of each recipe for all of your book club members to take home. You could even bind them together to create your own *The Summer Girls* cookbook!

Turn the page for an exclusive sneak peek of

The Summer Wind

BOOK TWO IN MARY ALICE MONROE'S
LOWCOUNTRY SUMMER TRILOGY

Available June 2014 from Gallery Books

CHAPTER ONE

SEA BREEZE, SULLIVAN'S ISLAND, SOUTH CAROLINA

July was said to be the hottest month of the year in Charleston, and after enduring eighty Southern summers, Marietta Muir, referred to affectionately by her family as Mamaw, readily agreed. She delicately dabbed at her upper lip and forehead with her handkerchief, then waved to shoo off a pesky mosquito.

Southern summers meant heat, humidity, and mosquitoes. But being out on Sullivan's Island, sitting in the shade of a live oak tree, sipping iced tea and waiting for the occasional offshore breeze was, for her, the very definition of summer. The ancient oak spread its mighty limbs so far and wide, Marietta felt cradled in its protective embrace. Still, the air was especially languid this morning, so thick and cloyingly scented with jasmine that it was a battle to keep her eyelids from drooping. A gust of wind from the ocean carried the sweet scent of the grass and cooled the moist hairs along her neck. Mamaw sighed heavily.

She set the needlepoint pattern on her lap so that she could remove her glasses and rub her eyes. Cursed old age. It was getting harder and harder to see her stitches, she thought with a sigh. Glancing at Lucille beside her on the screened porch of the guesthouse that Lucille called home, she saw her friend bent over the base of a sweet-grass basket, her strong hands weaving the fragile strands into the pattern, working each row tight with palmetto fronds. A small pile of the grass lay in her lap, while a generous heap sat at her feet in a plastic bag, along with another bag of longleaf pine needles.

Seeing a woman's hands lovingly weaving together the disparate grasses into an object of beauty made Marietta think again how imperative her challenge was this summer: to entwine her three very different granddaughters with Sea Breeze once again. They'd become more like strangers than sisters over the years. Half sisters, Marietta corrected herself, shuddering at the nuance of the term. As if by sharing only a father, the women's bond was somehow less. Sisters were sisters and blood was blood, after all. She had succeeded in corralling all three women at Sea Breeze in June for the summer, but here it was, the first of July, and Carson was already off to Florida and Dora was fixing on returning to Summerville.

"I wonder if Carson made it to Florida yet," Lucille said without looking up. Her fingers moved steadily, weaving row after row.

Mamaw half smiled, thinking how Lucille's and her own mind were in sync . . . again. Lucille had been hired as her housekeeper some fifty years back, when Mamaw was a young bride in Charleston. Lucille had never married and had become a part of the Muir family, helping to raise Mamaw's only child, Parker, and later, her three granddaughters. They'd shared a lifetime of ups and downs, births and deaths, scandals and joys. Old women now, Lucille had become more a companion and confidante than employee. Truth was, Lucille was her closest friend.

"I was just wondering the same thing," Mamaw replied. "I expect she has by now and is just settling in at her hotel. I hope she won't be away long."

"She won't be. Carson knows how important this summer is to you, and she'll be back just as soon as she finds out what's done happened to that dolphin," Lucille said. She lowered the basket in her lap and looked Mamaw straight in the eyes. "Carson won't disappoint you. You have to have faith."

"I do!" Mamaw exclaimed. "But I'm old enough to know how life likes to throw a wrench into even the most well-thought-out plans. I mean, really," Mamaw said, lifting her hands in frustration. "Who could have foreseen a dolphin tossing all my summer plans applecart-upset?"

Lucille chuckled, a deep and throaty sound. "Yes, she surely did. That Delphine . . ." Lucille's smile slipped at the mention of the dolphin's name. "But it weren't her fault, now, was it? I do hope that place in Florida can help the poor thing."

"I do, too. For Delphine's sake, and for Carson's." Marietta paused. "And Nate's," she added. She was worried about how hard Dora's son had taken the dolphin's accident. Only a young boy, he placed the blame on himself for luring the dolphin to their dock and getting it entangled in all that fishing line. In truth, they were all to blame. No one more than herself.

"For all our sakes," she amended.

"Amen," Lucille agreed soberly. She paused to sweep bits of scattered grass to the wind. "Don't you fret none, Miz Marietta. All will be well. I feel it in my bones. And in no time you'll have all your Summer Girls here at Sea Breeze again."

Marietta wondered about that. A voice called out from the driveway, dragging her thoughts from reverie.

"Hi, Mamaw! Lucille!"

"Here comes one now," Lucille murmured with a chuckle, returning to her basket.

Marietta turned her head and smiled to see her youngest granddaughter, Harper, jogging toward them in one of those skimpy, skintight running outfits that looked to her like a second skin. Her strawberry blond hair was pulled back in a ponytail, and sweat poured down her pink face.

"Harper!" Marietta called out with a quick wave. "My goodness, child, you're running at this time of the day? Only tourists are fool enough to run here under a mid-summer sun. You'll have a heat stroke! Why, your face is as red as a beet!"

Harper stopped at the bottom of the porch steps and bent over, hands on her hips, to catch her breath. "Oh, Mamaw, I'm fine," she said breathily, wiping the sweat from her brow with her forearm. "I do this every day."

"Well, you look ready to keel over."

"It *is* hot out there today," Harper conceded with a half smile. "A lot hotter than Central Park. But my face always turns red. It's my fair skin. I've got a ton of sunscreen on."

Lucille clucked her tongue. "Mind you drink some water, hear?"

"Why don't you jump in the pool and cool yourself down some? You look to be wearing a swimming suit . . ." Mamaw added. It made her hot just to see Harper's pink face and the sweat drenching her clothing.

"Good idea," Harper replied, and with a quick wave, she took off toward the front door. She turned her head and shouted, "Nice basket, Lucille!" before disappearing into the house.

Lucille chuckled and returned to her basket. "Only the young can run like that."

"I never ran like that when I was young!" Mamaw said.

"Me neither. Who had the time?"

"And certainly not dressed like that. What these girls parade around in today! That outfit left little to the imagination."

"Oh, I bet the young men can imagine plenty," Lucille said, chuckling again.

Mamaw huffed. "What young men? It's not as though she's getting any calls, and I simply cannot understand why. I've seen to it that she was invited to a few parties in town where other young people would be present. There was that nice boating party at Sissy's yacht club . . . Several eligible young men were invited." Mamaw shook her head. "Harper is such a pretty girl, with good breeding." She paused. "Even if her mother is English." Mamaw picked up her needlepoint and added archly, "Her father is from Charleston, after all."

"Oh, I wouldn't say she hasn't been asked out . . ." Lucille said, feeding more grass into the basket.

Mamaw narrowed her eyes with suspicion. "You wouldn't?"

Lucille's eyes sparkled with news. "I happen to know that since she's been here, several young men have called on our Miss Harper."

"Really?" Mamaw fumed silently, wondering why she hadn't been made aware of this. She didn't like being the last to know things, certainly not about her own grand-daughters. She reached for the *Island Eye* newspaper and used it to fan the air. "You'd think someone might've told me."

Lucille shrugged.

Mamaw lowered the paper with pique. "Well . . . why hasn't she had any dates? Is she being shy?"

"Our Harper might be a quiet little thing, but she ain't shy. That girl's got a spine of steel. Just look at the way she won't touch meat, or white bread, or anything I cook with bacon grease."

Mamaw's lips curved, recalling the row at the dinner table Harper's first night at Sea Breeze. Dora was driven to distraction by Harper's strict diet.

"She's only just been here a month," Lucille contin-ued. "And she's only staying another two. She don't have her light on, is all. And who can wonder? Harper's got a lot on her mind. I reckon dating a young man is low on her list."

Mamaw rocked in silence. Everything Lucille had said was true enough. It seemed everyone had a lot on their minds this summer at Sea Breeze—she certainly did. This summer was flying by, and if she didn't somehow patch things up among her granddaughters, Mamaw knew that come September she'd be sitting on the dock howling at the harvest moon.

The previous May, Mamaw had invited her three granddaughters—Dora, Carson, and Harper—to celebrate her eightieth birthday at Sea Breeze. Secretly, however, she had an ulterior motive. In the fall, Marietta was putting Sea Breeze on the market and moving into an assisted-living facility. She simply couldn't keep up living alone with the demands of an island house any longer, not even with Lucille's help. Her hope was that, once here, all three women would agree to stay for the entire summer. She wanted them to be her Summer Girls again—as they had been as children—for this final summer before Sea Breeze was sold.

Countless previous invitations of hers had been rebuffed by all the girls over the years, with just as many excuses—*I'd love to but I'm so busy! I have work! I'll be out of town!*—each sent with gushes of regret and replete with exclamation marks.

So this time, Mamaw had trusted that her granddaughters had inherited some of her ancestral pirate blood, and lured the girls south with promises of loot from the house. And the little darlings had come, if only for the weekend party. Desperate to keep them there with her, Mamaw had resorted to a bit of manipulation when she'd threatened to cut them out of her will if they did not stay for the entire summer. She chortled out a laugh just remembering their shocked faces.

Carson had just lost her job and was pleased as punch

to spend the summer rent free on the island. Dora, in the midst of a divorce, was easily convinced to stay at Sea Breeze with Nate while repairs were done on her house in Summerville. Harper, however, had thrown a hissy fit. She'd called it blackmail.

Mamaw shifted uncomfortably in her seat. Blackmail, really. Harper could be so dramatic, she thought as she rolled her eyes. Surely there was a more refined, gentler term for the actions of a concerned and loving grandmother set on bringing her granddaughters together? A smile of satisfaction played at her lips. And they'd all agreed to stay the summer, hadn't they?

But now, here it was only midsummer, and Carson and Dora were leaving again . . .

Mamaw closed her eyes, welcoming another soothing ocean breeze. She couldn't fail in her mission. Eighty years was a long time of living. She'd survived the loss of a husband and her only child. All she had left that mattered were these three precious jewels, her granddaughters. Mamaw's hands balled into fists. And come hell or high water—or hissy fits—she was going to give them this one, perfect summer. Her most private fear was that, when Sea Breeze was sold and she'd moved on to a retirement home—and later met her maker—the fragile bond between the sisters would break and they'd scatter to the four winds like the bits of sweetgrass that fell loose from Lucille's basket.

"Here comes another one," Lucille said in a low voice, indicating with her chin the sight of Dora rounding the corner of the house.

Mamaw's gaze swept over her eldest granddaughter

with a critical eye. Dora was dressed in a khaki suit and a blouse the same pale yellow color of her hair. As Dora drew closer, Mamaw noted that she was even wearing nylon stockings and pumps. In this heat! She could see pearls of perspiration already dripping down Dora's face as she dragged a suitcase behind her through the gravel toward the silver Lexus parked in the driveway.

"Dora! Are you off?" Mamaw called out.

Dora stopped abruptly at hearing her name and turned toward the guesthouse.

"Hey, ladies!" Dora waved upon seeing the two women sitting side by side on the front porch. She left her suitcase and came over to join them. "Look at you two, sitting there like two birds on a wire, chirping away the morning." Dora stepped up onto the porch. "Yes," she replied, fixing a smile. "I've got to dash if I'm going to get to my lawyer's appointment on time. It's going to be a long morning."

Mamaw set her needlepoint aside and gave Dora her full attention, studying her eldest granddaughter's face. Of all her three granddaughters, Dora was the one who could best mask her emotions. Had always done so, even as a child. On her wedding day, her father, Parker, had arrived at the church unforgivably drunk. Dora had bravely smiled as she had walked down the aisle with her stepfather instead of her biological one. She'd smiled through the whispers behind raised palms, smiled during Parker's rambling toast, smiled while friends escorted Parker to the hotel to sleep it off.

Mamaw studied that same fixed smile now. She knew too well the sacrifices a woman made to present the facade of a happy family. This divorce was striking at Dora's very core, shaking her foundation. Even now, Dora wanted to give the impression that she had everything under control.

"You look very . . . respectable," Mamaw said, choosing her words carefully. "But isn't it a bit steamy today for that suit and nylons?"

Dora lifted her blond hair from her neck to allow the offshore breeze to cool the moisture pooling there. "Lord, yes. It's so hot you could spit on the ground and watch it sizzle. But I've got to make the right impression in front of Cal's lawyers."

Bless her heart, Mamaw thought. That suit was so tight, she looked like a sausage squeezed into its casing.

Dora dropped her hair and her face shifted to a scowl. "Calhoun's being flat-out unreasonable."

"We all knew when you married him that his elevator didn't go all the way to the top," Mamaw remarked pointedly.

"He doesn't have to be smart, Mamaw. Only his lawyer does. And I hear he's got himself a real shark."

"You called the Rosen law firm like I recommended, didn't you?"

Dora nodded.

"Good," Mamaw said. "Robert will catch that shark on his hook, don't you worry."

"I'll try not to," Dora replied, smoothing out wrinkles in her skirt. "I still want to make a good impression, though."

Mamaw reached up to the collar of her dress and unpinned her brooch. It was a favorite of hers. Small pieces of bright coral embedded in gold to form an exquisite starburst. Her granddaughter needed a bit of starburst in her life right now.

"Come here, precious," she said to Dora.

When Dora drew near, Mamaw waved her hand to indicate Dora should bend close, and then she reached out to pin the large brooch to Dora's suit collar.

"There," she said, sitting back and gazing at her handiwork. "A little pop of color does wonders for you, my dear. The brooch was my mother's. It's yours now."

Dora's eyes widened as her facade momentarily crumpled. She rushed to hug her grandmother with a desperate squeeze. "Oh, Mamaw, thank you. I didn't expect . . . I don't know. It means a lot. Especially today. I have to admit, I'm nervous about confronting Cal after all this time. And his lawyers."

"Consider it ceremonial armor," Mamaw said with a smile.

"I will," Dora said, standing erect and smoothing out her jacket. "You know, I'm so tickled I can fit back into this suit. Between Carson not letting us have any alcohol in the house and Harper getting us to eat all that health food, I've actually lost a few pounds! Who would have thought?"

Dora's smile lit up her face, and Mamaw saw the dazzling young woman who once had enchanted all who met her with the warmth of that genuine smile. Over the past ten years, coping with an unhappy marriage and having a child with special needs, Dora had committed the cardinal sin of a Southern wife—she'd let herself go. But worst of all, her sadness had drained that sunlight from inside of her. Mamaw was glad to see a glimmer of it in her eyes this morning.

"Is Nate going with you?" Lucille asked.

Dora shook her head and grimaced. "I'm afraid not. I just came from his room. Mamaw, I begged him to come with me, but you know Nate when he's got his mind made up. He barely said more than one word—*no*. I don't think he likes me very much right now," Dora added in a softer tone. "It was like"—her voice choked with emotion—"like he couldn't wait for me to leave."

"Now, honey, don't pay him no mind," Mamaw said in a conciliatory tone. "You know that child's still hurting from what happened to that dolphin. It was traumatic for him. For all of us," she added.

"Carson should be calling with news soon," Lucille said comfortingly.

"And I just know it will be good news," Mamaw agreed, ever the optimist. "I'm sure Nate will come around."

"I guess . . ." Dora replied and hastily wiped her eyes, seemingly embarrassed for the tears.

Mamaw slid a glance toward Lucille. It wasn't like Dora to be so emotional.

Dora checked her watch, and gasped. "Lord, Mamaw, I've really got to go, or I'll be late," she said, all business now. "Are you sure y'all can handle Nate while I'm gone? You know how he can get squirrelly when I leave."

"I feel sure that three grown women can handle one little boy. We've sure handled him before. No matter how testy," Mamaw said, arching one brow.

Lucille chuckled while her fingers worked the basket.

"Yes, of course," Dora muttered, digging into her purse

for car keys. "It's just, he is particularly difficult now, because he's all upset I'm going to see his father."

Mamaw waved Dora off. "You go on and don't worry about anything here. We'll all be fine. You have enough to contend with getting your house ready for the market."

Dora's eyes narrowed. "Those workmen had better be there, or I'll raise holy hell."

Mamaw and Lucille exchanged a glance. That was the Dora they knew.

Pulling out her keys, Dora turned to go.

"Dora?" Mamaw called to her as she made to leave. Dora stopped, turned her head, and met Mamaw's gaze. "Mind you remember who you are. You're a Muir. The captain of your ship." She sniffed and added, "Don't you take any guff from the likes of Calhoun Tupper, hear?"

The brilliant Muir blue color flashed in Dora's eyes. "Yes, ma'am," she replied with heart, and straightened her shoulders.

The two old women watched Dora rush to her car, load the suitcase into the trunk, and roar out of the driveway, the wheels spitting gravel.

"Mmm-mmm-mm," Lucille muttered as she returned to her basket weaving. "That woman's hell-bent on taking her fury out on all the men in town today, it seems."

Mamaw released the grin that had been playing at her lips all morning. "I don't know who I feel more sorry for," she said. "The workmen at the house, or Calhoun Tupper."